DRY

DRY

NEAL SHUSTERMAN
and
JARROD SHUSTERMAN

WALKER
BOOKS

First published in Great Britain 2018 by Walker Books Ltd
87 Vauxhall Walk, London SE11 5HJ

Originally published by Simon & Schuster Books for Young Readers, an imprint of Simon & Schuster Children's Publishing Division, Inc.

2 4 6 8 10 9 7 5 3 1

Text © 2018 Neal Shusterman and Jarrod Shusterman
Jacket illustration copyright © 2018 Jay Shaw

The right of Neal Shusterman and Jarrod Shusterman to be identified as authors of this work has been asserted by them in accordance with the Copyright, Designs and Patents Act 1988

This book has been typeset in Bembo,
Brandon Grotesque and Neutraface Display

Printed and bound by CPI Group (UK) Ltd, Croydon CR0 4YY

British Library Cataloguing in Publication Data:
a catalogue record for this book is available from the British Library

ISBN 978-1-4063-8685-1

www.walker.co.uk

This book is dedicated to
all those struggling to undo
the disastrous effects of climate change

PART ONE
TAP-OUT

1) Alyssa

The kitchen faucet makes the most bizarre sounds.

It coughs and wheezes like it's gone asthmatic. It gurgles like someone drowning. It spits once, and then goes silent. Our dog, Kingston, raises his ears, but still keeps his distance from the sink, unsure if it might unexpectedly come back to life, but no such luck.

Mom just stands there holding Kingston's water bowl beneath the faucet, puzzling. Then she moves the handle to the off position, and says, "Alyssa, go get your father."

Ever since single-handedly remodeling our kitchen, Dad has had delusions of plumbing grandeur. Electrical, too. *Why pay through the nose for contractors when you can do it yourself?* he always said. Then he put his money where his mouth was. Ever since, we've had nothing but plumbing and electrical problems.

Dad's in our garage working on his car with Uncle Basil – who's been living with us on and off since his almond farm up in Modesto failed. Uncle Basil's actual name is Herb, but somewhere along the line my brother and I began referring to him as various herbs in our garden. Uncle Dill, Uncle Thyme, Uncle Chive, and during a period our parents wish we would forget, Uncle Cannabis. In the end, Basil was the name that stuck.

"Dad," I shout out into the garage, "kitchen issues."

My father's feet stick out from underneath his Camry like the Wicked Witch. Uncle Basil is hidden behind a storm cell of e-cig vapor.

"Can't it wait?" my father says from beneath the car.

But I'm already sensing that it can't. "I think it's major," I tell him.

He slides out, and with a heavy sigh heads for the kitchen.

Mom's not there anymore. Instead she's standing in the doorway between the kitchen and the living room. She's just standing there, the dog's empty water bowl still in her left hand. I get a chill, but I don't yet know why.

"What's so important that you gotta drag me out of—"

"Shush!" Mom says. She rarely shushes Dad. She'll shush me and Garrett all day, but my parents never shush each other. It's an unspoken rule.

She's watching the TV, where a news anchor is blathering about the "flow crisis." That's what the media's been calling the drought, ever since people got tired of hearing the word "drought." Kind of like the way "global warming" became "climate change," and "war" became "conflict." But now they've got a new catchphrase. A new stage in our water woes. They're calling this the "Tap-Out."

Uncle Basil emerges from his vapor cloud long enough to ask, "What's going on?"

"Arizona and Nevada just backed out of the reservoir relief deal," Mom tells him. "They've shut the floodgates on all the dams, saying they need the water themselves."

Which means that the Colorado River won't even reach California anymore.

Uncle Basil tries to wrap his mind around it. "Turning off the entire river like it's a spigot! Can they do that?"

My father raises an eyebrow. "They just did."

Suddenly the image switches to a live press conference, where the governor addresses a gathering of antsy reporters.

"This is unfortunate, but not entirely unexpected," the governor says. "We have people working around the clock attempting to broker a new deal with various agencies."

"What does that even mean?" Uncle Basil says. Both Mom and I shush him.

"As a precautionary measure, all county and municipal water districts in Southern California are temporarily rerouting all resources to critical services. But I cannot stress enough the need to keep calm. I'd like to personally assure everyone that this is a temporary situation, and that there is nothing to be concerned about."

The media begins to bombard him with questions, but he ducks out without answering a single one.

"Looks like Kingston's water bowl isn't the only one that's run dry," Uncle Basil says. "I guess we're gonna have to start drinking out of the toilet, too."

My younger brother, Garrett, who's been sitting on the couch waiting for normal TV to return, makes the appropriate face, which just makes Uncle Basil laugh.

"So," Dad says to Mom halfheartedly, "at least the plumbing problem isn't my fault this time."

I go to the kitchen to try the tap myself — as if I might have the magic touch. Nothing. Not even the slightest dribble. Our faucet has coded, and no amount of resuscitation will bring it back. I note the time, like they do in the emergency room: 1:32 p.m., June 4th.

Everyone's going to remember where they were when the taps went dry, I think. *Like when a president is assassinated.*

In the kitchen behind me, Garrett opens the fridge and grabs a bottle of Glacier Freeze Gatorade. He begins to guzzle it, but I stop him on the third gulp.

"Put it back," I tell him. "Save some for later."

"But I'm thirsty *now*," he whines, protesting. He's ten – six years younger than me. Ten-year-olds have issues with delayed gratification.

It's almost finished anyway, so I let him keep it. I take note of what's in the fridge. A couple of beers. Three more bottles of Gatorade, a gallon of milk that's down to the dregs, and leftovers.

You know how sometimes you don't realize how thirsty you are until you take that first sip? Well, suddenly I get that feeling just by looking in the refrigerator.

It's the closest thing I've ever had to a premonition.

I can hear neighbors out in the street now. We know our neighbors – run into them occasionally. The only time whole bunches of them come out into the street at the same time is July Fourth, or when there's an earthquake.

My parents, Garrett, and I gravitate outside as well, all of us standing, strangely, looking to one another for some kind of guidance, or at least validation that this is actually happening. Jeannette and Stu Leeson from across the street, the Maleckis and their newborn, and Mr. Burnside, who's been eternally seventy years old for as long as I can remember. And as expected, we don't see the reclusive family next door – the McCrackens – who have probably barricaded themselves inside their suburban fortress upon hearing the news.

We all kind of stand there with our hands in our pockets, avoiding direct eye contact, like my classmates at the junior prom.

"Okay," my dad finally says, "which one of you pissed off Arizona and Nevada?"

Everyone chuckles. Not because it's particularly funny, but it eases some of the tension.

Mr. Burnside raises his eyebrows. "Hate to say I told ya so, but didn't I say they'd hoard what's left of the Colorado River? We let that river become our only lifeline. We should never have let ourselves become so vulnerable."

Used to be no one much knew or cared where our water came from. It was just always there. But when the Central Valley started to dry up and the price of produce skyrocketed, people started to pay attention. Or at least enough attention to pass laws and voter propositions. Most of them were useless, but made people feel as if something was being done. Like the Frivolous Use Initiative, which made things like throwing water balloons illegal.

"Las Vegas still has water," someone points out.

Our neighbor, Stu, shakes his head. "Yeah – but I just tried to book a hotel in Vegas. A million hotel rooms, and not a single one available."

Mr. Burnside laughs ruefully, as if taking pleasure in Stu's misfortune. "One hundred twenty-four thousand hotel rooms, actually. Sounds like a whole lot of people had the same idea."

"Ha! Can you imagine the traffic on the interstate trying to get there?" says my mom, in a sour grapes kind of way. "I wouldn't want to be caught in that!"

And then I put my two cents in. "If they're diverting the remaining water to 'critical services,' it means there's still a little bit left. Someone should sue to get them to release a fraction of it. Make it like rolling blackouts. Each neighborhood gets a little bit of water each day."

My parents are impressed by the suggestion. The others look at me with an isn't-she-adorable kind of expression, which ticks me off. My parents are convinced I'm going to be a lawyer someday. It's possible, but I suspect if I am, it will just be a means to an end – although I'm not sure what that end would be.

But that doesn't help us now – and though I think my idea is a good one, I suspect there's too much self-interest among the Powers That Be for it to ever happen. And who knows, maybe there isn't enough water left to share.

A phone chimes, receiving a text. Jeannette looks at her Android. "Great! Now my relatives in Ohio found out. Like I need their stress on top of my own."

"Text them back: 'send water.'" My father quips.

"We'll get through this," my mom says reassuringly. She's a clinical psychologist, so reassurance is second nature to her.

Garrett, who's been standing quietly, brings his Gatorade bottle up to his lips … and for a brief moment everyone stops talking. Involuntary. Almost like a mental hiccup, as they watch my brother gulp the quenching blue liquid. Finally, Mr. Burnside breaks the silence.

"We'll talk," he says as he turns to leave. It's the way he always ends a conversation. It signals the conclusion of this loose little fellowship. Everyone says their goodbyes and heads back to their homes … but more than one set of eyes glance at Garrett's empty Gatorade bottle as they leave.

"Costco run!" says Uncle Basil late that afternoon, at around five. "Who's coming?"

"Can I get a hot dog?" Garrett asks, knowing that even if Uncle Basil says no, he'll get one anyway. Uncle Basil is a pushover.

"Hot dogs are the least of our problems," I tell him. And he doesn't question that. He knows why we're going – he's not stupid. Even so, he still knows he'll get a hot dog.

We climb into the cab of Uncle Basil's four-by-four pickup, which is jacked up higher than should be allowed for any man his age.

"Mom said we have a few water bottles in the garage," Garrett says.

"We're going to need more than just a few," I point out. I try to quickly do the math in my head. I also saw those bottles. Nine half-liters. Five of us. That won't even last the day.

As we turn the corner out of our neighborhood and onto the main street, Uncle Basil says, "It may take a day or so for the county to get the water up and running again. We'll probably only need a couple of cases."

"And Gatorade!" says Garrett. "Don't forget the Gatorade! It's full of electrolytes." Which is what they say on the commercials, even though Garrett doesn't know what an electrolyte is.

"Look on the bright side," Uncle Basil says. "You probably won't have school for a few days." The California version of a snow day.

I've been counting down the days for junior year to end. Just two weeks now. But knowing my high school, they'll probably find a way to tack any lost days on at the end, delaying our summer vacation.

As we pull into the Costco parking lot we can see the crowd. It seems like our entire neighborhood had the same idea. We do nothing but slowly circle in search of an empty space. Finally Uncle Basil pulls out his Costco card and hands it to me.

"You two go in. I'll meet you inside when I find a place to park."

I wonder how he'll get in without his card, but then, Uncle Basil finds ways around any situation. Garrett and I hop out and join the hordes of people flooding the entrance. Inside it's like Black Friday at its worst – but today it's not televisions and video games people are after. The carts in the checkout line are stocked with canned goods, toiletries, but mostly water. The essentials of life.

Something feels slightly off. I'm not sure what it is, but it hangs in the air like a scent. It's in the impatience of the people in line. The way people use their carts – on the verge of being battering rams to make their way through the crowd. There's a sort of primal hostility all around us, hidden by a veneer of suburban politeness. But even that politeness is stretching thin.

"This cart sucks," Garrett says. He's right. One wheel is

bent, and the only way to push it is to lean it on the other three wheels. I look back toward the entrance. There were only a couple of carts left when I grabbed this one. They'll all be gone now.

"It'll do," I tell him.

Garrett and I forge our way through the crowds toward the back left corner, where the water pallets are. As we do, we overhear bits and pieces of conversations.

"FEMA's already slammed with Hurricane Noah," one woman tells another. "How are they going to help us, too?"

"It's not our fault! Agriculture uses eighty percent of the water!"

"If the state spent more time finding new sources of water, instead of fining us for filling our swimming pools," one woman says, "we wouldn't be in this position."

Garrett turns to me. "My friend Jason has a giant aquarium in his living room, and he didn't get fined."

"That's different," I explain to him. "Fish are considered pets."

"But it's still water."

"Then go drink it," I say, shutting him up. I don't have time to think about other people's problems. We have our own to worry about. But it looks like I'm the only one who cares, because Garrett has already gone off to hunt for free samples.

As I push the cart, it keeps veering to the left and I have to lean heavily on the right side to prevent the bent wheel from acting like a rudder.

As I approach the rear of the warehouse, I can see that it's the most crowded spot, and as I reach the last aisle to see the water pallets, I realize I'm too late. The pallets are already empty.

In hindsight, we should have come straight here the moment the taps were turned off. But when something drastic happens, there's a lag time. It's not quite denial, and not quite shock, but more like a mental free fall. You're spending so much time wrapping your mind around the problem, you don't realize what you need to do until the window to do it has closed. I think of all those people in Savannah the moment Hurricane Noah made that unexpected turn and barreled straight toward them, instead of heading back out to sea like it was supposed to. How long did they stare unblinking at the news, until they packed up their things and evacuated? I can tell you how long. Three and a half hours.

Behind me, people who can't see that the water pallets are empty keep pushing forward. Eventually some employee will have the good sense to put a sign out front that says NO WATER, but until they do, customers will keep piling in, pushing toward the back, creating a suffocating crowd, like the mosh pit of a concert.

On a hunch, I maneuver my way to the side aisle, and to the racks of canned soda, which are also beginning to disappear. But I'm not here for soda. As I look around the stacks of drinks, I find a single case of water that someone abandoned there maybe yesterday, when it wasn't such a precious commodity. I reach for it, only to find it pulled away at the last second by a thin woman with a beak of a nose. She stacks it on top of her cart like a crown on top of her canned goods.

"I'm sorry, but we were here first," she says. And then

her daughter steps forward — a girl I recognize from soccer — Hali Hartling. She's annoyingly popular and thinks she's much better at soccer than she really is. Half the girls in school want to be like her, and the other half hate her because they know they'll never come close. Me, I just put up with her. She's not worth the energy for me to be anything but indifferent.

Although she always seems to bleed confidence, right now she can't even look me in the eye — because she knows, just as her mother knows, that I had that water first. As her mother pulls their cart away, Hali leans closer to me. "I'm sorry about that, Morrow," she says earnestly, calling me by my last name like we do in soccer.

"Didn't I share my water with you at practice last week?" I point out to her. "Maybe you could return the favor and share a few bottles with me."

She looks back to her mother, who's already moving down the aisle, then back to me with a shrug. "Sorry, they don't sell them by the bottle here. Just by the case." And then she gets a little bit red in the face, and turns to leave before it becomes a full-fledged flush.

I take in my surroundings. Crowds are still getting thicker, and things are vanishing from the shelves at an alarming rate. Even the sodas are gone now. Stupid! I should have grabbed some. I hurry back to my empty cart before someone else can take it. There's no sign of Uncle Basil yet, and Garrett is probably off stuffing his face with something greasy. The Gatorade he requested is all gone, too.

Finally I spot Garrett. He's down one of the frozen aisles, pizza sauce all over his face. He wipes his mouth with his shirt, knowing I'll comment. But I don't bother – because I see something. Just past the frozen vegetables and ice cream, there's a chest packed with ice. Enormous bags of it. I can't believe people are such limited thinkers that they haven't thought of this themselves! Or maybe they have, but denied that they could possibly be so desperate. I open the door and reach for a bag.

"What are you doing? We need water, not ice."

"Ice *is* water, Einstein," I tell him. I go for a bag, and realize they're a lot heavier than I had anticipated.

"Help me!" Together Garrett and I heave one bag of ice after another into our cart, until it's piled as high as it can get. By now other people have taken notice, and have crowded the ice case, beginning to empty it.

The cart is ridiculously heavy now, and almost impossible to push – especially with a bad wheel. Then, as we struggle with the cart, the jammed wheel scraping across the concrete floor, a man in a business suit comes up behind us. He smiles.

"That's quite a load there," he says. "Looks like you could use some help."

He doesn't wait for us to answer before grabbing the cart's handle, and wrestling it forward far more effectively than we did.

"Crazy here today," he says jovially. "Crazy everywhere, I'll bet."

"Thank you for helping us," I tell him.

"Not a problem. We all need to help one another."

He smiles again, and I return the grin. It's good to know that difficult times can bring out the best in people.

Bit by bit, with short but steady lurches, we get the cart to the front of the store, and into one of the snaking checkout lines.

"I suppose that's my workout for the day," he chuckles.

I look at our cart, and decide that one good turn deserves another. "Why don't you take a bag of ice for yourself," I suggest.

His smile doesn't fade. "I have an even better idea," he says. "Why don't you take a bag of ice for yourselves, and I'll keep the rest."

For a moment I think he's joking, but then realize he's dead serious. "Excuse me?"

He manufactures a heavy sigh. "You're right, that really wouldn't be fair to you. Tell you what, why don't we split it down the middle? I'll take half, you take half."

He says it like he's being generous. As if the ice is his to give. He's still smiling, but his eyes scare me.

"I think my offer is more than fair," he says. I begin to wonder what business he's in, and if it's all about cheating people but making them think they're not being cheated. It's not going to fly with me — but his hands are firmly locked on the handle of our cart, and there's nothing to prove that it's ours and not his.

"Is there a problem here?"

It's Uncle Basil. He's arrived just in time. He glares at the man coldly for a moment, then the man takes his hands off the cart.

"Not at all," he says.

"Good." Uncle Basil says. "I'd hate to think you were

harassing my niece and nephew. People get arrested for that."

The man holds eye contact with our uncle for a moment more before folding. He looks at the ice, his expression bitter, then leaves, not taking as much as a single bag.

Uncle Basil's pickup truck is parked illegally – halfway onto an island, having demolished a row of ficus. "Had to kick this sucker into four-wheel drive," he says proudly – probably the first time he's ever actually had to use it. Suddenly Uncle Basil's midlife crisis truck is a blessing rather than an embarrassment.

We load the bags of ice into the truck bed. "How about that hot dog?" Uncle Basil offers, trying to lighten the mood.

"I'm full," Garrett responds, even though I know that's a nearly impossible feat for him. He just doesn't want to go back inside. None of us do. And now there's a small crowd that's formed, watching us load the ice into the bed of the truck. Even though I try to ignore it, I know there's a dozen eyes on us.

"Why don't I ride in the truck bed with the ice?" I suggest.

"No, it's okay," Uncle Basil replies calmly. "Ride in the cab. Some nasty potholes on the way back. Wouldn't want you to bounce around back there."

"Right," I agree as I hop into the cab of the pickup. And although no one speaks of it, I know it's not potholes my uncle's worried about.

We pull onto our street, but for some reason it doesn't quite feel like the same block I grew up on. There's this strange-ness, like when you accidentally turn one street too early, and, because all of the cookie-cutter houses look the same, you feel as if you're in a parallel universe. I try to shake the feeling as I watch the houses go by through the car window.

Our neighbors across the street, the Kiblers, usually lounge in their lawn chairs and "supervise" their kids as they play, which in reality means gossiping over glasses of chardonnay while making sure their children don't get run over. However, today the Kibler kids play tag in the street without supervision. And even through the children's laughter there's this insidious silence that underscores everything; then again, maybe the silence was always there, and I'm only just noticing it now.

Uncle Basil backs the truck into the driveway and we get straight to unloading. Even with the sun getting low in the sky, it's still ninety degrees, and the ice is already melting. If we're going to get all of this ice inside in time, we're going to need to hurry.

"Why don't you go clean out the freezer so we can put some ice in it," Uncle Basil says as he grabs the first bag from the truck bed. "The rest we can let melt and drink today."

"Better yet, why don't you clean the downstairs bathtub," I tell Garret. "We'll let it melt there."

"Good idea," says Basil, although Garrett's not too keen on cleaning the tub.

Dad emerges from the garage, greasy wrench in hand, clearly still trying to squeeze water from the pipes. "Ice, huh?"

"They ran out of everything else," I tell him, keeping it brief.

Dad scratches his head. "Should have gone to Sam's Club," he says. "They keep more items stocked in the back of the store." Although Dad smiles it off, I can tell he's a little more disturbed than he lets on. I think he knows that Sam's Club has most likely been cleaned out of all of its bottled liquids, just like every other store.

Uncle Basil quickly changes the subject. "Thought you were going into the office today," he says.

Dad shrugs and grabs a bag of ice. "Best thing about having your own business is that you don't have to work Saturdays if you don't want to."

Except that Dad *does* work Saturdays. Some Sundays, too. A lot of people put in extra hours these days, considering how the price of produce has been rising – but even without that, Dad always told us that it takes a 24/7 commitment to build out a business. Yet apparently he'd rather haul ice than sell insurance today.

I pull more ice from the back of the truck, but find, even in a thick plastic bag, it's hard to grip now that it's starting to melt.

"Need some help?" says a voice from behind, and before turning around I know exactly who it is. Kelton McCracken. Your not-so-typical red-headed geek next door. Most kids of his strangeness are content killing zombies with an Xbox controller, but not Kelton. He prefers to spend his time practicing aerial reconnaissance with his drone, shooting critters with his paintball gun, and hiding in his tree house with a pair of night vision goggles, pretending to be Jason Bourne. It's like he never matured past sixth grade, so his parents just bought him bigger and bigger toys. But today I can't help but notice that there's something different about him. Sure, he's grown in this past year and looks a lot more mature – but it isn't just that. It's the way he holds himself. There's a bounce in his step, as if this whole water crisis excites him in some sick way. Kelton smiles, revealing that his braces are off and his teeth have been wrangled artificially straight.

"Sure, Kelton, we could use some help," says Dad. "Why don't you give Alyssa a hand?"

I go to hand him the ice, but as I hold it out to him, something comes over me, and I can't seem to let go of the bag.

Dad takes notice, confused by my hesitation. "Let him take the ice, Alyssa," he says.

I look down to the ice in my hands and then back to Kelton, realizing I'm still skeptical about allowing people to *"help."*

"Is there a problem?" Dad asks, in an intrusive, fatherly tone that demands an answer – which I don't give.

I force myself to hand the ice over to Kelton. "Just don't expect a bag for helping," I tell him, which makes my father give me a stern look, probably wondering what would possess me to be so nasty about it. Maybe later I'll tell him about that guy at Costco. Or maybe I'll just try to forget it ever happened.

As for Kelton, I expect him to have a snotty comeback, but instead he just stands there, genuinely thrown by my comment. I regain my composure and force a smile, hoping it doesn't look forced. "Sorry," I tell him. "Thanks for helping."

We go inside to set the ice in the bathtub, but Kelton grabs my shoulder to stop me.

"Have you sealed the drain?" he asks. "Not a good idea putting this ice in the tub unless you've sealed the drain. Even the tiniest leak and you'll lose it all in a few hours."

"I thought my uncle had done that," I tell him, even though none of us would have thought of it. As much as I hate to admit it, that's probably the smartest idea I've heard all day.

"I'll go get you some caulking," he says, and hurries off to retrieve the sealant from his garage, obviously happy for an opportunity to put his Boy Scout training into action.

Kelton and his reclusive family always seem to have a worst-case scenario plan for anything. Dad would sometimes joke that Mr. McCracken lived a double life, working as a dentist by day and preparing for the end of the world by night. But recently the joke is becoming all the more real. It seems Mr. McCracken now spends most of his time welding cast-iron contraptions late into the night, as if he were drilling into the cavity of the gaping monstrosity that is his garage.

Over the past few months Kelton's family has assembled an over-the-top surveillance system, set up a mini greenhouse in their side yard, and lined their entire roof with some kind of unregistered, off-grid solar panels. Most recently, Kelton – who's in far too many of my classes this year – is always bragging about how his father installed one-way bulletproof windows – bullets can shoot out from inside, but can't penetrate from the outside. Even though the rest of our class thinks he's completely full of it, I think it might be true. I wouldn't put it past his father to do something like that.

Aside from our complaints about the late-night welding, our families are generally amicable, but there's always been a sense of polite tension when my parents deal with them. We once shared an area of grass between our two houses, until Mr. McCracken installed a picket fence right through my mom's prize-winning vermilliades. The fence was obnoxiously taller than your typical whitewashed suburban barrier, but just low enough not to technically violate the rules and regulations of the Homeowners Association – which they always seem to be at war with. Once, they even tried to lay claim to the curb in front of their house as their own private parking spot, insisting that their property line extended a few inches into the street – but the association won that battle. Ever since then, Uncle Basil makes a point to park his truck right in front of their house whenever he can, just to mess with them.

Kelton returns in a few minutes with the caulking and gets right to sealing the drain. "This might take a couple of hours to harden, so be careful when you pack the ice in," he says, way more enthusiastic than someone ought to be about silicone sealant. There's an uncomfortable silence between us that makes me realize that I've never actually spent time with Kelton one-on-one.

Then something occurs to me that's not just a conversation filler, but something important. "Wait a second. Don't you guys have a big water tank behind your house?"

"Thirty-five gallons," Kelton brags, as he applies the caulking with the precision of a jeweler. "But that's inside our house. The outside one's for bodily waste, full of quaternary ammonium compound chemicals. You know, like that stinky blue soup at the bottom of a porta potty."

"Yeah, I get it, Kelton," I say, duly disgusted. "Well, I can't say you guys didn't think ahead." Which is the understatement of the century.

"Well, as my dad always says, 'We'd rather be wrong than

dead wrong.'" Then he adds, "I bet if your dad just thought ahead too, you'd probably be better off."

Kelton's clearly not aware how insulting he can sound sometimes. I wonder if he ever won a merit badge for being Most Annoying.

Kelton finishes up the job. I thank him, and he heads back home to shoot his potato launcher, or dissect bugs, or whatever a kid like him does with his free time.

In the kitchen, my mom is scouring every surface with 409. Stress cleaning. When something's out of your control, you bring order to the things you can. I get that. She's never been the type, though, to leave the TV on as background noise – but she has it blasting in the family room. I'm not sure where my dad and uncle are. Maybe back working on his car. I find it odd that I feel I need to know.

On TV, CNN is focused on the continuing crisis of Hurricane Noah. I don't begrudge those poor people the attention, but wish some of it would turn toward us, too.

"Any news about the Tap-Out?" I ask.

"One of the local stations has regular updates," Mom tells me, "but it's that brainless anchor I can't stand. And besides, there's nothing new."

Even so, I switch to the brainless anchor, who my dad says got his start in porn, although I don't want to ask him how he knows.

My mom's right; they're just showing the governor's statement from this morning, and trying without success to spin it.

I switch back to the national news stations. CNN, then MSNBC, then Fox News, and back to CNN again. Every national broadcast is reporting on Noah, and only on Noah. Slowly it dawns on me why.

There's no radar image for a water crisis.

No storm surges, no debris fields – the Tap-Out is as silent as cancer. There's nothing to see, and so the news is treating it like a sidebar.

I mention this to my mom. She stops cleaning for a moment, and watches the crawl of secondary stories at the bottom of the screen. Finally something comes up: *California water crisis deepens. Residents urged to conserve.*

And that's it. That's all the national news says.

"Conserve? Are you kidding me?"

My mom takes a deep breath and sprays the kitchen table again. "As long as FEMA does its job, who cares what the news says?"

"I care," I tell her. Because if there's one thing I know about the news, it's that it decides for most people – including the federal government – what *is* and what *isn't* important. But the big news stations won't give the Tap-Out the critical airtime it needs – not until there are images that are as dramatic as winds taking off roofs.

And if it takes that long for the Tap-Out to be taken seriously, it will be too late.

SNAPSHOT: JOHN WAYNE

Dalton loves the way planes take off from John Wayne Airport. It's a real trip. They call it a "modified noise abatement takeoff," and it was specifically implemented to spare Newport Beach millionaires from having to deal with airport noise. Basically, the plane powers up on the runway with its brakes on, then accelerates at full force into a ridiculously steep takeoff, followed ten seconds later by a sudden leveling off and throttling down of the engines, which sounds, to the uninitiated, like engine failure, causing at least one person on every flight to gasp, or even scream in panic. The plane then coasts out over the back bay, Balboa Island, and the Newport Peninsula before the pilot pushes the engines back to full and resumes the climb-out.

"They oughta call it John Glenn instead of John Wayne," Dalton once said – because taking off from there was the closest most people would ever get to blasting off into space.

Dalton and his younger sister are regular flyers, visiting their dad, who lives up in Portland, a few times a year – Christmas, Easter, most of the summer, and every other Thanksgiving. Today, however, it's not just the two of them traveling north. Their mother is coming, too.

"If your dad won't put me up, I'll be happy to stay in a hotel," she says.

"He won't make you do that," Dalton tells her, but she doesn't seem too sure.

A few years back, Dalton's mom had left him for a loser with nice pecs and a soul patch, who she subsequently kicked to the curb a year later. Live and learn. Anyway, when the marriage went south, his dad went north.

"You understand this is not about your father and me getting back together," she tells Dalton and his sister, but for kids of divorce, hope springs eternal.

Within minutes of the Tap-Out, his mom had gone online and bought three overpriced tickets on Alaska Air – one of the few airlines that flies nonstop to Portland on a plane that you didn't have to get out and push.

"Last three tickets," she told them triumphantly. "You've got an hour to pack. Carry-ons only."

The trip to the airport is bumper-to-bumper. What should be a fifteen-minute ride takes almost an hour.

The parking situation at John Wayne is the first indication that there's going to be turbulence up ahead. All but one parking structure says FULL. They get one of the last remaining spaces at the far end of the last lot. As they make their way to the terminal, Dalton notes all the cars circling, like it's a huge game of musical chairs, with no chairs left.

The TSA checkpoint is a madhouse, which never happens here.

"A lot a people are going on vacation," Dalton's seven-year-old sister, Sarah, says.

"Yes, honey," their mom responds absently.

"Where do you think they're going?"

Their mom sighs, too stressed to continue humoring her, so Dalton looks at the boards, and takes up the slack. "Cabo San Lucas," he says. "Denver, Dallas, Chicago..."

"My friend Gigi's from Chicago."

The security guy double takes on Dalton's passport, because his hair is brown in the photo, but now it's bleached blond.

"You sure this is you?"

"Last time I checked," Dalton responds.

The humorless TSA guy lets them get into the slow-moving crawl to the metal detector, which has issues with his facial rings. Finally they make it through security with just five minutes until boarding starts. Mom is relieved.

"Okay," she says. "We're here. We haven't lost anyone. No missing fingers or toes."

"I'm thirsty," Sarah says, but Dalton has already noticed that the concessions they passed all had NO WATER signs up.

"There'll be something to drink on the plane," their mother says.

Dalton thinks that might actually be true. After all, these planes all came from somewhere else. And he is getting a bit thirsty himself.

Then, just as they're about to start boarding, the gate agent comes on the loudspeaker and makes an announcement.

"Unfortunately, we're oversold on this flight," she says. "We're asking for volunteers with flexible travel plans who are willing to take a later flight."

Sarah tugs her mother's arm. "Mommy, volunteer!"

"Not this time, baby."

Dalton grins. Dad always tells them to volunteer because they give away hundreds of dollars in travel vouchers, which is always worth the inconvenience. But not today. Today it's all about getting out. Which is why they have trouble getting volunteers. The price of the vouchers goes from two hundred dollars to three hundred to five hundred dollars, and still no one is willing to surrender their ticket.

Finally the gate agent gives up. She gets on the loudspeaker, calling the names of the last people to buy tickets. Dalton, Sarah, and their mother. Dalton feels a twisting in the pit of his stomach.

"I'm sorry," says the gate agent, not sounding sorry at all, "but as the last to purchase, I'm obliged to reschedule you to a later flight."

Dalton's mom goes ballistic, and he can't blame her. This is one time they need to fight the Powers That Be.

"No," says their mom. "I don't care what you say! My children and I are getting on that plane!"

"You'll each receive a five-hundred-dollar travel voucher – that's fifteen hundred dollars," the agent says, trying to placate them. Their mom will not be bought.

"My children have court-ordered visitation with their father," she yells. "If you take them off this flight, you'll be breaking the law, and I'll sue!" Of course, this isn't their father's time with them, but the agent doesn't know that.

Even so, all the agent does is apologize, and look for later flights. "There's a flight tonight at five-thirty... Oh wait, no, that one is full, too... Let's see." She continues to hack away at her computer. "Eight-twenty ... no..."

Then Dalton turns to his sister and whispers, "Give her the eyes."

Their mom had always told both Dalton and Sarah that their big blue eyes could melt anyone into a puddle. Not so much Dalton anymore. At an awkward seventeen, a bunch of facial piercings, a biohazard neck tattoo, and what his father calls "weed-whacked hair," the general public isn't melted anymore. Only seventeen-year-old girls. But Sarah still has the magical melting effect on hardened adults. So he lifts her up for the agent to get a good look at her.

"Aw, you're cute as a button," she says. Then rips three new tickets from the printer. "Here you go – tomorrow morning at six-thirty. That's the absolute best I can do."

So they wait. They don't leave, because the crowd just grows, and they know they'll never get back through security. They spend the night sleeping in uncomfortable airport chairs, getting sips of water from anyone who'll share with them, and there aren't many.

Then, when morning comes, even with confirmed tickets, there's no room on the six-thirty flight for them. Or the next one. Or the next one.

And they can't get tickets to flights to other places.

And the airport gets so crowded that extra police are brought in to keep the peace.

And with traffic jams everywhere, trucks with jet fuel can't get to the airport.

And Dalton, his mother, and sister have to face the fact that they won't be blasting off anywhere.

---

2) Kelton

My dad always told me that there are three types of humans on this planet. First there's the Sheep. The everyday types who live in denial – spoon-fed by the morning news, chewed up by another monotonous workday, and spit back out across the urban streets of the world like a mouthful of funky meatloaf that's been rotting in the back of the fridge. Basically, the Sheep are the defenseless majority who are completely unwilling to acknowledge the inevitability of real danger, and trust the system to take care of them.

Next you've got your Wolves. The bad guys who abide by no societal laws whatsoever but are good at pretending when it suits them. These are the thieves, murderers, rapists, and politicians, who feed on the Sheep until they're thrown in prison, or better yet, belly up in a landfill alongside sheaves of your grandma's itchy hand-knit Christmas socks. The ones you ritualistically blow up every year with an M80.

And lastly, you have people like us. The McCrackens. The Herders of the world. Sure, our kind may look a lot like Wolves – large fangs, sharp claws, and the capacity for violence – but what sets us apart from the rest is that we represent the balance between the two. We can navigate the flock freely, with the ability to protect or disown as we see fit. My dad says that we're the select few with the power of choice, and when real danger arises, we'll be the ones who survive – and not just because we own a 357 Magnum, three glock G19's, and a Mossberg pump-action shotgun, but because we've been prepping, in every possible badass way, since as long as I can remember, for the inevitable collapse of society as we know it.

It's Sunday, noon, second day of the Tap-Out. It's boiling hot, like a forgotten soda can left out on summer solstice. I take to my personal "bug-out." Namely, the elevated tactical unit I built in the oak tree in our backyard. Some people might call it a tree house, but that would insult its fortified and functional nature. You don't do infrared reconnaissance and maintain a civilian arsenal in some namby-pamby tree house. It's nowhere near as cool as our real bug-out, though – a hidden safe house our family built deep in the woods in the event of a nuclear attack, or EMP, or any other end-of-the-world scenario. We all built it together, as a family, a few years back, before my older brother, Brady, left home. If things get bad, I'm sure we'll go there. But in the meantime, I make do with my tree-bug-out.

I've got quite my own stockpile of supplies, separate and apart from the stuff Dad has in our safe room. Weapons-wise, I've got a paintball gun, a tactical hunting slingshot, and a Wildcat Whisper pellet rifle. As far as supplies go, I have enough Mountain Dew to keep me awake for weeks if need be, not to mention chicken-flavored Top Ramen, my favorite comfort food – because it's comforting to know that in the event of nuclear fallout, my food has enough MSG and preservatives to out-survive all of mankind.

I look out the fort window and clock someone approaching

our house, so I pull out my binoculars to get an ID. The off-brown suit and bolo tie are dead giveaways. It's Mr. Burnside, the retired business executive who never exactly came to terms with the end of his career. With nothing better to do, he organized a silent coup and took over the Homeowners Association a couple of years back. He's been running it with an iron fist ever since. We're pretty sure he's a fascist. He's probably here to notify us that our windows are too bulletproof, or that our garage door is too titanium, or that our rooftop aerial drone helipad is too awesome. But upon closer examination I realize that he's not carrying the usual legal binder full of petitions and cease-and-desist paperwork. Instead he holds a gift, wrapped up neatly with a bow and everything. I'm skeptical, so I climb down and move to the side of the house, crouching behind a hedge where I can see him at the front door.

Burnside mats down his gray combover and knocks four times, then a fifth, because he's obnoxious like that.

My dad answers, but only opens the door partly. "Good afternoon, Bill. And to what do I owe the pleasure of your visit today?" my dad asks, when he really means, *What the hell do YOU want?*

Burnside forms a smile through a set of teeth too white to not be fake. "Just checking in on families in the neighborhood." He looks around our property, feigning enthusiasm. "I have to say, I'm coming to understand and appreciate some of your unique modifications."

"Such as our greenhouse, which the association is still disputing?" my dad says sharply.

"Water under the bridge," Burnside says with a cheap wave

of the hand, his retirement-earned gold watch and medical ID bracelet jingling together. Not sure what his medical condition is, but five'll get you ten he didn't stockpile the medication he needs.

"Haven't you heard?" my dad says. "There isn't any water under the bridge."

Burnside laughs, but rather than cutting the tension it just adds to it. So he hands my dad the gift.

"From me and the wife," he says. "Just a little something to help bygones be bygones."

"Well, that's awfully nice of you, Bill. I assume that means you and the board won't mind if I upgrade the security fences. I was thinking ten-footers."

Burnside gets a little bristly, but says, "I'll have a talk with the board. It shouldn't be a problem."

"Is there anything else I can do for you?" my dad asks, clearly enjoying the power position.

"Well, as I said, I'm out doing rounds to let everyone know that the Homeowners Association is making efforts to pool neighborhood resources. You know, to help each other out in this crisis …"

Rather than responding, my dad waits for him to continue, making him squirm.

"… I'm sure you and your family are doing just fine…" Burnside prods, showing those porcelain teeth again. "But of course there are some others that were caught off guard by this water situation."

"Exactly what are you asking, Bill?" my dad says, a little less jovial than before.

"We're asking everyone to make an inventory of supplies," he says, then adds, "I'm sure there are things you need that other people might have, and vice versa."

"From each according to his ability, to each according to his need. Isn't that the basic tenet of socialism, Bill?" my dad says. "Never thought I'd hear something like that coming from a dyed-in-the-wool capitalist like you!"

Boy is my dad enjoying this! Burnside's smile is starting to resemble a snarl. "No need to be insulting, Richard – we're all in the same boat here. We should all try to make the best of it."

"If everyone's making an inventory, why are *we* the ones getting a gift?" my dad asks.

Burnside takes a deep breath and releases it. "I know we've been adversaries in the past … but a little bit of goodwill on both our parts can go a long way."

Burnside then turns to go, but before he reaches the end of our walkway, my dad unwraps the present. It's a bottle of Scotch. The expensive kind.

"Thanks again, Bill," my dad shouts to Burnside with a sly grin. "I bet it will make an excellent Molotov cocktail!"

"On the rocks is best," Burnside shouts back, completely missing the joke. "We'll talk."

3) Alyssa

I wake up late on Sunday. I had been up most of the night texting friends, trading stories about the day. Mora, who marched on city hall with her family and a few dozen others, demanding satisfaction. Faraz, who spent the day with his dad trying to get their reverse-osmosis water purification system to turn urine into drinking water. Spoiler alert: It didn't work. And Cassie, who spent the day at her temple filling up water bottles for the elderly. "It's a mitzvah," she told me. "And our rabbi's son is hot."

Still only half awake, I go into the bathroom and, by force of habit, turn on the shower, then realize I forgot to get a towel. I get one and come back into the bathroom, only to notice that the shower isn't on. Oh. Right. Now I feel like an idiot. I was even thinking about the Tap-Out when I turned on the shower – but somehow in my glorified monkey brain, I didn't make the connection that the shower head is a tap, too. It's not that I didn't know it wouldn't be working – of course I did. But when you're on morning autopilot, routine and muscle memory know no reason. I turn the knobs, not remembering which direction is on and which is off. Until the water comes back on it's not going to matter anyway.

No showers. What fun this is going to be. I slather on more deodorant than usual and head downstairs.

"Good morning, honey," Mom says, and tells me breakfast is a quarter of a watermelon that's been sitting in a corner of our refrigerator for a week. Garrett's rind is still on his plate like a wide green grin. It's an odd choice for breakfast, but she points out it has a high liquid content, so consuming it is killing two birds with one stone. And besides, it's almost lunchtime anyway.

Before the water turned off, my plan for Sunday was to work on my paper on *Lord of the Flies*. My hypothesis is that had it been a group of girls abandoned on the island instead of boys, it would have gone a lot differently. When I suggested it to the teacher, the boys in class agreed – and were convinced that everyone would have died a lot sooner. My hypothesis was, of course, the opposite. I had procrastinated for over a week in writing the paper, and it was due on Monday. Suddenly it didn't seem to matter all that much. It was already announced that our school district would be closed tomorrow – and besides, try as I might, I couldn't bring myself to care about who held the conch shell, and who was tormenting Piggy – or Miss Piggy, in my theoretical version.

Still, I figure it's better to keep busy than to dwell on things. I resolve to seek out normalcy, and decide to hang out with another friend, Sofía Rodriguez, who wasn't answering texts last night. After a few more unanswered texts, I decide I'll just go knock on her door like I used to back when we were younger.

I slip outside and head toward her house, one street down from my own. As I walk, I take stock of the current state of my neighborhood. Most every car windshield is flyspecked and covered in dust. A large majority of lawns are neglected, or replanted with succulents. Some people even had their dead lawns painted green, kind of like the way funeral homes put makeup on dead people. The Frivolous Use Initiative wasn't just about banning water balloons. It also made it illegal to fill up private pools. The pool thing seemed like a good idea at the time – after all, in a time of drought, a pool is an extravagance. But since then, people with pools used the remaining water in them to wash their cars and water their lawns and such. Between that and evaporation, most pools are now totally empty. So what used to be mini neighborhood reservoirs are now all as dry as our sinks.

I arrive at Sofía's house and see her father strapping suitcases to the roof of their Hyundai. At first I try to tell myself that maybe he's taking another road trip for business, but as soon as I spot Sofía's favorite pink weekender bag strapped to the roof, I can't deny the truth. They're packing up and heading out.

"Sofía's inside the house," her father tells me, without taking even a moment's break from packing.

I enter their home through the garage door. On the inside everything looks normal. Same hallways. Same blue pastel walls. Same floral print couch. Yet for some reason everything feels different, as if it's not the same house that I practically grew up playing in... And then I notice why. The TV is off, and the air lacks that sweet smell of Mrs. Rodriguez's cooking. Family pictures have been taken down, leaving bright squares against the sun-faded walls like shadows of the memories those walls once held. It's as if the house has been stripped of all those little things that made it a home.

And then I think about *my* home. About how we keep all of our goofy family photos downstairs for everyone to see — and although I either hate my hair, or my smile, or my clothes in every picture I'm in, I couldn't imagine having to actually physically take them off the walls.

Sofía emerges from her bedroom, sees me, and gives me a hug, holding me for a second longer than normal, and then pulls back, smiling weakly. "I was going to stop by your house before we left…"

"Where are you going?" I ask.

"South," she responds. The short response strikes me as odd, because on any other day I couldn't pay Sofía to keep her mouth shut. I remember that she has grandparents somewhere in Baja – the western peninsula of Mexico – and it all starts to make a little more sense ... though I can't imagine Mexico being any better than Southern California right now. Most of it is a desert, too.

"Have you been watching the news?" she says. "They're saying even the Los Angeles Aqueduct went dry. It's been dry for weeks, and they kept it a secret. People are resigning and being fired left and right. They're saying LA's water commissioner could be brought up on criminal charges."

"Why don't they do something about it instead of spending time blaming people?"

"I know, right? Anyway, my father thinks it's gonna get worse before it gets better." She gives a nervous chuckle. "Of course, you know him – he's always overreacting."

I laugh, but it's more of an obligatory laugh than a real one. Mrs. Rodriguez enters the room, Sophia's five-year-old brother in one arm, a stack of Sofía's paintings in the other. "Which of your pieces do you want to take?"

"All of them," Sofía responds, without the slightest hesitation.

She puts the paintings down on a pile of them already resting on the dining room table. "Pick your three favorites." She kisses her daughter on the head and then smiles warmly to the both of us. Sofía's mother was always one of those women who was so pretty, people would mistake her and her daughter for sisters. She was youthful in every way. I always loved that about her. But today, she just looks tired.

Sofía sifts through the canvasses. "This one is yours," she says, turning to me. "You painted it for me back in seventh grade art class. Remember?"

"Yeah," I say. "It was a birthday present."

"I think you should keep it," she says.

"Well, let's just say I'm borrowing it back. For a week or so." I correct her.

"Yeah." Sofía smiles genially, even though her eyes tell a different story. She was always the glass half full type, but something about the way she looks at me now tells me that her optimism is running as empty as her pool.

My dad is that guy who avoids going to doctors at all costs. It's not that he never gets sick, or has a deathly fear of needles, but I think some part of him thinks that drawing attention to an issue makes it worse. Maybe it makes something imaginary real. And since a vast majority of illnesses eventually go away on their own, most of the time it works for him. It's how he handles all of his problems, from fights with Mom to a bad fiscal quarter for his business. So tonight he declares a Family Dinner, which is his favorite communal Band-Aid. Sure, throwing lasagna at the issue isn't always the answer, but I am a firm believer that when Mom and Dad cook together, it has the power to turn any day around. So I make sure to be home precisely at seven-thirty.

As soon as I walk in the door Mom puts me to work, as expected. She hands me an empty pitcher. "Get some water for the table."

A simple request that suddenly feels like I've been charged with a sacred duty.

"Sure," I respond. I go into the downstairs bathroom and dip the entire pitcher in the tub, and even after a day, there's still some ice. As soon as I return, I pour everyone a glass.

"Not too much," Dad says. "I'm thinking we each do six cups a day. I did the math and the amount that we have should actually be enough for about a week at that rate."

"I thought people were supposed to drink eight cups a day," Garrett says.

"Think of your two less cups as a long-term investment," he tells Garrett, who at this point could probably run his own company based entirely on Dad's cheesy business analogies.

"Plus Kingston needs water, remember? But just a cup twice a day," Mom adds.

I totally forgot about our dog – and feel guilty about it. I couldn't imagine rationing something as helpless as an animal. I look to his water bowl and notice that it's empty, so when no one is looking I pour him a little bit from the pitcher.

Uncle Basil arrives at the table last, and right away chugs his entire glass of water, giving himself a killer brain-freeze.

"Serves you right, Herb," Mom says, like he's a little kid. "That's all you get tonight."

"It's healthier to drink all your fluids ten minutes before you eat," he counters. "It allows your body to process the water separate from your food and absorb more nutrients." And whether that's true or not, I decide to write it off as bro-science. I think Uncle Basil gets all of his scientific factoids from his beer buddies. That, coupled with the only A he ever got in school, in biology, and you've got yourself a recipe for misinformation.

Despite Basil's words, everyone else takes their water slow. Perhaps because no one likes looking at an empty glass, which is true even when there's not a water shortage.

The lasagna is extra tough tonight, being that Mom boiled the pasta in Dad's red sauce in an attempt to use as little water as possible. Dad waits for our reactions before tasting it himself.

"I love it. Nice and crunchy," Garrett tells Dad. Of course he'd love it. Garrett, for some reason, hasn't really shed certain strange juvenile habits, like secretly eating cherry Chap Stick and raw pasta. Not necessarily together.

"It's good," I tell him with a smile. Unfortunately, Dad always knows when I'm lying, but I'm sure he appreciates the gesture...

After a few minutes of awkward crunching, Basil goes ahead and breaks the silence. "At least the water's cold," he says, which makes everyone crack up, eventually growing into uncontrollable giggles. It's the kind of laughter that forces its way out like a bad case of hiccups. It makes me feel a little bit better, and though at first I just kind of played with my food, the more I eat, the more the meal is starting to grow on me.

That's when the lights suddenly flicker off.

And then back on again.

It was only dark for a second. Maybe not even that, but it's enough to make everyone stop eating. Everyone is frozen. What's that expression? Waiting for the other shoe to drop? But it doesn't. The lights are on, they stay on. But it doesn't change the fact that they blinked. And now all the clocks angrily think that it's 12:00! 12:00! 12:00!

I finally look to Dad, and I see for the first time my father truly starting to worry. It's that maybe-I-should-see-a-doctor face – a line I've only heard him say once, five minutes before he was rushed to the hospital with appendicitis.

So now we all sit there, silent, forks in hand, trapped at the dinner table. And for some reason I can't bring myself to look anyone else in the eye, so I put my head down and I eat. After a few seconds, I realize that everyone else is doing the same. Shoveling food into their mouths like scared animals. And it goes on like that until our plates are empty. Not because we're that hungry, but because none of us wants to see that look on Dad's face again.

I'm just getting ready for bed a few hours later when I hear movement outside. Uncle Basil. My bedroom window looks out into the street, so I have the luxury of hearing his every coming and going. I check the clock. Midnight is a strange time for Basil to go anywhere. I travel downstairs, and when I get there I find him loading up the back of his truck.

"I didn't want to wake you," he says, already seeming guilty about something.

"You're leaving?" I ask.

He looks to me warmly. "It'll just be for a few nights," he says, though the giant suitcase full of clothes tells me otherwise. Just like with Sofía. "Besides," he continues, "I've already eaten you out of house and home. I don't want to use up all of your guys' water, too."

Uncle Basil has always been a little sensitive about having

to stay with us this past year. And this whole Tap-Out thing is another added dimension to his dependence on us. But I think the power threatening to go out was the straw that broke the camel's back.

"Where are you going?" I ask.

"Daphne's place. She's still in that big house over in Dove Canyon. Says they still have water there. Not sure how long that'll last, though, but at least it's something," he says, looking down.

I smirk. "Are you talking about the water, or you and Daphne?"

He chuckles. "Either/or," he says.

Daphne is his on-again–off-again girlfriend. They'd been together since before his farm failed. They moved down here right at the beginning of the "Big Bail," which is what they called the mass exodus from the Central Valley's farming communities. Daphne always refused to allow us to call him "Uncle Basil" in her presence. It was all Herb, all the time – which makes me think that deep down, she really does love him, even though they keep breaking up.

"Well," I say, "I hope the Tap-Out helps bring you two back together."

"She's not doing it for me," he admits. "She's doing it for you."

"Me?"

"All of you. To keep me from being a burden on your mom and dad."

"You're not a burden…"

He smiles. "Thanks for saying so, Alyssa."

I give him a tight hug goodbye, and watch him drive off. Then I go back inside, sad to see him leave like this, but at the same time, a little less worried than before. The fact that there's running water anywhere gives me hope that things might not be so bad after all.

SNAPSHOT: KZLA NEWS

"Tensions rise as the Southland enters the third day of the Tap-Out, but government officials say relief is on the way."

Local Eyewitness News anchor Lyla Singh reads her part, then defers to Chase Buxton, her co-anchor, who recites his line from the teleprompter.

"Meanwhile, the cascade effect that has left more than twenty-three million people without running water shows no sign of abating. For more, we take you to Donavan Lee in Silverlake."

As they cut away from the studio to the empty concrete reservoir that used to be Silverlake, Lyla reflects on the trials of her day. Getting to the studio from the Hollywood Hills was a nightmare. She had nearly missed the midmorning update, and now it looks like the news will be preempting more and more programming – which means she won't be going home anytime soon.

"Did you hear the head of FEMA was ignoring the governor's calls?" one of the cameramen had told her earlier. "No joke – Hurricane Noah is the only thing on FEMA's radar right now."

At that moment, their producer had passed by and admonished them both – as if Lyla had been doing anything more than just listening. "We deal in news, people, not rumors."

The control booth cuts back to the studio from the Silverlake report, and Lyla quickly brings her thoughts back to the here and now.

"Thank you, Donavan. In the midst of the mayhem, earlier today, the governor had this to say."

They roll a tape that the station has been playing over and

over throughout the day, and Lyla listens for the umpteenth time, still trying to figure out if there's anything in the governor's voice betraying a deeper truth that he hasn't shared with the press.

"Federal Emergency Management is aware of the situation," the governor says, "and we are told that tankers of potable water are on their way from as far as Wyoming to satisfy Southern California's immediate critical need."

Wyoming? thinks Lyla. *How long will it take water trucks to get here from Wyoming?*

"I want to assure the people of Southern California," continues the governor, "that help is on the way. Mobile desalination plants are going to be in place up and down the coast, to turn seawater into drinking water. Everything possible is being done to alleviate this situation. Thank you."

Then he leaves, as always, dodging a barrage of questions.

The camera's red light blinks on, catching Lyla a little bit off guard. But she's a professional. Rather than stumbling, she just pauses, making the moment seem intentional.

"At this time," she reads, "everyone is advised to stay indoors to avoid heat stroke, and stay tuned for more information."

"That's right, Lyla," Chase says. "And everyone should refrain from any sort of strenuous activity."

"Exactly. The best way to conserve water right now is to hold onto the water your body already has."

There were two full pitchers of ice water in Lyla's dressing room when she arrived that morning. Just thinking about them now makes her want a nice tall glass.

"We'll be back right after this."

Then they cut to a commercial.

Lyla relaxes, looking at her briefings of the upcoming stories. How the zoo is handling the Tap-Out. A man who was shot while trying to get water from a tanker truck heading for a hospital, and – just breaking now – the first official death from dehydration in San Bernardino.

Chase turns to her, raising an eyebrow. "This is bad," he says, with the same vocal inflection with which he might have said, "This is fresh," back in the days when he was a voice actor on fast food commercials – although rumor had it he did other sorts of work. But like their producer said, they deal in news, not rumors.

"And yet all we do is tell people to stay calm and keep watching."

"What are we supposed to tell them? Go scream bloody murder naked through the streets?"

"If it will help get them through this, then yes."

"Well," Chase says with an irksome smirk, "that would make quite the story."

When the afternoon report is over, Lyla goes to her dressing room, only to find that both pitchers are empty. Someone – or maybe multiple people – has pilfered her water.

"More is on the way," a nervous intern promises. "Ten minutes, max."

But ten minutes later, neither the water nor the intern are anywhere to be found.

In the hallway, Chase is on the line with his agent, the speakerphone blaring his personal business to anyone who cares. The agent's telling him that if he handles this just right, this crisis could propel him to the national stage. A spot on CNN, maybe.

"I hate that you're using this as your personal pole vault," Lyla tells him.

Chase just shrugs, and continues his conversation.

While Lyla has her own career ambitions, she's not the jackal that Chase is, scavenging a future from the bones of the present.

She looks out a window, trying to get a true view of this crisis from forty-three stories up. Down below there are crowds in the street. Are they demonstrating? Is it water distribution? From this high up she can't tell. Suddenly she feels claustrophobic in this tower. Isolated.

Then more reports of dehydration deaths begin to roll in as the afternoon churns on. They come fast and furious, and she knows they have to report them, and can only imagine what it would be like to be on the listening end, trapped in your neighborhood, wondering if someone on your street is going to be next.

And all this time, no water comes to her dressing room. Chase is dry, too. There doesn't seem to be water for anyone, and no one's promising anything anymore.

That's when she gets an idea. It's a long shot, but it's the only idea she's got.

"Put me in Sky-Three chopper," she tells her producer.

"What?" He looks at her as if she's become delirious. "Lyla, you're an anchor – you haven't done an aerial report since your days covering traffic."

"Riots, fires, and gridlock – the stories aren't in here, they're out there. People will respond to it," she says, pretending that, like Chase, this is all about ambition. "An anchor in the sky will hold their attention. Keep them on us instead of switching channels."

"No," he tells her. "I need you at your desk."

But once he's gone, she goes to the roof anyway.

Sky-Three chopper is on the helipad, as the traffic reporters' shifts are changing. For a moment she flashes to Vietnam, where some of the best reporting ever took place. Of course, it was long before she was born, but she can't help but look at that helicopter and imagine what it must have been like for those reporters desperately waiting to get airlifted out as Saigon fell.

Kurt, the same pilot who used to take her out in her early days with the station, leans against the stairwell shaft, having a smoke – which is not allowed so close to the chopper, but he doesn't care. She's hoping that's not the only rule he doesn't care about.

"Kurt, what's the range of your chopper?"

"About two-fifty on a full tank," he tells her. "Right now, probably closer to two hundred – why?"

She takes a deep breath. "I need a favor."

Five minutes later, they're soaring away from downtown LA, heading east. And once she feels they've put enough distance between themselves and the newsroom, she texts her producer.

Taking Sky-Three to Arrowhead. Will report on refugee situation.

She sends it. Thinks for a moment, then texts, **Cover for me, or fire me.**

There, it's done. Whatever happens now, she'll be in one of the few places that still has water. The high lakes might be below their usual waterline, but they're still lakes. She takes a deep, relieved breath, feeling a sense of connection to her fellow journalists all those years ago, as they boarded helicopters halfway around the world to escape the Viet Cong.

---

4) Kelton

No school today. No news on when classes will resume. With just two weeks left to the school year, I wonder if we'll be going back at all.

I try to keep busy by flipping through comic books, but for some reason they don't feel engaging today. I search online for hunting gear to add to my Christmas wish list – still not gripping my attention. So I go to watch YouTube videos of chess boxing – a hybrid fighting sport where you alternate between chess and a round of boxing. It's the one non-weapon-related sport that I excel in. It's also the only thing that's landed me in disciplinary Saturday school in my entire high school career – because after doing an oral report on it in English last year, I was cornered by a trio of nonbelievers, and forced to demonstrate the boxing aspect on one of their noses. I would have pummeled them in chess, too, but was hauled into the dean's office.

I watch a couple of videos, but today, even chess boxing is no match for how listless I feel. It's more than that, though. I'm troubled about the state of the world outside, even considering how prepared we are.

It started when Burnside showed up at our door with a gift. Sure, I love the idea of our family's arch-enemies turning into sycophantic suck-ups, but when the strange actually materializes into reality, it definitely leaves you reeling. Much like that what-now feeling when you look into the dark eyes of the first stag you've brought down – or the triumphant despair of shooting a game duck out of the air, only for it to fall down a cliff, never to be retrieved for all of eternity. And the more I think about it … the more I realize that everything can be effectively related to hunting. I mean, they do say our every action and inaction is related to some primordial fight or flight hardwiring…

For example, winning the affection of a girl is a lot like shooting a deer. It's important that you approach slowly and with caution – and preferably from a posterior angle, where they have little to no vision. Women, like deer, can be scared away by a strong musk, which is why it's important to always wear deodorant. Dressing in camouflage doesn't hurt either, because in my experience, girls find camouflage really cool. But all of that aside, I think the most important aspect of obtaining a girl of the opposite sex is knowing when to pull the trigger. Metaphorically, that is. You gotta make your move when it feels right, or else you'll come off as creepy. This I know from experience, too.

But when it comes to my next-door neighbor, Alyssa Morrow, she feels like the deer I've never been able to shoot. Like I'm so close to making a move, or at least telling her how I feel, but for some reason the moment never feels right. I always figured that if I was in the right place, the right time would present itself, so this year I hacked the school computer and arranged to get five of my six classes with her … I would've done all six, but that would have been too obvious.

On this particular morning Alyssa's finishing up yard work out front. It looks like she's trying to siphon water out of their irrigation system, but that's not going to work. Judging by their brown lawn, their sprinklers have been dry for months, just like most everyone else's. As far as timing goes, I'm starting to get the feeling that it's now or never, so I slip on a desert camouflage tactical vest and head next door.

I step outside and locate Alyssa heading toward her garage, struggling to carry some tools. I have positioning to my advantage, so I flank left. As I near, I swallow hard, my nerves making my throat go thick. "Need any help?" I manage to get out. I realize it's the exact same thing I said the other day when they were unloading their ice. I'm hoping she appreciates consistency.

"That's okay, I think I got it." Though clearly she doesn't. Perhaps she's trying not to look weak in front of me. So I push forward.

"Here, let me at least grab these for you," I say, as I take a few wrenches and store them in my pocket. Cargo shorts are essential. Girls love a guy with lots of pockets.

"Thanks," she says, as we put the tools away in their respective places in the garage. That's when I catch a whiff of something nasty coming from the house. I must wrinkle my nose, because she notices it and looks away, as if I might think the smell is coming from her.

"Septic problems?" I ask.

"We think sewer gas is backing up into our house because of the lack of water," she tells me. "My dad's working on some plumbing modifications to stop it."

This, I knew, was inevitable. Probably every house in the neighborhood but ours will be smelling the same right about now. But not everyone seems as diligent about doing something about it as Alyssa and her family. Of course, they're going about it all wrong.

"All you need is zero-evaporation trap seal liquid. Pour about a cup into every drain, and no sewer gas can get through." And then I add, "It's the stuff they use in waterless urinals."

She makes an "ew" face at me, and I realize that was too much information.

"Anyhoo," I say, stumbling over my words a bit, and looking away involuntarily, "I can give you a bottle. We've got plenty of it." Which is true, but when my dad finds out I gave it away, he'll chew me a new one.

But it's worth it, because Alyssa lights up. "Thanks, Kelton – that's really generous of you."

And after seeing her smile like that at me, something compels me to go all in. I hold out my canteen to her. "Here, have some," I say. "You look thirsty."

She cautiously takes the canteen. "Are you sure?" she asks.

I shrug like it's nothing. "What are friends for?"

She takes a few gulps and hands it back. Then I take a swig. Alyssa and I just shared a canteen. Considering the saliva exchange involved, that's almost like kissing. I suppress a little shiver at the thought.

"Thank you, Kelton," she says again. Then we stand there in silence, but for the first time the silence that lingers between us feels a little more natural. It feels good.

Without warning Garrett appears out of what feels like

thin air, and snatches the canteen from me.

"Thanks, Kelton!" he teases.

"Don't be rude," Alyssa says. "That's not yours!"

Just then their father enters with a box of dirty rags, and her mother just a few moments later. She smiles, barely able to contain herself. "News says there'll be desalination machines along the coast. They'll have a few up and running down at Laguna Beach by this afternoon."

"What's a desalination machine?" Garrett asks.

"It converts saltwater into freshwater," I tell him. "They've actually got a big plant down in San Diego, but it's not going to help us." Truth be told, it won't help San Diego much either now. It was forward-thinking of them to build it a few years back, so for once it's not a case of too little too late. Instead, it's too little right on time. Because at full capacity, it can provide enough water for eight percent of San Diego's population. Less than one in ten people. Not the solution they hoped it would be.

Alyssa's father wipes sweat from his brow. "We pay big taxes to fund organizations like FEMA. It's about time they stepped in and did something."

"Well, it's not like they can just let us die of thirst," her mother adds, as if this notion were preposterous, but then waits for someone to chime in with validation.

Her father nods in agreement. "It's a matter of numbers," he says. "After all, California is one of the largest work economies. They need us, and I don't think they would be so stupid as to neglect us."

Her father's words stick with me ... and though they have

merit, I can't help but hear my own father's voice echoing in my head, complaining about the thousands of cumulative mistakes that have led us to this point – the failed consumer rebates, conservation councils, and radical attempts to save water, like the millions of black "shade balls" Los Angeles released into reservoirs to prevent evaporation, which did nothing. And now I can't decide whether we're headed toward a real solution, or if we're desperately throwing water bottles at the problem...

I open my mouth to raise such questions, but then suddenly stop myself, remembering what my father always told me about the *sheep*. Their behavior. How their main instinct is to follow members of the herd directly ahead of them, and how being thrown off course even the slightest bit would elicit an overwhelming primordial sense of panic that can be deadly. I did a current events presentation once about a flock of five hundred sheep somewhere in Turkey that plummeted to their deaths one by one in a ravine, because each sheep followed the one directly ahead of it, never comprehending the bigger picture. Which is worse, I wonder – watching everyone you know fall into that ravine, or shaking their reality with such force that it ruins them.

5) Alyssa

Today the toilet is really getting back at us for all the years of cruel and unsanitary labor. It's been making strange gurgling sounds and expelling six-month-old-rotten-egg smells. So our current mission is to clean the toilet bowls the best we can, and

61

then pour in two cups of Kelton's trap seal liquid stuff, so our house can smell like a house again and less like a spiteful septic tank. And as supreme ruler of the household, Dad has elected Garrett and me to take care of the toilets.

This morning Dad has taken the liberty of delegating tasks through passive-aggressive Post-it notes hidden like Easter eggs all over the house. One on the fridge reads, "Six cups of water per day!" Another on our shower reads, "Dry bathing only!" which consists of shower gel and paper towels. But I think the worst one of all is the "Clean me please!" Post-it just above the toilets. Dad craftily installed bags under each toilet seat, which we are to throw out after using, like a giant camping nightmare. The bag thing is manageable, but having to actually clean the bowl in its current state is just cruel and unusual punishment.

Garrett and I start with the downstairs bathroom, seeing as our water is stored in the bathtub adjacent to the toilet. I take a look into the bathtub and realize that the water line has really receded since Saturday. This morning Mom discreetly gave away a couple of gallons to some friends around the corner. With desalination units being set up along the coast, she figures there'll be enough water for everyone soon enough, so why not be generous? If it were up to me, I'd probably do the same.

"How are we supposed to clean a toilet if we can't use water?" Garrett asks, as he crams his hands into those yellow cleaning gloves that squeak when you rub your fingers together.

"Dad said the cleaning supplies are under the sink. I'm sure you can figure it out."

I pinch my nostrils together, and dare myself to look into the toilet bowl. Black liquid bubbles to the surface.

"Why do I have to do it?" he nags.

"Because we're taking turns," I remind him, then appeal to his male ego. "Plus you're a guy; you're naturally going to be better than me at plumbing."

He nods in accordance, clearly satisfied to hear me say he's better than me at something. Then he fishes under the sink for the cleaning supplies.

"Bleach will do," I tell him.

He eventually settles on the green canister of powdered Comet, a bleach-based multipurpose cleaner, and goes to set it on the edge of the bathtub. The moment its bottom touches the edge, I can already see the worst-case scenario playing in my head, but it isn't until he lets go of the Comet that my worst fear materializes into reality. The container, sitting precariously on the uneven edge, begins to slip...

My heart quicksteps. "Garrett!" I yell, which is all I can manage to get out.

He spins around, and before he's even able to grasp the situation, the container of powdered bleach has already slipped down the side of the tub and splashed into the water.

He looks back to me, his face completely drained of color. And next comes the most torturous of silences.

He quickly goes for the Comet, but it slips from his grasp, only to float farther away. The water is already clouding with a swirling murk of poisonous multipurpose cleanser. And then reality finally hits me.

Garrett has just tainted the only water we have...

"Maybe we can save some of it," he says as he finally grasps the Comet can and pulls it out of the water upside down, dumping even more liquefying powder into the tub.

"It's already contaminated, idiot," I tell him sharply.

"It's your fault," he snaps. "You told me to use the bleach!"

"You've always been a klutz! Do you have any idea what you just did?"

But instead of coming back with another defense, his face constricts, his eyes take on a shiny squint, and tears begin to seep out, his body giving way to hopelessness.

My sisterly conscience kicks in and I'm suddenly wishing I could take back my words.

"I'm sorry," he says through snivels, burying his face in his hands.

"It's okay," I tell him, and I give him a hug — something I realize I haven't done in a long time. "We have the desalination machines down by the beach. Mom and Dad are going to stock up, remember?"

Garrett nods, collecting himself.

"Drinking from the bathtub was totally disgusting anyway," I say, and he laughs, disrupting the tears long enough to bring him back from despair.

I agree that I'll be the one to tell Mom and Dad about what happened to the bathwater, because Garrett argued that it would sound better coming from me. Of course, the real reason is that he's too afraid to break the news to them himself. For some reason he thinks our parents are a lot scarier than they really are … but then again, this isn't the routine spoiled dinner, stink bomb, or broken window. "I'll tell them, but I won't take the blame," I say to Garrett. "I know it was an accident, but you still have to own up to it." Because what kind of sister would I be if I didn't teach him the importance of taking responsibility?

I go downstairs to tell Mom and Dad, bracing for the worst – but they don't get angry. Which, I soon realize, is much worse than if they had.

"All of it?" Dad says – as if there were a way to divide the Comet water from the drinkable water.

"It wasn't Garrett's fault," I tell them, even though it was. "He was just trying to clean the toilet, like you told him."

I expect Mom to say something like, *Don't you go putting this back on us!* But she doesn't even return my slow lob. This isn't just a screw-up, I realize. It's an *Event*. Events bypass anger, straight to damage control.

"We still have the pitcher in the fridge," Mom says, looking at Dad.

Dad nods. "The desalination rigs should be up and running sometime today. We'll head out there as soon as we can."

"Maybe we can boil the water in the tub, one pot at a time," I suggest, "and collect the steam." We made a distillery like that back in seventh grade as part of a science lab. As I recall, we barely managed to get a test tube of water out of it – but I'll bet Kelton could make a functional one.

Did I actually just think about asking Kelton for help?

"That's a project for another day," Dad says, already over-whelmed with the weight of the news I just delivered.

"I'm sorry," I tell them. "It sucks, and I'm sorry."

"Don't cry over spilt milk, honey," says Mom.

"Or poisoned water," adds Dad, which makes me grimace, but I press my lips tight so they can't see.

I go upstairs to notify Garrett that he won't be put up for adoption, sent to a forced labor camp, or cooked into meat pies – but he's nowhere to be found. I check the bathroom, the backyard, and even the garage … and that's when I notice that his bike is missing. He took off without telling anyone, so afraid of what Mom and Dad would do.

Mom and Dad drop everything to find Garrett. They want us to split up and systematically search every place he might go. They're a little more worried than I thought they'd be. They're always overreacting when it comes to Garrett. He was born a month premature, and it sent my parents into this eternal hypersensitive protection mode; even to this day, if he so much as gets a scratch, it's like they've got the hospital on speed dial for an emergency skin graft. I try to tell myself that it's just my parents being parents, but today I can't help but worry a little, considering the circumstances.

I agree to check the parks where he and his friends like to hang out, and the bike trail that runs parallel to the freeway. I go to get my bike, but both tires are flat, since I haven't really used the thing in years, and the tires don't take air now, no matter how much I pump. All that's left is Garrett's GoPed, which I have no idea how to use, and a pogo stick – which was clearly invented by Satan right after he invented the unicycle. So after exhausting all options, I realize that I'm going to have to ask Kelton for some neighborly help. Maybe he'll let me borrow a bike – or create a work-around out of bubblegum and earwax.

I ring the doorbell and he answers, almost too quickly.

No time for small talk. I get right to the point. "I have a favor to ask. Garrett's missing, and I need a bike."

Rather than being weird, he responds like a regular human being. "You can use my dad's," he says. "I'll go get it."

He goes back in, and meets me at the side gate. It's a nice bike. Then I realize that he's bringing his own bike out as well.

"Two heads are better than one," he says. "And it's really not a good idea for you to be out on your own right now. Things might look quiet, but it's always that way right before a storm."

Scratch the normal human being thing.

"That's okay, Kelton. You don't have to come."

"The cost of borrowing my dad's bike is letting me come with you."

He's not mincing words any more than I am – and clearly, he's not negotiating.

"Fine," I tell him. Actually, I don't really mind, considering he's officially been moved down from orange to yellow on the threat-to-my-sanity scale.

We start with the back trails, which eventually spits us back out to the main road near Garrett's school – my high school being just across the street. Which gives rise to the thought that maybe he's hiding in the last place we'd expect; the place he despises more than cauliflower and piano lessons combined – Meadow Creek Elementary School.

I lean left, redirecting my bike's trajectory, but before I can even turn, a truck flies by, nearly running us over. At first I find myself pissed that someone could drive so recklessly, but as soon as I realize what kind of truck it is, my spine stiffens, and without even thinking, my legs stop pedaling.

It's a camouflage-green open-top military truck, packed with armed soldiers. My first thought is stupid. The kind of thing you think before your mind has time to run it past your brain.

"What the hell? Did my parents call the freaking national guard?"

"Quiet before the storm," is all Kelton says.

My brain has kicked in by now, and I realize that this is much bigger than my AWOL brother. It's pretty disturbing to see war machines traverse the neighborhood you grew up in – and if that's not troubling enough, the truck turns left, directly into the high school parking lot.

"What do you think's going on?" I ask Kelton, hoping that his extensive knowledge of useless military factoids will come in handy.

"I don't know," he says. "It's too soon for martial law…"

"English, please."

"It's when the military takes over," he says. "It means that government brass thinks the local police can't handle the situation by themselves."

"Well, that would be a good thing, right?" I say, really wanting to convince myself. I push back onto the seat of the bike. "It means we'll be safer…"

Kelton attempts to smile. "Could be," he says, even though I get the feeling he doesn't believe it could be a good thing at all. "Maybe."

Maybe. I'm so sick of maybe!

Maybe it's martial law. *Maybe* FEMA will bring in water trucks. *Maybe* everything will be fine tomorrow. Living in this world of complete uncertainty is more and more frustrating. So I ride forward and follow the transport truck. It's not just that I'm angry, it's because I have to know. I need to kill the maybe. Kelton is on the same wavelength, because he's pedaling right behind me.

We ride past lower campus, the football stadium, and then the tennis courts, just waiting to see where the truck will stop. But it isn't until we pass the aquatics center that we get our answer.

It's not just one truck, but a whole bunch of military vehicles. They've got the swimming pool on total lockdown … because high school pools were the only ones that were excluded from the Frivolous Use Initiative. They're the only pools left that still have water.

The perimeter of the aquatics center is now guarded by soldiers with automatic rifles. And spidering into the pool are a dozen thick fire hoses – which seem to be sucking up water and depositing it into a series of tanker trucks. Then one of the military guards spots us and locks eyes. I don't look away, but I don't get any closer either. *It's like somehow I'm the enemy.*

"I should've guessed it," Kelton says, upset at himself for not knowing everything in the history of everything.

"Those idiots think we're going to drink that?" I laugh. "I have friends on the water polo team. I've heard stories. They'd have to pay me to drink that water."

"If they can filter the salt and fish guts and whale turds out of ocean water, I'm sure they can manage anything left behind by the water polo meatheads," Kelton says.

And for some reason this strikes a chord, piquing a memory. Something that Garrett said when we were pushing that broken cart in Costco...

I gasp, and Kelton looks to me, wondering why.

"Garrett's friend Jason has a huge fish tank! I'll bet he went to his house to ask for water from it!" Though Garrett's always been hard on himself, he was never much of a sulker, so it makes perfect sense that he'd try to fix the situation rather than run from it. I reach for my phone and realize I don't have it. I left it to charge on my nightstand. Stupid.

"Can I borrow your phone? I should tell my parents. They can get there quicker."

He hands me the phone, but after a few moments of blankly staring at the screen, I realize that I don't even know my parents' numbers. In fact, I don't know anyone's number by heart, except my stupid eighth grade boyfriend's, who is the last person on this or any other planet that I'd call.

I don't want to admit to Kelton my current uselessness, so I just say, "We're not that far. Let's just go."

We circle the block that Jason lives on twice.

"You don't know where he lives, do you?"

"Just shut up, okay?" I snap, because I only kinda sorta know where Jason lives. "There's a huge tree in the front yard," I tell him. "Like, ridiculously huge."

But there are no trees that big anywhere.

"I'm sure it's this street," I say, after the third time around.

Kelton thinks about it. "So let's do some detective work," he says. "If the tree was that big, it probably was a huge violation of association rules — and believe me, my family knows about that, because everything we do is a violation."

"Your point?"

"My point is, not everybody doubles down on their violations..."

I finally get it. "A stump! We're looking for a stump!"

And five houses up, there it is!

Kelton smiles, pleased with himself. Under other circumstances it might have been annoying, but he deserves a moment here. Someone else might have just thought I was lying, or not remembering – but he accepted that I was telling the truth and went from there.

"That was pretty clever," I admit to him as we head to the house.

He shrugs with false modesty. "Just a simple deduction."

That's when my own simple deduction is confirmed – because, on closer inspection, I can see Garrett's bike behind a dead hedge near the front door.

We hop off our bikes and approach the house. The door's ajar. It feels weird knocking on a door that's already partially open, but I do. No response, so I push it open all the way.

I go in, and Kelton follows. There's a smell here. Awful. Rotten.

"Could be a dead body," Kelton whispers. I ignore him.

The living room looks pretty normal. Except for the gaudy Roman statue with the leaf-covered genitalia. No accounting for taste.

"I don't think anyone's home…"

Screw it. I cross the living room, heading deeper into the house. "Garrett…?" I call out… No response. "Anyone home?"

Kelton hesitates. "You know, it's perfectly legal to shoot someone for breaking and entering."

"Fine – you can say 'told ya so' when I'm dead."

Kelton initially follows behind me, but then he pushes his way in front – as if just remembering that Eagle Scouts probably shouldn't hide behind girls.

We continue down a hallway. The farther we get, the stranger the carpet underneath my feet begins to feel – the squishier it becomes. It's wet – and the smell is worse than before.

That's when something catches my eye—

A tropical fish – no, dozens of them. All dead, spread across the floor of the family room. I look up and realize why… The giant fish tank is broken. The enormous aquarium reaches all the way to the ceiling, the collections of rocks and coral that once were a part of the aquatic ecosystem still intact. This is definitely the tank that Garrett was talking about. I move closer to get a better look. A large portion of the tank's face has been smashed in, violently drained of all of its water – that is, except a thin layer at the bottom, maybe an inch, where a small clown fish sucks in water helplessly, its body partially exposed to the air. I pick it up and move it to another area of the tank where it has a better chance at survival—

"It was like this when I got here," says a voice from behind. I spin around and there's Garrett, standing in the kitchen doorway. "And it's saltwater, anyway."

I'm happy to have found him … but it isn't long until a thousand thoughts cascade through my head, bursting the levees that maintain my patience.

"Then what are you still doing here?" I say sharply, realizing that I'm pissed he would send us on a wild goose chase in the first place.

"Dad said he needed more pasta sauce, so I figured I'd borrow a bottle or two," he explains, avoiding the important questions, as he always does. He looks down and kicks an invisible rock. "Can't leave empty-handed, you know?"

"You have Mom and Dad worried sick. You had us *all* worried sick," I tell him, which I'm sure he already knows. I exhale my aggravation and look around the room, taking in the whole bizarre scene. "So what the hell happened here?"

Garrett shrugs. "I think they skipped town and someone must have broken in."

"Well," says Kelton, looking around at all the dead fish, "they definitely didn't come for sushi." It might have been borderline funny in a different situation.

Kelton then reaches down and picks up a shard of glass. He holds it up as if to inspect it, the shard glimmering in a ray of light … and that's when I notice what he already has. There's blood on the glass…

"Let's leave," Garrett says.

Kelton and I don't need a second invitation. We don't even bother to take the pasta sauce.

Once we're back, Mom and Dad don't punish Garrett, which in itself worries me a little. Instead they're scouring the house for empty gallon jugs to bring to the desalination machines.

"You think they'll let us get more than two gallons?" Mom says, to whoever's listening, her head stuck in the pantry.

"We can always go back for more!" Dad yells, probably from a closet somewhere.

Garrett emerges from the door to the garage with a large container usually reserved for camping trips. "Will this work?"

"Absolutely," Mom says. Garrett, in light of not being punished, is now trying his best to be a perfect son. I give it five minutes, tops.

"Take care of your brother," Mom says to me. "And be careful of the McCrackens. Remember, they invented ten-foot poles for people like that."

Dad swings through the kitchen and grabs the car keys from the bowl on the counter. "Listen to your mother," he says, having no idea what she even said.

"Kelton's not sooo bad," I say, suddenly realizing how strange that sounds coming out of my mouth.

Mom and Dad, with empty jugs under their arms, make their way toward the door. "Well, his older brother got out of there the second he could. His shoes left skid marks on the doorstep," Dad says.

Garrett holds the door for them graciously, and Mom kisses him on the head.

"See you in a bit," I say with a smile. They take Mom's Prius, since Dad's car is still convalescing in the garage. It's moments like these, seeing them together, that make me appreciate the family I have. When you're a teenager you spend so much time complaining about how lame your parents are, and then they always somehow seem to find a way to remind you that they're actually not as uncool as you want to believe. And now with the two of them gone, for some odd childlike reason, I find myself wishing I could have given them a hug goodbye.

6) Kelton

I decided not to tell my father about the military trucks we saw at our high school. It's not that I don't think it's a significant development, but seeing that we haven't yet been able to get in touch with my older brother, Brady, there's no point in rocking the proverbial boat if we're just going to wait here for him anyway, rather than take off to our bug-out in the mountains. With my dad, the embers of armageddon will quickly grow into a full-on blazing apocalypse in his head. He already got that crazy look in his eyes after hearing about the closures of so many school districts. Which, by the way, is no tragedy to me. Not that I hate school, it's just that when it comes down to it, I learn more just hanging out at home anyway. I'd probably be homeschooled if either of my parents had the patience to do it.

To take my mind off of things, I load up my paintball gun and practice in the backyard. I'm hitting every target on point, and I try to tell myself it's a good omen. The de-sal rigs down at the beach will do their job. No one will go thirsty. All will be well.

My dad steps out onto the patio. "Don't forget to exhale

with your shot," he says. He knows his stuff – after all, he did spend twelve years in the Marine Corps. My mom likes to make fun of his career as a jarhead – his "extraction missions," because technically he worked as a military dentist and never actually left his base.

After a few more shots, my CO_2 cartridge runs out. I go inside to change it, and right after I finish loading the new cartridge, there's a knock on the front door. My dad answers it – it's Roger Malecki, one of our other neighbors. The Maleckis just had a baby, so we never see them much. Actually, we never saw them much before the baby, either. We're not exactly social butterflies in our family.

"How are things, Roger?" my dad says pleasantly.

"Ugh, don't ask," Malecki says. "The car keeps overheating. Plus we're having problems with sewage. Whole house stinks."

"I hear ya," says my dad. "You know, the Morrows next door had the exact same problem." Although he doesn't offer Malecki any trap seal liquid.

Then Malecki begins to avoid eye contact. My father has no patience for beating around the bush.

"What can I do for you, Roger?"

Malecki heaves a sigh. "It's the baby. Hannah's still able to feed her, but she's getting dehydrated. I'm afraid she won't be able to breastfeed much longer. We have some powdered formula, but that's kind of useless without water…"

"I'm sorry to hear that," my dad says genuinely. "How can we help?"

"Well … we know you have survival supplies. Hell,

everyone knows you've got enough squirrelled away in there to survive the apocalypse." Then he laughs nervously, noticing my dad frowning a bit at the word "squirrelled." As if preparing for the worst is somehow worthy of ridicule. And just then I notice that Malecki's hands are shaking anxiously, like he went over this dialogue in his head a thousand times, and still screwed it up.

I know my dad well enough to know that he doesn't give "hand-outs." Plus, once you start giving things away for free it's a slippery slope. And if there's one thing my dad hates, it's slippery slopes.

My dad casually, strategically puts his hand on the door. Not to close it, but to give him leverage in case he needs to. "The key word there, Roger, is 'survival.' We have just enough to survive."

Malecki takes a moment to regroup his thoughts, and tries again. "All right, I get it," he says. "You have principles and you don't want to compromise them – but I'm begging you, Richard. There's got to be something you can do... I mean ... the baby..."

My dad weighs the possibilities. "I'm sure I could give you a few pointers," he says.

"Pointers?"

My dad motions toward Malecki's yard. "You've got a marvelous garden of succulents. You could grind those up and squeeze at least a gallon out of them. I could even show you how to make a condenser to extract the water."

"The cactuses?" Malecki laughs, incredulous.

My dad smiles graciously. "Cacti," he gently corrects.

"You could have fresh water by tomorrow."

Malecki's smile fades, realizing that my father isn't joking. "I have a family to look after. I don't have that kind of time!"

"Well, if you want water you'll make the time."

But rather than formulating a response, his eyes narrow and his lips curl with rage. He steps forward, getting into my dad's face. "Who the hell do you think you are?"

But my dad stays cool. Collected. "Roger, I'm offering you a gift much more valuable than a bottle of water. Self-reliance."

Malecki's expression darkens, and he gets this strange, wild look in his eyes.

"You're just going to stand there and let my wife's breast milk run dry?"

"How dare you get angry at me – as if *your* lack of foresight is my fault!"

"You're a son of a bitch, you know that?"

And my dad's done. He doesn't suffer fools lightly – and to him anyone who expects others to solve their problems is a fool.

"Why don't you come back when you're ready to behave like a functioning member of society." He tries to shut the door, but Malecki lunges forward across the threshold, blocking the door from closing.

"I should smack that grin right off your face," says Malecki, although my dad isn't grinning at all. My dad tries to shoulder him out, but Malecki has the adrenaline of a desperate man, and pushes farther in. He knocks my father off balance, and the door swings open.

That's when I raise my gun, exhale, and pull the trigger.

Three times. I shoot Malecki square in the chest. Right on target. The force of the blasts blows him back against the door jamb. All his bravado is gone. He wails, thinking he's dying. Then he reaches to his chest and examines the blue phosphorescent ooze on his shirt. My heart pounds probably as much as his. He looks up to me with this forlorn, bewildered look, as if I really had blown a hole in his chest. Then I reach for my backpack hanging on the rack near the front door. I cram my arm in, shift around, and produce a water bottle I bought at school, when it was something I took for granted. I shove it into his blue, dripping hands.

"Take it and leave," I tell him.

Malecki looks at the bottle of water and goes red in the face, embarrassed, like it wasn't too late for his humanity to suddenly come rushing back. He turns, and like that, he's gone.

In an instant my dad looks to me, his lip bloodied from the scuffle, now wearing this violently charged expression – and I can't tell if he's just worked up, or if he truly disapproves of what I did – not that I blasted the guy with paint, but that I gave him my water.

"This was none of your business," my father says sternly. "You shouldn't have interfered."

"Yes, sir," I tell him. "I know, sir." I always call him sir when he's pissed off at me.

Then he closes the door and strides away.

The thing is, I'm glad I did what I did. Not just because it has always been a fantasy of mine to blast our neighbors with my paintball gun – but because whether my dad knows it or not, I saw what was coming next. What would have happened if I didn't pull my trigger. Because at the apex of that confrontation, my dad's hand had instinctively traveled down to his belt … where his gun was nestled in its holster.

PART TWO

THREE DAYS TO ANIMAL

Camille Cohen has always had a problem with impassive bureaucracy and authority figures. Back in high school, she was extremely vocal in pointing out hypocrisies in the curriculum, or inequalities in their disciplinary system – and nothing has really changed now that she's a social ecology major at UC Irvine. The only difference is that now, she sees a path to actually changing the world.

It really didn't take a genius to figure out that we'd run out of water. If you just read the quarterly public water reports, as she had, the numbers were right there. But to successfully ignore those reports and misdirect people into thinking the problem was under control? That required the mastery of a very special skill set. These were the supervillains Camille hoped to bring down someday. Hopefully, sooner than later.

Weeks before the Tap-Out, Camille led a protest at the county government offices in Santa Ana, backed by a record number of participants – all members of her college's student body. But she knew it would take more than one protest. If there's anything her past efforts have taught her, it's that real change requires prolonged pressure and inspired action.

Raw. Tangible. Action.

Today's action will be inspired by what she sees on the road ahead of her. It begins with shock, followed by rage – because cruising ahead of her is a water supply truck owned by one of the various underperforming water municipalities. The ten-gallon bottles stacked in its bed are clearly visible, and are a let-them-drink-wine sort of slap in the face to an increasingly thirsty population. This truck is delivering water that isn't supposed to exist to some privileged place. It represents every single lie she's been fighting so hard to expose.

So rather than continuing west to the desalination center at the beach, she decides to crank her wheel right and follow the truck.

SNAPSHOT 2 OF 3: OCWD TRANSPORT

David Chen has been an employee of the Orange County Water District for nearly a year now – and lately they've given him increasingly stressful tasks. Today he's driving a truck full of drinking water, and riding shotgun is a guy with a shotgun. And a bulletproof vest. In fact, they've given David a vest, too. "Just a precaution," he was told. "Nothing to concern yourself with." As if he's stupid.

The vest is heavy and hot, and no amount of air-conditioning in the truck can cool him down. He's sweating in more ways than one.

With all the county's water mains on emergency shutdown, and endless glitches in the computers trying to redirect what water is left, he's been transporting water manually to high-priority facilities. Just yesterday he drove one of a dozen tanker trucks delivering the contents of a high school swimming pool to Camp Pendleton Marine Base. But desperate times call for desperate measures, and water managers are scrambling to keep the sky from completely falling.

It's late afternoon and David is only on his third delivery of the day. Traffic has been getting increasingly worse, and the GPS apps keep giving everyone the same alternate routes, just compounding the problem. Current protocol is that all water from municipal water districts will go to hospitals and government facilities first. Federal Emergency Management will provide relief for private citizens.

David already stashed away one of the blue watercooler-size containers for himself and his family. One measly container in the grand scheme of things won't be missed. He considers it unofficial combat pay.

It's reclaimed water. That's what they're down to now. All the water that was still in the sewer system when the water was turned off. All the water that was leaving homes ahead of the Tap-Out, and heading back to the Orange County Water District.

It's not like they just dump that water into the ocean. It's purified. Microfiltration, reverse osmosis, ultraviolet radiation, and abracadabra – they turned the county's last day of raw sewage into nearly fifty thousand gallons of drinkable water. Of course, no one's supposed to drink it. The policy is that it's only supposed to be used for public irrigation – because serving a litigious, finicky public reclaimed water, no matter how clean it is, would be a public relations nightmare.

But now no one cares where it comes from, as long as it comes.

This afternoon's delivery is a critical one. He's bringing water to the workers holed up behind the locked fence of Huntington Beach power plant. From what he understands, the plant, which only has about forty on-site workers at any given time, has become a refuge for Applied Energy Services, and Southern

California Edison employees. Now there are more than three hundred people within its gates. A spontaneous refugee camp of sorts. Hence today's delivery.

As he pulls off of Pacific Coast Highway, the plant wavers before him like an ugly industrial mirage, asphalt heat making it shimmer before him. But he has to halt short of the security gate, because someone's standing in his way, preventing him from proceeding. Not an employee, but a girl, no older than twenty. By the way she's planted her feet, and by the angry, thirsty look in her eye, he gets the feeling she's not going to let him pass.

Meanwhile, on the other side of Pacific Coast Highway, on the long strip of Huntington Beach, frustrated crowds waiting for desalination machines have begun to take notice of his truck.

SNAPSHOT 3 OF 3: PLANT MANAGER

When Pete Flores was a child, he always wanted to be a magician. As an adult, he found his magic in the manipulation of electrical currents. To him, he couldn't have landed any closer to his original dream, because now, as a power plant manager, he gets to create electricity out of thin air – literally – using natural gas. His Huntington Beach plant produces 450 megawatts of power, which is enough to power nearly half a million homes. But for the first time in all his years here, the station is facing an unprecedented situation.

Should he have refused to allow all of his employees safe refuge within the gates of the plant? Should he have refused when other electrical agencies requested sanctuary for their workers?

Should he have refused when they asked to bring their families?

The home office would have refused. Not because they were hardened, but because they were so far removed. They didn't see the human faces of this crisis. He might be reprimanded for what he did – might even lose his job, but he resolved not to regret it. He's accepted that the days ahead are going to be increasingly difficult, but the job brings him pride and honor.

This is nothing, he thinks, reminding himself of the nuclear power plant that melted down in Fukushima, Japan, after an earthquake, and the tsunami that followed. Generators flooded and shut down, and the reactors overheated, resulting in total nuclear meltdown. And what did that plant manager do? Rather than fleeing the scene, he decided to stay with his workers in spite of the danger, cooling the plant using seawater. It exposed them to lethal levels of radiation, but reduced Japan's nuclear contamination tenfold. That's how you hold the line when you have the fate of millions of lives in your hands. Sometimes being the hero means going down with the ship.

As the power plant is considered a critical water priority, Pete's request for food and water had to be honored. Which is exactly why all the families who are currently under his care came. Now he isn't just a plant manager, he finds he's more like a mayor. It's both terrifying and exhilarating. It makes him wonder if public office might be in his future once he gets fired for helping all these people.

Today his turbines are working at full capacity, because both the Redondo and Palomar power plants have gone off-line. The un-official word is that it was the result of employee attrition. Workers just stopped showing up. In a choice between taking care of the plants, or taking care of their families during the Tap-Out, they chose their families. It just reinforces for Pete that welcoming his own workers' families was the right decision. Still, the two plant shutdowns trouble him. If there are any more, it could cause a cascading failure in the grid – and with so many electrical workers AWOL, there's no telling when such a thing would be resolved.

Late in the afternoon, his control room supervisor alerts him that the water truck they've been waiting for all day is at the gate.

"But there's a problem," he says.

Pete is wary. While his job is all about solving problems, the issues he's been facing lately have been a bit out of his wheelhouse. "What sort of problem?"

"Maybe you should see for yourself."

Most of the security cameras show expected activity on the property. Technicians and machinery in restricted areas, and in the nonrestricted areas, their numerous guests go about their business.

But the cams at the main gate show something else entirely. Something that hits Pete like a thousand volts.

There are dozens of people at the gate, all amassed at the entrance. At first he thinks it's some sort of protest or strange demonstration – there have been plenty of those in this drought climate. But why here? And then he realizes the object of their attention —

It's the incoming water truck. And it's totally encircled.

This isn't just a protest, it's something far more dangerous – more desperate.

"How many guards do we have on duty?" Pete asks the control room supervisor.

"Three," he answers, "including the one at the gate."

"Get them all down there!"

"Should I call this in to the home office?"

"Are you kidding me? Call 911!"

And then on the screen, the crowd seems to explode into action. All of them, all at once. They're ripping bottles off the truck, smashing the windshield. Pulling out the driver. My God! It happened in the blink of an eye!

From the passenger seat emerges what looks like a security guard.

"Is that a shotgun?"

The man raises it, silently fires it into the air, and a second later Pete hears the delayed report of the gunshot, dull and distant. But the man who fired the gun gets off no more than a warning shot, because the mob rips the shotgun from him and pulls him down into a melee of angry hands.

The supervisor dispatches the other guards, and begins to frantically call 911, but it's too late – because that mob, in its righteous rage, is crashing through the gate and flooding into Pete's plant. And it's more than just dozens of people. It could be hundreds.

Helpless, plant manager Pete Flores watches the security screen, and realizes that, like electricity itself, this mob is a force as dangerous as that Japanese tsunami ... and it may be his turn to go down with the ship.

7) Kelton

As the hours pass, I start to get the feeling that Mom isn't very happy with the way Dad handled the confrontation with Malecki, because tonight she's making dinner an hour early – a nervous habit she's developed when things get tense at our house. Early dinner means she can get to bed early and end an undesirable day. My mom is also a compulsive "freezer" – and because we're trying to conserve the food we have, we somehow end up with defrosted honey-baked ham from Easter and half a green bean casserole that may have been from last Christmas, but don't quote me.

Mom fills all of our glasses with water. It's more than we're supposed to have, considering our rations, but it's not just that – she's filled our glasses to the brim, so that you can't lift them without spilling some. Another sign that she's angry at my father.

Dad takes his seat at his spot at the head of the table, for the moment oblivious to Mom's irritated overtures, and begins making incisions in his ham. The sound of scraping cutlery. The ticking clock. No one's talking, the tension so thick in the air you'd need a machete just to make it to the refrigerator and back. Finally my father notices it. He looks at my mom, looks at me, then continues cutting.

I try to lighten the mood with something positive. "Is Brady coming?" I ask anyone who'll answer.

Dad responds. "We still can't get ahold of him."

So much for lightening things. I realize that Brady's lack of response is yet another trigger-point of stress. Brady's never been good with phones. Or e-mails. Or any sort of communication at all. These days he only gets in touch when he feels like it, and only responds when he has to. I thought with the Tap-Out that might change, but apparently not. "We're going to wait for him, right?" I ask. "I mean, before we leave for the bug-out?"

Dad chews intensely. "We shouldn't stay here much longer," he says. "You can see how things are already breaking down."

Mom refills my half-drunk glass back to the absolute brim.

"Marybeth, this water is supposed to last us," he finally says, pointing with his fork.

"Your *son* is thirsty." Though I'm not really.

"Good. Being a little bit thirsty will *remind* us why we need to *ration*," he rebuts, his anger beginning to fill to the brim.

"We have plenty," Mom reminds him. "And if we're not going to *share* it, we might as well drink it *all ourselves* until we *burst*." Since I was a child, I always knew when my parents were having crypto-arguments in front of me because they start over-emphasizing words.

"We've shared every day," my dad says. "I taught the Clarks how to make a portable greenhouse, and even gave them some of the materials. I showed *your* friends down the block how to set up an outhouse."

Mom gets up and throws away her paper dinner plate, even though she's barely touched her meal. "Well, I don't see the harm in sharing a few necessities like water if we're going to be leaving it behind anyway, once we leave for the bug-out."

My dad takes a deep breath, which signals a lecture.

"You know how it works, Marybeth. If we start giving away free water, people are going to start demanding we give more. And when things get violent they'll just take. And as you can clearly see," he motions in the direction of the Maleckis' house, "even sharing information is dangerous past this point."

"They're our neighbors!"

"When it comes down to survival you don't have neighbors!"

"We're going to have to live with these people when this is all over."

"*Live* is the key word here! If this is as bad as I think it is, not everyone is going to make it — and if we're going to remain among the living we need to stick with our survival plan, and keep a tight lid on our supplies. You want to give things away? Fine. Leave the door wide open when we leave for the bug-out, and let the marauders strip this place down to the wall studs."

Mom breaks. Dad pushed just the right button. The one in between the commands for "yell" and "cry" — the same one he always pushes — the power button. Mom totally shuts down, clamming up and falling silent. Chances are she'll be like this all night, and maybe even tomorrow.

I take up her defense, though speaking in a way my father can understand. "As herders we're supposed to be a source of guidance, but we're doing nothing to help the sheep," I say.

"Before we can help anyone else, we need to make sure we're secure."

"And when will that be?"

"I'll tell you." And with that he folds his napkin, guzzles his water in audible gulps until the glass is empty, then exits the kitchen, leaving me alone with my crashed mom and the bizarro Holiday Dinner from Hell.

Fights like the one my parents had at dinner have been a regular occurrence at my house for as long as I can remember. It's one of the reasons why Brady left after he graduated from high school. Plus the fact that he got into Stanford and refused to go. That alone set him up as an Enemy of the People in our father's eyes. For the few months before his graduation, Dad would not leave him alone about it. *Do you realize the opportunity you're getting?* my father would say. *You're throwing your life away for some girl!* Because that's why Brady said he wasn't going. His girlfriend was going to Saddleback – our local community college – and he wanted to be where she was.

That wasn't the real reason, though. I know Brady better than my parents do. The real reason he didn't go to Stanford was because he was scared. I'm not exactly sure what he was scared of. Being on his own? Not measuring up? Living with strangers? Maybe a combination of all those things. Anyway, he moved out, got a job at GameStop, and now he only comes home for holidays. He stopped coming with his girlfriend, which means either she can't stand our family, or he broke up with her. Brady hasn't said either way.

My dad might not see eye to eye with him, but I know how much he still loves him – because even though we're constantly rekeying our doors, Dad always leaves a key hidden in the yard for Brady, just in case he comes home. He's the one person in the universe allowed to bypass all of our security.

The day of the Tap-Out, I texted Brady and called him, just as my parents had, leaving a message that he needs to come with us to the bug-out, but like I said, he's not the most responsive person. Our primary form of communication now is online RPG games. He's a knight, a mercenary, or an assassin, depending on the game. I'm always his sidekick. I've been getting online, hoping to catch him playing, but so far nothing.

Today's parental dispute has left Mom sitting on the couch, blank-faced, hopped up on Xanax and watching the news while defiantly downing a full gallon of water. My dad has retreated into the garage again, welding and sawing with full-tilt intensity, so I take it that they haven't quite made up yet.

"You okay?" I ask Mom.

"I'm fine, Kelton," she says. "Just tired." And I know her definition of "tired" can fill volumes.

I'm guessing that my father is working on one of the booby traps we planned out a couple of Saturdays back – which I'm sure will turn out awesome. My dad always makes the best weapons when he's angry. Nevertheless, this is my cue to get out of the house. I decide to go check in on Alyssa.

I find Alyssa and Garrett on their back patio. It's toward the end of twilight now, and they're wrestling with a black plastic trash bag, a bucket, and their barbecue. Seems as if they're working on a condensation trap to purify some water, and though I'm thoroughly impressed that they even know what a condensation trap is, they're going about it all wrong.

"Hey," I say coolly.

"Hey," Alyssa responds from behind the trash bag.

"Don't you think it would be best to do that during the day, seeing as the sun is nearly down? Evaporation and all…"

Alyssa throws the bag in frustration, "We started this during the day," she snaps. "Day or night, it doesn't matter, because it's not working."

She leans up against the wall of their house and goes to take a sip from a water bottle that's down to the dregs.

"Save what you've got and have some of mine." I extend my canteen graciously. Alyssa takes it without hesitation and drinks.

"How much are you gonna charge for that sip?" she asks. "Ten bucks? Twenty?"

I just smile. "Don't worry about it. I've got a thirty-five gallon tank, remember?"

She hands my canteen back to me. "I'm sorry," she says. "I'm just on edge. Our parents went down to the beach and they're not back yet."

"It's been six and a half hours," adds Garrett, taking his cue to worry from Alyssa.

I realize it's my job to be the optimist here – which isn't a role I'm used to, but in difficult times, you gotta be flexible.

"I'm sure they're fine," I tell her. "The lines must be massive, and getting back might take a lot longer than going."

"They're not answering their cell phones," Garrett says.

"I told you, their phones are probably dead," she tells her brother. "Mom's phone never holds a charge long, and you know how Dad's always forgetting to charge his."

"Also," I suggest, "it could be a system overload. Cellular frequencies get jammed in densely populated situations."

"Like at a concert!" Alyssa says, unable to hold back a wave of relief.

"Exactly."

"Then right now we'll just have to sit tight and hope for the best," Alyssa affirms for herself. I'm glad I can at least inspire the idea of hope.

Their dog, Kingston, who's looking sluggish, comes up to Alyssa and nudges her with his nose. His nose is way drier than a dog's ought to be. I pour some water out on the patio for him to lap up, which he does.

"Hey – I've been thinking about it, and I figured out a new way for you to get water." I say it mysteriously, like a magician presenting his next act.

"How?" Garrett asks.

"I'll show you!" Then I usher them into their house and stop in the kitchen. "The freezer. Have you scraped the ice from the walls?"

"Tried that the first day," Alyssa responds, folding her arms. "It's a frost-free refrigerator. No ice."

I open the freezer slightly. "It's only frost-free if you leave it closed. If you leave it ajar, water will eventually condense and freeze against the walls. Then you can scrape it off and melt it."

"Hey, that's pretty smart," Garrett says earnestly.

I lean nonchalantly up against the refrigerator, accidentally closing the freezer all the way again. "I *am* ranked second in our junior class."

"Not first?" Garrett teases.

It's Alyssa who smiles at that. "Don't tell me," she says. "Zeik Srinivasar-Smith."

I sigh at the mention of my nemesis. "Zeik Srinivasar-Smith." An exchange student from God-knows-where who's probably a genetic mutation.

It seems as if we might be on the verge of bonding, because she seems ready to tell her own Zeik story – because everyone in school has one Zeik story or another – but her attention is grabbed by something on the living room TV. A news report. There's footage of raging brushfires, and riot police in downtown Los Angeles. And the news anchor – only one instead of the usual two – says, "As a precaution, residents are instructed to stay in their homes, and remain calm." But in direct opposition to the anchorman's attempt to soothe viewers, the crawl below reads, *Southland declared official FEMA disaster zone.*

Then the TV suddenly goes off. It's Garrett – he's turned it off. He keeps the remote out of reach, just in case his sister or I want to turn the TV back on. "I don't want to watch that – they're just trying to freak us out!"

"They're saying we should stay calm," Alyssa points out.

"Yeah, that's what they said to people on the *Titanic* when they already knew it was going down."

And he's right. As far as authority is concerned, calm people quietly dying is a lot easier to deal with than angry people fighting for their lives.

We all stand there in uneasy silence until Alyssa gets down on a knee to Garrett. "It's going to be okay," she says, not as sure about it as she's trying to sound. "It's too dark to do anything now. If Mom and Dad aren't back by sunrise, I'll go find them."

And after hearing those words, seeing the look on her face, something suddenly takes me over – this strange, innate force. Kind of like the feeling I had when I shot Mr. Malecki in the chest to save him – a sense of knowing what to do, and doing it, regardless of the consequences. "We'll go together," I tell her. "And I'll stay here tonight, so you don't have to worry about this alone."

Alyssa shakes her head, smirking. "Uh … thanks, but no. I'm sure you need this for some sort of merit badge, but I'm not a damsel in distress."

I find myself getting angry. Is that what she thinks this is about? Last week, maybe. But today, it's the furthest thing from my mind.

"Look," I tell her in complete honesty, "I know I'm not your first choice for a friend, but remember, there's safety in numbers. There are a lot of thirsty people out there, and things can get sketchy pretty quick. If I stay, we can take turns keeping watch, and you can get some sleep."

"Do you really think we're going to sleep tonight?"

"You had better," I tell her, "if you plan to go after your parents tomorrow."

She considers that, and is clearly waffling – irritated by the fact that she knows I'm right.

… And just then the lights begin flickering.

We all kind of brace – like you do when you think you

might be feeling an earthquake. Then the lights go out.

"Oh crap!" says Garrett. "Oh crap oh crap oh crap!"

"It's okay," Alyssa says. "This happened the other day. They'll come back on. You'll see."

But they don't – and the silence now is true silence. The hum of the refrigerator, the breath of the air-conditioner, all gone. And the finality of that silence is so eerie, it's terrifying. I feel a tight grip on my arm. It's Garrett. He was closer to me than he was to Alyssa. I'm the closest port in his storm.

Now we begin to hear voices. Neighbors wondering what the hell is going on, and what the hell they should do.

What had seemed to be very surreal now has become vividly, luridly real.

Our eyes begin to adjust to the dim afterglow of twilight lingering in the western windows.

I know what I have to do.

"I need to go…"

But before I can finish, Garrett cuts me off. "No! You said you'd stay!"

And although she doesn't say anything, I know Alyssa is just as freaked by the blackout as Garrett is. As I am.

"I need to go," I say again, "but only for a minute. I need to check on my parents, but I'll be right back." And then I take a step closer to Alyssa. I can't quite see her face in the dim room, which is better for what I'm about to say. "I know you can take care of yourself. I know you don't *need* me here. But even so, it'll make the night a little bit easier."

"Okay," says Alyssa. "I just want to make sure … I mean, I don't want you to think…"

I know where she's going with this, and I save her the trouble. "Alyssa, just because I'm offering to stay overnight in your house, don't get any ideas about *me* getting ideas."

She sighs, relieved. "Thank you, Kelton," she says, then adds, "If it means anything, you've been officially lifted from 'creepy dude next door' status."

"You thought I was creepy?"

Alyssa shrugs. "Kinda."

I consider that. "Yeah," I say, "I kind of am." Then I leave, reminding them to lock the door behind me.

My house is a beacon of light in the darkness. Off-grid, totally self-sustainable. Inside, my mom's asleep on the couch, and my dad is still welding away in the garage. They have no clue that the power's down in the rest of the neighborhood. I don't engage them, because there's nothing to say. I leave a note in my room that I'm spending the night at Alyssa's to help her out until her parents come home. My mother will like it, because it's something social that doesn't involve video games and guys who believe deodorant is optional. My father won't like it, but he also won't embarrass both of us by coming to retrieve me. I'll get an earful in the morning, but I'll deal with it then.

I place the note on my comforter, then kneel down, reach an arm under my bed, and fish around until I find what I'm looking for. I slide out a black metal case and crack it open, revealing, in all its glory, my silver forty-five caliber Ruger LCP pistol. I pull it out and load the magazine, trying not to be overwhelmed by its beauty and its power – the way its sleek silver barrel reflects light, contrasted by a black matte grip so dominant, it absorbs any and all light that hits it. It's perfect in its dualistic nature. Light and dark. Today, I feel like I'm something in between the two. And that's okay. It's what I need to be right now, if I'm going to be the first line of defense for Alyssa and Garrett. I tuck the handgun into my belt, and hurry down the stairs and out the front door to head back to Alyssa's … but what I see as I come out our front door causes almost every joint to lock up—

Although every other house is now blackened by nightfall, I swear I can make out figures in the street, faintly illuminated by a low-hanging moon. Most everyone in the neighborhood has stepped out of their home to marvel at our light – like moths entranced by the lick of a hot campfire flame. By having our own electricity supply, my family has made itself the unexpected envy of the neighborhood. And a target. So I stand, body trapped in the doorway, stuck between the threshold of what my life once was and what it will soon be, staring into the dark, a hundred eyes glowing back in the night.

And I'm scared to the bone, because right now I can't tell if I'm looking into the eyes of sheep, or wolves.

DAY FOUR
TUESDAY, JUNE 7TH

8) Alyssa

The next morning I wake up to an obnoxious digitized symphony – the alarm on my phone, which, miraculously, held its charge overnight. It's 5:45 a.m. Sunrise. At first I couldn't sleep at all – every sound was my parents coming home, or someone breaking in. But neither of those things happened. Twice I went downstairs to find Kelton doing the Boy Scout thing – reading a book by flashlight, while keeping watch for the nonexistent bad guys he was so sure would be crashing through our windows to suck the moisture out of our veins. It all seems so silly now in the light of day.

Except for the fact that my parents still aren't home. No amount of happy sunshine is going to change that.

Garrett, who had insisted he was okay sleeping in his room, had, at some point, surrendered all macho pretense and crawled in with me. Now he sleeps and is in that blissful place where his only care in the world is what to feed Spider-Man and the various Pokémon who just came over for dinner – or whatever it is that ten-year-olds dream about. I don't wake him as I slip out of bed and head downstairs.

I half hope that my parents came in while I was asleep and didn't want to wake us, but no such luck. In the living room is Kelton, snoring away on the sofa. So much for keeping watch. He was supposed to get me a few hours ago to relieve him, but he tried to soldier through the night on his own.

That's when I see the gun. It's resting on the end table beside him, like it's part of the décor: lamp, family picture, pistol. He must have hidden it from me when he came back from his house, knowing I wouldn't approve – and I don't. It makes me consider demoting him back to "creepy dude," but worse, because now it's "creepy dude with a gun."

I pick it up and right away find that it's much heavier than I had anticipated – and then I get a little freaked out realizing that I've never actually held a gun before. This thing ends lives. I put the pistol down, but slide it out of Kelton's immediate reach, and shake him awake.

The moment he's conscious, he bolts up.

"What? What happened? Is everything okay? Did I fall asleep?"

"It is, and you did," I tell him. "And now you're going to take the bullets out of that goddamn gun."

He looks at me, then looks away.

"It has no bullets," he says. "The magazine is in my pocket – I'm not an idiot."

"The jury's still out on that one," I tell him, then hold out my hand. "Give."

Reluctantly, he hands me the magazine of bullets – and although I don't want it in my pocket, I'd rather it be there than in his. Then I look at the gun again, furious that it's even here.

"I marched against these!" I inform him. "How could you bring one into my house?"

"You marched against assault weapons," he says, far calmer about this than I am. "I can respect that. But this is not that. This is a defensive weapon. We may need it to protect ourselves."

He doesn't reach for it and override my objections with bravado. Instead he waits for me to give him permission. The fact that he's deferring to me makes me feel better about it. But only a little. I reach out and push the pistol a few inches in his direction.

"You want to keep this for show, fine. But you're not shooting anybody today."

"Understood. But a gun is worthless if you're not prepared to use it," he says – probably something his father drilled into his head.

I look out the window. The street's empty, but it's not even six a.m. I'm not expecting anyone to be out there. All I can think about now is my parents, and all of the worst-case scenarios that probably didn't happen but still haunt me all the same. I try their phones again. Mom's goes straight to voice-mail, but Dad's rings a few times first, which lets me know that at least it's on.

Kelton makes a quick trip home to get tire sealant so we can take all three bikes, and when he returns, he's suited up in what looks like a duck hunting outfit, fully loaded with survival rope, and a million pockets. I don't have the energy to make fun of him now, and I've come to trust that there's a reason for everything he does. We actually might need the rope, and whatever other stuff he has hidden away in those pockets.

Truth is, we need him – plus when it comes to water, he's

the person to know; without him, I'm not sure we'd have the rations to safely make the journey down to Laguna Beach and back.

I had packed a backpack last night for the road. Beef jerky. The rest of our water, a kitchen knife, although I'm sure Kelton has something much nastier than that hidden in his outfit. I don't ask. Anyway, I might as well have my own way to protect myself, so I don't feel I have to rely on Kelton's Krav Maga, or whatever other lethal martial art he knows. I pet Kingston, and give him a ration of water that I know is not enough but is all I can spare. Then, just before heading out of the house, I flip on a light switch to check the power again. No luck. I wonder how many other neighborhoods are without electricity right now.

With the bikes now fully operational, we wheel them outside, manually pull down the garage door, and take to the streets. Looking around my neighborhood, I half expect it to be in ruins, but everything appears just as it always was, and I realize the wreckage is more internal.

We push forward down our street, keeping the dawn to our backs.

"There's a path that runs down Aliso Creek Canyon that goes all the way to the beach," I tell Kelton. "Although I've never taken it all the way down, so I don't know how smooth it is."

"Bad idea," Kelton says. "It's all wilderness, and we'll be isolated. Targets for anyone who might jump us for our water."

I want to tell him that he's being paranoid, but I know he might be right, and it pisses me off.

"The more we keep to civilization, the more likely that people will be civilized," he says. Then adds, "At least for now."

I turn to Garrett as we leave our neighborhood and take to the bike lane of a major avenue. "How are you doing?" I ask him.

"Better than you," he brags. "I ride my bike all the time, and you don't, so try to keep up." The fact that he's being a brat answers my question – he's in good spirits.

It isn't long before we come to an overpass for the 5 freeway. As I look down, I can see a typical snarl of cars, but somehow this is different. This is bumper-to-bumper traffic like I've never seen before. Morning rush hour is usually all about heading north toward LA – but today the traffic is at a horn-blaring standstill in both directions, as far as the eye can see – which eventually disappears into a thick crimson haze, swallowed whole by the sun cresting over Saddleback Mountain.

Not our problem, I say to myself, a little creeped out. I try to focus straight ahead as we pedal across the overpass, but I can't pull myself away from the reality all around me.

"Where is everyone going?" Garrett asks.

"Anywhere but here," Kelton answers.

"Yeah," says Garrett. "Well, it looks like they're not gonna get there."

I don't think he realizes how deeply that truth resonates – and on every level. But Kelton does.

"When it's time to bail, there are nontraditional routes that most people don't know. They won't be gridlocked like the freeways."

The fact that he said "when" rather than "if" stays with me far longer than I want it to.

About five minutes later, Garrett pulls his favorite and most frustrating travel maneuver. "I gotta go to the bathroom," he says. I tell him to pee in the bushes somewhere, but of course, it's not that kind of bathroom he's talking about. I imagine, considering the horrific state of our toilet, even with Kelton's waterless fix, Garrett has been holding it in rather than dealing with it. But there comes a point at which nature takes over. And always at the worst time.

There's a familiar gas station with a convenience store up ahead. And although I'm sure its bathroom will be even worse than ours, I don't tell Garrett that. We pedal toward it.

The three of us roll up to the store and step inside, taking in our surroundings. Like the rest of the world, the store is a slight aberration of normal. Bleak and dusty, the air is so thick it coats your throat. The AC's off, which we already knew, since we hadn't hit a single functioning streetlight between home and here. Refrigerators that usually contain soda, energy drinks, and water are empty, as expected. But what I don't expect is how barren this place is, devoid of not just products, but even the hope of them. Only one in ten items still remain on the shelves – one type of chips, one brand of gum. It reminds me of pictures I once saw in class of a destitute market in a war-torn country, where your only options were between canned beans or bread, and if you hesitated, you didn't get either. All the while, the grimness is mocked by fifties doo-wop music that echoes from an old battery-operated radio somewhere.

At the far end of the store, the clerk sits behind the register. Someone I don't know. The thing is, I know this store. Mom and I would always stop here on the way home from soccer practice to get a Powerade and corn nuts. Kind of a little ritual of ours. I thought I knew all the clerks who worked here – but not this one. He looks like the guy your parents warned you about. The one with a white windowless van rolling slowly past the park. He looks like Santa Claus after two tours in Vietnam. His shifty eyes are fixed on us, with one hand hidden below the counter.

Garrett heads toward the bathroom, and the clerk shouts, "Gotta buy something to use the crapper." And so, as Garrett closes the bathroom door behind him, Kelton and I move down an aisle to get something, and to get out of the guy's line of sight.

I settle on a bag of peanuts. As I approach the checkout, I get a closer look at the clerk – he looks worn, the skin around his eyes thick and heavy.

"I haven't seen you here before," I say, as he tallies up my items.

He studies me coolly. "I'm new."

"How long have the cars been like that on the freeway?" I ask, changing the subject.

He scratches his neck. "Middle of the night, I imagine. Brought a lot of customers here. Some were cool, others thought they could just take whatever they wanted."

"Why didn't you just call the cops?" I ask.

The man chuckles, but it comes out as a hiss. "Haven't you heard? You can't get through. 9-1-1 lines have been jammed since yesterday." He grins, like it's funny. "That'll be forty dollars," he says.

At first I think he's joking. But then I realize that, no, he's dead serious.

"Free-market economy," he says. "Supply and demand. And right now there's a whole lot more demand than supply." He leans closer. "So like I said, that'll be forty dollars."

Kelton comes up beside me with a Clif Bar, having not heard any of my exchange with the clerk. That's when I notice the cash register. It's been smashed open. And I realize this guy isn't wearing the ugly blue and yellow shirt that the clerks here always wear. The more I try to comprehend what happened here, the more I don't want to know.

Garrett comes out of the bathroom, and I grab the Clif Bar from Kelton's hand, throw it down on the counter, and before he has a chance to object, I grab Garrett's hand, knowing that it will startle him into submission, and I hurry all three of us out.

"Gotta pay for the goddamn bathroom!" the man inside yells, but we are already gone.

I hop on my bike and we race off, but I keep in the lead, setting the pace, and the pace is fast. A few blocks away I slow down enough for Garrett and Kelton to catch up with me. I stop and look back, to make sure that the guy from the convenience store isn't chasing us.

"What was that all about?" Kelton asks.

I don't tell him. Not because I don't want to, but because the particulars don't matter anymore. "That gun of yours – it's in your backpack, right?"

"Yeah…"

"And you know how to use it?"

"Hell, yeah."

I reach into a side pocket of my own backpack and pull out the compact cartridge of bullets. The *magazine*, Kelton had called it. I look at it. Think hard about it. It represents everything that I hate about the world. But this isn't the same world it was yesterday. Finally I hand him the magazine, then I start pedaling again, because I don't want to see him snapping it into the pistol.

SNAPSHOT: INTERSTATE, NORTHBOUND
6:30 A.M.

When Charity first learned to drive back in the sixties, she was taught to leave one car length between you and the car ahead of you for every ten miles per hour you're traveling. That way, you'll give yourself ample time to brake.

But when no one's going anywhere, your bumpers all might as well be touching.

Gridlock.

Or maybe something worse, if that's even possible.

At first it's the typical rush hour stop and go, but on this particular Tuesday things start to feel different right away. There's a thickness in the air that reads like claustrophobia; it's evident in the positioning of the cars, more tightly squeezed than ordinary traffic, and soon there's even a sixth lane that was once a shoulder that cars have started funneling into. And stopping.

Charity left her apartment just before five a.m., hoping to beat traffic on the way to Henderson, Nevada – where she planned to spend the worst of this crisis with her daughter and grandchildren – but it looks like she wasn't the only one with plans to get away.

She looks to the other side of the highway, noticing that drivers going in the opposite direction seem to be in the same predicament, perhaps even worse, since there are a few cars stuck facing in the wrong way – something she's never seen before. Clearly the traffic got so bad, people turned around on the road and tried to go the other way, hoping that backtracking would actually cut their losses. Then again, this is probably the kind of elliptical logic that jammed up the highway in the first place.

Charity takes in her surroundings. An impatient man on a Harley trying to work his way between traffic, like threading a needle. A family in a minivan. A cable repair truck. She passes the time by thinking about who these people might be and what their stories are. Where they're coming from and where they're going. Sure, the water crisis is bad, but not every one of these people could possibly believe it's so bad that they'd need to leave for greener pastures.

Charity looks to an old black and white image of her and her late husband wedged into the dashboard. *If he were still alive,* she thinks to herself, *he'd probably be kicking and screaming by now.* For decades the two of them owned a pawn shop, where Charity would handle the customers – she was always the cool-tempered one. Her parents had named her Charity, one of the seven virtues, and she had always tried to live up to that name, giving her full heart to whoever she encountered – rare in the pawn business, but it was what it was. She added a ray of light in miserable circumstances. However, now, staring into the endless snarl of automobiles, she's starting to wish they had named her Patience.

Another half hour and still no movement. Not an inch. People start to get restless, standing on the roof like packs of meerkats, all trying to get a better view of the highway ahead. A man and his young son walk down the row past Charity. She rolls down her window.

"Getting out for a stretch?" she asks.

The father smiles weakly. "Gonna check things out up ahead – see if anyone knows what the hold-up is." The fact that people are doing something active to help the situation makes her feel a little bit better. And things could be worse. In between lanes, kids now play tag, weaving in and out of the landlocked cars, while their parents play cards on the hoods. It makes her think of her own daughter. How she always worries when Charity makes the long drive to Nevada. At this rate, she might not get there till dark.

Another forty-five minutes. The sun beams down now – any impatient honking has stopped. Most of the cars' engines are off. There are people in cars around her who seem to have given up hope altogether, but are hanging tough in their vehicles. Some even huddle together by the side of the road, or lie down in the shade between cars, as if going to sleep and then waking would magically make this situation disappear. Charity taps her hand on the dash, anxiety growing. The man and his son never returned to their car. It will have to be towed and will add that much more pain to the process. Charity locks her doors and leans back, resting her eyes for a brief moment...

Thirty minutes later her eyes snap open as she's awakened by the sound of screams ricocheting between cars, originating from God knows where – and then someone sprints past her window. And then someone else, and before she knows it, the scene is total chaos. Everyone abandons their cars and runs south, the complete opposite direction of traffic. What would compel every one of them to run in the opposite direction of where they were headed?

Charity steps out of her car to get a better view, walking north, against the stampede ... and finally sees what everyone is running from.

A fire.

Black smoke billows and swirls in the morning sky, and below it, maybe fifty yards ahead, is a single car that has caught on fire. It's a valid reason to flee, because if that car explodes, and if the explosion is large enough, it could set off a chain reaction of exploding cars up and down the freeway. But if Charity has learned anything in all her years, it's to keep a calm head – especially in the face of utter chaos. She is a child of the sixties; following the pack blindly has never been her ethos. Instead, Charity decides to ask herself the contrarian questions of the world, because unique questions will always yield unique answers.

She marches forward, against the current, even as the mob grows, cascading in an avalanche of panic that picks up everyone else in its path – including those who don't even know why they're running. Charity moves toward the fire, the hysteria heightening. People are trampled. Bruised. Bloodied.

But where everyone else sees disaster, Charity finds opportunity. Back when she and her husband had the pawn shop, Charity learned a thing or two about junk. It was always about looking closer. Finding the treasure in the trash. Identifying the true diamonds that were worth more than the fake gold ring that held them.

She searches the dozens of cars for anything that could help her put the fire out. *What kind of car would have a fire extinguisher?* she thinks to herself. She goes to the TV cable truck and opens up the back double doors – but with no luck. Just boxes of wires and junk. And then the situation escalates even further with the sound of a blast. The car that's on fire up ahead has exploded, blowing off the hood and setting fire to a couch in the bed of a nearby pickup truck. This is rapidly going from bad to worse.

Charity scans the rows of cars one final time and sees an

electrician's van, with the electrician long gone. She quickly pops the back doors open – and bingo! A fire extinguisher, right there strapped to the door. So Charity marches toward the blaze, extinguisher in hand, a fire in her eyes hotter than any earthly inferno.

---

9) Alyssa

We ride down Laguna Canyon Road, a main street that we've always taken to get to the beach. I try to transport myself back to one of the times that I enjoyed the ride, but it's just not the same. The arid wind cuts at my face. The burn in my legs feels less like exercise and more like a dreadful punishment.

Passing neighborhoods on a major main street does allow me to peer in from a safe distance, and I'm noticing that a few areas still have electricity, which is somewhat comforting to see. It makes me think that they're working on solving these problems. Maybe cell phone towers are out because they have no power. I try to convince myself that's the reason why I get nothing every time I try to call my parents.

"You should stop calling," Kelton tells me. "You're draining your battery, and you might need your phone later."

"Maybe it's just really crowded there," Garrett says, doing his own rationalizations. "Like when people were camped out for days for that last *Star Wars* movie."

But would Mom and Dad camp out at the beach waiting for water, when they knew that Garrett and I were home waiting for them? As much as I want the answer to be something simple that we'll all be able to laugh about later, the longer we don't hear from them, the harder it is for me to paint a rosy picture.

We arrive midmorning at Laguna Beach, where the marine layer still creates an overcast haze, keeping the shoreline mercifully cool. I can smell the ocean and feel the salt air making my clothes cling to my skin. Waves thunder in the distance, and although the ocean's cadence has always been comforting to me, the silence that lingers in between each crashing wave now strikes me as odd. Still, I push forward on my bike, flying down the last stretch of road, which dead-ends into the Pacific Coast Highway and the beach just beyond. I don't feel the blisters on my hands anymore, or the ache in my legs. I have to see that beach. I have to know that my parents are there, and that they're okay.

But once I'm across PCH, at the edge of the boardwalk, I hit my brakes hard and stop dead in my tracks – because before me isn't a beach populated by families retrieving water rations, but a vast, sandy wasteland. It's virtually deserted, with just a few random people who seem to meander aimlessly. Farther out, toward the water's edge, are machines hitched to the backs of trucks – maybe half a dozen of them spread out along the beach – but they're not producing water. They're not doing anything. In fact, one of them is spewing black smoke, and another one is lying on its side.

I drop my bike and step down from the boardwalk to the sand, with Garrett and Kelton close behind. My eyes dart around, searching for my parents, desperate for even the slightest sign of them.

And then Garrett says, "Alyssa, do you hear that?"

I do – it's a sound almost musical, and eerily electronic, that lingers just beneath the sound of the waves. I walk across the sand, and the sound gets louder, until I realize it's not just one sound, but many, all blending together. And all at once I realize what it is.

Cell phones.

The ringtones of cell phones.

There are dozens of them lying in the sand around us, creating an eerie eight–bit symphony. The lost calls of a thousand souls.

None of us knows how to react. We just watch the phones as they vibrate and ring, trying to overcome our shock. And suddenly I realize that until just a short time ago, I was on the other end of one of those lines, calling nonstop, desperately hoping that someone would answer. I see one vibrating, halfway out of the sand, and I dare myself to grab it… I hold it in my hand and after one more ring, I answer, pressing the sandy iPhone to my ear.

"Hello?" comes the voice of a child on the other end of the line. "Mom?"

He couldn't be any older than Garrett. I try to choose my words carefully. "This isn't your mother," I tell him.

"Where's my mom?" begs the child. "Who is this? Why do you have her phone?"

I pause, not sure what I can say to calm him. "I'm at the beach," I tell him. "Your mom dropped her phone at the beach."

"She went there to get water…"

"I don't think there's any water here," I tell him. "Can you tell that to an adult? Please tell that to an adult."

"Where's my mom?" the kid cries.

I try to formulate the best response I can, but it's like I've lost my ability to put together coherent thoughts. I have no answer for him, any more than I have an answer for myself. "I'm sorry," I tell him. Then I hang up and drop the phone in the sand, and when it rings again I bury it. I bury it deep enough so at least there's one phone I can't hear ringing anymore.

"What happened here?" asks Kelton. And bit by bit the clues emerge. They are in plain sight around us, right there in the sand. It's as if a tornado had passed through, depositing debris everywhere – debris that looms like a shadow of terrible events I can't even begin to imagine. Plastic tables and chairs are overthrown, trash all around, being picked at by seagulls. A single abandoned shoe, which somehow seems creepiest of all. And the sand is peppered with black aluminum cans – dozens of them. I'm hit with a wave of the most awful stench, like bleach mixed with snot. It stings the insides of my nostrils, so I hold my nose, but it hardly helps. Kelton reaches down and picks up one of the cans, holding it at a safe distance.

"These are tear gas canisters," Kelton says. "There must have been a riot squad here…"

And then there are the machines. We approach the closest one; I can see that it's torn to shreds. All of them are. This one's stainless steel facade has been peeled back, exposing its innards as if it were decomposing from the inside out. Tubes and wiring herniate from the opening, all leading to a series of dials and gauges, connected to three ruptured vats, and behind it, a series of arrested pistons.

Could people have done this? Could we have fought each other over these lifesaving machines, reducing them to scrap metal? Could we be so desperate for drinkable water that we're willing to destroy the very machines that could create it, just to get that first sip...? And if so, were Mom and Dad among them?

Now I can see that at each ruined desalination machine stands a police officer in riot gear with an automatic rifle, warning people to keep away – as if there's still something to protect.

"What happened here?" I ask the one closest to us, keeping a safe distance.

"You need to leave the beach, miss. Go home. Wait there for further instructions."

"What happened to the people who were here?" I demand. "Were they sent somewhere else? A different beach?"

"It isn't safe to be here," he tells me. "You need to go home."

I back away, right into Garrett, whose eyes have teared up, and it has nothing to do with the tear gas.

"Make him tell you where they went!" Garrett says, as if he can order me to make demands of an armed officer.

"Uh ... guys?"

I look over to Kelton, who's standing closer to the water's edge. I follow his gaze to the spiteful ocean and direct all of my hate toward it. I can't stand the way each crashing wave of undrinkable water mocks us.

"What is that?" asks Kelton. He points to something that's floating, moving forward and backward with the rolling surf – a dark outline in the rolling water, visible for only moments between waves. "Is that..." Kelton squints. "Is that a body?"

And I know that whatever it is, I've had enough. It's more than not wanting to know. I don't even want to know the depth of the things I don't want to know. I grab Garrett and pull him away, and call to Kelton.

"Kelton! We're leaving!" Because maybe I can't order a crowd control officer, but I sure as hell can order Kelton. Especially when it's for his own good.

I will not think about my parents now, because if I do, I will crumble. Getting home will be an uphill ride in more ways than one, and that has to be the focus of all my mental energy right now. Getting us home.

We get to our bikes back at the boardwalk.

"We have to DO something!" Garrett insists. "We can't just leave!"

And I turn on Garrett with a fury I didn't even know I had. *"Garrett, if you don't shut your mouth right now I'm going to shut it for you!"*

And that just brings forth a deluge of tears from him. But I can't cry. I have to hold it together, and I'm sorry, so sorry that I took my frustration out on him. I take him into my arms and hold him. I let him sob. I don't say anything. I just let him sob, because I know that's what he needs. And he knows I didn't mean it. He knows because of how tight I'm holding him. And I won't let go until he's ready for me to.

"Alyssa, we should go," says Kelton, looking even more freaked out by the unidentified floating object than I am.

Garrett pulls away from me gently. "Let's just go," he says, tired, defeated.

The plan is to travel back the way we came, but even before

we get started, something across the street grips my attention ... the sound of shouting voices. It's a trio of kids our age, or maybe a year or two older. They're in front of the abandoned Laguna movie theater. They've formed a circle, playing some sort of game – as if this were a time for fun and games. I turn to ride toward them, hoping that maybe they can give us some information about what went down here, but as I come around a parked car, I can see the truth of the situation. They aren't *playing*. They're pushing around an older man, who's maybe in his sixties. It's three on one and he's helpless to defend himself. Without thinking it through, I jump off my bike, my hands curled into fists, and I'm marching toward them.

"Alyssa, wait," Kelton calls, but I'm already committed.

"Hey!" I yell. "What do you think you're doing?"

The tallest of the kids turns to me. He has tousled bleached-blond hair and glacial blue eyes. He's rough-hewn like a jock, but his multiple piercings tell me he's not.

"Mind your own business!" he says.

The man they're pushing around stumbles to the ground. And the kid kicks him. He actually kicks him!

"Leave him alone," I yell, "or I'm getting those officers from the beach!"

"They won't care," says one of the other kids. "They won't even leave their posts."

"You're monsters!" I yell, and the blue-eyed kid goes feral on me.

"Monsters? *We're* monsters? You don't know me!"

"I know all I need to know! You're beating on some poor defenseless man!"

"Do you know what this asshole did?" yells the blue-eyed kid. "We saw him hide a bottle of water in his car! And he won't share a drop of it!"

"So?" I counter. "It's his water! You have no right!"

"We have every right!"

Only now do I see how dry his lips are. Not just dry but parched and chapped to the point of bleeding. None of these kids look right. Their skin is thin and almost leprous gray. The corners of their mouths are white with dried spit. And the look in their eyes is almost rabid.

The tall kid turns and kicks the man again. "Give us your goddamn keys!"

"Please," pleads the man. "I need that water! I need it for my family!"

"So do I, asshole! You think because you drive a freaking BMW your lives mean more?"

Before he can kick the man again, I hurl myself into the middle. His foot connects with my calf. It'll give me a charley horse, but at least it may have saved this guy from getting a broken rib.

"You don't have to give them anything," I tell the man, but he's too frightened to fight them anymore. He fumbles in his pocket, and holds the keys out to the blue-eyed kid. But before the kid can snatch them out of his hands, I do instead, and hold them tight in my fist.

"You're not getting these," I tell the kid.

The man, no longer the focus of their fury, scrambles away, not caring about his BMW or his water; he just wants to get out of this alive. And now I realize that I'm the one who might not. The blond kid grabs me. He has a neck tattoo that seems to practically throb with his fury. It's a biohazard symbol.

"Mess her up, Dalton," says one of the other boys.

"Hey – maybe she's got water, too!" says the third.

The blond kid – Dalton – tries to wrench the keys from my hand, but I won't let go of them. I refuse to allow this sorry excuse for a human being have them. His unnerving blue eyes dart back and forth across my face, and his cracked lips peel into a truly terrible grin. Deranged and dangerous.

"You're sweating," he says. "Which means you've been drinking water…" And then the grin vanishes. "Where is it?"

"Get away from my sister!" I hear Garrett yell. He runs toward us but one of the other kids grabs him. I try to pull out of Dalton's grip, but I can't get free, no matter how hard I try.

"Where's your water!" he demands.

And then something comes over me. My own animal nature. "Right here," I tell him. And I spit in his face.

It doesn't faze him at all. And I'm suddenly hit with this strange sensation, like there's an emergency alarm echoing in my head, and my brain is helpless to identify its source. But as this boy wipes the spittle from his cheek with his free hand, the awful feeling becomes identifiable. It's a horror that makes me sick to my stomach. I know what he's about to do before he does it.

He looks at his fingers, glistening with my spittle … and he licks it off. I try to struggle free, but Dalton pushes me hard against the wall and locks eyes with me.

"Do it again!" he demands. And when I don't, he presses his body against me. I can't move. *Do it, or I swear I'll suck it right out of you!"* And he moves his terrible dry mouth toward mine.

Then from a few yards away, comes a voice of salvation.

"Let her go, or I'll blow your goddamn brains out!"

10) Kelton

I didn't want to have to pull out my gun, but the second that creep got too close to Alyssa, it's like some protective instinct kicked in. Now my Ruger is pointed right at his head. I'm supposed to point it at his chest, but at this angle all I have is his back, and a bullet in the back could go straight through him and into Alyssa. But he's taller. A head shot will miss Alyssa.

The instant the other two creeps see my Ruger, they drop Garrett and bolt. But the tall blond kid still grips Alyssa.

"I said let her go!" My hand trembles. I reach up my other hand into a two-handed grip, but it doesn't help.

Now he turns to see the gun, and Alyssa uses the moment to break free, instantly distancing herself and going straight to Garrett to protect him.

The creep just stands there, looking at me as if he doesn't care if I pull the trigger. As if he's already resigned himself to death.

I stare him straight in those ice-blue eyes, and then focus back on my aim. Now my hands aren't just trembling, they're shaking. Violently. I try to stop them, but it's like my brain can't seem to send the signal that far down my arms – like I'm disconnected from my own body. And now I'm struck with a crippling wave of panic that starts in my chest and pulls like a lethal gravity, collapsing my lungs until I've imploded so deep within myself, I can't breathe. I can barely gasp.

"He'll do it!" Alyssa screams. The sound reverberates and echoes. "You better run like your friends."

"No," he says. Just "no." And then he takes a step toward me. Or does he? I can barely tell because now my vision is going spotty, as my brain misfires, shutting down piston by piston.

"Do it, Kelton! Do it!" Garrett yells.

But I can't. With all the training, with everything I've been taught about self defense and the wielding of weapons, something inside me blows a critical fuse. I can't bring myself to pull that trigger.

And the kid knows it.

He lurches forward, knocking me back, and the gun flies out of my hands. I can't let him get it! He'll kill all of us! He's that crazy – I know he is!

The weapon lands in the trash-filled gutter. We both scramble for it. I don't know which one of us is more desperate to get it. And when I get to where I thought I saw it land, it's not there. Instead, there's a girl standing there as if she appeared out of nowhere. A girl I've never seen before – and she's holding my gun. Pointed directly at me.

She cocks it, loading a bullet into the chamber with expert precision, and I realize that even if I had pulled that trigger, nothing would have happened, because I never even took the safety off. She smiles, almost seductively – and it's in this moment I realize that the gun isn't pointed at me at all. She has it trained on the ice-eyed creep who's right behind me.

She brushes me out of the way with a deranged sort of confidence and puts the muzzle of the gun to the kid's forehead.

I look to Alyssa, who, just like me, is shocked by the appearance of this mysterious girl, and terrified by what her intentions might be. I struggle to force my anxiety attack away.

The kid winces as she presses the gun harder against his forehead, a lot more terrified of her than he was of me. He stammers excuses – anything to buy time. "It's them, not me – they have the water – why me?"

"Why you?" she says, oddly pensive. "I guess I don't really like your face. Bet it was once pretty though. Pretty beach boy. I got dumped by too many of those." Although I can't see why anyone would dump her. She's not just tough, she's stunning in a wild kind of way. Dark and mysterious. But then maybe they dumped her because she's freaking psychotic.

She blows a long strand of black hair away from her face, revealing inscrutable dark eyes that pierce in a very different way than the kid's blue ones.

Then she holds her free hand out to Alyssa, keeping the gun against the kid's head.

"The keys, please," she says, and when Alyssa doesn't move, she adds, "The keys or I'll kill him."

I start to add everything up. If this girl knows about the keys, she wasn't just walking by when this happened. It means she saw everything. That she was watching, and waiting to make her move. But if she saw, then why does she think that Alyssa will save this kid?

And suddenly I realize why.

Because Alyssa will. This girl read that about Alyssa in just a few seconds of seeing her.

"Please," cries the kid. He'd probably wet himself if he had any water left to expel. "Please … my mom and sister – they're counting on me to bring back water. If you kill me, you kill them, too!"

"Wow, that sucks," the girl says, and presses my gun harder against his head. "Keys, please," she says again to Alyssa.

"Okay," says Alyssa, trying to placate her. "No one has to die here."

"No!" complains Garrett. "Just let her shoot him!"

But Alyssa ignores him and puts the keys in the girl's hands.

She immediately pulls the gun away from the blond kid's forehead, plants a foot on his chest, and pushes him over backward. Who the hell is this girl? She acts gleefully impulsive, but in reality, I don't think there's anything impulsive about her. I think she's calculating, and smart.

As for the blue-eyed kid, he stays on the ground, curled up in fetal position, broken and sobbing, which is how I imagine he'll spend the rest of eternity.

11) Alyssa

I saw her first. The way she flew out from a hidden doorway the instant Kelton lost his grip on the gun. That grin on her face when she picked it up. It all happened too fast to react, and all I wanted to do was protect Garrett – who seems to be the only one of the three of us who wants a stranger's brains splattered on the sidewalk today. I will not think about that. Our new threat is this girl.

She's dressed in black with long, dark hair. Sort of an olive complexion. Hard to tell her ethnicity – kind of like Garrett and me. No one ever knows what we are either, which has its ups and downs. She's fit, muscular. She's also bruised in a few places, with a cut on her arm. God knows what that's all about. There's a strange flush to her cheeks – a heat about her that's different from thirst. Not sure what that's about either. All I know is that she's cross-wired enough to put a gun to that kid's head like it was nothing. She did save us, but why? Was it only to get those keys? And she still has Kelton's gun. So how safe are we, really?

"That was awesome," Garrett says, stars in his eyes like he was just rescued by Wonder Woman.

She strides away, but I go after her, Garrett and Kelton following in our wake.

"Hey – that gun is ours," I tell her. She doesn't even slow down.

"I don't think so. I saved your asses from the water-zombie, so I get the gun. Fair trade."

"Water-zombie…" says Kelton, thinking about it. "That's exactly what he was."

"The human body is about sixty percent water," the girl says. "But I would say he was down to forty-five percent. I'm not sure what percentage makes you toast, but he's well on his way."

I take a moment to look back at the kid crumpled in front of the theater. How could he be so terrifying just a moment ago, and so helpless now? And how many more so-called water-zombies are we going to encounter between here and home? And without any way of defending ourselves. Suddenly the safe and sane world I thought I knew is filled with terrifying unknowns. So which is worse, those unknowns, or the freaky girl who just saved us?

"Hey – if you're going to take that car," I say, "the least you could do is give us a ride."

She spins toward me, temper suddenly raging. "What are you, sixteen? An entitled cheerleader type from a perfect family? Think everyone in the world owes you a favor?"

"What's your problem?" Now I'm kind of getting pissed off.

She takes another step toward me, getting dangerously close. I can see in the corner of my eye that her hand is tightening around the gun. I try not to show any fear.

"Just tell us what happened here. We came looking for my parents and we can't find them."

Hearing that seems to notch down her attitude just a bit. Maybe she has a soul after all. "Can't help you," she says. "It wasn't pretty. That's all I know. Best if you crawl back under your rock, hunker down, and wait this out."

And then Kelton, who's been pretty subdued since losing the gun, says, "That cut on your arm is infected, isn't it?"

She turns to him. "It's just a cut."

"I know an infected wound when I see it. It's bad."

She scrutinizes him, suddenly not so cavalier. "So?" she says.

"So if the infection gets into your blood, you'll *wish* you were just dying of thirst… But I have antibiotics at home. Take us there, and you can have all you need."

The girl twirls her hair around her finger, considering. I try to peg her age. Nineteen maybe. Going on thirty. Is this really a good idea? No. But currently ideas are all coming in various shades of bad.

"You got names?" she asks.

"I'm Alyssa. This is my brother, Garrett. That's Kelton."

"Kelton," she mocks. "Who names their kid Kelton?"

Kelton sighs. "I ask myself that question all the time."

She smiles at that. It only looks half psychotic. "I'm Jacqui. You better not be lying about those antibiotics. Now let's get the hell out of here."

I look to our bicycles lying in the street, and realize that if they end up the only casualties from this morning, that's fine with me.

12) Jacqui

It's a powerful feeling – daring the universe to end you. We all know that sensation. It's that feeling you get when you think for just a split second about steering into oncoming traffic. Or jumping off a balcony. Or playing Russian roulette with the revolver that your father thinks you don't know about. It's not like you'd actually do any of those things, but the feeling is there, like a wind at your back on the edge of a cliff, gently urging you. *What if… What if…*

It's what my psychiatrist, better known as Dr. Quack,

called the Call of the Void. It's a real thing – defined in psychiatric journals, and everything.

I know that feeling intimately. It's where I live. I eat, sleep, and dream of the void, and whenever it calls my name, I'm there in the front row ready to answer.

I imagine that the bleached-blond surfer twerp caught a glimpse of that when I stuck the gun between his eyes. Not that I would have actually pulled the trigger, but what if…

Threatening him wasn't even my plan in the first place. None of it was. I'm no savior or martyr or a hero in any way. Too much unnecessary attention. I was originally just going to wait out the confrontation until the three kids beating up the old guy got his keys and led me to the car and his stash of water. But the girl and her little entourage showed up, complicating things. The second I saw the geek with the gun, I knew this was not going to end well if I didn't intercede. So now I have a car and a weapon and maybe some water. Nice work for a Tuesday morning.

If Alyssa and company had any sense, they would have run as soon as I took the spotlight off her, just as the blond kid's "friends" had. Or at least, that's what I expected they'd do. Then again, the Tap-Out has made people remarkably unpredictable.

There's a reason why I won't tell her what happened at the beach yesterday. It's because nothing I could say would help her face the reality of it. Call my silence compassion if you want.

I was there yesterday. Not early enough to get water, but early enough to see things go south. See, I had been staying for about a week in a beach house on a cliff that overlooked one of Laguna Beach's smaller coves. Big iron D on the chimney. I think it once belonged to Bette Davis – my favorite old-time actress, because she wasn't beautiful, but damn was she sexy! I don't know who owns it now, but they're not around this summer. See, obnoxiously rich people do this obnoxiously rich thing where they buy real estate just so they can park their money somewhere. And if they're rich enough, they can't be bothered to rent it out, so at any given time, maybe one in five of the cliffside homes in Laguna Beach are vacant. And burglar alarm signs only about half the time mean there's actually an alarm. Add locksmith skills and a keen ability to keep a low profile, and I trip into the lap of luxury on a regular basis. Usually I stay for a week maybe, then clean up, like it was an Airbnb, and take off without the owners ever realizing I was there. Except for the fact that they do – because I always leave a note on a Hello Kitty greeting card, thanking them for their hospitality, and telling them that I've stocked the fridge with Dr Pepper for their next uninvited guest. What's the point of life if you can't mess with people?

I cut my arm breaking into the upstairs bathroom window of my current place. The gash wasn't really a big deal – that is, until the Tap-Out. I was caught off guard just like everyone else, which was stupid of me, because I'm usually more on the ball. Then, when they announced that they'd be making drinking water out of the seaweed swill of Southern California's beaches – and that the nearest location was just up the road – I took about a dozen empty water bottles and shoved them into my backpack – also Hello Kitty, because, okay, I've got a thing for Hello Kitty. It's a guilty pleasure, kind of like the macho biker dude who secretly wears women's underwear.

I arrived, like, an hour before they said the operation would start, but there were already lines up and down the beach and boardwalk, past the movie theater, running down all the side streets. Hundreds, if not thousands of people. On principle, I do not wait in lines. Instead I merge. Usually toward the front of a line, and do it with the skill of David Copperfield making the Statue of Liberty disappear. I just needed to find the right opening, so I lingered on the beach and observed.

The desalination machines were smaller than I had expected. The attendants who worked them looked like FEMA personnel – but they weren't wearing the official cobalt blue outfits. These were sky-blue. Turns out they sent the FEMA volunteer corps. Which really pissed me off. Did they misjudge this water crisis so badly that they dismissed how dire it was, and left it in the hands of volunteers? I know they were stretched thin, but you can't leave an entire relief effort to a bunch of wannabe feds. Not only is it a recipe for disaster, it's a recipe with half the ingredients missing.

The machines worked at first, and the volunteers seemed to know what they were doing ... that is, until the first machine started to smoke. That's when it became clear that the attendants' entire skill set was limited to opening the spigots and closing them again.

"It's the seaweed," I heard some fat know-it-all say. "These morons didn't take into account the seaweed."

Apparently the machines were designed to process *filtered* seawater. And although they tried to create makeshift filters, the machines were fouling and overheating one after another.

"Calm down," the clueless volunteers told the angering crowd. "Technicians are coming to take care of the problem. There'll be enough water for everyone." But of course no one came, and pretty soon only two of six machines were still working.

Then the guy in charge made the next in a long series of mistakes. He told the people in front of the broken machines to get in line *behind* the people at the machines that were still working.

If f-bombs were nukes, we'd have wiped out the planet.

Are you effing kidding me? We've been effing waiting in the effing hot sun for three effing hours!

As they say in the Old Testament, there was much consternation and gnashing of teeth.

People tried to defy orders and merge themselves into the functional lines, but without any of the finesse that I would have brought to the endeavor. And the people who were already there pushed back, and the mergers pushed harder.

Get lost! We've been waiting in this line all day!

Yeah, well we've been waiting in THAT line all day!

So go back there and wait till they fix your stinking machine!

And in an instant the lines were gone. It was just a single crush of people pressing forward.

I didn't see the first fight, but I felt it – because the entire mob surged and I was nearly knocked over. The crowd now pushed so hard that one of the two working machines was knocked over on its side – and even then, people rushed it, tried to fill their containers, but all they got was black sludge.

I had enough sense at that point to break away toward the waterline, but I was trapped there, forced to watch it all play out. One fight gave way to another, and another, and suddenly everyone's brain seemed to shut down at once.

There's this thing that happens with a mob. It's called "deindividuation." It's the kind of thing that happens when a cop puts on a uniform, or when you wear a pair of sunglasses so people can't quite see your eyes. It's like you slip out of your normal self – and it makes you feel different. Behave different. So what happens when you're just another thirsty soul in a sea of water-zombies? You become one.

I saw an old man get trampled to death. I saw a mother steal water from someone else's child. I even saw a man pull out a knife and murder a stranger in cold blood. The mob stormed the machines, attacked the attendants, some of whom had guns and started firing into the crowd.

Soon riot police stormed the scene, pushing against the crowd with riot shields as if they were going to push everyone into the sea and drown them. And some people did. Some people had nowhere to go but into the waves. And the weak ones, or the ones who couldn't swim, went under. The riot police shot rubber bullets, hurled tear gas, beat people with batons.

I was able to wade my way out of it, and climbed on a rock farther down the beach, me and my Hello Kitty backpack still full of empty bottles. At this point, I was already feeling a fever coming on, and I knew it was from that lousy infected cut. I stayed back, watching all those people give in to the Call of the Void.

After almost an hour of complete chaos, and after hundreds of arrests, the mob began to thin, which finally allowed paramedics to come in to help the wounded and haul away the dead. By sunset the beach was pretty much deserted, and the riot officers who were left behind were firing warning shots at anyone who dared to come close to the ruined machines. I think maybe one or two of those shots weren't just warnings.

I decided not to go back to the beach house. There was nothing for me there. No water. No supplies. I realized my best chance at survival wouldn't be hiding from people, but being among them. Because that's where opportunity was. People can be played, moved, and sacrificed. So in that way I guess you could say I'm a people person. Moral of the story here: Bad news is sometimes best not broadcast. At least not by me. Because when it comes to Alyssa and Garrett's parents, the truth is, between all the spilled blood and all the spilled water, they could be anywhere right now. Even the morgue.

We search the surrounding streets for the BMW, all the while my fever making me feel even more miserable. We pass vacant storefronts and small parking lots, and I'm pressing the panic button on the keys, but with no luck.

Alyssa and her brother keep looking around, and I know it's not the BMW they're looking for.

"What kind of car were your parents in?" I ask.

"A blue Prius," Garrett says.

I laugh. "Good luck with that. That's, like, half the cars in Laguna." I hold the keys in the air and press the panic button again.

"If you hold the keys to your chin you'll get better range," Kelton says. "The electrical current travels up the fluids in your brain, turning your head into an antenna."

It doesn't work, but he smiles nonetheless, clearly proud of his ability to spout useless information. Book smarts are nice like heelies are nice: They'll only get you so far, until you have to use your freaking feet. In fight-or-flight situations it's street smarts that will get you out alive. I'm exceptionally lucky, because I have both. I've been on my own for a couple of years now and I've managed without a permanent address or a regular paycheck. Whether it was staying with the boyfriend of the month, or in a foreclosed home, or luxuriating in a mothballed beach house, I've done fine. Life on the fringe suits my personality. Even back in school it was the same. I didn't have the melodramatic self-centeredness to be a goth, or show up to class enough to play the geek. I didn't have an IQ low enough to tolerate the popular crowd … and I'm pretty sure I would have preferred impalement on the school's flagpole than be a hipster.

My parents – who have so many of their own issues that they were determined I have issues too – kept bringing me to therapists and psychopharmacologists, who all told them that my problems stemmed more from environmental dysfunction than from chemical imbalance. Which always pissed them off. What could be dysfunctional about a mother so spiteful that she intentionally undercooks her husband's chicken, and a father so narcissistic he gets a face-lift at forty? Eventually, however, they managed to find the one guy who would give them the diagnosis they wanted for me: Psychodissociative

Disorder with Nihilistic Tendencies. Which basically means that I'm not a happy camper. And then they medicated me for it. Thank you, Dr. Quack.

It was great. For them. I didn't have motivation enough to have opinions, or energy enough to care. The thing about medication is that it's a true lifesaver if you actually need it. But if you don't it's just a pain in the ass.

When Mom finally grew a pair and announced that she wanted a divorce, I got out of there. This was one dog and pony show I did not need to witness, no matter how good the seats. I call every once in a while to make sure they haven't eaten each other or joined a Kool-Aid cult. Other than that, we keep on our own sides of the demilitarized zone.

Being on my own over the past two years has brought me close to being a victim of human trafficking, and closer to being dead – and that was even before the Tap-Out. Great fodder for the memoir that I'll never live to write.

So now I'm a chauffeur for three annoying kids. Which may ultimately be the most dangerous situation I've ever encountered.

We eventually find the BMW parked in an abandoned back lot. It's silver, sleek, and looks incredibly expensive, which means there's a chance this car is loaded with water, just as the blond kid said. The idea of it gets my adrenal glands pumping. But when I look inside, the car is a total mess. Mounds of useless junk. Sheaves of paper, trash, DVDs that would probably never be played again... This can't be it. What kind of second-rate hoarder brings trash rather than supplies? I search under the seats, between the seats – even the trunk is bursting with junk. It isn't until I pop open the glove box that I find salvation – well, at least sixteen ounces of it. I start to guzzle down the water, with no intention of sharing, because I know these kids have water of their own. I have to force my lips from the bottle to breathe.

I take a deep breath and look through some of the junk. Dozens of pictures of the guy who this car belonged to – a glossy family portrait, each family member dressed in uninteresting matching turtlenecks. Hell, their photos might as well have just come with the frames. But for some reason, the more I look through the portraits the more it begins to affect me, which is weird and stupid because I never knew this guy. It's more the items that get to me. The fact that these were the last things this man packed. These were the things he chose to keep before leaving his home, maybe forever. It's a desperate feeling I can understand and relate to. And with all of these emotions, the gravity of our situation comes crashing back to me. I feel woozy. It's the fever. I try to steel myself for the drive. This is no time for sentiment or sickness; it's time to rally.

I take another swig from the water bottle and catch Alyssa staring at me.

"You should conserve," she says. Like she's reciting something she heard on a public service announcement while watching cartoons with her idiot brother.

I glare at her. "Kelton sits shotgun," I declare, "because at least when he's irritating, it's informational." The real reason, of course, is that whoever sits in the front with me will be my biggest threat – and right now the dorky ginger who can't bring himself to fire a gun is the lowest risk. In fact, he seems hell-bent on being helpful.

"I'll navigate," he says. "We may have to go off-road."

Alyssa looks at me skeptically, and then opens her big mouth again. "Who put you in charge?"

"I did," I tell her, as I start up the car. "If you don't like it, you can go back to your bikes and ride home."

Alyssa eventually gets in the car, backing down as I knew she would. Because at the end of the day she needs me more than I need her. And I don't need her at all. The only reason she and her brother are in this car is because Kelton probably wouldn't come without them – and Kelton's the man with the antibiotics. That is, unless he's lying. But I don't think he is. He's honest to a fault. The kind of honesty that could get him killed.

As for Alyssa, I trust her just about as much as she trusts me. Which is fine, as long as I stay in control. Survival means not leaving any factor up to anyone else's jurisdiction. But now, catching a better look at Alyssa in the rearview mirror, I sense something I hadn't picked up on before. When I first met her I figured that she was all bark, no bite – but now in the car as sunlight refracts across her face, illuminating what I could not see before, I realize that her eyes aren't as dull and vapid as I had first thought. She's shrewd. Which means she could be a problem.

13) Alyssa

I can't help but notice the way Jacqui's eyes constantly glance back at me in the rearview mirror. I don't like her or trust her and she knows it. She makes me think of something I learned in biology. How pack animals that go rogue are always hungrier and nastier, because it's harder to hunt food without a pack – and when it comes down to it, you have no idea what they did to be excluded from the pack in the first place. Jacqui is an unknown quantity in an unmarked bottle, and we are currently at her mercy. For all I know, we've just been kidnapped.

Up front, Kelton flips on the radio. It's on a satellite country station, which somehow seems obscene. Luke Bryan's singing about rain, and whiskey, and his girl gettin' frisky.

Jacqui looks over at him and says, "If you don't change that, I will shoot you, and then shoot myself."

He quickly obliges. "What kind of person puts on a song about rain today?" Kelton says, switching to an AM news station.

" – as the Tap-Out continues to plague the Southland, the governor and local officials have assured residents that evacuation centers —"

Jacqui reaches over and turns the radio off.

"Hey! That could be important!" I remind her.

"They keep looping the same broadcast – I've been listening all morning," Jacqui says. "There aren't any 'evacuation centers.' At least not yet, anyway."

"Leave it off," says Garrett. "I don't want to hear anything anymore."

Neither do I, really. I just don't want to be stuck with my own thoughts. The only thing worse than my thoughts, though, are Kelton's.

"Things are gonna fall apart pretty quickly now," he says. "Critical services shutting down, unreliable communication – any minute it'll all give way to urban Darwinism. See, there's this theory called Three Days to Animal, which says —"

"I don't want to know what it says, Kelton," I tell him. "So just shut up about it."

"Fine," he says. And then doesn't shut up. "It's just that we're on day four – so I think the theory's only one day off."

I hate the fact that he's probably right. Disaster is one thing, and a riot is another, but the total disintegration of society? Is that what we're witnessing? My head spirals into visions of a post-apocalyptic reality that I never imagined could arrive quicker than the expiration date on our milk.

"You kids crack me up," Jacqui says. "All you do is bitch, bitch, bitch at each other. Next you'll start asking, 'Are we there yet?'"

To which Garrett replies, "Are we there yet?"

I rap him a little harder than I meant to, but he doesn't really react. He just slumps, and looks out the window, probably trying to avoid his own thoughts, too.

"You keep calling us kids," I say to Jacqui, "but you don't look any older than eighteen."

"Nineteen."

As we cross over the freeway, the same cars are still on the roadway below, and now there's clear evidence of abandonment. I force my thoughts away from it.

"So, where'd you go to school?" I ask Jacqui, interested only inasmuch as her answer will distract me from darker thoughts.

"Mission," she says, which surprises me, because that's where I go. It means our time there would have overlapped. I don't remember her, though – but then, Mission Viejo High is a pretty big school.

"So you're a Diablo, too?" Kelton says, equally surprised.

"Was," says Jacqui. "Until I bailed."

And then Kelton gasps. "You wouldn't happen to be Jacqui Costa, would you?"

She turns to look at him. "How the hell do you know my name?"

"Are you kidding me? You're, like, legend." Then Kelton turns to me. "She's on this plaque in the office – the school's SAT record – a near perfect score!" Kelton turns back to her. "I've been hating on you all year!"

"Well, now you have a face to hate, too."

"So why'd you drop out?" I ask her, now genuinely curious.

But of course she deflects the question with, "I had better things to do."

"Hmm," I say. "Sounds to me like your tap-out started a long time ago."

I catch her eyes again in the rearview mirror. A quick, cold glance. I have to remind myself not to antagonize her. She's got the gun, and a shriveled raisin of a conscience, if she has one at all. I imagine her to already be animal, without needing three days to get there.

* ★ *

As we turn in to our neighborhood, part of me begins to relax, while another part becomes more tense. Returning home means a measure of safety, but it also means failure. Unless Mom and Dad returned while we were gone. I hold onto that hope like the frayed end of a lifeline, because I still refuse to face any of the alternatives.

Rows of houses bake in the sun, their occupants nowhere to be seen – pretty much how we left it. I'm crooking my neck, pressed against the tinted window, to get a better view of our house. We're half a block away but I can already see our driveway. Mom's car is still gone. Garage door is still down. Side gate still shut.

But the front door is open!

Before Jacqui even throws the car in park, Garrett and I have jumped out and are running to the front door.

"They're home!" Garrett yells. "I knew we should have just waited! I knew it."

But if they're home, why would they have left the door wide open?

As we hurry toward the door, I can see there's a note taped to it. For a brief instant I think it might be from our parents, but it's just a flyer calling for an emergency community meeting later today. That's when I realize there are chips of wood lying on the doorstep and all over the tile in the foyer. The door isn't just open – it was kicked in.

"Dad?" Garrett yells. "Mom?"

He wants to believe it so badly, he's in complete denial. He looks at the busted doorjamb. "Maybe they lost their keys. Or

Uncle Basil came back and couldn't get in."

But he's grasping at straws. This was a break-in. And then I realize—

"Kingston!"

The thought of our dog having to face intruders propels us inside.

The house is not exactly ransacked, but things aren't right. There's a thin steel band on the floor, pieces of copper piping, greasy footprints on the carpet, and as we come around a bend, we see our hot water heater lying like a shipwreck in the dining room. It's been ripped out, ripped open, and lies dead on the dining room table like a patient that didn't survive the operation.

"Kingston?" Garrett calls. "Kingston! Where are you!"

And to my relief, Kingston appears in the doorway between the kitchen and the dining room.

"Come here, boy!" I call to him. "Did you chase them away?"

I extend a hand to pet him, but he doesn't come. Instead he whimpers and hesitates, not necessarily out of defiance, but something else...

"Kingston?" I say, still trying to process his reaction. I realize that he must be hungry after a morning without food, so I reach into my pocket and pull out the beef jerky I had packed for the ride.

As soon as I do, another dog emerges from the kitchen, having smelled the meat. It's the Rottweiler that belongs to a family across the street. Strange. Why is this dog here? He must have made his way in through the open front door, searching for water. I always remembered him to be friendly, but he doesn't look all that friendly right now.

Unnerved, I stand up, rip the jerky in half and toss a piece to both dogs – but they just sniff at it. It's not what they want. I know what they want, but right now my canteen is empty.

… And that's when a third dog emerges. One that I don't recognize. It's a Doberman, and it's eyeing me like I'm a much more attractive proposition than the jerky.

I'm so startled I almost jump out of my skin. "Garrett, stay back," I say.

Then the Doberman starts growling.

"Kingston!" I call out. But Kingston stands with the other two dogs, and won't come. It's as if he's no longer our dog. Because we betrayed him by not giving him enough water. This is his new pack.

The Doberman's muscles tighten, like it's ready to charge, so I grab Garrett and race back out the door.

"No!" Garrett yells. "We can't just leave him! We can't just leave Kingston!"

But behind us the dogs have started barking, and I can't tell if they're pursuing us into the street, or just chasing us from their territory. So I pull Garrett along, knowing that I can't take the time to explain this to him. That Kingston, a dog that, under any other circumstance, would have been loyal to the end, made an instinctive choice for his own survival.

14) Kelton

Alyssa and Garrett race out of their house, and practically hurl themselves back into the car, slamming the door – and it only takes a moment for us to realize why. A pretty lethal looking Doberman Pinscher comes out the front door, followed by Kingston and another big dog. They follow the Doberman's lead as it circles the car. Alyssa explains what happened, and Jacqui pulls out my gun.

"No!" I tell her. "Let's just see what they do."

Kingston puts his paws up on the back door, looks sadly in the window at Garrett, whose eyes are clouding with tears. Then Kingston follows the other two dogs back inside the house. Alyssa breathes out her relief.

"So you're just going to give up your house to a pack of dogs?" Jacqui says.

Alyssa doesn't respond. She won't even look up. It's like her brain's processor just froze with this last straw.

"It doesn't matter," I tell Jacqui. "We're going to my house. We'll all be safer there anyway."

Of course, convincing my father to take them in will be fun and a half. Considering the way things have escalated today, he's probably gone full commando by now – guns locked and loaded, with the truck all packed for our pilgrimage to the bug-out, and pissed off to high heaven that I left this morning with nothing but a note. But I'll stand firm that going with Alyssa was the right thing to do.

And Jacqui? Well, she's a necessary gambit. That's a chess term. It's the sacrifice of an important piece early on in the game, with an eventual long-term gain down the line. But sometimes that's what you have to do to win. Take risks. I know that bringing Jacqui here was a big risk. But despite Alyssa's obvious mistrust of her, Jacqui's the only reason we're still alive right now, whether we like that or not. I'm just glad I noticed her infection – because I knew she wouldn't pass up antibiotics. I can't help but feel that her decision to join us was a gambit of her own. And now I can only hope that Jacqui won't turn on us the second she gets what she wants.

We park in the driveway, and I lead them toward my house. I can already tell that my father's been busy. The spider holes in our yard are covered and ready to be manned, booby traps are set, and the security shutters are down. Dad's even lined the perimeter with additional surveillance cameras.

Jacqui looks around in sheer awe, stepping off the cement path and onto the grass, and when her foot touches the ground, the dirt gives way. I grip her arm and catch her so she doesn't fall into the pit, which is only a couple of feet deep, but lined with nail boards, like something out of an Indiana Jones movie.

"Booby trap," I say. "Be careful where you step."

Jacqui shakes her head, too cool to be horrified. "And how long have you been preparing for the apocalypse?"

"A while," I say. "The end of the world is our family hobby."

She glances around, captivated by the grim awesomeness of our yard. "Beats knitting," she says.

Now the hard part. I approach the front door, take a deep, deep breath, fumbling with my keys – but before I slip the key into the lock, I freeze up, remembering that Jacqui still has my gun. If my father sees it, the hell that's already going to break loose will become exponential. The fact that it's now in her possession doesn't just make me wildly irresponsible, but one hundred percent culpable for whatever the hell she ends up doing with it.

And then the door opens before I use my key – it's my dad. It's like he was waiting for us.

"Welcome home," he says, with deadpan coolness. "Have fun out there?"

"Not at all," I tell him. "It's just like you predicted."

"And the freeways?"

"Gridlock," I report.

That's when Mom rushes out, throwing her arms around me, in a deeply embarrassing hug.

"Kelton! Are you all right? Don't you ever scare us like that again!" I don't even have to look to see Jacqui's smirk.

Dad gestures for Mom to go in and let him handle this. Then he turns to the others. "Brought your friends, I see. Hello, Alyssa. Garrett."

They offer awkward greetings.

Then he gives Jacqui the once-over. "And who's this?"

"Name's Jacqui. I'm the one who saved your son's ass out there," she responds, fearlessly stepping forward. "I'm here for the antibiotics he promised me."

My dad's face swells with anger. But instead of yelling he takes a deep breath, bottling it up. He nods, keeping his composure, filing his fury away for another time. "Is this true, Kelton?"

"Yes," I say. "She saved our lives, and got us home safely."

"Thank you for that, Jacqui," my father says. "But unfortunately, our antibiotics are not my son's to give away."

Jacqui glares at him, practically growling like the Doberman in Alyssa's house, and my mind is already racing, knowing this won't end well. She takes a threatening step toward him.

"Yeah, that's not gonna work for me," Jacqui says.

I think about the gun concealed in her waistband. What my father would do if he saw it. How he can never find out. Before the moment ignites, I step in between the two of them. "Like Jacqui says, she saved my life!" I remind my father, pretending to be indignant, and then realizing I don't have to pretend because I am. "Are you saying my life isn't worth some lousy antibiotics?"

"Kelton, you're missing the point —"

"Next you'll probably tell me that we can't take Alyssa and Garrett in!"

"They have their own home!"

"Which was broken into, and is unsafe! And now their parents are missing!"

Then he gets closer to me, speaking quietly. Not quite whispering, but not loud enough for anyone but me to hear.

"We're not having this conversation. You know how things are."

And I blow it up, yelling, so that Mom can hear inside, and probably anyone else in listening range.

"Yeah, I know exactly how it is! And you're right, we're not having the conversation. Because I'm out of here."

I turn and storm toward the BMW.

"Kelton!" yells my father.

I can't fight the urge to halt when he calls my name like that – but I use it to my advantage. I turn back to him. "Now I get why Brady got the hell out of here the second he could. But I'm not waiting until I'm eighteen." Then I look at the others. "C'mon, we're leaving. Jacqui, we'll get your antibiotics from someone who gives a shit."

I'm hoping that Jacqui gets what I'm doing and plays along – because in a real situation, this girl would never take an order from me.

But she does get it – because she looks to my dad with a smile and a shrug and says, "Later, dick." And for a moment I wonder how she knows my dad's name. And then I realize that she doesn't.

We make it halfway to the car – then my mother comes storming out of the house.

"Kelton!" she says with even more command than my father. "Don't you dare get in that car!"

I turn to her, waiting for this to play out.

"Alyssa, Garrett – of course you can stay with us," she says. "You too, Jacqui. We have all the water and food you need." Then she turns to my dad, and says with thrilling defiance, "*And* antibiotics."

She hustles Alyssa and Garrett into the house right past my father, who's powerless to stop her.

"Marybeth, can we talk about this?"

"No."

And she pushes past him, his authority overridden.

I feel triumphant, and worried at the same time, because

152

my dad keeps a tally of slights. I know this will someday come back to bite me. But not today.

Jacqui saunters past my father, slathering him in sarcasm. "Thank you for your hospitality!" Mercifully, she doesn't add "dick" this time, but she does grab the pink community meeting flyer taped to the door and hands it to him – like she's doing him a favor.

As for me, I keep a poker face and don't look at my dad as I pass. But inside I'm smiling – because, for the first time in my life, I've made fear a tailwind rather than a headwind.

My circle of friends is usually limited to Scouts, preppers, or the random offspring of other dentists – so having Alyssa, Garrett, and Jacqui here is kind of a minor big deal for me. I give them the grand tour, starting with my favorite place in the house – our safe room. It's where we keep all the supplies that we are never usually allowed to touch. First-aid kits, water jugs, guns, ammunition, and nonperishable canned food. It's behind a hinged bookcase. I tug on a book that pulls back like a handle, and the entire shelving unit swings open.

"My dad modeled it after an old James Bond movie," I tell them, hoping to maybe redeem my father for them. They are duly impressed. This is also where Dad stashed the antibiotics – various vials and pill containers in Ziploc bags.

"Any antibiotics allergies?" I ask Jacqui.

"No."

I hand her two orange pill bottles of Keflex. "One round should do it, but if not, a second round definitely will." I hold the two containers out to her, and she looks at them as if maybe it's a trick. Then she snatches them from my hand, opens one of them, and pops two pills dry.

"Finally." She exhales, stuffing the bottles in her pocket. Then she smiles at me, and for the first time it doesn't come off as mad-creepy. "Thank you, Kelton," she says, and I think she actually means it.

Alyssa looks around. "Is there a lock on the door?" she asks.

"Only on the inside," I say. "It's a safe room, remember. Why?"

"Because," says Jacqui, "she thinks I'm going to raid it in the middle of the night and take off with all of your stuff."

"Not everything's about you," Alyssa says, but the way she evades Jacqui's glare tells me that this time it is. And maybe for good reason.

"No worries," I say, with a secret wink to Alyssa. "There's a motion-sensor alarm inside, so if anyone goes in during the night, we'll know." Which isn't exactly true, because all the motion sensors are on the perimeter of our property, but Jacqui doesn't need to know that.

I lead them out back, showing off my target practice area. And point out the porta potty. "We're not wasting water on internal toilets, so that's where all business is done." And although no one loves a porta potty, none of them complain.

In the kitchen, I show them the stainless steel drum that holds our primary water supply. I unscrew the rubber safety stopper and prep the tap. "My dad will ration the water," I say, looking around to make sure he's not around. He's back out in the garage being diligent again. "But for now you guys can fill up."

Jacqui's practically salivating, eyes large like saucers. I can tell she's already warming up to the place.

Alyssa and Garrett fill up the canteens I gave them. Jacqui fills up her water bottle. I notice, though, that Alyssa's not drinking. She's just looking down the dark hole of the canteen's mouth.

"What's wrong?" I ask her, just after her brother and Jacqui leave the kitchen.

"Nothing." She tries to shake it off, bringing the canteen to her lips, but as soon as she does — her eyes begin to well up, and I sense a pressure building within her until suddenly her floodgates break. She throws her arms around me, hugging me tightly. And I hug her back — not with the girl-next-door kind of infatuation I maybe would've had in the past, but with a sincerity that I hadn't felt before. It both surprises me and makes total sense. She pulls away quickly, embarrassed. "I'm sorry. I'm being stupid."

"What? No…" I say. I'm not exactly sure what to do in a situation like this.

She wipes her wet eyes. "What a waste of water." And she laughs.

"We all need to waste a little water sometimes," I tell her. "Better than wetting the bed." Which may be the stupidest thing I've ever said to another human being, but it makes her laugh some more. Not *at* me, but *with* me. Or at least next to me.

"Last week I would have called your house bizarre," she admits, "but now I think it's pretty incredible." She meets my eyes. "Thanks. For everything. For putting yourself on the line back there so we could stay."

I give her a slanted grin. "Eagle Scout, remember?" I say, trying to get a smile out of her. It works. "And anyway, I had to do something to make up for being so useless at the beach."

"You weren't useless," she tells me.

"We had to have our asses saved by the Queen of Darkness," I remind her.

"Would it have been better if you actually pulled the trigger and killed that boy?"

That gives me pause for thought. My father always told me you should never draw a weapon unless you are fully prepared to use it. I was not prepared. And maybe that's a good thing.

We catch up with Jacqui and Garrett, who have already gone upstairs and are checking out our game room. Jacqui's in the middle of a game on the classic *Twilight Zone* machine. "My life, in convenient pinball form," Jacqui says, slamming the flippers and keeping the metal ball bouncing. Garrett's examining a Pac-Man console, and declares it lame.

"Forgive him, Lord, for he knoweth not what he says," I say to the ceiling. Alyssa challenges him to a game. He plays it once and is addicted.

I notice that Jacqui, however, has given up on her own machine, with a ball still in the chute. She's sprawled out on a beanbag, looking even more feverish than before.

"You okay?"

"I'm fine," she says. "Leave me the hell alone."

I go to the bathroom and come back with some Advil for her. "The antibiotics will take a day or so to kick in. This'll bring down the fever."

She takes the bottle and downs three with a swig of water. She doesn't thank me this time. Maybe she rations gratitude the way the rest of us ration water.

I go downstairs to watch TV with my mom for a bit. She's not watching the news; instead she's watching *Back to the Future*, which you can't *not* watch when you channel surf across it. Doc Brown's talking about the 1.21 gigawatts needed for time travel, but mispronouncing it "jigawatts," which always bothered me.

It doesn't surprise me that she's not watching the news, which always emphasizes the gloom and doom. We get enough of that from my father. My mom generally subscribes to the more positive, optimistic school of thought, and my dad believes the doomsayers are underplaying the truth. I guess you could say they balance each other out.

Mom lowers the volume and turns to me. "You need to make things right with your father," she says.

"Now?"

"It will only be harder later."

And I know she's right.

I find him welding something new in the garage. Some sort of hybrid shovel with an ax at the opposite end. I'm not sure whether it's a tool or a weapon. It doesn't look very practical for either. I stare at his back for a while, cogitating, unsure of how to begin.

" – Dad," I finally manage.

He disengages the welder without turning around. "Yes, Kelton?" he says frigidly.

"I need to talk to you about what happened at the beach."

157

"Let me guess – the desalination plants failed and people rioted."

"Was it on the news?"

He lifts his visor and shakes his head. "There are too many things to report now for the news to catch it all. But if you look at the history of crisis mismanagement, it's an easy prediction."

"Yeah, well, we didn't actually see it go down, but by the looks of it, it was pretty bad." I clear my throat and finally get to what I'm really there to say. "I'm sorry I put you on the spot back there. But you really didn't give me much of a choice."

"We're leaving tomorrow morning," he says quickly, neither accepting nor rejecting my apology.

"The bug-out?" I say.

He nods. "It's time."

"But what about Brady?"

"We can't wait for him anymore, Kelton." I can tell that this was not an easy decision for him. "I have to believe that he took at least some of the lessons we taught him to heart," my dad says, "and that he kept his own emergency supplies – maybe even has his own bug-out."

"What about Alyssa and Garrett?" I say, less worried about Jacqui than I am about them. But I knew the answer before I asked.

"We can't bring them," my father says firmly. And this time I know there's no getting around him.

"Then let them stay here," I suggest. "There'll be water and food – and we can teach them how to use the security system."

Dad considers. He doesn't shut me down, which is a good sign. I give one more push.

"We can't just throw them out on the street..."

Then he meets my gaze, but rather than his typical bone-chilling glare, his eyes are different. Shimmering and glassy. Vulnerable. An honest display of emotion that I've never seen before. And in this single look I feel as if I've opened his personal .zip file; suddenly years of compressed emotional information comes bursting out, and I'm hit with an overwhelming truth. This is what lies beneath his indignation. All of the larger-than-life doomsday toys I adored as a kid, the anger and manipulation that pushed away Brady and threaten to push away my mother, are all just the threads of a veil woven to hide his own terror.

As a kid you idolize your parents. You think they're perfect, because they're the yardstick by which you measure the rest of the world, and yourself. Then as a teenager they just piss you off, because you realize that not only are they not perfect, but they may be even a little more screwed up than you. But there's that moment when you realize they're not superheroes, or villains. They're painfully, unforgivably human. The question is, can you forgive them for being human anyway?

Like an exposed raw nerve, he just stands there, holding that bizarre hybrid terror tool, and I realize that thing is the physical manifestation of everything he fears. And I don't know what to say except, "The booby traps work."

He's caught off guard by that. "They do?"

"Yeah, Jacqui almost fell into one. Never saw it coming."

He snaps out of his zip-file state and smiles, as I hoped he would. "Awesome!" he says, like some little kid. "I mean, it's reassuring to know that it worked."

"She thought it was really cool," I tell him. "Even if it almost maimed her."

He looks to his weird tool thingy. "Let me finish this," he says, the tension between us dissipated. "I'll be out in a bit, and I can show your friends all the features of the house."

I decide not to tell him that I already have.

15) Alyssa

"All circuits are busy now. Please try your call again later."

The voice sounds like Siri crossed with Google Maps. Cheerful, sure of itself, and utterly soulless. I'm trying to call hospitals near Laguna Beach, hoping to track down my parents, but that would require actually getting through to the hospitals. I hang up and try again.

"All circuits are busy now. Please try your call again later."

So is Verizon as dead as most people's phones now? How can circuits be busy if most phones in Southern California have run out of juice? I hang up and send a text to Garrett.

Ignore this, I'm just testing the system.

The text goes through. He texts back **K**, because "OK" is too long for our modern world. Satisfied that at least some cell towers are still in operation, I try one more call. I dial 911.

"All circuits are busy now. Please try your call again later."

I fight the urge to smash my phone, knowing that the momentary satisfaction will not be worth the loss. There's a bright side to this, though, that is actually a little bit comforting. Because if I'm trying this hard to find my parents, it's likely they're trying equally hard to get through to us. It would be much worse if phone service was working perfectly and we still didn't hear from them.

I try to take my mind off it all by checking what the others are up to. Jacqui's still passed out on a beanbag. Kelton's father is out in the garage making masculine metallic noises, and Kelton seems to be everywhere at once, like a watchdog obsessively checking that everything in his world is secure.

"You okay?" he asks for, like, the third time in an hour, as I pass him on the stairs.

"Yeah," I tell him. "Still good."

It's endearing that he's worried about me, but enough is enough. Kelton McCracken, endearing? I have stumbled into a very strange universe.

I can see Mrs. McCracken out in the greenhouse, busy with their hothouse tomatoes, and whatever else they're growing out there. While my mom stress-cleans, it looks like Kelton's mom stress-gardens. Then I spot Garrett in the dining room, staring blankly out the window. I watch as he picks up a decorative bowl from the dining room table and moves toward the front door. I have no clue what he's up to. He pushes through the door, and as much as my big sister instincts want to stop him, he moves with such intent, I just watch to see what he'll do, quietly shadowing him.

He goes out the front security gate and to our driveway next door, where he puts down the bowl, takes the canteen that hangs over his shoulder, and pours its entire contents into the bowl. And now I get it.

It's water for Kingston.

Garrett just stands there, not wanting to go all the way up to our front door. It's still wide open, and though I don't see or hear any of the dogs, they could be anywhere. They could be gone for good, and it pains me to think we might never see Kingston again.

Garrett, turning around, finally sees me. His cheeks go rosy, embarrassed. "It was always my job to make sure Kingston had water," he says, unable to meet my eye. "But I always forgot, so Mom would do it for me. But now she can't."

I can tell that he needed to do this for a whole lot of reasons. And although it's not our water to give, sometimes doing the right thing means doing the wrong thing first. With that in mind, I realize there's something that I have to do, too. A thing where the right far outweighs the wrong. But I realize I'll need an accomplice.

"Garrett, I have a mission for you."

"A mission?" Garrett is instantly interested.

"I need you to ask Kelton what chess boxing is."

He looks at me, confused. "I don't want to know what chess boxing is."

"It doesn't matter. I need you to have Kelton show you."

Knowing Kelton, this should buy me at least an hour out of his scrutiny. And with Mrs. McCracken occupied in the garden, and her husband playing with sharp objects in the garage, I'll have just the window I need.

Garrett agrees, not getting it, but trusting me.

*　*　*

We slip back into the house and I immediately locate the little trash bin near the foyer. I dig through tissues, wrappers, and bits of paper until I finally find the pink flyer – the one that was on the door, giving the specifics of the community meeting.

I read it over, this time more carefully. It's at the Burnsides' house. It started half an hour ago.

I grab Kelton's backpack, empty out the school stuff, then, making sure the coast is clear, I go to the bookcase near the stairs – the entrance to the safe room.

I can't remember which book opens the door, so I have to try a whole bunch of them until I find it. Finally the deadbolt disengages, and I pull the door open, revealing the treasure trove of survival gear. Weapons, tools, canned food, and most importantly, cases of bottled water.

I start stuffing half-liter bottles into the pack. I'm able to fit only ten in. Then I freeze, suddenly realizing that I'm not alone.

Kelton's mom stands in the doorway.

Caught, I stammer, trying to come up with some kind of explanation, because I know how bad this must look – but Mrs. McCracken's face softens. She offers a light, encouraging smile.

"You can fit two more in the side pockets," she tells me, and hands me the bottles. "The meeting's already started, so you'll have to hurry."

I'm so caught off guard, I can't respond. Then, without another word, Mrs. McCracken steps away from the doorway and quietly disappears into another room, as if she never even saw me.

Walking down my own street after the events at the beach this morning has me on edge. I have this vulnerable feeling, like if I stand outside too long, something's going to gobble me up. It's the same way I feel when I'm waist deep in the ocean and I think I see the outline of a shark. I know it's all in my head, but the feeling lingers all the same. So I deal with it, and wade deeper down the street. I don't want to be seen coming out of the McCracken house, because anyone who sees me will know I'm not as thirsty as they probably are. But even if they don't see me leaving the house, maybe they'll know I'm hydrated just by looking at me.

There's a kid coming down the street. My age. I know him, but not well – his name is Jacob something-or-other. I dread the moment he passes. Never have I felt so completely antisocial.

He's dragging something on the ground. A stick of some sort. It hisses on the concrete as he drags it. He doesn't make eye contact. He seems as uncomfortable passing me as I do passing him. And I notice that it's not a stick that he's dragging, but a golf club. A wooden driver.

"Hey," he says as we pass.

"Hey," I say back.

He goes his way, I go mine. I don't look back. I have no idea what he plans to do with that golf club, but I know it has nothing to do with golf.

The Burnsides' house is just around the corner. Mrs. Burnside used to have a prize-winning garden. Roses, azaleas, and bougainvillea climbing the trunks of tall palms. All that's left are the palms, which aren't dead yet, but everything else is gone. What was once a lawn is now a tricolored mosaic of river stones, creating an image of Kokopelli, the hunchbacked flute player of American Indian mythology – an idea Mrs. Burnside probably got on a visit to Santa Fe, or Taos, or someplace like that. I'm sure her stone-scape will win awards, too.

The door is closed but unlocked. As I enter I see that their large living room is packed with people. It seems for the most part, there's one representative from every neighborhood family that hasn't already left.

They're taking stock of pooled resources, both physical and intellectual. Mrs. Jarvis claims her sister is a legitimate dowser, and can find water for a "nominal fee." Roger Malecki says he put his entire cactus garden through his Magic Bullet blender, and extracted a gallon of water from it.

Mrs. Burnside sees me hanging by the door, and comes over to me, giving me a hug. "Allison, I'm so glad you came." I can tell she's genuinely pleased to see me, so I don't correct her. "How are your parents? I was hoping to see them here."

I take a deep breath and say, "They're not home right now," which is true, and doesn't elicit either questions or concern – neither of which I could deal with in the moment.

"Well, please give them our regards, and tell them to stay safe! Things are getting strange out there."

I heft the pack on my back and take a few steps forward. In a lull in the conversation, I try to get Mr. Burnside's attention.

"Excuse me," I say, but not loudly enough, because no one seems to hear me. They go on to talk about the heat, and someone suggests the cooling effect that evaporating alcohol has on the skin – although I suspect any alcohol is being otherwise employed.

"Excuse me," I say a little louder. "I have some water."

I have never in my life seen an entire room turn in my direction. Never have I commanded such complete attention.

"You have water?" someone says.

I flip around my backpack, open the zipper slightly, and pull out one of the bottles. "I mean – it's not enough for everyone, but it's better than nothing."

They stare at me. They stare at each other.

"How much do you have?" asks Stu Leeson, with both suspicion and expectation.

Then Mr. Burnside takes control again. "Well, this is good news," he says, and offers what I think is a bible quote, or at least a paraphrasing. "'And a child shall lead them.'" Then he does a head count of the room. "We have seventeen households represented here. How much water do you have, Alyssa?"

"Twelve bottles. Half a liter each."

Silence for a moment.

Then someone points out the obvious. "That means five of us won't get bottles."

"Now hold on," says Burnside. "That's not necessarily the case."

And now everyone has an opinion.

"The math gives everyone seventy percent of a bottle."

"That's ridiculous!"

"Families with young children should get a full bottle!"

"That's discriminatory!"

"My wife is pregnant."

Burnside puts up his hands. "All right, calm down!"

But the genie is already out of the lamp. Everyone begins talking among themselves. I can see alliances forming, lines in the sand being drawn – all within seconds, and all because I announced that I have a limited supply of something that all of them desperately need.

"We'll pour it into a pot, and every family gets a measured scoop."

"How is that fair? There are five in my family."

"So we'll count everyone and divide it that way."

"What about pets?"

"Pets? Are you serious?"

"Let the girl decide!"

Everyone considers that.

"Yes," someone else agrees. "It's her water, let her decide who gets it."

And for the second time in five minutes, they all turn to me.

I am not the kind of person who is easily intimidated. I can stand in front of a class and deliver an oral report fearlessly. I can debate anyone into the ground on any subject I'm passionate about. But never before have I held the fate of other human beings in my hands. Suddenly I'm timid. I'm never timid.

"Well ... I think ... maybe we should ... I mean..."

And then Stu Leeson shouts out, "Are you seriously leaving this in the hands of a teenage girl?"

And then before I can stop myself, I blurt out, "Well, that makes sixteen instead of seventeen I have to decide between, doesn't it?"

I don't mean that. Or maybe I do. I don't know. Now I *have* to give a bottle to the Leesons because I said that. But if I do, I'm denying somebody else. Is that fair?

"Alyssa, honey," says Vicky Morales, who I barely know, "we trust your decision, dear. We know you're a smart, honest girl."

"Well, you're just brown-nosing now, Victoria!" says Miss Bouman. "Do you really think she'll favor you just because you're kissing ass?"

"All right, we're all in the same boat here," someone else says. And it's true. But, as Garrett said the other day, that boat is the *Titanic*. One lifeboat left, and I'm it. I don't like this. I don't like it at all, and although I know this is terrible, I begin to wish I never came here with water.

These people look a lot like the kid at the beach. Their lips are white and raw. They're anxious, irritated, and their irritation is turning on me like a spotlight.

"Well, what's it gonna be?" a man I don't even know says, at the end of his patience. "We don't have all day!"

But I don't respond, because for a split second his eyes flit, and I catch that wild look in them – a look that I'm starting to learn how to identify – and I think I know what comes next.

Then Mr. Burnside signals to his wife, and apparently they communicate in that telepathic way that married couples sometimes do, because she comes up behind me and gently takes the backpack.

"Why don't you go, Alyssa," she says, this time getting my name right. "We'll figure it out. Thank you for the water – and I'm sorry you got put in this position. It's our problem, not yours."

I don't argue. I don't even ask for the bag back. I don't care. I just want to get out of there.

It's only after I leave that I remember that it's Kelton's backpack, with his name stenciled right on it. If they didn't already know the McCrackens have water, they sure do now.

The sun sets and we convene for what I'm anticipating to be the most awkward dinner of my life. Even the food is surreal: corned beef and cabbage with pumpkin pie that's still frozen in the middle for dessert.

"Don't ask," Kelton leans over and whispers. Which is just fine by me.

In spite of the off-grid electrical system that Kelton is always so proud to brag about, the lights in the house are turned off, and Mrs. McCracken has lit candles for the dinner table.

At the head of the table sits Mr. McCracken, who glowers at everyone as if he were a lord presiding over his fiefdom. I imagine he's one of those overbearing parents who makes you ask to be excused, and only after you've finished all your peas and carrots. Though right now his glare is focused more on Jacqui – who's already helped herself to three servings of corned beef. She stuffs her face, gleefully irreverent, and eventually motions with her fork. "So what's with the candles?"

"Good question," Mr. McCracken mutters to his corned beef, but with a tone that tells me he's talking to his wife. "I wonder that, too."

"We don't want to flaunt our electricity to the neighbors any more than we already have," Kelton's mother says too calmly.

"It took us six months to install our power system. I'd like to use it," Mr. McCracken says. "Besides, it's going to take more than a few scented candles to ward off our neighbors."

"We wouldn't have to worry about neighbors if we practiced a little more compassion," his wife comes back.

"Maybe we should just invite them all over for supper," he says.

"Maybe we should," she says, calling his bluff.

He looks around at the rest of us like a prosecutor making an argument to a jury. "You share nothing, or you share everything. There's no in between."

"Thank you, Master Yoda," says Jacqui.

I don't think this is the first time Kelton's parents have had this argument, because Kelton is quick to react. "It's called the psychology of scarcity, and deprivation thinking," Kelton says, feeling the need to defend his father – although it really feels more like he's apologizing for him. "Add that to mob dynamics, and you get a mob that will keep taking until you're just as bereft as they are."

"Bereft," says Jacqui. "Good word. You'll catch up with my SAT score in no time." Then she grabs more corned beef.

"Well, it's a bankrupt, self-serving way of thinking," says Mrs. McCracken.

"But he's right," I hear myself say, which is a surprise to everyone – even me. I think back to the way our own neighbors handled the division of those water bottles, and how so many of them were ready to turn against me, the one who brought it. As much as I hate to admit it, I see Mr. McCracken's point. It's not like it's their fault, but I can see how, when people feel a threat to their lives, they'll exercise any option they have.

If you don't want it to be at your expense, you have to take yourself off the table as an option.

"Either you open your doors wide, or you lock them," I say regretfully. "People are too complicated to trust with anything in between."

Mrs. McCracken studies me, perhaps feeling a bit betrayed. Mr. McCracken looks at me, surprised – almost proud – which gives me a queasy, uncomfortable feeling, like my journey to the Dark Side is now complete.

He clears his throat. "It doesn't matter anyway," he says. "We're leaving for our bug-out come daybreak."

"What's a bug-out?" Garrett asks.

"It's an emergency shelter," Kelton explains. "A secret place to go in the event of a major disaster."

"So when do we leave?" Jacqui says, through a mouthful of food.

Kelton doesn't respond, and just from his silence I realize that we're not part of the McCracken equation.

"There's only room for us," says Kelton's father. "I'm sorry." And I think he actually means it. To be honest, I myself haven't even put any thought into a world past this dinner. There hasn't been time to project any sort of future – even short term. Then Mr. McCracken surprises me.

"I'm going to leave the keys to the house with you, Alyssa."

"What?" I accidentally blurt out.

"I'll show you how to use the security system, and make sure you know where all the booby traps are. The whole place will be yours for the duration," he says. He glances at Jacqui, and reluctantly adds, "All three of you."

I wonder what his rationale is for giving me the keys to his castle. It makes me think of the way my mom used to always leave a television on when we'd go on vacation so would-be robbers would think someone was home. Maybe this is just an elaborate version of that. Was it Kelton who persuaded him, I wonder – or was it because I corroborated his abysmal view of humanity?

I think about the days ahead. This has to end, doesn't it? "The duration," as Mr. McCracken called it, can't be more than just a week or two – if that. Then, just as I begin projecting forward to a hope of better days, things suddenly get a whole lot worse.

Every phone vibrates and dings in unison, a strange and troubling cacophony. We all lift up our phones to see the identical message, which reads:

EMERGENCY ALERT: MARTIAL LAW DECLARED IN LOS ANGELES, ORANGE, VENTURA, RIVERSIDE, SAN BERNARDINO, AND SAN DIEGO COUNTIES. STAND BY FOR FURTHER DIRECTIVES.

16) Kelton

It's all happening just as all the books on prepping said it would. I take no comfort in that. Not even a little. Doomsday scenarios are only fun when doomsday is just a hypothetical. Now I wish that they were all wrong.

Martial law is the last step before everything falls apart.

Now it could go one of two ways: 1) Martial law will be

effective; there will be enough military might to counteract the chaos; riots will be flashpoints, rather than widespread; things will break soft, and recovery will be relatively easy. 2) Martial law will fail; the military will underestimate the need, or not be able to scramble fast enough; riots will be systemic and severe; Southern California will break hard, and recovery will take years, if at all.

"So what happens now?" Alyssa asks, before we all bed down for the night.

I don't share with her the two possibilities. "We'll have to see," I tell her.

I know Alyssa is capable, and I don't worry that she can maintain things here in the house after my parents and I leave, but I do worry about Jacqui. She'll want to take charge, and I don't see that as a good thing.

These are the thoughts I take to bed with me that night. I think they'll keep me awake, but sometimes your own body does you a much-needed favor. I'm so exhausted, I'm out within minutes of hitting the pillow.

I'm jolted awake by the drone of our motion detector alarm. We have second-generation motion detectors; they only trigger if the moving object is large enough to be a human being – which means someone has hopped our fence. I check the clock. Just before five a.m. I move to the game room, where Alyssa, Garrett, and Jacqui are already up and on high alert.

"What the hell is that?" Jacqui asks.

"Intruder alert," I say, realizing that sounds far more sci-fi than I mean it to. "Where's my dad?"

No one responds, but I hear Dad call for me downstairs. That's when Jacqui goes to a window, and whatever she sees out there makes her turn to me with bug-eyed concern – something I didn't even know was in her emotional repertoire.

"This can't be good…" she says.

I look out the window to see lights – dozens of them in the predawn darkness, constellated like stars. I rub my eyes, allowing them to adjust … and now I'm able to make out shapes. People holding flashlights – and they're all moving toward our house.

"What's going on?" Alyssa asks.

That's when I hear pounding.

Bang Bang Bang!

There's someone at our front door.

"Stay away from the windows," I tell them, and nearly throw myself downstairs.

My dad's in the dining room, one step ahead of us, with an array of weapons already sprawled across the table. Guns, ammo, knives, and an assortment of other tactical tools, some of which I don't even recognize.

I can see my mom in the safe room, frantically moving things to make room for us.

Bang Bang Bang!

The wolves have finally arrived. My stomach goes sour and knots up. I remind myself that the front door is reinforced, and that all the windows are bulletproof. Our house is impenetrable and no one is getting in. But if all of these things are true, why the hell am I so afraid?

"Kelton!" shouts my dad, as Alyssa, Garrett, and Jacqui

come downstairs behind me. "Get your friends into the safe room. Then go get your gun."

But the command doesn't compute for me.

He reads the look on my face. "Where's your pistol?"

"It's right here," Jacqui says, flashing the butt of the gun, which protrudes from her waistband.

My father looks from the gun, to Jacqui, to me, calculating how this unthinkable thing happened – and perhaps assessing Jacqui's threat level. Ultimately, he decides that the threat outside our home is more imminent than Jacqui, who clearly will not part with my gun – so my father doesn't ask how she got it. I'll get reamed for it later, I'm sure.

Dad opens the electrical panel in the downstairs hallway and throws the master switch, killing the floodlights outside, and any lights on inside as well, other than his own flashlight. Then he attaches infrared scopes to what guns he can, so he'll be able to see but the intruders won't.

The banging, which had stopped for a few moments, changes timbre and direction. Now it's coming from the back door instead of the front door, and is even more insistent than before. Our back door has a captive double-cylinder nickel-silver deadbolt, but my dad has complained that the door frame isn't thick enough. Deadbolts are only as strong as the frame that holds them.

My mom tries to move the others to the safe room, but Jacqui's not going – neither is Alyssa, and Garrett won't move without his sister.

My father loads the weapons and takes off any safeties.

"Richard, what are you doing?" Mom says, horrified. It's

one thing to see the weapons laid out. It's another thing to see them being loaded.

"Protecting my family." The pounding on the back door is more frantic than ever.

"Let's not jump to conclusions," Mom says, her voice quivering.

But Dad is single-minded. He straps on his Kevlar vest. "Get everyone into the safe room."

My mom is frantic now. "Come with us into the safe room! You don't need to do this!"

"Like hell I don't!"

My dad keeps on loading guns, and I can see now that his hands are shaking. The only thing keeping him from imploding right now is his collection of deadly toys.

"At least see what they want!" she yells, desperate.

"You know what they want!"

His gaze finally connects with Mom's, letting her see him, truly, for the first time in a long time. The person I saw in the garage earlier. Not an indignant, violence-seeking monster, but a human being, honest and raw — trapped in this house with us, and scared to the bone.

He chooses the shotgun and goes into the kitchen, taking a position across the room from the back door. No one has gone into the safe room. Everyone wants to be here. To see what happens. To see how this goes down — as if somehow being here will keep it from happening.

More banging on the back door. The knob rattles violently, but doesn't turn.

Meanwhile the voices coming from the street grow louder.

I hear our security gate come crashing down. I hear someone scream as they fall into a booby trap in our front yard, but there aren't enough booby traps to stop this onslaught.

Then the pounding at the back door stops.

My dad takes a deep breath and digs in deep. He raises his gun, pointed at the door, preparing himself for whatever comes next. I can't take my focus from that door – like when I was a kid and was convinced there was a monster in my closet. I'd stare, unmoving, unblinking, to make damn sure I would see whatever came out of there before it could see me. *This door is locked,* I tell myself. *It's locked. No one's getting in.*

Then there's a sound that's familiar and terrible. A deadbolt disengaging. The knob turns. The door opens. We've been breached.

And now everything comes in quick, disjointed images, like reality is violently strobing around me.

The door swings wide.

A figure moves forward.

Dad screams and pulls the trigger.

The world explodes with the shotgun blast.

The intruder is blown back against the door frame.

Blood splatters everywhere.

On me.

One eye stings from it.

The intruder bounces off the door frame.

He hits the kitchen floor, face down, in front of the open door.

And in that door –

There's a key in the lock.

A single, solitary key.

Dad catches his breath, still in shock from having pulled the trigger.

But then Mom steps forward, in some kind of trance...

Then Dad drops the gun...

And falls to his knees...

And now I finally start piecing it all together.

As I realize the body lying face-down on the ground isn't a murderous, thirst-crazed marauder.

It's my brother, Brady.

Dad, wailing in agony, rolls him over, confirming the inevitable truth. It hits me hard, but in a strange, hollow kind of way. I lose control of my senses. I'm outside of myself now, watching everything unfold, like an observer wrapped in someone else's skin.

Mom hurls herself over Brady's limp body. Her white nightgown absorbing his blood. Dad pats Brady's face over and over again in denial, as if to wake him up from a bad dream.

"No no no no no no no..."

I'm so fixed on the scene that I have failed to realize what's going on in the house. People have started flooding through the back door. The neighbors. The marauders. They pass like shadows, scavenging the entire house. Their eyes are wild and rabid. They come armed with shovels and fireplace pokers and baseball bats.

But Mom and Dad are completely oblivious to it. What does it matter? What does any of this matter? My big brother is dead.

Brady got our messages. He knew we were leaving for

the bug-out this morning, and, as usual, showed up at the last minute. And when he saw the approaching mob, he tried to warn us, frantically pounding on the door, trying to get in.

We should have known it was him when the doorknob turned. We all should have – because of the key my father always left for him, hidden in the same place it always was since the time we were both little; in a hollow in the back porch railing. The intentional flaw in our security measures.

Alyssa yells to me from behind, but it takes a few seconds for her words to register.

"We need to leave! Kelton, we have to get out of here!"

But I'm not leaving. I'm not abandoning my brother any more than my parents are. My legs are churning and I'm moving past her and toward the center of the room. My hand reaches for something, and I grip it. The shotgun my father dropped.

I load another round into the barrel.

I look into the wolves' many glowing eyes.

They're going to die today. Every last one of them.

I take aim at the head of a figure carrying a case of water.

I clamp the trigger.

Then suddenly everything goes black.

17) Jacqui

I've never seen anyone get knocked out with a picture frame, let alone a picture of themselves. But hey – there's a first time for everything. The metal frame was heavy enough, and Alyssa brought it down over Kelton's head with the right amount of force. Just in the nick of time, too, because Kelton was actually going to do it. He was actually going to start blowing people away.

All I can make out is the blinding flurry of flashlights beaming in every direction. I keep my hands light, fingers to my gun – but I'm not about to waste a bullet unless I absolutely have to.

Alyssa turns to me and produces a pair of keys. The keys to the BMW. She must have grabbed them during all the chaos. While the rest of us were gripped with shock, Alyssa was already calculating our escape.

"We have to get out of here now." She motions to Kelton's limp body. "Take him."

She clutches the keys tightly, and I realize they've become leverage in a power game.

"Who put you in charge?" I challenge, but with the house being stripped bare all around us, it's not like staying is much of an option – and if that bug-out thing will now be more than available, we're going to need Kelton to show us how to get there. In sum, she's right, and I hate that.

Alyssa races back into the kitchen; she tries her best to get Kelton's parents to leave with us, but they won't budge. All they want to do – all they're capable of doing now – is pointlessly comforting what I now realize is their dead son.

"Go," they tell Alyssa through their grief. "Just go…"

While around us, the intruders scavenge like jackals.

What happened here was inevitable. They had to flaunt their electrical system and their resources. Kelton's father had to be the family hero. It's like he was so obsessed with protecting the house that he forgot the main objective was to actually protect everyone inside of it.

I grab Kelton under the shoulders and pick him up. I shoot a glance to Garrett, who's been hiding, crouched by a sofa. We drag Kelton down the hall toward the front door, Alyssa leading the way. As we make our way there, I try to take stock of what's actually happening around us, but it's too dark — just shapes and outlines. But I can hear everything: the defeated whimpers of Kelton's parents, underscored by dozens of scurrying feet that squeak, click, and scuff against the hardwood floor. A door somewhere is kicked open — I hear wood chips splinter. Jars clink and crash in the kitchen as they're knocked from pantry shelves, or fall from overloaded arms. A water jug we had brought up earlier tumbles down the stairs and bursts across the floor. This place will be ravaged and picked apart until all that's left is the carcass of a home.

Alyssa opens the front door, and more people flood in. A veritable cross-ventilation of water–zombies.

Just as we get out the door, one man raises a baseball bat, threatening to swing at Alyssa. He holds it there for a moment and lowers his weapon, recognizing her.

"They left us no choice!" he says, as if it can excuse his actions.

But Alyssa doesn't acknowledge it. In fact, she doesn't give him even the slightest satisfaction of a human moment. She pushes past, toward the BMW in the driveway.

Garrett and I stuff Kelton's limp body inside — it feels like we're kidnapping him, and then I remember we technically are. Alyssa climbs in after to tend to him in the back seat, so Garrett climbs into the front to sit shotgun. Today I wish the passenger seat weren't called that.

I get behind the wheel, close the door, and hit the lock button, hearing the satisfying sound of locks thudding down. Although the marauders are too crazed to even notice our exit.

I reach a hand back to Alyssa. "If you want me to drive, you're going to have to give me the keys."

Still she won't give them to me. She holds them tight in her fist. "It's a keyless ignition — just push the button."

Damn BMWs. As long as the key is in the car, it will start, regardless of whose grubby little hand it's in. Again it looks like I don't have much of a choice. I start the car, back out past the water-zombies that lurk around us, then speed headfirst into darkness, nearly forgetting to turn on the headlights.

A left. Then a right. Then another right. Then a left.

I'm driving too fast and I know it, but I can't seem to slow down. Adrenaline has turned my foot to lead. I run over a piece of debris in the road. I hear it scrape against the bottom of the car. I pray to God it didn't puncture our gas tank.

"I'm gonna throw up," says Garrett. "I think I'm going to throw up."

"Swallow it down and man up!" I tell him.

"Don't you talk to my brother like that!"

I turn right. I don't know why; I'm at a T in the road and I have to choose. I put my brights on because I want to see everything that's ahead of me. I don't care if I blind oncoming traffic. There *is* no oncoming traffic. Anyone who's going anywhere has already gotten there, or has given up.

I chide myself for even getting into a situation like this. I should have found a way to get the keys back during the night from Kelton's father, but I gave in to the comfort and safety of a well-stocked home. False security. There was nothing safe about that place; all those supplies, all those pissed off, thirsty neighbors. The place was a lightning rod in a shit storm, and they couldn't see it. Well, what do you expect when you bunk up with a family of angry nerds? That's what Kelton's family is. Nerds who traded in their Comic-Con passes for gun show tickets. Instead of *Star Trek* trivia, they could probably tell me about every application of a weapon, yet could never even begin to fathom what it feels like to actually end a human life. Well, now Kelton's father can. Nerds with guns. Now I've seen everything.

"Where are we going?" Garrett asks, successfully not hurling.

"Away from that goddamn house," is the only answer I can give. We drive down another identical suburban street, past endless rows of tightly spaced homes, once full of life, but now their facades look like dead faces with sagging eyes seething despair. This place feels like the eerie, abandoned suburban neighborhoods that surround nuclear power plant leaks. It feels bleak. A place where hope goes to die.

I make a left. It's just another residential cul-de-sac. Dammit! I nearly do a donut at the end, and head back out.

"We can't just keep driving in circles!" Alyssa says from the back seat.

"Fine!" I snap. "Then navigate."

"To where?"

"Anywhere!"

Alyssa leans forward and looks around us. We can barely see a thing, but she seems to know where we are.

"All right. Take a right. Not here, but the next one."

Two more turns, and we're finally out of the neighborhood and on a major street. Although I'm not sure what that buys us.

I glance in the rearview. Kelton is propped up against the door behind Garrett. He's still limp and lifeless.

"Wake him up," I say.

"I want to let him sleep it off," Alyssa responds.

"How do you know he's not dead? You hit him pretty hard."

"He's breathing," Alyssa says, annoyed by my suggestion. "Dead people don't breathe."

Garrett turns around to look at him. "Maybe you're both right. Maybe he's brain-dead." Which really pisses Alyssa off.

"He might have a concussion. We won't know for sure until he wakes up."

"So wake him up," I say again. This time Alyssa reaches over and shakes him. He wakes up, and I think I'm just as relieved as Alyssa is.

Kelton coughs, rubs the back of his head, and blinks a few times, still woozy.

I wonder if he knows he got knocked out cold and dragged to the car. I wonder if he remembers what happened in his house. Sometimes when you have brain trauma, it wipes your short-term memory. You lose the last few minutes like a lousy Word doc that you forgot to save.

It takes a moment to clear the fog, but clearly he does remember, because he goes berserk.

"No!!! What are you doing? We have to go back!"

Alyssa grabs him with both hands, but he wrestles her off. "We have to stop them!"

"It's too late for that, Kelton!" Alyssa says.

He pulls on the door handle, fully prepared to leap out of the moving car. It's only sheer luck that his child lock is on, and the door won't open.

He wails in fury and kicks the door handle until it breaks. But the door still doesn't open.

I change lanes sharply to force him away from the door. It works. He gets thrown back onto Alyssa, who holds him with more strength than I thought she'd have as he thrashes.

"But my parents!"

"I tried to get them to come – they wouldn't."

"Those people might kill them!"

And then Garrett says something that's actually kind of wise. "Prolly not," he says. "I mean, they weren't fighting back. Water-zombies just want one thing, right? If you don't get in their way, I bet they leave you alone."

It seems to calm Kelton down a little bit. At least enough for Alyssa to trust letting him go. He slumps back into the seat again, shaking his head.

"No no no no. We can't … we can't…" But he doesn't have the conviction of his words anymore. He's quiet for a moment as his fury rolls out, and the real emotion behind it surges in.

"My brother's dead…"

I don't say anything. What can I say? It can't be undone, and all you can do is die or deal. Kelton would probably choose the former right now. I leave compassion to Alyssa. I'm sure she's much better at it. I can only imagine the dark, messed-up things that are going on in Kelton's head right now. I keep playing the events of the last fifteen minutes over and over in my head, and the more I let the mental merry-go-round spin, the more I realize that Garrett had the right idea. I feel like I want to barf, too. What happened in that house – I've never experienced anything so savage, anything so inhuman.

"I'm sorry, Kelton," Alyssa says. "It sucks."

And that just makes him go psycho. "Sucks? It *sucks*? No, Alyssa. Failing a midterm sucks. Dropping your phone in water sucks. My father just shot my brother in the chest and I watched him die! Don't insult me by saying that it sucks!"

And then he kicks the back of the seat so hard I almost lose control of the wheel. "And I will never forgive *you* for knocking me out!"

"Me?" I say. "As much as I'd enjoy rendering you unconscious, I wasn't the one who hit you."

"*I* hit you Kelton," Alyssa says. "I had to – you were about to kill Stu Leeson."

"So what?" says Kelton. "I wish I had! He deserves to die! They all do!"

"Trust me, Kelton – you'll be glad I stopped you later."

Kelton hardens his jaw and turns away from her. His eyes are red and clouded with tears. He catches me looking at him in the rearview mirror.

"Don't look at me, bitch!'

Normally that would be met with severe punishment, but Kelton's not himself. Grief can twist people in ways they're not supposed to twist. So I'll give him a pass.

The road ahead curves. Dark fast food places on either side. Then, just past a major intersection, I see scores of cars and tents amassed around a Target. It's probably some sort of relief center that hasn't actually seen any relief yet.

"You think there's water there?" Alyssa asks.

I shake my head. "Not a chance. But they're all waiting for it like the second coming." There are so many of them there. *Misery loves company,* I think, but then again, so does hope. If it didn't, I wouldn't be here with these fine idiots.

As we pass the Target tent city, I have to do a reality check. This is the same planet I was on last week, and yet how could it be? I never would've imagined that "perfect" Orange County could go so utterly insane. Funny how my disdain for this place once left me wishing that God Almighty would plague it with locusts and leaking breast implants. But now that the whole of Southern California has actually been plagued, I'm a little disappointed. Not that I want to endure any more than I already have, but I'm disappointed by people – how weak they are, how frail their psyches must be to allow a water shortage to turn them into murderous mobs. If there's one thing I know for sure, it's that I don't want be in the same league as them – hell, I don't even want to be in the same ballpark.

Not to say that I'm any sort of saint. I've broken my share of windows. Raided countless fridges and supply rooms. I've made a hobby out of breaking into houses, living the high life and moving on. The difference is, I did that by choice, and not at the expense of others. I mean, yeah, my crimes weren't entirely victimless, but the victims barely noticed what they were missing, and when they did, they had good insurance. I do the scofflaw thing with a wink and a smile. I don't think I could ever be part of a mindless mob that raids a house. Instead, I'd be the one who takes the truck where the mob just stashed all the stuff they stole, leaving behind a Hello Kitty note that says, "See you, suckers." To me, that's the Bette Davis move.

"Look at that!" says Garrett. He's pointing ahead, where a church is lit by hundreds of candles. The door is wide open, the sanctuary is packed, flowing out to the street. Dozens of families, huddling close, praying for deliverance from thirst. My grandmother believed in the power of prayer. There's a trite saying among the faithful, goes like this: "God answers all prayers. And sometimes his answer is no." My grandmother hated that. "God never says no," she told me. "He just says, 'Not today.'" Which is exactly the answer raining down upon this candle-lit vigil.

Behind me, Kelton has gone entirely silent. Right now his brain is beyond short-circuited, and I'm realizing that he's going to need a full reboot if he's going to make it out of this situation alive.

Garrett, seeing Kelton's shell-shocked state, offers him his canteen. "Here, have some," Garrett says. "You'll feel better." Funny how in all of that chaos, Garrett was the only one who remembered to grab the most important thing.

Kelton doesn't even acknowledge his offer, as if water is the enemy that got his brother killed. I guess in a way it was.

When Kelton doesn't take the canteen, I take it instead — but rather than acting like a water-zombie, I take a brief, measured sip and hand it back to Garrett. Alyssa glowers at me and purses her lips – probably to stop herself from saying something stupid. Then she asks Garrett for the canteen and takes her own measured sip.

All this time, we still don't have a destination. I'm not driving in circles anymore, but it doesn't change the fact that we have nowhere to go.

"Kelton, where's your bug-out?" I ask.

"Up your ass," he says.

"Ooh, look who's suddenly become a potty mouth," I tease. He responds with an expression an Eagle Scout type like Kelton shouldn't know.

"Leave him alone," says Alyssa.

"Give me one more order," I tell her, "and I'm throwing you out with a 'drink me' sign taped to your back."

Which actually gets a very slight snort from Kelton. Good. Progress.

Now, to our right are dozens of families, migrating in droves – as if they're all partaking in some kind of divine pilgrimage. At least these people are taking action rather than sitting and waiting for someone to save them. It's like everyone has divided into camps, all with their own theories on what course of action to take.

"Where do you think they're going?" Garrett asks.

"I'm not sure they even know," I answer.

"Just like us?" Alyssa points out.

And then Kelton points ahead, where the light of dawn crests the distant mountaintop. "They're going to Lake

Arrowhead," he says, "But they won't get there. There are two mountain ranges and two counties between here and there."

Looks like the pilgrimage has brought him back to planet Earth. I take this opportunity to tease more information out of him.

"Is that where the bug-out is?"

He shakes his head. "No … it's in Angeles National Forest. Much closer. Due north rather than east." He redirects his gaze. "But we're not going to be able to get there in this car. We're going to need something with an elevated chassis. Four-wheel drive."

"You mean a raised truck?" Garrett suggests. "Like Uncle Basil's?"

"Exactly like Uncle Basil's," Kelton responds.

"He's staying with his sort-of ex-girlfriend," Alyssa says. "In Dove Canyon."

And finally we know where we're going.

PART THREE

THE CHASM BETWEEN

18) Henry

There's a very specific way that one must think if one wishes to achieve true success. You could run the best textile company in the world, design a new propulsion system for NASA, even paint the next Mona Lisa – and at that point you may be rich, but you'll still be one important skill set away from being *wealthy*.

That's because wealth is a mindset.

Or, as my mentor, Vice Principal Metzer, always says, "Rich is an adjective, wealth is a verb." Actually it's a noun, but that's beside the point.

True wealth is only established after you've disciplined yourself to invest in assets that generate enough income to cover your expenses. Right now my expenses are minimal, and my new hydration business has taken off, launched through the roof, and shot into the stratosphere.

My parents and I live in a gated community called Dove Canyon. And when you're living in upper-middle-class Orange County – and especially in a canyon – elevation is everything. That's why my mom and dad invested in a house near the top of the hill. It's one of the biggest in the community, with a panoramic view, presiding over the golf course and most every other house that shares our zip code. And since my parents left on vacation last week, I've been looking after our home all alone, even through these difficult times.

The Tap-Out has not only contributed to my growth as a person, but has proven to be a fantastic learning experience in business and commerce. A while back my father encouraged my mother to start a business of her own; instead she let one of her friends talk her into buying sixty cases of ÁguaViva, a pyramid scheme where you spend a ridiculous amount of money to purchase seven hundred twenty bottles of alkaline-infused goji berry mineral water – only for it to sit in your guest room for six months because nobody wants to buy alkaline-infused goji berry mineral water. However, now that the value of water has exponentially risen, I've been turning a substantial profit on the ÁguaViva.

If I've learned anything in my studies, it's that the greatest investors capitalize in times of crisis. And though at first it may sound cold, it's the giants' duty to continue to stand tall and generate profit, which will lead to spending, and ultimately stimulate the economy for the greater good.

I'm eating red licorice and leftover cookies from my father's most recent company party when the doorbell rings. Another customer! I answer the door, and to my surprise it's Spencer, a kid who lives a few houses up. I never particularly cared for Spencer; his house is at the very top of the hill – higher and bigger than ours, but technically ours is taller. Back in elementary school we'd open lemonade stands across the street from each other. When we were a little older, we would silently compete for magazine subscription sales for school fund-raisers, and if it looked like he wasn't going to win, his parents would buy *Readers Digest* magazines for every friend on their contact list – something that my parents refused to do, and as a result, I would always come in second. It used to bother me; now I just see it as an early lesson in the inherent value of healthy competition. But I still don't like him.

"Hi, Henry."

"Hey, what's up, Spencer? C'mon in."

I welcome him into my home and lead him to the living room. I notice his slow, irresolute movements as he walks.

"Can I get you anything?" I say, as a formality, and as a way of opening negotiations.

He takes a seat on the leather couch. He's looking weak. Feverish. A lot of people have been that way. I think it's a little bit more than mere dehydration.

"You okay?" I ask, knowing that he's not, but wondering if he'll admit it.

"The water from the old tank on the hill," he says. "I don't know, I think it was bad or something."

While everyone else in SoCal was scrambling for water, Dove Canyon thought they had it made. Although our primary water tank was down to the dregs before the Tap-Out, there was an older one on top of the hill that had been taken out of service. Someone had the bright idea of reconnecting it, to get to the last of its water, and bingo! We had water two days longer than anywhere else. The problem is, now everyone's getting sick from it. Everyone but me, that is, because I never trusted tap water – even when it was supposed to be good. And besides, in sales you not only have to believe in your product, but live by it.

Spencer heaves a heavy, achy breath, rolls his neck, and says, "So I heard you have water."

"I do," I tell him, as I sink deeply into the adjacent couch, letting the moment become intentionally awkward.

"I'll give you the autographed Peyton Manning ball," he says, making the first offer, which already puts him at a disadvantage. Even if he thought it was his best offer, it's now just the floor of the negotiation.

"Barely worth half a bottle," I explain to him. "And you know I'm not really into football. Besides, I've already checked – that ball is only valued at two hundred and fifty dollars."

He thinks quickly. "The ball *and* a bottle of Johnny Walker – King George Edition," and he adds, "for your father."

A nice gesture, but I have to turn him down. The problem with most people in a barter economy is that they're just trading one consumable for another. But if you truly want to build wealth, you need to be trading up for appreciating assets. My father has always stressed the importance of diversification, and I like to think that I've acquired a diversified portfolio from my hydration business – a portfolio I plan to turn for a profit on eBay. So far I've acquired a surround-sound system, a vintage vinyl record collection, a Thomas Kinkaid painting, an autographed first edition of *The Maltese Falcon*, and a yellow-scaled ball python.

So what does Spencer have that's worthy of adding to my collection?

"How about my Xbox?" he asks.

I shake my head. "Everyone's offering me Xboxes."

He knows what I want, and this dance is just winding us closer to it. Because in his bonus room hangs a framed auto-graphed Michael Jordan jersey – the baby blue one, from when he was in college; very rare, valued at nearly two thousand dollars.

He won't say it. He won't offer it. He's going to make me ask for it. Fair enough.

"The Jordan jersey," I say. "A case of water – that's twelve one-liter bottles – for the Jordan jersey."

"I can't! My father'll kill me!"

"That's the offer," I tell him with a shrug.

He grits his teeth and squints like he's taking a painful crap, then says, "Two cases," and I know that I've won.

I stand up, feigning ending the negotiation. "If you're not serious about this, I'm gonna have to ask you to leave."

"A case and a half?" he says.

I sigh. "Fine," I say. "But only because we go way back." I would have actually made the deal for two cases, but like I said, I don't like Spencer.

I reach under the couch and pull out a bottle of water that I typically have reserved for samples. There's only a third left, so I toss it to him. "First drink's free," I tell him. "Consider it a bonus."

And he's instantly guzzling.

"ÁguaViva is pumped from an artesian aquifer in Portugal, nearly a mile beneath the Earth's surface," I inform him as he drinks. "It's then ionized, for perfect pH balance to increase oxygen in your blood and maintain energy throughout your day. And just before bottling, it's infused with antioxidant-rich goji berries that not only detoxify your liver, but improve immune function."

Spencer finishes the bottle and looks at me like he's in love. Maybe he is. I've heard that about him, but right now I think it's the kind of *agape* you feel for your personal savior.

"Tell you what," I say. "I'll give you a case and a half for the jersey, the ball, *and* the bottle of Scotch."

He nods, caving like a sinkhole. "Yeah. Yeah okay. Thanks, Henry!"

I smile cordially. "You're welcome, Spencer." And I mean it. If you ask me, there's nothing better than a win–win.

19) Alyssa

Just outside the Dove Canyon gate is a fountain. When the drought was just a normal drought, before the intense water restrictions, the fountain attracted mountain lions. They came out of the hills like house cats to a water bowl. That really should have been a red flag to anyone who was paying attention.

Then people began abandoning farming communities in California's Central Valley, when it became the Pacific Dust Bowl, overcrowding the already overcrowded cities, like the big cats abandoning the dry hills. As much of a warning as that was, it still didn't sink in as deeply as it should have – because the official responses were, well, literally, a drop in the bucket. Fines for people who watered their lawns. The Frivolous Use Initiative. Public service announcements reminding people to conserve water. None of that mattered. The water still ran out. Now the Dove Canyon fountain was empty. The mountain lions had either died or migrated, and the humans were now facing the same two alternatives.

There's only one way in or out of Dove Canyon: a single gate guarded by rent-a-cops. Some are friendly, others act as if they were members of the Secret Service guarding the White House. Today none of them are there, and the gate itself has been knocked off its hinges.

"Talk about your false sense of security," says Jacqui. "That gate probably got rammed on the first day."

"Alyssa, look," says Garrett, pointing.

There's a bizarre makeshift barricade just beyond the broken gate.

We pull over to the side of the road, leaving the car, and walk through the abandoned entrance, puzzling at the barrier that must have been put in place after the gate came down.

"It looks like it was done in a hurry," Kelton notes.

The barricade is made up of all the junk pulled from every neighborhood garage. Ladders and old furniture, Ikea bookcases that have seen better days. Lawn chairs and rusty bicycles. Basically all the clutter that would have been sold off in garage sales if the homeowners association here actually allowed garage sales.

"Our uncle said that Dove Canyon still had water after the Tap-Out," I tell the others.

"Yeah," says Garrett. "The people here probably had to repel invaders."

The thought of the soccer moms and country clubbers of

Dove Canyon repelling invaders almost makes me laugh … until I remember how our own neighbors attacked the Mc-Cracken house.

Since the barricade was designed to stop vehicles, not pedestrians, we're able to walk around it. And all this time, we haven't seen another soul. It's unnerving.

"You would think," says Jacqui, "if they built a barricade, they'd at least have someone manning it."

"You'd think," echoes Kelton. Neither of them wants to follow the thought to a logical conclusion.

Suddenly my brother begins to freak. "Alyssa, I don't like this. Let's just go."

"We can't," I remind him. "We need Uncle Basil's truck.

"No we don't!" insists Garrett. "We passed plenty of four-wheel-drive trucks on the way here. We can hotwire one of those. I'll bet Jacqui knows how to do that, right?"

Jacqui glares at him. "I'm insulted that you assume I know how to do criminal things."

"Do you?" I ask.

"Yes," she responds, "but I'm still insulted."

I look ahead at the tree-lined street. The grass on the community greenbelts is still mostly green. Uncle Basil told us that the canyon used its own recycled water to irrigate. Like the McCrackens' house that glowed bright when everyone else's electricity was off, the greenbelts of Dove Canyon made the place a target.

"Our uncle's place isn't far from the gate," I tell the others. "Just a right at the first stop sign, and maybe a quarter mile from there." Then I add, "Hotwiring a car will be plan B."

Jacqui lifts the edge of her blouse to show she still has Kelton's pistol concealed there. "In case we run into trouble," she says.

It just ticks me off. "If we run into trouble, we'll behave like civilized people."

"She doesn't mean she'll use it," says Kelton. "Just showing it will get most people to back off."

I take a deep breath and decide not to argue. I'm surprised to hear him not take my side – especially against Jacqui, and especially on the subject of violence. But then again, he's the one who brought a gun into our equation in the first place. Maybe it's less surprise than it is *concern*. After seeing that look in his eye when he picked up the shotgun, I don't know who's the looser cannon now, him or Jacqui.

Daphne – our uncle's sometime girlfriend – has a big house here that was left to her by her mother. Before coming down here, she was a realtor up in Modesto, the same town where Uncle Basil had his almond farm. But almond trees use more water than almost everything – and with rationing set so low, the almond farms failed first. He declared bankruptcy, let the bank take the farm, and moved in with Daphne – who for a whole five minutes thought she was on top of the world, because she had a ridiculous amount of real estate listings. But since no one in their right mind was buying homes there anymore, she couldn't make a single sale. Property values plunged. Then they started calling the Central Valley the Pacific Dust Bowl, and that put the last nail in the region's coffin. I imagine Modesto is mostly a ghost town now, along with Bakersfield, Fresno, and Merced. Anyway, they had the sense to leave before the Big Bail, and beat the rush. They packed up their belongings in a U-Haul and moved in with Daphne's mother, who was conveniently dying and left Daphne the house in Dove Canyon.

Then she kicked Uncle Basil out, and he moved in with us. Twice.

I get it, though. I mean, I don't blame her, that is. See, it wasn't just that Uncle Basil couldn't find work – it's that he really wasn't looking. I think he was kind of broken from losing the farm. She cared about him enough to give him a second chance, but I guess it was just more of the same, because he was back in our house again – and the second time, we were pretty sure it was for good.

"Until I get on my feet," he always told us. But how can you get back on your feet when your life's been cut off at the knees?

We get to Daphne's street. All the while we haven't seen a single person.

Although the community greenbelts are still alive, people's lawns look like the lawns in our neighborhood. Some are just plain dead. Brown grass and leafless trees. Others have been replaced by desertscape – cactus, succulents, and river stones. About a third of the homes have ridiculously green artificial turf. A suburban pretense that nothing is wrong. Daphne's house is the latter kind. It's easy to spot because it also has a fake ficus tree, taking the fiction a step beyond absurd. It's the only green leafy thing on the street, which makes it kind of embarrassing.

Uncle Basil's truck is not in the driveway. I figure it must be in the garage.

"What if they're gone?" says Garrett. "What if they bailed, like they bailed from his farm up north?"

It's something I should have considered but hadn't. I don't answer him. Instead I go up to the front door, ring the doorbell, which of course, doesn't ring. Duh. Then I knock. Loudly.

Nothing for a few moments. I begin to wonder if maybe Garrett was right, but then the door creaks open, and there's Uncle Basil.

"Alyssa? Garrett?" He's both surprised and pleased to see us, but his response is muted. "What are you doing here? Where are your mom and dad?"

It's a question I don't want to think about. I've compartmentalized it in a corner of my mind to keep me functional. I can't even say *we don't know* out loud without my eyes clouding with tears, so I don't answer him.

"Can we come in?"

"Yes, yes of course." He steps aside and we file in. The house is hot. Uncomfortably so. Daphne's house has a southern exposure with lots of windows, and not enough blinds to cover them. Sheets have been tacked up to keep out the light and the heat, but they're not doing a very good job. And there's a smell about the place. Musty and gamey, like a sick room that hasn't been aired out. That should be my first hint that something is wrong – but it's just one more thing in a long list of not-my-reality that has become too numerous to count, much less process.

Our uncle looks dehydrated. Worse than dehydrated. He's pallid, and his face seems to sag, like his skin has grown tired of clinging to the bone. His eyes are dark and a little sunken.

He looks like a drug addict, but I know that's not it. Aside from the occasional weed, Uncle Basil's not that way. No, this is something else.

"You want water?" he asks us. "I've got plenty."

"You do?" says Garrett, just as surprised to hear that as I am.

"Hell, yeah, I'll have some," says Jacqui, with no hesitation.

He leads us to the kitchen, where there's a box of bottled water. Six bottles are left. He gets some plastic cups and pours us all a small drink. But after he pours, he hesitates, gripping the counter and closing his eyes, wincing a bit. He seems weak on his feet.

"Uncle Herb?" I say, using his real name instead of our nickname for him. "Are you okay?"

"I'll be fine," he says. Which means that at this moment, he's not okay.

"You don't look fine," says Jacqui, annoyingly blunt. "You look like crap."

"It's nothing," he insists. "I've just got the runs, is all."

The runs. Maybe he ate something from the fridge that had spoiled once the power went out. Our uncle was always scavenging our refrigerator for leftovers that my mom would toss if she got to it first.

"Where's Daphne?" I ask.

"Resting," he tells me. "She's not feeling well either."

Kelton gives me a worried look. I'm not sure what it's about, but as I lift the water to my mouth, he stops me. Then he checks his own cup, sniffing it, then taking a sip.

"It's good," he says.

"Why wouldn't it be?" I look at the bottle our uncle poured from. It's ÁguaViva, which, as I recall, is ridiculously expensive. You can buy wine for less.

"You hungry?" our uncle asks. "Still got some canned stuff. Not much variety, but what are you gonna do?"

I take a look in the pantry just to see how well stocked they are. It's mostly condiment bottles – like a dozen different kinds of salsas. There are Sara Lee cake mixes, and the types of canned goods that sit for years until you need them. Things like pineapple chunks and sliced olives. Plenty of them, but no one's choice for a meal.

"No thanks," I tell him. "We're good."

And upon seeing what's there, no one disagrees. We're all hungry, but had eaten well at Kelton's house the day before. And if this is all they have for themselves, I don't want to take it.

Then Kelton does something weird. He goes to the faucet and turns it on. Of course nothing comes out, but then he sniffs the spout. He turns to our uncle. "So I hear there was water here after the Tap-Out."

"Yeah, for a while," Uncle Basil tells him. "They hooked up the old water tank. Kept the water flowing a couple of days. Just dribbling really. Not enough to bathe with, but enough to drink."

Kelton nods, then turns to me again. "Alyssa, could I talk to you for a minute?"

Then he takes my arm and leads me into the dining room.

I shake his hand off once we get there. I don't like being pulled places. "What's so important that we couldn't talk in there?"

"Alyssa, we have to get out of here," he says in an intense whisper.

"I'm working on it," I tell him. "I can't just show up, take his truck, and leave."

"You don't get it!" he says, in that same whisper that's almost maniacal. "Don't you think it's strange how quiet the streets are?"

And come to think of it, I did find it strange. Everywhere else we've been, however quiet, it still pointed toward life, but this place doesn't even show the slightest trace of it.

He gets closer to me. Not as loud, but still just as intense. "I'm pretty sure that the tap water was bad. Worse than bad. I think your uncle has dysentery. Maybe all of Dove Canyon has."

I don't know much about dysentery, other than that it's seriously bad diarrhea that people in third world countries get.

"So ... what do we do?"

Kelton shakes his head. "There's nothing we *can* do. Not without a whole lot of medicines we don't have." He takes a moment to gauge me, making sure he has gotten through. He has, but it doesn't mean I have to like the message.

"We shouldn't touch anything," he says. "And definitely shouldn't eat anything."

"It's all in cans!" I argue, even though I have no intention of eating it.

"Yes, but anything he touches could be contaminated!"

I can't argue with it. As paranoid as it sounds, it's probably true.

And when we go back into the kitchen, Uncle Basil is

serving Garrett a bowl of pineapple chunks.

"It wasn't me!" Garrett says. "Uncle Basil insisted."

Our uncle puts a spoon in front of him. "You need your energy. I know it isn't much, but I won't let you guys go hungry on my watch!"

Resigned, Garrett reaches for the spoon.

"Don't!" I say sharply. I almost slap the spoon away. I turn to our sick uncle. My action spoke pretty clearly, so I don't hide my reason.

"It's the tap water that made you sick, Uncle Herb," I tell him, to cut through any denial he might be in. "It's dysentery – which could be contagious, so we shouldn't eat anything you've touched. I'm sorry."

He sighs, realizing I'm right, and maybe mad at himself for not considering that already. "Then open a fresh can. I have some hand sanitizer."

But Garrett pushes away from the table, no appetite for anything.

"It's okay, I'm not very hungry anyway."

I'm realizing now that our uncle has no idea how sick he and Daphne might be. And then Jacqui says, "I'll take you up on that hand sanitizer." As I look to her, I can tell she's having a flash of fever again. She points to her wound, which is oozy, and clearly needs redressing. "And gauze too, if you have any."

"Sure," my uncle says. He grabs the hand sanitizer, but first cleans his own hands and the bottle before handing it to her with a pained smile. "Upstairs, second door on the left. Should be a first-aid kit under the sink."

I watch her go upstairs, and then I realize something. Jacqui has antibiotics. I'm not sure where they are now. In her pocket? Still out in the BMW? Or, in the commotion, did she leave them back at Kelton's house? Would I take them from her to give to my uncle? No, I tell myself. I might not like Jacqui all that much, but I won't steal from her. I would never hurt one person's chances to help another – even if that other person was someone I cared about. If I did, I'd be no better than the marauders.

"You should leave," I tell my uncle. "Both you and Daphne. They're setting up shelters. They might not have water yet, but they'll have medicine – I'm sure they will."

But he swats the idea away. "I don't think Daphne is really up to travel. And we've gotten through the worst of it already."

I don't know if he means the worst of his sickness, or the worst of the crisis. Either way, my response is the same.

"I think the worst is still coming…"

Still, nothing I say will persuade him. "We'll be fine."

And more than anything, I want to believe him. But my days of sitting still and hoping for the best are over. Now hope is a thing in constant motion, like a shark.

20) Jacqui

I find the bathroom, shut the door behind me, and reach into my pocket, pulling out one of the two orange containers of antibiotics. I can't remember which one I started with, but why does it matter? I examine the little two-tone green capsules.

Astonishing to think that these tiny pods rolling around in the palm of my hand mean the difference between life and death. I'll bet they're worth their weight in gold a hundred times over right now. Then again, you can never put a price on human life – so it's down the hatch they go.

Next comes the bandage. I find the first-aid kit right where Basil or Herb or Dill, or whatever the hell his actual name is, said it would be. The bandage sticks to my arm as I peel it off, the wound healing into the cloth itself. Well, at least it's healing. I clean it thoroughly, and painfully, with alcohol swabs, careful not to touch anything that might infect me, then redress the wound. Good as new.

I wander a bit upstairs, checking the place out. This is some house. The kind I wouldn't mind squatting in under different circumstances – although the decor is a little too prissy for my tastes. Basil's girlfriend must be the doily and lace type. What was her name again? *Should be Rosemary,* I think, which makes me chuckle.

I make my way back toward the staircase, passing the double doors to the master bedroom, and notice that one is slightly ajar. Through the crack, I can make out the silhouette of a woman lying motionless in an all-white bed. There's an acrid smell wafting from the room. Dark and decrepit. Where anyone else would walk away, I'm pulled closer, drawn to the scene with a gravity I find hard to resist. The Call of the Void. I push the door open wider and take a single step over the threshold. It's like leaning into the wind at the edge of a cliff.

Over the bed flows one of those decorative mosquito nets fit for a queen, but here, it seems to be keeping disease in rather than out. Daphne – that's her name. This ailing empress must be Daphne.

The silence in here is overwhelming. And then I realize why.

The woman isn't breathing.

Now it's more than just the void pulling at me. It's the scene of a car crash. It's the rubble after a tornado. I have to get closer. I won't touch her. I won't cross the barrier of that net, but I have to see. I have to look at her chest to see if it rises and falls. I need to know. And the smell now, it's terrible. Bile and sulfur and all the fetid organic stenches we fight all our lives to keep at bay.

Then, before I'm close enough to get a good look, she moves, shifting slightly beneath the covers. My heart pounds in my chest so loud that I think she hears it, because she slowly lolls her head in my direction, and when she looks at me, her eyes are dark and glassy. She's too weak to speak, or even to wonder what a stranger is doing in her home.

She's not dead, but her body doesn't know it, because I think it's already beginning to decompose – and although she still looks at me, our gazes somehow don't connect. That's when I realize that it's not me she sees at all.

She sees the void.

A few moments later, I'm downstairs again with the others, but I'm quiet. To myself. Because over everything, I see Daphne's image burned across my retina. Alyssa is trying to convince Basil to go with Daphne to an evacuation center, but of course, he refuses. And the more she tries to convince him, the further he's pushed away. I wonder if he realizes how bad off Daphne is. On some level he must. And although he's holding it together for his niece and nephew, I don't think he's all that far from crawling into that bed with her and letting the end come. Then I realize with a shiver that the scene upstairs is likely happening in many of the homes around us. This gated community has become a high-end morgue.

Alyssa hasn't asked for her uncle's keys yet. This polite streak of hers is going to get her killed, and us along with her. Apparently Kelton's patience has also run out, because he's the one who cuts to the chase.

"If you're not leaving, then let us borrow your truck. We need four-wheel drive to get us where we're going."

"I would if I could," he says, embarrassed, some color actually returning to his face. "But I traded it."

"You what?" I blurt out.

"For that ÁguaViva you've all been drinking. I'll get it back as soon as this whole thing blows over," he says, looking down. "I mean, I'm sure a thing like that can't be legally binding."

"Who'd you trade it to?" Alyssa asks.

Again, he looks down, ashamed. "Some kid up the hill."

The house is obnoxiously huge, like the rest of the houses around it, built out to as close to the edge of the property line as allowable by law. It's freshly painted in an off-brown color, like someone tried to give it a Brazilian spray tan. It's what's commonly referred to as a McMansion. An ostentatious home thrown up in an assembly line fashion while you wait.

The garage door is cracked open about three inches

from the ground, and spewing fumes. I can hear a generator inside – which means the house has its own electricity source. Apparently, actually putting the generator outside where it belongs leaves it open to theft. This kid's no idiot. Over the drone of the generator I can hear electronic dance music playing inside the house. Okay, maybe he is.

Alyssa ignores the big brass Oz-like knocker and pounds directly on the door. Nothing – I can tell she's getting pissed, because she starts pounding and doesn't stop until the door finally opens, revealing a good-looking, well-groomed kid in a dark blue letterman jacket from Santa Margarita Catholic High School, and a polo shirt underneath. A letterman jacket in this heat. Yes, the generator is keeping the air-conditioning on, but the jacket still seems off. I tuck it away in my weird-crap-I-don't-care-enough-about-to-question file. Basil told us that the kid's parents were out of town. A silver-spoon preppy type left home alone. God help us all.

He smiles brightly. "How can I help you?" he says, like we were about to order a cheeseburger and fries from his McMansion.

"I'm here for my uncle's truck," Alyssa demands.

He exercises his right to refuse service to anyone. "I'm sorry, I can't help you." Then he quickly tries to shut the door. That's when I jam my foot in. He leans against the door, keeping pressure. "One foot in my home constitutes trespassing!" he belts, trying to sound much more intimidating than he really is. Maybe the Oz knocker is appropriate. "There are severe legal ramifications if you don't get your foot out of my door."

I lean my shoulder into it. "Open the door, asshole."

Alyssa and Garrett join in, applying pressure.

"My father is a lawyer — he'll shove a lawsuit so far up your —"

Before he can even finish his idle threat, Kelton hurls himself against the door as well, and his added force sends the door flying open, knocking the preppy kid down. He scrambles to his feet, treading Persian rug.

Then he suddenly turns, reaches into a foyer credenza drawer, and produces a gun.

Dammit.

No sudden movements, I think, as my hand very slowly creeps toward the gun hidden in my waistband.

"That's right, stay back. Hands where I can see them," he says, quoting something I'm sure he saw on TV.

We all freeze — except for Kelton. Instead Kelton strides toward the kid. *He really has lost it!*

The preppy kid tightens his grip on his gun and shouts, almost maniacally, "I'm fully within my rights to shoot! I swear I'll do it!"

But Kelton is fearless. He suddenly lurches forward, grips the boy's wrist, and all in one motion, twists his arm behind his back.

The kid yelps, but Kelton isn't finished. He pushes the kid's arm up behind his back and twists him around so his own momentum is his enemy. His arm is now bent at an obscene angle, and we all hear a *POP.*

The preppy kid falls to the floor screaming bloody murder, and Kelton holds the gun. For a moment he looks just as surprised as we do. As if he's saying to himself, *Holy crap, it worked.*

While the kid still writhes on the floor, Kelton examines the gun.

"Kelton, are you out of your mind?" Alyssa says. "He could have killed you."

"Nope," Kelton says. "This is a WG Panther. It's an airsoft gun, which means it's nothing but a toy. Look, the orange tip is colored black with a Sharpie."

I'm so infuriated that I was tricked by a freaking airsoft gun, I get the sudden urge to kick this kid in the gut. And then I remember that his arm is totally popped out its socket. Serves him right.

Kelton gets down on one knee to help him, but the preppy kid scrambles back and points with his working arm. "No! Keep that psychopath away from me!" he screams. It's refreshing to hear someone else be called a psychopath for once. Ironically enough, this guy should be thanking Kelton for what he did. Because if he hadn't disarmed him, I would have done it myself. And real guns don't shoot plastic pellets.

"Let him help," Alyssa tells the kid. "He knows what he's doing." And for some reason, he listens. People seem to trust Alyssa, for better or worse. I trust her like I trust kung pao chicken in a frat guy's mini-fridge. Just enough to not vomit.

Kelton has the kid lie on his back, and firmly holds his arm. "Take a deep breath and hold it," Kelton says, gripping tight. "Ready? One … two —" And on three Kelton pops his shoulder back into place. The kid yelps, but a little less loudly than when it was first dislocated.

He then sits up and leans against the wall, sweating. "Ice. Get me ice, will you?" he demands, to anyone.

The words almost don't even register. Ice? This kid has ice? Come to think of it, he has a lot of things that other people don't.

"In the kitchen," he says, mistaking our shock for stupidity.

"Sure thing, Roycroft," I say with a smirk, and nod to Garrett, who goes off to get it.

The kid glares at me, now as confused as he is angry.

"Don't be so surprised," I say. "Your name's on your jacket."

"Oh. Right."

"There, now we're on a last-name basis."

"I still don't know your name."

"No, you don't. Funny how that works."

I look around, trying to calculate our current situation, but the numbers just aren't adding up. It's an embarrassment of riches. A stack of laptops, multiple Xboxes – who has multiple Xboxes? There's a bunch of signed sports memorabilia – and at the far end of a hall is some sort of tank with a giant—

I spin around, barely even able to look at it.

SNAKE!

I center myself – take a deep, calming breath, reminded of the one thing I have in common with Indiana Jones besides proficiency with a whip. But that's another conversation.

I turn to him. He's moved himself to a leather sofa, still holding his shoulder.

"So what's with all this stuff?" I ask.

He somehow manages to flash a cool smile, even in his most emasculated state. "Assets that I've acquired, fair and square."

Alyssa steps forward. "Was it fair when you took my uncle's truck?"

"Of course," he replies, taken aback by the mere suggestion of impropriety. "I have all the paperwork."

"You took advantage of him!"

"The price of water has gone up," he says, getting defensive. "Don't tell me that's my fault."

Alyssa curls a fist, ready to dislocate more of his body parts. Which I'd actually pay to see.

"He came to *me*," the preppy kid says, still offended by the indictment of his character.

Kelton is already growing impatient. "The water here is tainted. What's the point of having all of this junk if you're just going to get sick like the rest of them?"

"I didn't drink it; I have my own means of hydration."

"You haven't left here, have you?" Kelton realizes. "You haven't seen what it's like out there."

And this seems to give him pause for thought. It must be true; this little prince has been living on his own personal planet since the Tap-Out.

"Why are you here alone, anyway?" I ask.

"My parents are on a cruise. They left me to watch the house. I'm sure they'd come home if they weren't in the middle of the Atlantic Ocean."

"Lucky them," I say.

Garrett hands him a skimpy bag of ice, and he holds it to his shoulder.

"Have you been watching the news at all?" Alyssa asks.

He shakes his head. "The TV drains too much power from the generator."

He leads us to a family room that looks more like a home

theater, with a sixty-inch TV which, as he said, eats up so much juice from the generator, the lights dim when he turns it on. Kelton grabs the remote and finds the local news channel – except now the entire channel is just color bars.

Kelton tries the other local channel.

Static.

I want to believe it's a problem with the provider, and not with the stations themselves. Kelton flips to a national broadcast – CNN – and we finally see a report. But I almost wish we hadn't. Although it shows us what we already know, somehow seeing it in huge high-def color makes it worse.

There's a map of southern California, a circle around it, like the highlighted path of a hurricane. *SOUTHERN CALIFORNIA TAP-OUT COVERAGE* is what the chyrons read at the bottom, like this was some kind of event for everyone else's entertainment. I've been on the receiving end of broadcasts like this from other places – but this is the first time in as long as I can remember that I'm standing in the epicenter of the disaster area.

I turn to the others and realize that they're all just as shaken as I am – even the preppy kid.

"It's finally happened," says Alyssa. "The rest of the world finally noticed and is taking the Tap-Out seriously."

"The rest of the world is too late," says Kelton. And he's right. You don't wait nearly a week until mobilizing serious resources for a disaster of this magnitude. The reports flash across the screen and blend together – my brain hardly able to register it all:

A reporter in a chopper flies over downtown Los Angeles,

showing rioting that makes the LA riots of the '90s seem like a tea party. There's a journalist reporting from the fringes of Riverside, at a safe distance, peering inside the fishbowl of chaos – afraid to travel too deep. A group of elementary school kids in Florida hold a bottled water drive – as if any of their water will actually get here in time to make a difference. There's a shot of FEMA officials – actual FEMA, not just their reserve volunteers – handing out water in an evacuation center, but a wider shot reveals more crowds than they can possibly handle. Rock stars plan relief concerts to raise funds. Celebrities promote charities. All the usual self-congratulatory stuff. The only difference is that we're the victims now, rather than the ones sitting comfortably in our homes, sending five bucks on a charity app and patting ourselves on the back because we're so goddamn generous.

"If you're getting this report, and you're in the Southland right now – there is a mandatory evacuation," says Anderson Cooper. His image is accompanied by shots of military personnel helping families evacuate onto massive trucks, handing out water to long lines of people. "Evacuation centers are being set up throughout Southern California in school gymnasiums, churches, and malls – but there seems to be a staggering number of people who are choosing not to cooperate with these government mandates."

"Look on the bright side," I say. "At least malls have a purpose again."

The next shot shows mobs of people flowing like a human river down a winding mountain road, and disappearing beneath a forest canopy. "These families are making their own way toward Lake Arrowhead and the Big Bear Lake area, but reports on the ground tell us that people who have been entering many of these woodsy areas aren't coming out on the other side..."

Everyone watches silently, and then I turn to Kelton. "Hey, bug-out boy – if they're not making it through the forest, what makes you think we will?"

"I told you, we're not going where they're going."

And that's good – because if all those people aren't getting to the high lakes, there's only one of two places they're going. And neither of them are places you come back from.

21) Henry

Dealing with irrational people takes focus, intelligence, and extreme discipline – you have to maintain a sense of true emotional stasis – as outlined in one of my favorite books, *Transformative Power*, by Pearce Tidwell. One must learn to manage one's emotional state in order to consistently operate from a place of resourcefulness, thus producing desirable outcomes. You have to be *actionary*, rather than *reactionary*.

Which is why, instead of giving into the god-awful throbbing pain in my right shoulder, I channel it – using the pain as a tool to sharpen my focus. *(It really hurts though, sweet Jesus how it hurts.)* I won't allow it to control me. My current agony will not define me. Instead, my profound discomfort will be a springboard that will propel me toward a better reality.

Until now, I have mostly avoided watching the news; it's

always so manipulative. But now I can't help but acknowledge that the Tap-Out is a tragedy, and the relief effort a travesty. The cities are clearly hit hardest – the crumbling impoverished areas packed with marginalized people unequipped for societal disaster.

But there is always opportunity in misfortune. So the question is: How do I turn this to my advantage? Because, after all, you can't work for the greater good unless you have all of your own ducks in a row first.

All considered, it may be in my best interest to fly the coop rather than sit on my current nest egg. Then again, if the state of things has really devolved to such a degree, my water must be worth more than ever. Everything that I've traded for thus far will be peanuts compared to what my next transactions will bring. I'm busting inside! But I keep my cool... One must never overreact to the spoils of one's windfall. I decide it's best to take an inventory of my current "liquid assets," so I get up and head to my dad's home office, where the rest of my ÁguaViva is.

"Where're you going, Roycroft?" the toughish girl with the perpetual smirk says. I say toughish, because I doubt she's as tough as she wants everyone to think. But I won't deny that there may be a screw or two loose.

"To get more ice," I reply.

Which they all buy, because they don't follow me. They're still glued to the television screen. I guess with my arm like this, they don't see me as much of a threat. Which is a big mistake. As long as they underestimate me, I have an advantage.

I close the door to the office, ensuring my privacy, and pull out the last box of ÁguaViva. It's a fairly large box, containing two cases. I pry the box open to reveal a new and unexpected wrinkle to my current situation.

Life is rife with many moments of misfortune, which we must learn to see as opportunities. Misfortune, oh, say, like opening up a box that you think contains forty-eight water bottles, only to find that it's full of ÁguaViva independent multitiered distributor brochures instead.

In these situations, one must keep a level head.

A very. Level. Head.

I hold on to the one positive in this personal debacle: At least now I won't have to struggle to make a decision as to whether to stay or go. I don't have much of a choice now; I'm going to have to leave here. My generator will soon be out of gas anyway – and I can hide my acquired assets in the attic behind the boxes of Christmas ornaments. Except, of course, for the python – but that thing can go for weeks without food, plus I assume it's well-acclimated to hot climates. Ultimately, a place of greater safety might not be a bad idea – and if Dove Canyon really is the bacterial petri dish my uninvited guests are making it out to be, I'd imagine any place will be better than this.

In which case, their arrival is a lucky thing indeed.

But I could have done without the dislocated shoulder.

I seal up the huge cardboard box as securely as I can with strapping tape. And then I tape it again and again, so it'll be virtually impossible to open. That's when one of them comes in. It's the more reasonable, less snarky of the two girls. The one who's laying claim to her uncle's former truck.

"I thought you were getting ice."

"All out," I say convincingly. "Which reminded me to check my water supply." I rap on the box and point to the giant ÁguaViva logo on the side.

There's a brief lull in the conversation. And I know exactly where this is going. It can only go one way. The truck. They're not going to leave until they get what they want. There's four of them and one of me. Clearly I'm not going to be able to overpower them – especially with their psychotic red-haired pit bull around. I just have to write the truck off as a short-term loss leader, because when it comes down to it, I'm no longer in a position to negotiate. But she hasn't realized that yet, and right now it's just the two of us. So I beat her to the punch.

"We never officially met," I say, turning on the charm. "I'm Henry." I extend my left arm to shake, since I can still barely move my right.

She hesitates, a little skeptical. Understandable. "My name's Alyssa."

"Pleasure to meet you, Alyssa." I smile and clear my throat. "I'll tell you what. I appreciate the passion that you have for your friends' and family's well-being, and can see why you might feel entitled to that truck."

She crosses her arms, but she's still listening.

"So I'm prepared to give it to you." I pause for effect. "But only under one condition."

She lifts an eyebrow.

"You take me with you."

She thinks it over, but I can already feel things tipping in my favor. I once read in *The Thriving Executive* by R. J. Sherman that the number one way to sustain a job in this day and age is to make yourself indispensable. Or at least make people *think* you're indispensable. She deliberates − and just when I sense that I've reached that tipping point where her emotions and better judgment teeter ever so precariously, I give her the gentle tap that ensures which way she'll fall.

"I'll bring this ÁguaViva box," I say, with an ingratiating smile.

"We could just take your ÁguaViva," she points out.

"True … but you're not that kind of person. The others might be, but you're not."

And I can see by the look in her eye that she's freefalling toward a unilateral decision. If they take me, they get what they want and I get to ensure my own survival. Another win-win.

The toughish girl, whose name I find out is Jacqui, insists on driving. Fair enough. For now. As we drive down my street, I begin to think I may have totally underestimated the effect of the water shortage on this community.

It's one thing to see rioting on TV in dense urban areas that are more prone to social conflagration, but quite a different thing to see homes with broken windows in an upscale community like Dove Canyon. Not that the affluent are any better − I mean, human nature is human nature. However, where personal space is at a premium, tensions are apt to spike much more quickly than in a place where one's battle cry reaches maybe ten neighbors instead of a hundred. Which means that in the suburbs and exburbs it's hard to generate the critical mass needed to ignite truly bad behavior.

Or maybe not.

Because as we drive off, there's more evidence of bad behavior than just broken windows. There are shattered mailboxes, cars that have jumped curbs into hedges, and the kind of random debris that one generally doesn't find in a turnkey community like this one. Not because people here aren't slobs – I'm sure a lot of them are – but they're so obsessively worried about their property values that they'd rather die than allow the detritus of civilization to sully their curb appeal.

"I'm worried about leaving my uncle," says Alyssa, who sits beside me in the back seat. She's a buffer between me and the psychotic redheaded kid on her other side. I would have preferred to sit in the front seat, but Alyssa's brother called it, and if we don't adhere to the convention of calling shotgun, what rule of law is left to us?

"Uncle Parsley will be fine," says Jacqui. "And even if he's not, there's nothing you can do about it. You asked him to come and he wouldn't. End of story."

Alyssa accepts the wisdom, but doesn't seem comforted.

"Well, he's got plenty of ÁguaViva," I point out. "Even if it's going right through him, he'll still get the benefits of the electrolytes. In fact, its proprietary formula is proven to improve quality of life."

"Great, just what we need," says Jacqui. "An infomercial with good hair."

This is what one calls a backhanded compliment. I choose to see the positive, because that's how I roll. "That information could save lives," I tell her. "And so can good hair in the right situation."

The truck is still hot. The air-conditioner has been blowing since we got in, but it's no cooler. Jacqui notices that too, because she starts checking the controls.

"What's wrong with this thing?" she asks.

"That's right, I forgot – the air-conditioner doesn't work," Alyssa informs us. "Our uncle kept saying he was going to get it fixed, but never got around to it."

Jacqui glares at her. "You could have told us that before."

We all crank down the windows, but it's just as hot outside as it is in the car. The digital thermometer on the dashboard reads ninety-eight degrees. Body temperature feels so much hotter when it's outside of your body. Her uncle should have disclosed that the air-conditioner didn't work when he made the deal with me. Legally you have to disclose things like that.

Then Alyssa's brother turns around and asks me, "What sport did you letter in?"

I point to the patches on my jacket, which is increasingly wrong for the weather, but I refuse to shed it. "This one's soccer," I say – which seems to grab Alyssa's attention, although I can tell she's trying not to show it. "And this one's lacrosse."

"Lacrosse," says Jacqui. "I'm not surprised you're good with a stick."

I choose not to comment.

Alyssa looks at another patch. "Captain of the debate team?"

I shrug like it's nothing. "I make a good argument."

"How about the tattoos on your wrist?" asks Alyssa's brother, pointing to the words peeking out from beneath my sleeve. "What are they?"

"They're not tattoos," I tell him. "It's just standard ink."

"So what do they say?"

I pull up the sleeves of my letterman's jacket a bit, and try to lift my arm to show him, but my shoulder throbs. My dislocation is a gift that keeps on giving. I'm able to get it high enough for him to see the words, though. He reads them haltingly.

"Con-fla-gration. De-tri-tus."

"My words of the day."

Alyssa looks at me, a bit amused. "You write vocabulary words on your arm?"

"'One's vocabulary needs constant fertilizing or it will die,'" I say, quoting Evelyn Waugh. Not that I know who Evelyn Waugh is, but knowing the source of a quote is what counts. "By the time it fades, the word is permanently committed to memory."

"*I* got a few words I'd like to write on your arm," says Jacqui.

As we come to the gate of my community, I can see that it's blocked by a barricade of sorts; another sign of how deep the crisis has cut. It must have been designed by a committee because it's a fairly pathetic barrier. Like something beavers might have erected if they had opposable thumbs and lots of upper body strength.

"I forgot about that," says Jacqui.

"Maybe we can just roll over it," suggests psycho-ginger. "This truck has a pretty high chassis."

"Why risk damaging her uncle's truck?" I say. "We'll get out and dismantle it."

It's really the only reasonable course of action, but by saying it first, it helps to move me a few inches closer to a position of leadership.

We all get out to clear a path to the gate. I'm not as effective as I'd like to be, however, and Jacqui notices.

"What's the matter, Roycroft? Is heavy lifting beneath your pay grade?"

"Leave him alone," says Garrett. "His shoulder's messed up."

I grin and give her a one-shouldered shrug.

With enough of a path cleared, we get back into the truck. I get back in next to Alyssa. It's a bit cramped in the back, but to be honest, I don't mind.

"Look at that," I say as we drive out of the gate. "Someone actually abandoned a BMW by the side of the road."

"Yeah," says Jacqui. "What idiots."

As we pull away from Dove Canyon, I take a moment to do a more in-depth assessment of my travel companions.

Alyssa seems to be the one calling the shots, although Jacqui wants to be. Then there's Alyssa's little brother, who stood up for me back at the gate, so I think I've already won him over. And then there's the crazy kid. He's the part of this equation I wish would just cancel out. I know the type. Angry. Sadistic. Sociopathic. He's probably a drop-out, on the way to being a career criminal. Drug dealer type. Yeah. The kind of guy who beats up Eagle Scouts for fun.

I won't even try to gain his confidence. For now I focus on Jacqui. I try to decipher her. A lot of people probably think she's Latina because of her complexion, but she's not. Her intonations and body language point elsewhere. Her eyes and the cast of her brow feel more European.

She catches me in the rearview mirror watching her, so I don't shy away from it.

"Italian?" I ask, taking a wild guess.

"Greek," she answers. "But I can't see how that's any of your business."

"Greco-Roman, then," I say. "I wasn't entirely wrong." Then I add, "You have a classic look. If Venus de Milo had arms, she'd look like you."

"If Venus de Milo had arms, she'd slap you around," she responds.

"How about us?" asks Alyssa's brother.

"Garrett, don't even bother," Alyssa says. "Nobody gets it right."

But still Garrett waits for me to try. I'm on shaky ground here, because, considering the volatile nature of our society, if I get it wrong, I'm likely to offend.

"I would say your family hails from multiple continents."

Alyssa is impressed. "That's ... sort of right."

Then Garrett chimes in with: "We're a quarter Dutch, a quarter French-Canadian, a quarter Jamaican, and a quarter Ukrainian!"

"A fine melting pot!" I say. "What my father would call 'a full-flavored stew.'" Actually, my father would call them "mutts" but my father can be an asshole. His is a tree I strive to fall increasingly farther from. "Anyway," I say, "it's a much broader genealogy than your Viking friend here."

"We're not Scandinavian!" snaps Kelton. "We're Scottish and English. I have an ancestor who came over on the Mayflower."

"Really?" I ask. "A rat or a roach?"

Which I feel safe saying because Alyssa's between us – although he might make me pay for it later when no one else is looking. But it makes Garrett laugh, and Garrett's laughter makes Alyssa smile, so it's worth the risk. With the exception of Mr. Mayflower, I'm beginning to feel at home with this little group. They say that intense communal experiences can create lasting friendships. I think there's real opportunity here.

"What about you?" Alyssa asks.

"I have no idea," I tell her. "I'm adopted."

As we drive, the desolation around us makes it hard to keep spirits up. Everywhere things seem as hopeless as my neighborhood. *At least the people out here don't have dysentery*, I think – but if "not having dysentery" is where the bar is set, that's pretty low.

Morale is everything in difficult times – it's the only thing that can keep stress from becoming toxic – but morale doesn't just happen. It starts with management and trickles all the way down. I see it as my responsibility to ignore the emptiness of the streets, the nonfunctional stoplights, and the occasional clusters of walking dead. You can't get caught up in that kind of stuff. If my decisions reflected this abysmal reality, how could things ever get better? I realize that this group needs more than just a competent leader. They need a hero. I resolve to do my best to rise to the occasion.

Alyce Marasco isn't new to the skies, but has never before flown her chopper as a first responder. However, now that martial law has been declared and the national guard has been activated, Alyce has been called on to airlift drinking water to evacuation centers.

Like everyone else, she has come late to the realization that this crisis, from a human standpoint, is just as severe as any natural disaster, because of the sheer number of people affected and the desperate position every single one of them is in. Yes, there was warning – years of it, in fact – but public service announcements about conservation are a whole lot different from a total stoppage. There was no warning at all that the water would simply. Turn. Off.

Alyce often visits an uncle with dementia who lives in a nursing home in Tustin – a community right in the heart of the affected area. And because Alyce hasn't been able to confirm that he's been safely evacuated, she finds herself pulled slightly off-route and flying in the direction of his nursing home. Even though she wouldn't be able to make out much from this altitude, she needs to get a sense of things; an overview that can at least give her a little bit of comfort. She scans the streets below, not even sure what she's looking for. She remembers reports of how, during disasters, nursing homes are among the hardest hit. They don't command the resources or attention that hospitals do, and often they're severely understaffed, leaving such places barely equipped to deal with a normal day, much less a crisis.

There are Facebook pages for dozens of neighborhoods where people have started checking themselves in as safely evacuated and with access to water – because those two things don't nec-essarily go together. Those pages have actually become the most accurate registry of evacuees. She's been checking it for people she knows, but hasn't come across any – least of all her uncle, to whom social media means sitting in a crowded room reading a newspaper.

Her uncle's neighborhood looks just like most others. Lifeless except for overcrowded, overflowing evacuation centers, looking like anthills spaced out at five-mile intervals. The lifeless places look fake from an aerial view, like a miniature with plastic trees or a felted architectural model. She can't take the time to find the specific building, but even if she did, what could she do? When her copilot points out that they're slightly off course, she adjusts their direction and lets it go.

Up ahead is one of those swarming pockets of life. Thousands of people all congregating in a shopping center parking lot. From this altitude it appears the way Coachella or any major festival would look – which is disturbing to her, because entertainment is the last thing these people want right now.

They've cleared a huge circle in the lot. Crowds have pushed themselves back to create a landing pad. A makeshift heliport for her supply of life-giving water.

But there's nothing Alyce can do for these people.

This isn't her destination.

This isn't even an official evacuation center.

And then she's hit with a gust of emotion, an inner turbulence that shakes her to her core. She starts doing the math: At this point, there are about two hundred evacuation shelters. Even if only half the population went to a shelter, that means that nearly

12 million people would be there, waiting for water. That's sixty thousand people for each shelter. And yet the choppers in service can only provide enough water for about six thousand people per shelter per day.

Which means that nine in ten people won't get water today.

And that's just in the *official* centers.

Tears begin to cloud her vision, but she wipes them away. Maybe the water in her chopper is just a drop in the bucket, but it's going to help someone somewhere. And for the others, there's nothing she can do.

And so she passes over the crowded parking lot, but not before saying a silent prayer for the souls below.

SNAPSHOT 2 OF 2: TARGET

Six.

That's how many helicopters have soared right over Hali's head since she got to the Target parking lot yesterday. Everyone says that the military helicopters are transporting water. That they're going to land here and save everyone. That's why the people "in charge" keep clearing places for the choppers to land. That's why every family has someone waiting in a long, winding line – just in case there's something to line up for.

The sound of another chopper rises in the north. Everyone looks up in anticipation. The sound peaks. Its shadow crosses the lot. That's the closest it comes. The sound of its engine fades as it disappears to the south. That makes seven.

"We won't get the military deliveries," a woman beside her

says to anyone who'll listen, or maybe just to herself. "But the *other* helicopters – they're coming to unofficial drop points." She lights a cigarette to console herself. "There's more nonmilitary choppers out there, anyway."

Where? Hali wants to ask her. *What helicopters are you talking about?* Certainly none that are big enough to ship water. Most small choppers can barely hold a handful of passengers, and water is heavy. Does this woman really think some sightseeing company is sending them water?

She returns to her mother, who has staked out a position in line, only about thirty from the front – folding chair and all. She doesn't have the spot because they got there early, but because she saw a friend in line when they arrived, and offered to hold her place when she went to the bathroom. The friend had since abandoned the parking lot for the hope of greener pastures, leaving Hali's mom to inherit the spot. That's the way her mom has always been. She finds ways to get what she wants.

"Bastards," Hali's mom mutters under her breath, as Hali sits on the ground next to her. No explanation of which bastards she's referring to. It's obvious. The bastards in the helicopters that fly by, and everyone else ignoring this lot; the water gods rolling dice to decide which way that water will go.

"Next one will be for us," Hali tells her.

She offers Hali a slim smile. They both know it's wishful thinking that borders on delusion, but right now it's all they have. They have no choice in the matter. Water MUST come to them, because they're not going anywhere. Her mom is NOT abandoning her place in line.

They had water on the first couple of days of the Tap-Out.

Her mom had ripped a case out of the hands of one of Hali's soccer teammates back at Costco. "Ya snooze, ya lose," her mom said, once they got to the checkout line. "Let that be a life lesson."

But there were clearly life lessons that her mom had missed. Like, "Don't wash your hair when all you have is bottled water." And, "Skip your morning jog when sweat is the enemy." And maybe the most obvious one of all, "Let the houseplants die."

That case of water lasted only two days.

Out on the street, just beyond the parking lot, a little red Volkswagen bus pulls up. The kind of thing you might have seen at Woodstock. A minivan, built before there was such a thing as a minivan. It was here yesterday, too. Twice. Today three girls around her age, maybe a little bit older, get out. She can't see the driver, but she knows it's a man. She knows this instinctively.

"Hali, honey," her mother says, trying to shield her eyes from the sun, "why don't you go into the shade where it's cooler, against the side of the building. Maybe listen to what people are saying, maybe get some information."

"What people say is useless," Hali points out.

"Mostly, yes, but every once in a while there might be something worth listening to."

She hates leaving her mother sweltering here, but she's been given a mission, and so she goes, all the while thinking of the things the two of them have had to do over the last couple of days to get this far.

When they were still at home, Hali's mom flirted with Mr. Weidner – a neighbor who had gotten divorced last year. Truth was, Hali's mom always flirted with him – but when she realized he had water, she flirted with him just a little bit more. He was polite about it, and although he didn't really flirt back, he did offer them a bottle of water.

"Mission accomplished," her mother had said when they got home, although she had trouble looking Hali in the eye when she said it.

The next morning, Hali took a page from her mom's survival book, and taught some soccer moves to the obnoxious little kid across the street who she couldn't stand, but whose family was rumored to have some water. In the end, the kid's mother gave Hali a Dixie cup of water. Hali sweat more out playing with the little brat, but it was better than nothing. She brought half of the cup to her mom, who refused it and insisted that Hali drink it all.

Now, as they wait helplessly for relief, a lame inspirational quote keeps looping in her mind:

You've got to do something you've never done, to have something you've never had.

It was something that a soccer coach told her at some point in her life. However cheesy, it stuck. She assumes it applies not just to things you've never had, but things you've had and lost. Things you still desperately need.

On the shady side of the Target, Hali runs into her friend, Sydney, who is famous for talking an awful lot but saying absolutely nothing.

"Is this crazy or what?" Sydney says. "It's, like, what the hell, right? Give me a break or something! But it is what it is, I guess."

"I hear you," which is generally the best way to respond to her.

Then Sydney leans close, and says, "You wanna see something?"

She surreptitiously opens a pouch in her backpack to reveal a small water bottle. The sight of it takes Hali's breath away. Suddenly Sydney is her BFF.

"C'mon, I'll give you a sip," she whispers.

They go off toward some bushes, and Sydney pulls out the bottle, shielding it from anyone who might see, like it's something illegal, and lets Hali take a sip. The sip turns into a gulp before Sydney pulls the bottle away. She's not mad or anything. She must know how hard it is to stop drinking once you've started.

"Where did you get it?" Hali asks. "You didn't have any when I saw you yesterday."

Sydney nods off to the side, and Hali turns to see that she's indicating the red Volkswagen bus. The driver is leaning up against it now, having a smoke. Late twenties or early thirties. Ponytail. Bushy sideburns. Torn jeans that don't read as a fashion statement.

"He's giving out free water," Sydney says. "But he's kind of picky about who he gives it to. I mean, he can't give it to everyone, you know?" Then Sydney lets off a nervous little chuckle that gives away the cold, hard reality that there's no such thing as free water – and Hali realizes why she hasn't seen Sydney until now. She was one of the three girls who just got out of the little red bus.

"He's not mean or anything," Sydney says. "He even gave me a bottle to take to my family..."

Hali watches as a pretty girl she doesn't know gets into the van. The ponytail guy holds the door open for her, pretending to be a gentleman instead of slime.

Hali turns to Sydney. "Thanks, but no thanks," she says, and tries to stride away with sufficient indignation – but Sydney grabs her arm.

"Don't be stupid, Hali. Haven't you figured it out yet? No one's coming to help the people here! They're probably all going to die of thirst. You don't want to be one of them!"

But Hali still can't let herself believe that. These things just don't happen here. But Sydney still won't let her go. She looks desperate now.

"Why do you even care what I do?" Hali blurts out. "You got your water, why don't you just leave me alone?"

And Sydney finally spills her true motive. "He said he'll give me another bottle if I bring him someone. Someone like you..."

Hali wrenches her arm away and runs, not looking back.

But before she gets to her mother, there's a sound up above. A chopper! And this one is louder – closer than any of the others! Everyone stands up, looking to the sky like a starry-eyed mob waiting for the rapture.

The helicopter appears over the treetops. It isn't big. It's one of the nonmilitary ones that the woman was speaking of. It circles above the mob. It circles again. It circles a third time, and by the third time, Hali realizes that it's just a news helicopter. It's come to show the world the drama of crisis and the true meaning of desperation. She wonders if the news crew up above even realizes the hope they're shattering by their mere presence here.

Once more around, and the chopper leaves. People keep on standing, refusing to believe it's gone. As long as they stay standing, it might come back. It might. It might.

"Bastards!" says her mother.

Hali looks at her. She looks to the curb. She looks at her mother again.

You've got to do something you've never done, to have something you've never had, Hali thinks. Or something you may never have again.

"I'll be back," she tells her mother. "I promise."

Then she heads toward the little red Volkswagen bus, where the man with the ponytail opens the door for her. Like a gentleman.

---

22) Henry

The secret to a successful group collaboration is a dynamic, responsive leader, and the key to being a good leader is acute observation and subtle manipulation – so subtle that no one knows they're being manipulated. Come to think of it, that's also the key to a successful government.

As we drive, I stay quiet, which is against my nature but necessary at the moment. I watch. I listen. I take mental notes.

"So we have our four-by-four," Jacqui says, and turns to Psycho Ginger beside her. Where do you want me to drive it?"

"I told you," Kelton says, "Angeles National Forest."

"So, how. Do. We. Get. There?" Jacqui asks with a vague but persistent threat in her condescension.

"I'm not sure – I've only been to the bug-out twice – but I know exactly where it is on a map."

Alyssa instinctively takes out her phone, but gets an error message as she tries to open the app.

"Damn," she says. "Maps isn't working."

"So use Waze," suggests Garrett.

Although I want to laugh at that, the way Jacqui does, I say very graciously, "I think what your sister means is that there's no service. But maybe there's an actual map in here. Some people still use those, believe it or not."

"Right," says Alyssa, "and our uncle might be one of those people."

I smile. Point for me.

There's nothing in the glove compartment but the registration, gum wrappers, and a lint roller. The door pockets yield only an empty can of Red Bull, a leaky pen, and more gum wrappers. And then Kelton checks in the center compartment between the front seats. There's no map, but he does pull out a questionable sandwich-size Ziploc bag.

"What the…?" He tosses it to Alyssa like it's a hot potato.

Alyssa examines it. No question: It's a bag of weed. She turns to her brother and they say, simultaneously:

"Uncle Cannabis."

"Well," says Jacqui, "we might be dying of thirst, but now we won't even care."

The mention of thirst makes Garrett open his canteen, only to find it's dry as a bone.

"The forest is north of Pasadena, right?" I say. "We can take the 241 to the 91 to the 57 to the 210. That will get us close."

"Not gonna happen," says Jacqui. "The freeways are dead. Both directions. All of them."

"There are other ways to get there," says Kelton. "Non-traditional ways … but we'll need a map to get us started."

Suddenly, up above, a military helicopter roars past at a low altitude. We pass a military truck heading in the opposite direction from us, but other than that there are very few cars on the road. Then, up ahead, we come to a roadblock – also military. Soldiers in camouflage are gesturing to the left, and yell to us.

"This road is for official business only! Take a left! Signs will lead you to the evac center!"

"Don't listen to him," says Kelton. "The last place we want to be is an evac center right now."

"What do you suggest I do?" asks Jacqui. "Crash through the roadblock? Do you even see the size of the guns they're all holding?"

"Turn left," I say before Alyssa can say it. "Do what he says for now, until we find a way around the roadblocks." And although Jacqui clearly doesn't want to take any orders from me, she has to. There is no other viable choice except to follow, and reinforce my benevolent leadership.

"I agree," says Alyssa. Point for me.

We turn left, heading down El Toro Road. There are a few more cars on the road with us now, and more roadblocks. It seems that any and all civilian traffic is being directed onto this road.

"We should be going in the opposite direction," says Kelton.

"Don't worry," I tell him, forcing a big-brotherly tone. "Two steps forward sometimes requires one step back."

"What, did you get that off of a motivational poster in your counselor's office, Roycroft?" says Jacqui. "How about this one? *Sometimes in life you're just plain screwed.*"

"All right, can we just kill the attitude?" says Alyssa. "It's not helping anything."

It's the perfect set-up for what I'm about to say next.

"It's all right, Alyssa," I say, with an infinitude of

understanding. "Jacqui's just stressed and scared. It's how she deals with it."

"Don't you dare analyze me!" she snaps, which just proves my point.

Alyssa glances at me, and I offer her a small grin and a shrug. In return, she offers me a commiseration of raised eyebrows – which is one step before a friendly smile. A fine turn of events! I'll admit that she's still in charge here, but she's beginning to see the two of us as a team. This is excellent progress toward a sustainable dynamic. Once she starts deferring to me, I'll know that I've slipped into the virtual driver's seat, regardless of who's actually driving.

Now there are more cars on the road around us, and all traffic is detoured right. I begin to realize that we have entered a funnel – a funnel leading directly to El Toro High School, where they've set up an official evac center. I don't think I've ever seen so many people in one place. Crowds in the parking lot, crowds in the fields and the tennis and basketball courts – except for one set of courts that's being used as a helipad. The military helicopter we saw before idles there, offloading water behind an entire gauntlet of armed soldiers.

Up ahead of us, a soldier motions for us to pull over to the side of the road, along with the other cars.

"We can't let ourselves be herded and corralled like sheep," says Kelton. "This is how it all starts. This is the beginning of the end."

"Wow, that's bleak," Jacqui comments, which says a lot coming from her.

But Kelton holds firm. "We'll have to tell them we got

lost. Then we'll turn around before it's too late."

A soldier raps on Jacqui's window, and she has no choice but to roll it down.

"Park here," he says. "Then follow the crowd."

"We're here by mistake," Jacqui says, heeding Kelton's warning.

"Yeah," adds Kelton. "We have somewhere else to go."

The soldier isn't buying it. "Then why aren't you already there?"

And then Garrett, giving his best puppy-dog eyes, says, "My grandma! Please, we have to get my grandma! She's waiting for us!"

The kid's clever, I'll give him that.

And then he adds, "She wouldn't leave her dogs," which is the perfect cherry on his story. This kid should run for office. Hell, *I'd* cast an uninformed vote for him.

Then the soldier says, "Give us her address, and we'll send someone for her."

That leaves Garrett completely speechless, and before any of us can keep his little fiction balloon from popping, the soldier leans in, looks down at Garrett, and says, "Mind telling me what *that* is?"

We all look down to the bag of pot in Garrett's lap. Garrett says, "Oh shit," and another promising political career goes down in flames.

The others speak up now, but everything they say just makes it worse.

"It's not what you think!" says Alyssa.

"It came with the car!" says Kelton.

"It's just oregano," says Jacqui.

Graves rarely get so deep.

"All right, out of the truck!" says the soldier using his no-nonsense boot-camp voice. "I SAID OUT! NOW!"

And so we scramble to do what he says, because red-handed is red-handed, and this is martial law, and Jacqui's motivational poster is truer than anything right now. We are screwed, and I cannot see a way out of this.

He takes the keys from Jacqui, leaving us with without wheels.

"Turn around!" he demands, waving his weapon. "Hands up against the vehicle."

I try, but I grimace.

"I SAID HANDS UP!"

"I can't," I tell him. "I dislocated my shoulder."

"It's true," says Kelton. "I dislocated it."

"Just keep your hands where I can see them," he says, mercifully not forcing my arm out of joint again. But now I'm scared. Truly and honestly scared, because I can see that there are others who are sitting handcuffed on the curb. Troublemakers or brawlers, or other sorts of unpleasant characters who required restraint, and God knows where *they* go under martial law. I try to hold it together, because leadership requires at least a pretense of grace under pressure.

And then Alyssa opens her mouth – and what comes out is downright magical.

"So you're going to arrest a bunch of kids for having pot? It's legal now, you know!"

"Not in a moving vehicle," the soldier says as he begins

to frisk us. "And you're all underage!"

But Alyssa will not be deterred. "Really? Is this your top priority in the middle of this crisis?"

"Be quiet!" the soldier orders. He pats Kelton down, and is about to move on to Alyssa.

"This is the physical and psychological intimidation of minors – not even martial law allows that!" she yells. *"I'm sure my cousin at the* LA Times *is going to love this story!"*

And, miraculously, he backs off. But not before grabbing the bag of weed. "I'm confiscating this!" he says. "Now move it! Get in line with everyone else!"

And just like that, we're free. With so many people to process, I guess arresting us just wasn't worth the hassle. We hurry away from the soldier, passing all the forlorn people handcuffed by the curb, and join the mob heading toward the school, all of us breathing a communal sigh of relief.

"That," I tell Alyssa, "was masterful." And it's not even like I'm sucking up. I mean it. "You completely saved us back there – and you didn't even have to lie!"

"Actually," says Alyssa, "I don't have a cousin who works for the *LA Times*."

And suddenly I think I might be in love.

23) Alyssa

Maybe, I think, *maybe this will be okay.* Now that the Tap-Out is being taken seriously – now that all these resources are being mobilized – it will be okay. We won't have to brave the journey to this mysterious bug-out, which always sounded sketchy to me anyway.

But Kelton is like an animal in a trap, and he's ready to chew off his own foot to escape. He halts, refusing to walk any farther, standing in the middle of the path. The four of us have to fight the current of people to not get swept away with it.

"We can't be here!" he insists.

"But we are," Jacqui tells him, butting back. "Deal with it."

Considering all that Kelton has been through, I think he needs better than a tough-love approach from someone who doesn't actually love him, so I try to be a little bit gentler.

"Maybe this is a good thing," I tell him. "It's not like we're prisoners – they aren't making us stay if we don't want to. And who knows, maybe we *do* want to."

But now that we're standing here like boulders against the relentless flow of people entering the evac center, it doesn't feel like much of a choice at all.

"Maybe Mom and Dad are here," Garrett shouts over the clamor of helicopter blades. Though I think if they were here, they would have left to come to get us. Or maybe, like the soldier was going to do for our imaginary grandma, they sent someone to get us, but we were already gone.

"It's possible," I tell Garrett, because I don't want to shatter his hopes.

And then Jacqui yells, "Where the hell is Roycroft?"

I look behind us, and he's not there. He's vanished completely.

"Forget about him," growls Kelton. Someone knocks into

him and he almost loses his footing. "If he wants to stay here let him, but we can't!"

"Stop it!" Jacqui yells. "This is stressful enough without you freaking out."

Kelton grits his teeth, anger growing. "You all have no idea, do you?" He points to the football field, which is just up a small hill. "You think there are no prisoners here? Take a look at that fence! Go up there, and ask the people on the other side how long they've been waiting. Go on!"

And just to placate him, I do. "I'll be right back," I say. "Stay together." And I push through the crowd and up the grassy embankment. As I reach the football field, I'm hit by just how crowded it is. The stands, the track, the field. You can't even see the grass – it's all people. There are umbrellas and awnings set up to keep them in the shade, but not nearly enough.

The fence is fairly high. All high school football fields have fences. They're to keep the fans of opposing teams from getting into fights with each other, and to keep out people who didn't pay for a ticket. Today, at every gate, there are multiple armed soldiers. As much as I hate to admit it, Kelton's right. In the here-and-now those fences are all about keeping people in. They've quarantined water-zombies. Thousands of them.

"Excuse me," I call through the fence to anyone who'll respond.

A bony woman with long, unkempt brown hair comes over to me. "Did you see?" she asks. "Did you see where they took it?"

But I'm not sure what she's asking.

She gets impatient. "The water! Did you see where they took it? We all saw the helicopter, but where did they take the water?"

I did see them beginning to unload it, but I don't know where the water went. There are so many staging areas around this school, it could have gone anywhere. "No," I tell her, "I'm sorry, no."

She slams her hand against the chain-link fence and it rattles. She bites her lip. She squints and starts blinking, and I realize what she's doing. She's crying. She's crying but there are no tears left in her.

Finally I ask the question I came to ask. "How long have you been here?"

"We came yesterday afternoon," she tells me. "This is only the third helicopter that's come since then, and the line never moves! We haven't seen any water. You have to find out where it's going!"

And then I hear Jacqui behind me. "The gym," she yells over the crowd. "I saw them taking it to the gym. There's a lot of people there, too."

The woman desperately grabs the fence so tightly her fingertips turn white. "You have to get some for us! You'll do that, won't you? You'll go to the gym and bring us some of that water?"

There's nothing I can say to her.

"Please promise you'll do it. Please!"

"Alyssa, let's go."

"I'm sorry…" I say. "I'm … I'm…"

Then Jacqui gets in front of me, blocking my view of

the woman, and moves me backward, down the hill. "Don't engage," she tells me. "It won't help anyone, least of all you."

I think to the box of ÁguaViva in the bed of the pickup, hidden beneath a blanket. Is it still there? Did it get taken? Should I open it and start hurling bottles over the fence? But then I remember what happened yesterday when I brought water bottles to the Burnside house. And these people are far thirstier than that.

Don't engage.

How do you just walk away? And yet I do. I have to.

"So what did you find out?" asks Kelton, when we get back to him. He already knows the answer from the look on my face.

24) Henry

I hadn't planned on leaving the others – I was just too busy being observant, taking in the situation around me, and when the line diverged, I went the other way. But that's okay. I know where the others are, and although, under any other circumstances, I'd be better off as a free agent, I'm thinking our strange little fellowship might be worth maintaining. Or at least the Alyssa part of it. We'll see.

I focus on the situation at hand. There are opportunities in every circumstance – even a circumstance as complex and troubling as the one around me … but as I take everything in, I'm finding it hard to see any opportunity whatsoever. Thousands of thirsty people. Water barrels being carried into the gym, with a heavily armed entourage, and people trying to push their way through to those barrels with all the anguish of a baroque painting.

My heart is still racing from the encounter with the soldier back at the truck, but everything I see just makes it worse. The line I'm in is driving people toward the baseball field, but I can see it stopping before the entrance. That field is full, too. What the hell are they going to do with all these people?

As the line devolves into a great milling mob, I slip away. There are soldiers everywhere, but plenty of spots are unguarded, and so far I haven't heard gunshots, so I'm assuming they're not shooting people who live outside the lines. I make my way to a less crowded area, keeping an eye on the entrance to the gym, and those water barrels. My father always said when you want to go somewhere you're not supposed to be, just walk in like you own the place, and nine times out of ten, you'll get in. But I'm pretty sure this is that tenth time. And if I do get in, what then? I'm just one of thousands of people waiting for a taste of that water. That's not an opportunity, it's a dead-end deal.

As I round a corner, I get a glimpse of the pool. Empty. They ran off with all the water in high school pools to use elsewhere, before they realized they'd be turning some of those schools into evacuation centers. There is no limit to short-sightedness in this world. But it's not the lack of pool water that troubles me. It's what I see on the pool deck.

There are body bags there.

Not just one or two, but at least a dozen. And something tells me there's going to be more.

All right. All right. This isn't funny now. All right. All right. Maybe it never really was. All right. All right. There are dead people. In bags. And the helicopter flies away, and I have no idea when it will be back with water to keep other people from finding their way into bags. And I've never wet my pants, and I never will, but I swear to you, I come really, really close.

"Hey! You! You're not supposed to be here!"

I don't need to be told again. I double back, heading to the place where people are still walking and breathing. Kelton was right. We can't stay here. And now I know exactly what I have to do. This is going to be a tough one – but if there's anyone who can swing a deal to end all deals, it's me.

25) Alyssa

The line suddenly stops moving. More people come in behind us, and we're pushed up against the people in front of us. All crammed like cattle. I keep a hand on Garrett, just to make sure we don't get separated. It's the soldiers behind us – they've begun to press against the crowd to clear a path in the road – and then empty school buses pull in, like it's just an ordinary school day.

"Your attention please!" a voice blares over a sibilant bullhorn. "This evacuation center is at capacity," which is an understatement if ever there was one. I don't think it was equipped to handle even a fraction of the masses here. "These buses will take you to an overflow facility."

"Where?" someone yells. "Where the hell are they taking us?" But no one gives an answer.

As the parade of school buses continues to pour in, the soldiers make room for them in the lot. We're all uncomfortably close together, and I can smell everyone's breath, which isn't particularly good. Kelton doesn't even have to lean in to whisper within earshot. "They won't answer because they don't know," he says. "They're probably still trying to figure out where to send the buses – but wherever it is, it's not an evac center. They don't have the time or the manpower to set up any more. All they can do is dump people in 'overflow facilities.'"

Jacqui has her elbows out, trying to keep her personal space. "Why is it that you know all the answers?"

He doesn't bother to answer her. Instead he says, "Do you know the concept of social triage? No? Because I do. In a mass emergency, you help the ones you can, and the ones you can't help, you move out of the way." Then he looks to the first bus, where people are already beginning to obediently board. "I can guarantee you that half the people who get on those buses are going to die, because wherever they're going, it's away from water."

I stand on my toes and look over people's heads at all the soldiers moving the giant herds. One of them kindly helps an elderly woman onto the bus. It's not like it's their intention to kill anyone, but after days without water, death needs no invitation.

"There are no fences around this parking lot," I point out. "We're not trapped yet."

But before I can formulate a plan, Henry comes into sight, bounding out of nowhere, out of breath and eyes wild.

"Lookie what I got," he says, and holds up Uncle Basil's key chain, stupid rabbit's foot and all. It changes everything.

"How did you do that?" I ask, hardly able to believe my eyes.

"I made a deal," he says. "But we have to hurry. Come on!"

We run after him, fighting the current of people heading toward the buses. "Wait – you traded with the guy who took the keys?" Garrett realizes, profoundly impressed. "He was going to arrest us, how did you make a trade with him?"

"Because it's what I do!" says Henry. "Come on, we don't have much time."

We get to the truck, and I immediately see the blanket in the back has been overturned, and the box that was hidden beneath it is gone. "The water!"

At the mention of water, a dozen eyes turn in my direction.

"Forget about it!" insists Henry. "That's what I traded for the keys."

Jacqui looks at him, incredulous. "You traded the last of the water for keys? Did it occur to you that we could hotwire it – or run the hell away from here and find another truck? One that actually has air-conditioning?"

But before he can answer, another voice broadsides the conversation.

"Hey! Roycroft! Wait up!"

It makes Henry scramble even faster.

A muscular meathead type pushes his way through the crowd. Chapped lips, glassy-eyed, but not quite a water-zombie

yet. He grabs Henry by the shoulder and turns him around –
then the kid looks at Henry a little funny.

"Hey, wait a second – you're not Trent Roycroft…"

Henry ignores him, and turns to the rest of us. "Just get
in the truck!"

But the jock will not be ignored. "Who the hell are you?
Why are you wearing Roycroft's jacket? Where's Roycroft?"

Henry fumbles with the keys and drops them. They skid
underneath the truck.

"Hey!" says the meathead. "I'm talking to you."

Then Henry dives underneath the truck, not like he's
trying to get the keys, but like he's trying to escape. And now
I realize that Jacqui is gone.

"Alyssa!" says Garrett. "He said to get in!"

The door isn't locked, and Garrett climbs in the back seat
with Kelton. I look for Jacqui but can't see her anywhere.
Damn her! Henry emerges from underneath the car on the
opposite side from the meathead, but right by the driver's door,
and he has the keys again.

"Hey, I asked you a question!" the meathead calls to him.
And now with a car between them, Henry gives him an answer.

"Go screw yourself."

Then Henry gets in, slamming the door hard.

The meathead is more stunned than angry. "You know,
I don't even think you go to Santa Margarita High School!"

Henry starts the truck, and I jump into the passenger seat.

"We have to wait for Jacqui!" I insist.

"We don't have time!"

It's like something's snapped in Henry. If his name even

is Henry. I have no idea of anything anymore. He throws the car into reverse, and we smash into the Toyota behind us that's boxing us in. He throws it in drive and does the same to the Audi in front of us. Then he reverses into the Toyota again, forcing the cars apart to give us space to pull out.

And then I finally see Jacqui. She's running toward us. And she's carrying the ÁguaViva box!

"Noooooooooo!" yells Henry when he sees her. Finally he's created enough damage and made enough room to pull the truck away from the curb. He lurches forward, scattering people heading toward the buses. By now the soldiers have taken notice – and the one who made the trade is chasing Jacqui, but she's too fast.

Henry swings a violent U-turn that takes down a little crepe myrtle tree on the island between lanes, and we're beached there, spinning our wheels, kicking up leaves and pink flowers.

It gives Jacqui enough time to reach us. She throws the box in the back, and, realizing Henry has no intention of waiting for her to hop into the cab, she climbs the bumper and jumps into the bed along with the box and whatever other junk Uncle Basil has back there.

Henry stomps on the gas, cursing, and rather than telling him what to do, I reach over and engage the four-wheel drive.

Now when he hits the gas, we lurch forward, making sawdust of the little tree, and careen away from the school, leaving gawking people, and frustrated soldiers who don't seem to be following us. They're just glad we're no longer their problem.

"Are you insane?" I scream at Henry. "You nearly killed us back there!"

He looks at me with those wild, snapped eyes. "Killed you? *Killed* you? I just saved your lives! At least you could show some gratitude!"

"Slow down!" I demand. He's so frenetic, he can't seem to find a lane. If there were more cars on the road, we'd have totaled the truck by now.

He grips the wheel tightly, looks straight ahead. "All right. All right," he says, taking a deep breath. He steadies the car, eases up on the accelerator. "All right, all right. It's all under control now. It's all good." Then he turns to me. "There were body bags, Alyssa. Some of them were already full, but there were stacks and stacks and stacks of empty ones."

"There were?" says Garrett, wide-eyed, like someone just proved to him that the boogeyman was real.

"Do you see why I had to get us out of there, Alyssa? Do you? I had to save us, because if I didn't, no one else would have. Do you see?"

I nod. "Just keep your eyes on the road."

He turns to face forward. "All right. All right," he says again, tamping down his panic. Pretending it wasn't panic at all. He's not driving well, but who would under these circumstances?

And then Kelton says, "There's nothing scary about a body bag. They're for transport and to prevent the spread of disease. I have one in my room; I use it for laundry."

There's a rap on the little back window of the cab. Jacqui's hair is windswept and she doesn't look happy back there.

"Stop the car," I tell Henry. "Let Jacqui back in."

"I will be happy to let her in once we're far enough away from that place."

And apparently twenty more yards down the road is far enough away, because he eases on the break, and pulls over to the side of the road. Jacqui hops out of the truck bed and storms to Henry's window.

"Get the hell out, I'm driving!"

"In the back seat or not at all," Henry tells her.

"Not gonna happen," says Jacqui.

"Fine, then not at all," and he throws the car in gear and pulls out, leaving her behind in a cloud of dust.

"God DAMN it!" yells Jacqui, running after us.

"You can't just leave her here!" I yell.

"I'm not!" he tells me, now calm as can be. "This is a negotiation and I'm playing hardball." He stops the car to let Jacqui catch up with us. "If you want to tie down a loose cannon, you can't give it much rope, follow?"

Jacqui catches up with us, spewing wholly original combinations of foulness. Henry is not fazed.

"In the back seat," he says. "Or I drive off, and we part company for good."

Disgruntled, Jacqui hops in the back, pushing Garrett into the middle, and slams the door. "Remind me to kill you in your sleep, Roycroft."

And then I remember she wasn't there when the jock blew Henry's cover. Henry, having found his comfort zone again, remains unfazed.

"So who's Roycroft?" I ask.

Henry doesn't even hesitate. "An asshole who traded me his letter jacket for two bottles of ÁguaViva."

"Wait, what?" says Jacqui. "You mean you've been lying to us all this time?"

"I never said my name was Roycroft – you just assumed. And I just went with it."

"So what *is* your name?" I ask.

"You know my name."

"Not your last name."

"We're on a first-name basis, so why does it even matter?" Then he turns around to glance at Kelton. "So how do we get to the bug-out?"

SNAPSHOT: 13 RIDGECREST, DOVE CANYON

Herb was relieved to see his niece and nephew this morning, and glad they were okay – but he worries about his sister and brother-in-law. They would never have sent Alyssa and Garrett here without them. There was clearly something his niece wasn't saying – and who was this new girl? She was not one of Alyssa's usual friends. Kelton he could deal with. Everyone had a weird-but-mostly-harmless neighbor kid to contend with. But this Jacqui had a red flag vibe about her.

He closes his eyes and steadies himself against the banister at the bottom of the stairs. The ache of his fever, and the weight of his own body, is telling his brain that the staircase might as well be Mt. Everest. He takes a deep, shuddering breath, and sighs. One crisis at a time. He can't wring his hands over his sister now, or about his niece's choice of traveling companions.

Besides, the fact that Alyssa and the others haven't come back is a good sign. He heard the unmistakable sound of his truck driving down the street. He'd bet a pretty penny that they were in that car when it left.

He takes the stairs one step at a time, pausing for a breath between each one, all the while chiding himself for trusting the tap water once they switched the source to the old tank on the hill. Everyone in the neighborhood was so full of their own cleverness at having jury-rigged a solution to the Tap-Out. And so they drank. And Herb drank. And Daphne drank. They sated themselves on stagnant water that had been sitting untreated in a dark tank for who knew how long.

It didn't taste bad. Didn't make you spit it out, grimacing. Yes, it was a little bit earthy, but that was all. He wondered if anyone had the good sense to boil it first before drinking it. Probably not. There's a false sense of security when you turn on a shiny chrome tap in your own kitchen. Yes, you expect it not to taste quite as good as filtered water, what with all the fluoride, and chlorine, and whatever the hell else they treat the water with – but you don't expect it to kill you. How could anyone have known?

Now the community has been unusually quiet. It took a while for him to realize that such a semblance of peace was the biggest indication of how bad things had really become. No one's coming out of their homes, because, like him and Daphne, they're just too sick and weak.

Halfway to the top of the stairs now.

He holds a bottle of ÁguaViva in one hand and grips the banister with the other. The only reason he's still able to stand is that he's been keeping the ÁguaViva down. Yes, it goes right through him, but while it's coursing through his troubled intestines, some of it must get absorbed. It gave him the strength to keep himself mostly together for Alyssa and Garrett. They didn't see how hard he was struggling just to stand. Besides, the sight of them did give him an adrenaline boost.

Now he's paying for that though, as wave after wave of weakness hits him.

The top step. He stands there catching his breath, and trying to ignore the throbbing in his joints. He thinks this might be the last time he attempts the stairs.

For a while. Just for a while.

He steps into the master bedroom, where the stench has

gotten worse. He's already changed the sheets twice today. He doesn't know if he has it in him to change them again, but he knows he will.

He doesn't announce his arrival. Herb stopped talking to Daphne yesterday. It just became too painful to do once she stopped talking back. So now he silently cares for her, feeding her small bits of soft food, hoping she'll finally start holding it down, and drizzling ÁguaViva into her mouth, which makes her cough and gag, then comes right back up onto the white sheets.

He sits on the edge of the bed, touching her pale skin, so thin now he can see the veins beneath. Her eyes are like dull marbles that stare through him. They don't even blink.

He listens but can't hear her breathe, so he puts his head to her chest, listening for a heartbeat. It's there. Weak. Strained. She's climbing her own Everest, without even moving. He wonders what he'll do when he puts his head to her chest and hears nothing.

Then, as he prepares to get up to change the sheets, something catches his eye by Daphne's bedside.

There's a little orange prescription bottle that wasn't there before. Did someone leave it here? Who could have done that?

Herb was never one to believe in miracles. Certainly no miracle came to save his farm, or for that matter, anything else he had lost in his life. But when he sees that pill bottle – and the label reading "Keflex" – he has to reevaluate his whole concept of reality.

———————————————————————————————

26) Kelton

Strangers. I'm in a car with strangers. Jacqui, mysterious and deranged. Then there's Henry, who isn't who he says he is. Even Alyssa and Garrett are question marks. Because it's like I don't know anyone anymore. But the biggest stranger is me. Sure, I know my name. I know where I live – or lived, because I don't know if I even live there anymore. I have all the same memories, but the new memories – the ONE memory that keeps playing in my head along with the sound of that shotgun blast, has rendered everything that happened before that moment completely irrelevant.

Just before dawn this morning, when it came to fight or flight, my body finally chose fight. When it's flight, you're swept away by a force – but when it's fight, you're giving in to an even stronger one. I would have done some heavy damage if Alyssa hadn't knocked me out. At least now I'm filled with confidence that the fight function exists within me. And maybe now that I know what it is, and what it feels like, perhaps I can start to control its power.

As a result, I do find myself giving in to more violent, de-structive thoughts. Like how when that soldier pointed his gun at me, a part of me wanted him to blast my brain into the next county. I wanted Henry to run people over on the way out. I want things to explode and I want everyone to feel the shrapnel as deep as I do. I know it's wrong. But the feelings course through me, and who am I to try to stop them?

But then my mother's voice comes to me. My mother, who might be dead, for all I know. And she says, *Things pass. Even big things. And when they're far behind us, they don't look big anymore.*

And my father's voice, too. Sterner, but still with the authority of experience. *Everything in life is a lesson, Kelton. Learn from it. Better yourself. Become stronger.*

The best way to honor them is to listen to them. To believe them. But it's hard, so very, very hard.

"So how do we get to the bug-out?" I hear Henry ask. And I realize I have a mission. To take the blast. To be strong enough to block the shrapnel from hitting the others. Yeah, a part of me wants everyone to feel the pain, but I'm better than that. Stronger than a shotgun blast. My brother is dead. But I am not. And I will do what I have to do today.

"We need to find Santiago Creek," I tell him. "It won't be far from here."

"A creek?" Jacqui questions, now suddenly interested by the notion of water.

"It's all dried up," I inform her. "And besides, it's an urban creek," I explain. "So expect a lot of concrete and graffiti."

"I thought you said we needed a map."

"It would help, but I'm pretty sure I have the waterways memorized. There's a map with the aqueducts and drainage channels all marked up in our garage."

Henry looks at me like I'm from another galaxy, and I start to feel defensive.

"We've been preparing," I explain.

"If you haven't noticed by now," Jacqui explains to him, "the Tap-Out is like Christmas for Kelton."

Which pisses me off, because maybe at one point she would have been right – but now it's just a nightmare. And she knows that. I shoot her a death glare that, if there was justice, would make her head explode. And for the first time, I think she gets the picture, and actually shuts up.

As we continue north it becomes increasingly apparent to everyone else what I already know: There's no escaping the military takeover. We pass an open canopy truck crammed full of soldiers. Random humvees are parked on corners. Helicopters tear through the sky overhead. Then we dead-end at a traffic-jammed road. There's another roadblock up ahead, and soldiers directing people down another suburban funnel that leads either back to the high school, or to an "overflow facility" that will be the last place to see water. There are no roads left in all of Southern California that go anywhere we want to be.

Alyssa turns to Henry, alarmed. "We can't get caught in that again."

"I thought your doomsday dog was navigating."

I don't know whether to be annoyed or flattered that Henry Not-Roycroft is spending all his mental energy coming up with nicknames for me.

"Didn't you say you had the map memorized?" Jacqui says to me.

"I have the map of the *aqueducts* memorized, not these roads. And on paper you're technically supposed to be smarter than me, right? So why don't you tell us how to get out of here."

"Not my neighborhood," Jacqui shrugs. "But I'm glad we established that I'm smarter than you."

"Do you want to find the aqueducts," Alyssa interjects, "or just snipe at each other until they put us on a death bus to nowhere?"

"Wait," Garrett says. "Is it like a concrete ditch where kids skateboard?"

And now we're all looking at him. "Yes!"

"I know where it is! Turn right here, and then left at the ugly cow. Then look for a Jack in the Box. It's in the back, behind the parking lot."

We follow Garrett's directions and come to a corner where there's a mom-and-pop ice cream place on the corner. On the roof is the saddest looking plastic cow I've ever seen.

"Should I turn left," says Henry, "or is there an uglier cow up ahead?"

He turns without waiting for Garrett's answer, and we see a Jack in the Box a few dozen yards ahead.

We pull into the empty parking lot and to the far back fence, where there's a concrete aqueduct stretching as far as the eye can see in both directions. It's amazing how places like this can be here, cutting right through your own neighborhood, but for most people, it's completely off their radar. Unless you're a prepper. Or a skateboarder. The concrete is mottled salt-and-pepper, stained from the sediment of old storm surges, but Santiago Creek hasn't had running water for a few years now.

We come to a stop, and I can see that there's no visible entrance – it's blocked off by a tall chain-link fence topped with barbed wire. My father would know where the entrance would be, but that's no use to us now.

"I used to fit in through that hole right there," Garrett says.

"That's not big enough for the truck," Alyssa says, pointing out the obvious. Just looking at the fortified nature of the fence, even if we had the luxury of time, I doubt we would find an opening big enough, and I doubt even more that Alyssa and Garrett's uncle has bolt cutters in the back.

"I've seen kids on bikes down there…" Garrett says. "They've got to get there somehow."

Another helicopter soars overhead, the relentless beat of its blades making me anxious. Searching for an access point large enough for us might take hours.

"We're going to have to bust through it," Jacqui says, not even trying to hide the excitement in her voice. I question her intentions, as always, but it's not like we have any better options right now.

Now all eyes are on Henry in the driver's seat. He looks back at us, the pressure getting to him. "Even if we can get through, it's kinda steep."

Which is definitely an understatement. I look down into the crevasse and instantly get that sick-to-my-stomach feeling, like that terrifying moment before chickening out of dropping into a halfpipe. Sadly, I have intimate relations with that moment.

The aqueduct is shaped like an upside-down trapezoid,

with a steep downslope that abruptly levels off for twenty yards, then slopes upward again. The flat portion in the middle always reminds me of the racing scene in *Grease*. Only I'm sure John Travolta is a much better driver than Henry. Hell, his car flies in the end.

Henry throws the car in reverse and begins to back up, like a bull before charging a matador.

"Are you sure we want Henry to do this?" Alyssa asks. "What about his arm?"

"It's fine now," Henry says.

Which is a lie – I'm sure it still aches, but it probably won't affect his driving. Still, I'm just as wary as Alyssa. "I think Jacqui might have more experience driving," I suggest.

"No, I do," he insists.

"You're what? Seventeen," Jacqui points out. "How much experience could you have?"

"I've been driving since I was thirteen," he says. "Don't ask." So we don't. After all, he did manage to maneuver us out of the high school. Granted, he damaged a bunch of cars and killed a defenseless tree in the process. Under normal circumstances that would not be considered skilled driving. But these are not normal circumstances.

I calculate the metrics of it all. "You'll want to hit the fence with enough speed to break through, but not enough for us to lose control and flip into the channel."

"So how fast?" He coughs, trying to hide the little quiver of fear in his voice.

I weigh the variables and make a guess that sounds far more educated than it actually is. "Thirty miles per hour.

And since we don't have much of a runway, we'll need to accelerate quickly. Once we get down there, you'll want to turn left."

Henry takes a breath and finds the closest thing he has to a happy place. "Okay, are we ready?"

"YES, just do it already!" Jacqui yells from the back seat.

"All right. All right."

And like that, we're off.

Henry increases pressure on the accelerator. I can hear the tires peeling out beneath us. We rocket forward. My body presses back against the seat with the acceleration. We're closing the distance between us and the fence quickly – but just before we do, Henry suddenly hits the brakes, bailing, the way I bail from halfpipes.

But it's too late. We're moving too fast.

We collide with the chain-link fence, but rather than busting through it, it holds … and then I realize it's slowly bending forward. I can hear the metal brackets that hold the fence to the support poles begin to snap. The fence clangs and twangs like a weird musical instrument, and the nose of the truck begins to dip forward, revealing a gorge like a roller-coaster drop.

The slope is much steeper than it had seemed. *We're going to die,* is all I can think. Suspended over the edge, the car hangs in the fence like someone in a hammock – then the fence finally gives way. We fly down the slope, and the nerves in my stomach flutter up into my throat, like I'm about to puke.

I brace myself, and we hit the level concrete, the shocks absorbing most of it. Still, we're slammed back into our seats, and everything bounces.

Henry cranks the wheel left, as instructed, and we fish-tail, until he manages to gain control, straightening out, then punches the gas.

And we're gliding on the concrete riverbed.

I look out the window. We're carving the aqueduct like we're surfing. After that rough drop, it feels so smooth! I find myself laughing out of disbelief, and Jacqui screams out of excitement. The others are just relieved.

"That was awesome!" Garrett bursts out, looking to Henry, starry-eyed. But as cool as Garrett thinks Henry is, it doesn't change the fact that this was wildly dangerous. If we had leveled out with any more speed, or at any steeper an angle, we would have totaled, or even flipped.

Henry smiles, pleased with himself. "I knew thirty miles per hour was just too fast," he says – like hitting the brakes was the result of calculation and not fear. But I'm so thankful to be alive right now, he could take credit for the faked lunar landings and I wouldn't care.

But then I realize – "The ÁguaViva!" I twist in my seat to get a better look at the truck bed through the rear window.

"It's still there," Jacqui reassures us all.

"Some of the bottles could have been damaged…" Garrett notes coyly. "Maybe we should open up the box just to see…" But I know exactly where this is going. I think we all do. Henry puts an end to it.

"ÁguaViva bottles are made of durable low-density poly-ethylene, and are BPA-free," Henry informs us. "I promise you nothing in that box will leak."

And although agreeing with Henry on any level makes me

cringe, I say, "Besides, we don't want to open that box until we have no choice." Temptation is not our friend right now. There will be more than enough water at the bug-out. We'll need to save our reserve for emergencies. I'm still surprised that we got that ÁguaViva box back, anyway. I find myself shaking my head and smiling at Jacqui.

"You were totally insane to go after that box, you know that?"

And she grins, knowing that I mean it as a compliment – something I'm not sure she's used to getting.

"So are you," she responds. I choose to take it as a compliment as well.

I wonder what it would've been like if I had crossed paths with Jacqui in other circumstances – then again, I highly doubt that would ever happen. This girl lives on a totally different dimensional plane than the rest of us. If the Tap-Out never happened, she would be nothing but a name on an SAT score I couldn't beat.

Realizing that my thoughts are no longer nagging anxieties, I finally take a moment to breathe. We all do.

Jacqui leans forward and turns on the radio. Nothing but emergency broadcasts, telling people where to go, where not to go, and to remain calm. A one-size-fits-all relief effort that doesn't actually fit anyone.

"Our uncle has satellite radio," Alyssa points out, and switches to the satellite stations. Suddenly "Smooth Criminal" assaults our eardrums, which, in this place, in this moment, sounds like the best song in the world. Impulsive as ever, Jacqui reaches forward and opens up the sunroof, then stands, her entire torso protruding dangerously out of it, indulging in the high of another adrenaline rush.

After a little while, Alyssa tugs at Jacqui's blouse. "Enough." And then as soon as Jacqui comes down, Alyssa, all smiles, jumps up and pops her head through, too. Jacqui shoves her like she would a bratty sister. Then Garrett, of course, demands his turn. Sharing. What a concept. If we're a messed up, dysfunctional family, I guess this can go down as our single functional moment.

I roll down my window and stick my hand out. I close my eyes and open up my fingers, letting my hand cut through the wind. I look through the window and marvel at the world outside. Hazy afternoon sunlight pours down from the sky. The light glimmers against the concrete path like ribbons of gold … and I'm realizing that this is the first time we've felt relatively free in a long time. Like we weren't escaping from the place we once called home. Like this wasn't a suburban apocalypse. I can't forget the events of the past twenty-four hours, but here, speeding along a concrete wash, I can let them trail behind me, if only for a few moments. It's the briefest hint that no matter what happened, or happens, life might actually go on.

It's Henry who brings us back to reality. "There's a junction coming up," he yells over the whipping wind.

"Stay left," I tell him.

It's Alyssa who points out that we're heading southwest – toward the shore, not the mountains.

"It's okay," I tell her, "we're traveling a river system. We have to go down this tributary until we reach the main river."

Henry bears left at the junction.

"When we reach the main riverbed, we'll make a hard right, and take that river all the way up to the mountains," I tell everyone.

I used to brag to everyone that I had a photographic memory, but this is the true test. The channel we're in loses its brutal edge, and becomes natural for a while. Wild, like a true riverbed. Then we're riding on concrete again, in an area more industrial than before.

Another junction, Henry makes the hard right, and the dashboard compass shows that we're now heading north. We're in a much wider channel now: the Santa Ana River, although it's really just the memory of a river. All Southern California waterways have become like phantom limbs. We might feel that they're still there, but it's just an illusion cast in cement.

I have a better idea of where we are on the map. There are even some landmarks along the way that help guide us: Angel Stadium, the Honda Center. Which reminds me that we're not too far from Disneyland. I can't even imagine what kind of madness is going down there right now. Last year, as a show of community support, and shrewd marketing, they drained their artificial waterways. The jungle cruise became a VR ride. Pirates and Small World were converted to magnetic levitation, and they opened up Grand Canyon Land in the dry moat around Tom Sawyer's Island. So anyone who thinks they can jump the fence now and suck down the guano-tainted blue-dyed water will have a rude awakening.

As we travel this expansive concrete channel, it feels to me like the world has torn in two, and we're traveling the seam of that tear. The chasm between what was, and what will be.

We're no longer part of any world. Or at least I'm not. Everything that used to mean something to me is on the outside, hopelessly out of reach. I think about my brother. I think about my parents. I feel numb now. Like how, after a really bad burn, once the pain subsides, you lose all sensation in the spot. That's because the nerve endings are dead. And yet, I think right now the best place for me to be is the chasm between the tattered edges of life as we knew it.

The chasm takes many forms as we travel. In some places we have to slow down because there are rocks, branches, and other obstacles that I imagine were swept up in a current when this place actually transported water. Other parts we have to crawl at an excruciatingly slow pace, because of rocks bulldozed into five-foot berms, intentionally formed into a maze designed to direct the flow of water. It's as if the chasm itself is an obstacle course created to defeat us. But we will not be defeated.

Another hour in, and we encounter a dam.

"Was this on your mental map?" Jacqui asks.

I don't answer that. Instead I say, "Dams always have an access route for heavy machinery to reach both sides." We drive along the face of the dam, then double back for about a hundred yards and find the access path. It's gated, but the gate is pretty rusty.

We ram it, doing fifty, which was probably overkill, because the gate flies off its hinges.

Jacqui whoops with excitement, invigorated. Alyssa endures it, Garrett's all smiles, and Henry remains all business, keeping his hands gripping the wheel at ten and two. Me, I'm still numb.

Crashing the gate barely raised my resting heart rate.

The gate on the other side of the dam is open, so Henry doesn't have to do a repeat performance as we descend the accessway. We find ourselves in a sprawling flood basin, which means we've crossed from Orange into Riverside County.

Now my eyelids are becoming heavy. It must be the sleep debt I owe my body – the accumulated hours of missed rest over the past four days. Then I imagine the water debt we've all worked up by now. We were hydrated yesterday, but we've also been sweating a great deal in this heat. The last water we had was just the little bit that Alyssa's uncle gave us early this morning. Now it's way into the afternoon – almost evening. Water deprivation in hundred-degree heat doubles, maybe triples the dehydration clock. I'll be glad when the sun sets. I can only hope we'll reach the bug-out by then.

There's a smell of smoke in this flood basin. Faint, but constant. Probably from the various brush fires we heard about on the news. Bad air tends to settle in basins.

"Is this it?" Henry asks. "Is the bug-out somewhere around here?"

"Not even close," I tell him. "We're in the Prado flood control basin. Three rivers feed into here – or at least they used to. Take the left-most one."

"Great," says Jacqui. "Let's find out what's behind door number one."

We bounce and rattle over the dusty tumbleweed-ridden terrain, until we see another concrete channel up ahead, not quite as wide as the Santa Ana River. This one has sides that are straight up and down, no slope at all. There's the normal stuff you'd expect to see in a drainage ditch: old tires, rusty shopping carts, broken sofas that seem to have fallen from space – a brand new obstacle course. There's not enough junk to stop us, just to keep us on edge as we weave a serpentine path around it all.

"This is like the crap that gets caught behind furniture cushions," Jacqui comments, "but on a cosmic scale."

There's more graffiti on the walls of the ditch here, too. Colorful tags like "Rong" and "OrGie" and "Stoops," and others so stylized they seem written in an alien language, adding to the feeling that we're in a completely different world.

About an hour into this channel, we come across people who have set up camp on either side of the aqueduct, and it doesn't look like a new occurrence. There are dozens of pitched tent dwellings made of tarps and blankets and make-shift supports, like some sort of skid row. I think of what Jacqui said, and realize that it's not only *things* that get lost behind the cushions of the world. People do, too.

With the sun sinking low and shadows getting long, the place looks even more eerie than it would in the bright light of this hot day. The closer we get, the clearer it becomes that this is a permanent homeless encampment. If it is, they definitely haven't read *The Art of War*, which points out that setting up camp in a ditch is a death wish. High ground offers visibility, low ground leaves you open for an ambush. Still, I get the feeling that ambush is not high on their list of worries.

Alyssa keeps her gaze straight ahead. "Don't slow down," she says.

"I wasn't intending to," says Henry.

She keeps her eyes forward, refusing to even look at the people in the encampment. It seems out of character for her, and makes me think about how she agreed with my father yesterday. Either you give everything, or nothing at all – and I realize why she's refusing to look. For a girl like her, whose first instinct is always to fix a situation, the "nothing at all" choice isn't easy. It's painful. But after everything that's happened, she realizes that her and Garrett's survival requires the kind of aggressive hardness she usually reserves for the soccer field. Today there's no taking a knee for the players who fall.

As we slowly drive through the encampment, some of those lost souls emerge from their tents and watch us go by. They don't stop us, they don't bother us, they just watch. I think they're just being vigilant – making sure we don't stop to harass them. I look at their weathered faces, their worn clothes, and I wonder what their stories are and how they landed here. If there's anyone thinking about them, or wishing them well. Then I realize that by the way they're looking at us, they're wondering the same.

Soon we're past, and I hear Alyssa release a breath of relief.

"How much farther?" Henry asks, about forty-five minutes past the homeless encampment.

While it's not quite dusk, the entire channel is now in shadows. I squint. There's absolutely no signage on these aqueducts, let alone the fact that I can barely see, now that the sun has practically gone down.

"Just keep going," I tell him. "Eventually we'll get to the Foothill Freeway. The Angeles National Forest is just past that."

The compass now reads northwest, and everything feels

right – until we pass into a tunnel that at first I think is just another underpass – but there's no other side. We're suddenly in complete darkness. Henry hits the brakes, and we come to a stop.

"Turn on the headlights!" Alyssa says.

"I can't find them!"

I can hear Henry frantically scratching away at dials until he eventually finds the headlights. He flicks them on, and for the briefest, crazy instant, I expect to see something like a T. rex glaring through the windshield. I don't know why my brain dredges up that image, but when the lights flash on, I jump. Of course there's nothing there. Nothing but a drainage culvert. All we can really see are the ribbed walls around us, flaking with dried moss, and the tunnel ahead lit by our headlights. Correction. HeadLIGHT. Only one is working. Great. So much for nighttime visibility.

"So," Jacqui says to me, "is this part of the urban river experience, or are we lost?"

"Quiet, I'm thinking."

Like I said, I'd only been to the bug-out a couple of times – but we took normal roads. Dad had once brought us this way virtually, in an annoyingly detailed PowerPoint, but I think I would have remembered the endless black tunnel portion of the presentation.

"We must have missed a turn," I am forced to admit. And the thing is, I have no idea where that turn would have been. I know we took the correct path out of the flood basin. That was hours back. If there was a hidden fork it could be anywhere between here and there.

Then I begin to wonder if the walls deeper in the tunnel

might be moist. What if there's water down here? Which makes me think about the many species of animals that have most likely infested these parts, no matter how contaminated the water. Then I think about how many humans might have wandered in with the same intentions, and I realize that my brain short-circuited and kicked out the wrong image. It's not dinosaurs we need to be worrying about ... it's people.

"Turn around," I tell Henry. "Get us out of here."

But a U-turn is an impossibility. Henry kicks the car in reverse, and we roll backward until we're out of the tunnel. It's twilight now. Harder to see much of anything, and the channel is still too narrow to make a turn, so we reverse back the way we came. Slowly. Carefully, with nothing to guide us but our dim red taillights. Half an hour later, we still haven't found another fork.

"Are you sure we weren't just supposed to go straight?" Alyssa asks. "Through the tunnel?"

"Yes," I tell her. "No," I say. "I don't know," I finally admit.

"Maybe we can just back our way into the homeless camp," Jacqui says, oozing sarcasm. "I'm sure they'll be more than happy to help us."

We continue to wind backwards for a few more minutes, then Alyssa cries out.

"There! Do you see it?"

And there it is: a spur in the channel heading off to the right, due north. The mouth is choked with weeds, and there's some bright graffiti to the left – which pulled our attention the first time we passed. I'm incredibly relieved. If we couldn't find it, I had no idea what we would do.

Henry takes us out of reverse and steers us down the proper path, but not long after we begin our new route, the channel forks again. And now I'm questioning if we're even in the right aqueduct to begin with. Like they say, *When it rains it pours.* However, when the heavens have no water left to give, I'm starting to realize the Powers That Be just find the next best way to screw you over.

Because the low-fuel light pings on.

Of course. In all this time driving we never once thought about gas. I might have been to blame for misdirecting us, but for this, I blame Henry.

"How could you have not checked the gas gauge?" I say.

"Excuse me, but I've been a little busy!"

"What's the big deal?" says Jacqui. "Wasn't there an access path leading back up to the streets a little ways back?"

"What use is that?" Alyssa says. "The gas stations aren't pumping, and we'll be facing military detours again."

"Spoken like a true prisoner of lawful behavior," she says.

Alyssa doesn't get it, but I do. "So we siphon gas from an abandoned car."

Jacqui nods. "And I'm sure there are plenty of them on the freeway we just passed under."

27) Alyssa

Our entire dynamic has definitely changed since we brought Henry on. I can't tell whether that's good or bad. He's not the best driver, but he's competent, and keeps his eyes glued to the road. He did manage to get our keys back so we could get away from the evac center – and he seems to genuinely want to help us. On the other hand, he was taking advantage of the people in his neighborhood – including my uncle – and he kinda-sorta pretended to be someone he wasn't. I'm not quite sure what to make of him, and it's annoying that he's not all that unpleasant to look at, because that could cloud my judgment.

We have to backtrack a little farther than we would like to find the accessway to the street, and I'm just happy the truck hasn't run out of gas yet. We barely make it up the concrete path, which is so narrow that looking out of the window, I can no longer see the ground beneath us, and the steep drop to the bottom just continues to grow. If our right tires slip off the ledge, we'll flip multiple times before reaching the bottom.

Finally we make it to street level. I have no idea where we are, and the fact that so much of Southern California looks alike is disconcerting. I know it's not home, but it's familiar in its unfamiliarity. The neighborhood is older than ours, with aging ranch style homes, but a strip mall on the corner looks no different here than in my neighborhood. The air tastes acrid and burnt, and it's heavy to breathe in. It's smoke from the fires. They call this part of California the Inland Empire, and it's always smoggy, because whatever nastiness is in the air gets blown here and caught against the mountains. I feel like I played a soccer tournament in this town. Or maybe it was another town a hundred miles away that looked exactly the same.

We roll up to a freeway on-ramp, and Jacqui suggests that we reverse in, to get our gas tank as close as possible to which-ever car we choose. Funny how Kelton knows everything about this anarchic world, but it feels like Jacqui's already lived it.

Turns out, backing in isn't necessary, because, surprisingly, the on-ramp isn't congested with abandoned cars – but then, I guess that's not surprising at all. Anyone who realized that traffic was at a permanent standstill would eventually be able to back out. You'd have to be deep into the massive automotive clot to feel that abandoning your car was your only course of action. So the freeway is pretty much empty for fifty yards or so, until we hit the first abandoned cars, and finally the full-on clog through which there is no passage, and from which there was no escape.

Some cars are turned at bizarre angles. Some face in the wrong direction entirely. There are broken windows, doors wide open, an empty car seat on a roof. Up ahead I see an abandoned yellow school bus. The scene isn't quite like it was back at the beach, where the evidence of panic and violence painted a chilling story – and yet the abject nature of this abandonment is just as disturbing. People walked away with nothing but the clothes on their backs and their kids in their arms. Any vandalism must have come after the fact – and that implies that there might still be marauders smashing windows, and water-zombies wandering the labyrinth.

"First we're going to need to find a hose," says Jacqui, as we pull to a stop. We fan out, looking for a gardening truck or something that might have a hose, but no luck. Then, on a hunch, I check the back of Uncle Basil's truck. There's a lot of junk back there. Things that our uncle didn't have the strength to care about when he made the deal with Henry, so they just went along with the truck. Tumbled among the stuff that had been tossed around in our rough ride, I find his hookah. Mom always made him keep it in the backyard because she didn't want the thing in the house, and I remember him once mentioning that Daphne refused to allow it in her sight at all. So it stayed in the back of the truck, its four-foot hose hiding in plain sight. Hopefully, it will be long enough to do the job.

Henry backs toward one of the cars at the edge of the clot, and only after getting out to look for its gas cap do we realize he's not going to find one. It's a Tesla. Jacqui notices it first. She taps me and points it out, but doesn't tell Henry, who is still looking for a place to stick the hose. The rest of us get it now, but wait to see how long it takes for Henry to catch on.

I find myself smiling at the irony of it. Not just the Tesla, but Henry, in his entirety. The world goes dry, yet we find Henry totally oblivious, living in his own little oasis. He let us think he was someone else, for no apparent reason. He's clearly smart, but lacks basic common sense in the strangest of ways. He doesn't seem entirely trustworthy, but when you look in his eyes, you really want to trust him. It's like he *wants* to be trusted — as if the very act of trusting him will suddenly make him worthy of it. I want him to be worthy of our trust. So does that mean I have to trust him first? I can't help but be a little intrigued by his unknown quotient.

"Isn't anyone going to help me?" Henry finally asks, exasperated.

"No," says Jacqui. "Keep looking."

Maybe it's the smirk on her face that makes Henry re-evaluate and glance to the Tesla logo on the car.

"Right," he says. "Duh."

Garrett laughs, and I can't help but grin.

"Glad I could be tonight's entertainment," Henry says. "It's just one of the many services I provide."

I notice that although Henry left the keys in the ignition, trusting us, they're now in Kelton's hands. He gives them back to Henry so he can start the car and move us to a vehicle that actually runs on gasoline, but there's an unspoken message there. I'm not sure whether it's about distrust on Kelton's part, or power, or both.

We drive around the snarl of cars until we come across a gas-guzzling minivan. Jacqui gets out to guide us in. This time when Henry turns off the gas, he tries to take the keys, but Kelton hops out of the truck and blocks him from opening the driver's door wide enough for him to get out.

"Keys, please," Kelton says.

Henry forces the door open anyway, but Kelton stands in his way. I find myself irritated by Kelton forcing a confrontation now, when all we're here to do is get gas.

"What am I going to do?" Henry asks. "Drive off and head for the hills? a) We don't have gas; and b) You're the only one who knows which hills to head for."

But Kelton isn't up for negotiating.

Henry throws a quick glance in my direction, and says, "Fine," then tosses the keys to me instead of handing them to Kelton.

Kelton bristles at having been blatantly slighted. He looks to me like I'm going to give him the keys, but I'm not. Because he's the one being an ass right now. Instead, I slip them into my pocket. If Henry sees me as the voice of reason among us, so be it. If he trusts me, maybe that makes me trustworthy.

Mercifully, the little door over the gas cap is one that opens by hand, rather than having to be popped from inside the van.

"Okay, what now?" I ask Jacqui.

But she defers to Kelton. "I don't know – can't you Mac-Gyver something?"

He shrugs. "You're the criminal mind," Kelton says.

"What's a MacGyver?" asks Garrett.

Jacqui sighs. "An '80s TV guy with a mullet who could make cool crap out of nothing."

But none of us have either the mullet or the knowhow to do this. All we have is a hookah hose. I realize that we are, all of us, out of our element – even Jacqui. For all of her street smarts, siphoning gas is something she's clearly never done, and for all of Kelton's survival skills, he's useless in this particular pinch.

"All I know," I say, "is that you stick the hose into a gas tank and you suck on it." This is truly the blind leading the blind.

After four failed attempts and a mouth full of gasoline, Jacqui throws the hose to the ground, uncrowning herself the queen of thievery. I idly wonder if she had an urge to swallow the gasoline she got in her mouth, and it reminds me of my own thirst, but I push it to a back burner.

Meanwhile, everyone has an opinion on why the siphon isn't working – but our knowledge of this lost art is limited to fifth-grade science labs and movies. With everyone giving their two cents, I realize I haven't heard a peep from Garrett. In fact, I haven't seen him since our first siphoning attempts.

"Garrett?" I yell.

Crickets. Wind. Silence.

I check the pickup. Around the pickup. I run back to the Tesla. Nothing.

"Garrett!"

Kelton shushes me, and I know why – the distressed voice of a girl is a bleeding wound in a sea of sharks – but I don't have time to formulate a better course of action here. I have to find my brother.

Before I know it, my feet are churning, and I'm hurrying off – diving deep into the maze of cars. I'm weaving in and out, screaming his name, but in a whisper, which is as useless as it sounds. My head is spinning. The freeways are deathtraps, I know, Kelton's pounded it into our heads. And even if I'm not alone, if someone has Garrett right now, his well-being takes priority, and I must be fearless.

Then I see smoke swirling in the air up ahead. A fire. It's somewhere farther down the highway. I know there've been brush fires everywhere, but on the freeway? I push forward, climbing, sliding over cars – I trip and fall, but I won't let it slow me down. And now I have a better view.

It's a campfire in a trash can. And around it at least a dozen people.

And they have Garrett.

When Garrett was five, he wandered off the safari jeep tour at the zoo. I had to rescue him from getting kicked in the head by a giraffe. When he was six, he almost went home with another family at the mall because their kids had cooler toys. When he was nine, he wandered off at the Ikea showroom and decided to nap in a race car bed, in an attempt to become a permanent resident of the store — and I had to track him down before Mom and Dad found out and called in the national guard. Disappearing is what Garrett does, he always does it at the worst possible moment, and for some reason I always feel responsible. But this time, I'm more frightened than furious, because I've seen the monsters out there — and I suspect I'm going to see worse ones before this whole thing is over.

He stands in the middle of strangers who could be as hostile as the marauders that raided Kelton's house. I scan their faces, trying to get a read on the situation. People of all ages. Then Garrett sees me, and he smiles.

"There she is — that's my sister."

My heart is still tolling out danger. My head throbs, and I feel woozy from exerting myself. It's the lack of fluids. I approach cautiously — then a woman steps forward. Silver wavy hair, a soft complexion. Her eyes seem to glow, but it's only the reflection of the fire.

"Welcome," she says.

"Garrett, let's go," I order him.

"It's okay," he says, walking over. "I went looking for a bucket — you know, to drain the gas into — but I got lost. They found me."

I let my guard down a little.

"You must be Alyssa," the older woman says warmly.

"Who are you?" I ask, still on edge.

A little girl holding folded linens stops in passing. "We call her the Water Angel."

The older woman smiles kindly. "Oh, stop it. The name's Charity. Which is a much more charitable name than I deserve, but there it is."

Now having calmed down a bit, I get a better look at her. She's as old as my grandma, maybe seventy, though there's something youthful about her, too. The way she holds herself. Her sharp, radiant gaze.

Jacqui, Kelton, and Henry catch up, but keep their distance, still reading the situation.

"You could say we've taken up residence here," Charity says, addressing us all. "At least for the time being."

I look around and notice that there isn't just one campfire, but several, constellated across the span of the traffic-jammed freeway, in different clearings. This is nothing like the homeless encampment we saw before; these seem like people from many walks of life who have decided that staying here in the midst of the crisis is better than being anywhere else.

Kelton shakes his head. "But you're totally exposed out here. Isn't it dangerous?"

"At times," says Charity, "but we've found a way to keep everyone safe and hydrated."

That last word pulls us all in.

Jacqui takes a step forward. "You have water?"

"There's water everywhere," Charity says with a faint grin. "You just have to look in the right places." She examines our dirty clothing, and probably reads how exhausted we are, both emotionally and physically. "Why don't you stay with us?" she asks, and when we hesitate, she says, "Your brother seems to like it."

"This place feels okay," Garrett says. "Safe-ish."

And although safe-ish is probably the best we're going to get, Kelton is skeptical. "We have somewhere we have to be," he says.

"Well, at least stay the night. It's getting late. You can set out in the morning." Then she returns to the campfire, leaving us to talk.

Henry opens the discussion. "I say we stay. Rest. Hydrate."

"We have your entire box of ÁguaViva in the truck," I point out, and realize to my horror that we left it in the truck bed unattended. "Why don't we lock the water in the truck, accept their hospitality, and maybe even have these people help us siphon gas. Then we can leave."

"And go where?" Henry argues. "Back to those nasty-ass aqueducts, just to get lost again?"

"We weren't lost anymore," Kelton tells him. "And there's not that much farther to go."

And then Jacqui tips the balance. "The aqueducts will be easier to navigate during the day. Right? So let's accept the Water Angel's invitation and spend the night. It's not like we have to join their little cult."

Everyone agrees it's the best solution. Even Kelton, as reluctant as he is to trust anyone or anything.

I leave them to go find Charity. She's tending to a boiling pot. She's boiling water to purify it. "Okay, we'll stay the night," I tell her. "But do you think there's anyone here who can help us siphon gas?"

"Of course," Charity says with a wink. "How do you think we get these fires started?"

"And maybe some of that water, when it cools?" Jacqui says, coming up beside me.

But instead of responding, Charity steps forward and closely examines Jacqui's face. Then she takes Jacqui's hand and pinches it with her thumb and forefinger.

"OW! What the hell was that for?"

"I'm sorry, but I can't give you water now," Charity says. "Your skin is still elastic, which means your dehydration isn't critical yet."

"She's right," Kelton says, and Jacqui sneers at him, whispering "traitor" beneath her breath.

Charity looks to Garrett, who's still sitting with another kid he found, then to the rest of us. "I know how difficult it is to be thirsty, but I can't give you water in good conscience when there are others here who need it more. We can feed you though."

Food! I forgot about food. And now I can feel my stomach roiling, eating at itself. I'm hungry – but even if I'm given something to eat, it would be hard to chew, because my mouth is dry and raw. Even swallowing water right now would hurt like needles. And then there's the growing pressure in my head. If I'm not worthy of water in this state, then I can hardly even imagine what it's like to be worse off.

"We'll help you with your car trouble, give you shelter and something to eat," the Water Angel says. "That will have to do for now." Then she turns to a few rugged-looking men playing cards around the campfire.

"Max? Do you think you could help them out? They need gasoline."

"Sure." One of them stands. He's large and hulking, clad in leather like the leader of a biker gang. At first I'm apprehensive, but as I've come to learn, looks can be deceiving – because at the end of the day, no matter what the person's exterior, there's only one thing that defines behavior, and that's water. In my other life, I might not have trusted this guy. But here and now, I do. Because I know he's not a water-zombie. He hasn't turned yet.

I suddenly feel guilty for doubting their intentions.

"In return, however, I will ask you to contribute to our little effort," Charity says. "We'll be collecting supplies from the northbound lanes pretty soon. While Max here is fixing your car issues, perhaps a few of you could join us."

"I'll go," Henry says, stepping forward.

Garrett looks to him and follows his lead. "Me too," he says quickly.

My gut reaction is to volunteer just so I can look after Garrett. To make sure that he doesn't wander off again, or get into any trouble. But I stop myself. Lately Garrett hasn't gotten us into trouble at all. Maybe I owe him a little more space. A little more trust. And if he's trying to contribute to something larger than himself, shouldn't I allow him that dignity? So I let my sisterly guard down, tell Garrett to mind Charity, and I join Jacqui, Kelton, and the jolly gargantuan biker to fill up the truck.

We follow Max to a small, white landscaping truck, where he pulls out an empty red plastic gas can and a gardening hose – the kind we couldn't find when we were looking before.

"It's really hard to siphon directly from one gas tank into another. You need a gas can like this so you can position the hose lower at this end. You know, gravity."

"Gravity..." Kelton mutters, clearly annoyed that he couldn't figure that out himself. Garrett had figured that out instinctively, because he had gone looking for a bucket. We've all had an opportunity to feel stupid today.

We zigzag back toward the truck. My body has grown heavy, which makes each step weightier than the previous one. And it seems our exhaustion is a little more obvious than I'd like to believe, because Max takes notice. "Here." He reaches into his pocket and pulls out a little plastic-wrapped pastry.

"It's a MoonPie. Currently our staple food."

"Thanks," Jacqui says, opening the wrapper and biting into the chocolate marshmallow spongy thing. She chews on it dryly, realizes there's only one, and reluctantly breaks the rest of it in half for me and Kelton to share.

"*Bon appetit*. We found a whole truck of 'em two days ago," he says. Then adds, "A few years back, I remember hearing about a stranded cruise ship. They airdropped them Spam and Pop-Tarts. I don't know about you, but I'd rather have MoonPies."

"Is that how long you've been here?" I ask. "Two days?

"Three," he says. "I wandered onto the freeway two days after the Tap-Out. I had it worse than most people on account of my blood pressure meds make me sweat like a racehorse. Dehydrated real quick, and I couldn't get a drop of water for the life of me. I wandered onto the freeway, determined to either find water, or drop. I dropped. But the Water Angel found me. Charity gave me water, and when I was strong enough, put me to work. Before long there were dozens of us, all working and taking care of each other."

"Kind of like a commune," Kelton says.

"Yeah, I guess it just kind of evolved into that. We all have our own skill sets. Turns out I'm pretty handy," he says with pride.

"Well, you're a lifesaver," I tell him.

"Thank you, but we have a medic for that." He chuckles. "Others gather supplies. Just yesterday they found a semi full of new linens and pillows."

Just the thought of it makes me long for my comfortable bed.

"We have folks who keep a watch at the perimeter around the clock," Max continues. "Those are the ones who found your brother."

We reach the truck, and luckily the ÁguaViva box is still in the back. Max settles by a nearby Hyundai to siphon gas, and while I keep him occupied, Kelton and Jacqui move the ÁguaViva to the back seat of the truck, locking it in. Since it's not my water to give, I get around the crisis of conscience that would come from withholding the ÁguaViva from the Water Angel. Still, I feel guilty about it, but I'll live with the guilt. If that makes me a bad person, I'll care on a different day.

Jacqui and Kelton probably feel that urge to rip the box open – I know I do – but as Charity said, we're thirsty but not desperate. And Kelton has drilled into our heads that an emergency supply is for emergencies. Although I can't help but sense that desperation is right around the bend.

28) Henry

I have found that the elderly can be either deranged or saga-cious. It's a complex equation made up of their life experiences, the advanced nature of their years, plain old genetics, and how pissed off life has left them. The Water Angel is of the sagacious variety – wise beyond her years, which says a lot, considering how old she is. She has figured out a simple, brilliant way to collect water – water that's been right under everyone's noses all along, but is so far out of most people's boxes that they could die of thirst inches from the source and never consider it.

Washer fluid.

Not the actual fluid, but the containers that hold it, which are in every car. Most of the time people fill them with that blue Windex-y stuff, which is positively toxic – but every once in a while people can't be bothered with the good stuff, and use water instead. Who would have thought it would be that lazy substrata of society that would save us? Even if the Water Angel isn't willing to share with us, having the knowledge is enough. Teach-a-man-to-fish kind of thing. Of course, our truck doesn't have either water or washer fluid. It's completely empty, as I discovered when I tried to clean bugs off the wind-shield earlier.

We're sent in teams of two to search cars on the north-bound side of the freeway, maybe a quarter mile up, because all the closer cars have already been inspected. We're accompanied by a paunchy pair of twenty-something iden-tical twins. Tweedle-dum and Tweedle-dumber. There's a nagging mother and her seemingly mute child, and an older couple who have been married for so long they've morphed into near identical androgynous versions of each other. Each team is given a backpack, a flashlight, a coat hanger, and a crowbar. Many of the cars are locked, which means the hoods are unable to be popped, so we use the coat hangers to try to pop the locks, and if all else fails, use the crowbar to smash a window.

"It's not like we're destroying property that matters anymore," Charity told us before we left. "Chances are these cars will be bulldozed to clear the freeway when this is all over."

Although we've been instructed to be on the lookout for items that may benefit the greater good of the collective, I've been more interested in a wider variety of things.

See, in the heat of the moment, when people were escaping these freeways – something truly interesting happened. There was a cataclysmic shift in values. Kind of like a market crash. External events combined with mob psychology and generated a positive feedback loop. Well, not positive for them. Their only goal was to survive – which meant people were quick to forget items of high value that didn't improve their immediate chances of said survival. Watches, jewelry, cash – you'd be amazed by the things that turn up in cup holders and glove compartments. Not that these things were left on purpose, but stuff simply got forgotten because they were no longer on the radar of critical possessions. Sure, most cars contain nothing but junk, but I manage to acquire a few unexpected assets that would otherwise go to waste.

"Look what I found," says Garrett, looking in the rear window of a hatchback. Garrett indicates a bag of diapers in the back seat. "I remember there was a woman with a baby sitting back by the fire."

"Good thinking," I tell him, because value comes in many forms. "She'll appreciate that." And, I realize, so will the rest of us.

The door is, of course, locked, and multiple attempts to unlock it with the coat hanger are less effective here than elsewhere.

"I guess we're just going to have to break the window," I say.

To that, Garrett almost involuntarily gives a mischievous smile. That smile speaks volumes. It says he wants to break things, but never had permission. He wants to be wild, but has never been off the leash. I know that feeling – and I realize that I can save him years of future therapy by one simple action.

I hand him the crowbar. "You do it," I say.

He looks a little scared. "Are you sure?"

I shrug. "Charity said we could if it was the only way in, right? Go on, give it a shot."

Garrett hefts the crowbar, gives that involuntary smile again, and swings it at the window. It shatters with the first blow – not an explosive sound, more like the popping of a light bulb, followed by the patter of safety glass pellets. I'm actually surprised by how much force he put behind it. I thought the first swing might be timid.

"Well done!" I tell him. "Try another."

Without hesitation, he turns to the car behind us and swings again, smashing the closest window.

"My turn," I tell him. I see a Mercedes with a hood

ornament. The car looks like my asshole neighbor's, who sued us for building a retaining wall two inches onto his property. I take a swing at the ornament, fully prepared to see it fly off like a golf ball, but instead it gets knocked over and pops back up into place. Darn. I forgot that Mercedes ornaments do that – so they don't get ripped off in car washes. I take a second swing, and it pops up again. It makes Garrett laugh.

"It punked you!" he says.

"Oh yeah? Take that," and I smash off a side mirror.

Suddenly there's one of the Tweedles lumbering up to us. "Hey!" he yells. "You're supposed to be looking for water!"

"We couldn't get in," I inform him. "Had to smash the window."

He glances at the dangling side mirror. "That's not a window."

"Guess I missed."

Garrett snickers, and the Tweedle glares at me. "Stay on task!" Then he lumbers back to his brother, who has been gingerly trying to get into a Buick for five minutes.

I turn to see Garrett grinning at me – and I realize he's looking at me in a way that he doesn't his sister. He's clearly never had an older brother figure in his life. It puts me in a unique position.

I lean against the car and speak casually. "Your sister would kill me right now if she saw what we were doing."

"Who cares?" He reaches for the crowbar, but, as a surrogate big brother, I hold it out of reach, indicating that's enough. For now.

"Funny how she treats you like you're just a kid," I tell

him, "even though you're the one with most of the good ideas."

He looks to me, just a little bit wide-eyed. "You think that?"

"Are you kidding me? If it weren't for you we wouldn't have found the aqueduct. And aren't you the one who found these good people? Thanks to you we have a safe place to spend the night."

"Yeah, I guess so."

"We all have our skills. Yours is seeing things that the rest of us don't."

It's true, and I can tell he appreciates that I've noticed what others overlook – just like him. It's a nice bonding moment. One that serves a purpose...

"So tell me," I put to him, "what other things do you see that the others don't?"

He considers it, then says, "Well, I don't think Jacqui is as horrible as Alyssa makes her out to be."

"Really, what makes you think that?"

"Well, it's like the girls on her soccer team. Alyssa always trash talks about the ones she kind of sees as a threat. I'll bet Jacqui and my sister could be friends if they weren't both so set on hating each other."

A sharp observation. Useful, too. If I can keep them turned against each other, they're not turned against me. Or at least, Alyssa isn't. After nearly stranding Jacqui at the evac center, I doubt I'll ever win her over, but I may not have to. "How about Kelton?" I ask him.

He laughs. "He's just glad to be in the same car with my sister. Kelton's had a serious crush on Alyssa since, like, forever!"

I feign shock. "Get out of here!"

"No, seriously. When they were in elementary school, he'd hit balls into our yard on purpose, and when they were in eighth grade, I caught him spying on her with one of his helicopter drone cameras. He paid me ten bucks not to tell her!"

Not quite the information I was fishing for, but when you catch a boot, you never know what else might be lurking inside.

"Spying how?" I ask.

And he sits on the big pack of diapers to spin me a nice little story.

We return to camp to join the others about an hour later – and though Garrett and I didn't find any washer reservoirs that contained water, some of the others did. But we pulled our weight in other ways. We found some painkillers, a Bluetooth speaker fully charged, binoculars, and of course, the diapers.

Charity travels around, picking and choosing who is most in need of the water she has, while our little group is brought to five cars near the guarded perimeter, the back seats of which have been spread with linens. Someone has left a MoonPie on each pillow. Real concierge service.

"There you go, Garrett," Alyssa says, "didn't you always want a car bed?"

Garrett is not amused.

Jacqui looks at her MoonPie. Banana flavored. "How can we even digest these without water?" she says. "And how do I know I won't die of thirst in my sleep?"

"You won't," Kelton says. "You'd have to be a lot worse

off. You'll feel more and more tired – but then, right before the end, you'll get a sudden burst of energy. It's the body's last stand. After that, it's all over."

"TMI, Kelton," she says, not wanting to think about it. "TMI."

We should all call it a night, but we're at that state where we're too exhausted to sleep, and none of us is looking forward to sleeping in this heat – which seems only a few degrees cooler than the day. I take my acquired letterman jacket off and set it on my lap, wishing that its manufacturers could have had the good sense to use a fabric that breathes.

The five of us now hang out in a small clearing in between the cars to wind down. The trash can fires are out, and the moon paints everyone in blue shadows.

"I really don't get it," says Jacqui. "How are these people not tearing each other apart, like in every other place we've been?"

"They created a system," Alyssa says. "Not everyone can do that."

I feel a need to enlighten them. "Communism only works in theory, and goes against human nature. This place won't last."

"It doesn't have to," Alyssa points out. "Only until the crisis is over."

"They'll turn on each other," Jacqui says. "Everyone does eventually."

Alyssa throws her a glare. "Everyone like you, maybe."

"Oh, are you gonna tell me your neighbors weren't like these people? Fine, upstanding citizens, until they started eating their young?"

I glance to Garrett, who just shakes his head knowingly at me. Jacqui and Alyssa will never agree on anything.

"People suck," Kelton says, adding his own two cents. "Always have, always will."

"I don't see it like that," Alyssa says. "People might do whatever they can to survive, but once they don't have to worry about that, they're different."

"Sometimes," Kelton argues. "Sometimes not. Some people are always like that and just pretend to be civil."

He says that looking at me. I'm not sure if that's intentional, but it still pisses me off.

Jacqui bounces her knees, amused. "Ooh, looks like we've got ourselves a classic Hobbes versus Rousseau philosophical quandary."

It catches me off guard to hear Jacqui make such a reference. Especially because I don't precisely know who Hobbes and Rousseau are – but not knowing and admitting you don't know are two completely different things.

"Yes, that's one way to see it," I tell them. "But I think you're both wrong. People are nouns, actions are verbs. Apples and oranges."

"Ding! Ding! Ding! And we've found our Machiavelli!" Jacqui announces, like a showman. And then suddenly, as absurdly and unexpectedly as she pulled philosophers out of her ass, she pulls a gun out from God knows where. A gun. A real. Freaking. Gun.

We all jump out of our skin, but maybe me more than the others. Did she have that all along? And now I'm thinking back to the dozens of times she could've shot me today – like when I pulled that airsoft gun on her. Not my best move.

"Dammit, put my gun away!" Kelton says, adding one more layer to this crazy cake. Did he say *his* gun?

She just ignores him, marveling at the weapon, turned on. Invigorated. "Tell me, Henry, if I put one of these bullets right into your head and got your brains all over Kelton and his MoonPie, would I be a noun or a verb?"

"Jacqui, put that away before anyone else sees it!" Alyssa growls.

But it only energizes Jacqui. She will not be controlled, and now I get why Alyssa sees her as a threat. Because she is.

"C'mon, Henry," Jacqui taunts. "I thought you were the captain of the debate team – or at least pretended to be." Then she points the gun at me. "Convince me that I am not my actions. That doing something bad doesn't make me bad."

I talk fast, trying to pretend I'm not a thumb-pull away from oblivion. I don't know if that gun has a safety on it. Hell, I don't even really know what a safety is. "You wouldn't be good or bad, right or wrong, because concepts are fluid, and subjective, and it would flip depending on whether or not killing me was the right thing to do, but it's not – it most definitely is not!"

Jacqui holds there. Everyone else is frozen. No one wants to jump in and maybe accidentally set the gun off. Finally, she withdraws her arm and tucks the gun away, suddenly disinterested. "You're no fun," she says.

Jacqui goes back to eating her pastry, speaking with a full mouth. "You're a bunch of scaredy-cats anyway – there was no bullet in the chamber," she says. "Or was there...?"

Mental note: There are now two confirmed psychopaths in our party of five. Kelton and Jacqui will have to be taken down if I am to assume my rightful place in charge, and protect Alyssa and her brother.

29) Alyssa

I lie in my makeshift bed, eyes peeled open. At least I think they are. I don't have the energy to sleep, or to be awake. So I toss and turn, in and out of consciousness in a delirium of anxieties that haunt both states. Thoughts of Jacqui. The gun. My parents. Mixed with nightmares of marauders raiding the freeway like they raided Kelton's home – led by Hali on my soccer team and her mother, who's now fifteen feet tall and steals everyone's water. Then it starts to rain blood, and Kingston is there, lapping it all up. The rain resolves into a tapping noise… My eyes snap open. It's Henry, and he's standing just outside my car, tapping on the half-open window. It's still dark. I'm not sure whether it's somewhere around midnight, or closer to dawn.

"You were talking in your sleep," he says. "I could hear you from my car."

"Oh. Sorry." To be honest, I'm glad he woke me up. As tired as I am, I'll take him over the hallucinations, so I open the door and get out, stretching.

"Have you noticed that it's snowing?"

"What?"

Sure enough, there are snowflakes settling gently around

us. But it's got to be almost ninety degrees. Now I know the world has gone crazy.

"Don't catch them on your tongue though," Henry says. "I don't think they'll taste very good."

I catch one with my hand, and rub it between my fingers. It's ash.

"The brush fires have grown up," he tells me. "They're full-fledged forest fires now. Pretty far east of us, but the Santa Ana winds are bringing the ash our way."

As I look around, the cars are beginning to grow a fine layer of gray dust.

We lean against the side of my Cadillac, watching the "snow" settle.

"It's so quiet now," I say. "It almost makes you forget what's out there."

"Nothing out there but people," Henry points out.

"People can be monsters. Whether it's just their actions, or whether it's who they really are, it doesn't matter. The result is the same."

Henry shrugs, as if it doesn't bother him. I wonder if he's really so nonchalant about it, or if it's just an act for my sake. "Sometimes you have to be the monster to survive," he says.

I shake my head at the thought, then grimace at the pain that comes with moving my head. "I could never be that kind of monster," I tell him. "No matter what."

Rather than commenting on that, he lets another "snow-flake" land on his palm, studying it for a few moments.

"I wanted to apologize," he finally says, "for not telling you the truth about not being the guy my jacket says I am – but with all that was happening, there didn't seem to be a right time."

No apology is complete without its "but." Well, at least he's trying. So I decide to let him off the hook. I know it's stupid of me to trust him, but I decide to do it anyway.

"I get it. Common courtesies have gone the way of running water," I tell him. "No one's acting the way they usually would."

He smiles. "You're a very forgiving person." His smile seems genuine, and I look away from his gaze. I wonder if it's possible to see a blush in ashen moonlight.

"Not really," I tell him. "I just don't hold grudges." Which isn't entirely true; I hold plenty of grudges. But right now it would be a waste of valuable energy.

"But you *are* forgiving," he insists. "You let me come with you, even after acquiring your uncle's car. And it looks like you're beginning to forgive Jacqui for … well, for just being Jacqui. You even forgave Kelton after the whole drone thing."

I get caught on that last part. "What?"

"You know. How he used to spy in your window with his drone?"

But I don't know. I have no idea what he's talking about. My stomach begins to fill with a weird, greasy feeling.

"Who told you that?"

"Garrett may have mentioned it in passing. But don't get him in trouble. I only bring it up to add evidence to my argument about your forgiving nature." Then he grins. "I did pretend to be captain of the debate team, you know."

But right now, I don't feel forgiving at all. I feel stupid.

And embarrassed. And violated. My face must be turning a much more visible shade of red now, because Henry says—

"Wait – you mean you didn't know?"

Why should I be the one who feels embarrassed? Kelton's the creep here! And before I know it, I'm abandoning Henry, and I'm storming over to Kelton in his stupid little hatchback, pounding on the door, then kicking it, until he pops his nasty little orange head up and opens the door.

"What? What is it? What's happening?"

"Did it feel good, Kelton?" I growl. "Did it? Was it fun? Was it everything you thought it would be?" I know, in the midst of everything going on, that this is not the highest priority right now, but it feels like it. It feels *huge*.

"What? What are you talking about?" he stammers as he scrambles out to face me.

"Did you or did you not spy on me with your drone!"

He hesitates. That's all the answer I need. I push him back against the car. "You lousy! Stinking! Creep!"

"Alyssa, it was in eighth grade!"

"There is NO statute of limitations on being a certified DOUCHE!"

"And I only did it once!"

"It doesn't matter how many times you did it! The fact is you did it!"

"Alyssa…"

"Don't you say my name!" I yell at him. "Don't you even *think* it. *Ever*!"

I storm away from him, because I know if I stay I'm just going to keep on screaming, and that will wake up half the people here and make them come running, and I don't want this to be any more of a federal case than it already is. There's a battle in my head now. Part of me wants to file this away and deal with it when we're not in a crisis. His brother is dead. There are more life-and-death challenges we have to face. Yet there's the other part of me that will not be silenced or ignored. The *normal* part, which won't let such an unacceptable act slide just because there are bigger things to worry about. No matter what else is going on, I have every right to what I'm feeling!

I go back to my car. I'm thirsty, and I'm angry, and I think maybe I'd rather face the nightmares than this, after all.

Henry appears at the window. "Alyssa, I'm sorry. I didn't mean to upset you…"

"Well you did!" I snap. Then I feel guilty about it. So I speak a little more gently. "I know I shouldn't blame the messenger, but it's hard not to."

"I understand." Then he puts his hand on the door handle. "Can I come in?"

I actually consider it. But right now I want to keep all of humanity at a ten-foot-pole distance. "I'll see you in the morning," I tell him.

"Okay," he says. "Sleep well."

But we both know there's zero chance of that.

PART FOUR
BUG-OUT

30) Kelton

Alyssa isn't talking to me, Garrett won't look at me, and Jacqui seems to find that amusing.

Henry says nothing, silently smug behind the wheel.

Garrett confessed what he told Henry, and Henry didn't waste any time sharpening it into a weapon to use against me. I occupy my mind thinking of all the painful moves I can inflict on Henry once we reach the bug-out. Dislocate his other shoulder, snap his arm, kick out his kneecap. I know the moves, and am pretty confident I can execute them. All he has to do is give me a reason. Exposing my middle-school creepitude to Alyssa should be reason enough, but that was really just my own karma coming back to bite me. As much as I want to, I can't make any sort of move against Henry until he proves himself to be the clear and present danger I suspect he is. But I can't act on a feeling. Especially when Alyssa trusts him a whole lot more than she trusts me.

It's been half an hour since we left Charity's little freeway commune. We cleaned up our camp at dawn, folded the linens and returned them. It felt good folding the linens. It felt decent. Funny how that used to be my least favorite chore. We said goodbye to some of the friends we made during our brief stay, like Max the handy biker. Then the Water Angel sent us off with more of those marshmallow sponge cakes, and then gave each of us hugs. Standing there in her embrace, in a weird, childish way, I didn't want to let go.

I know that Alyssa didn't want to leave. I was actually surprised that she didn't decide to stay, just to be rid of me. I mean, she would have gotten water there. Or at least she would when she got dehydrated enough. Maybe she couldn't bear the thought of me getting to the bug-out, and getting water before she did. Or maybe she didn't want to part with Henry. Why bother breaking a limb? I could jam the heel of my hand into his nose and drive his nasal bone into his brain.

We had to move the ÁguaViva box back to the bed of the truck to make room for all of us in the cab – which was hard to do without raising suspicion. There was a quiet discussion as to whether or not we should pull a couple of bottles from it to drink now – and this time, even I was willing to do it ... but there was no way to open the box without revealing to Charity and her freeway folk that we had water.

"If they know about it, you know what'll happen," Jacqui said. "She'll claim it's community property, divvy it out to her minions, and there goes our emergency supply."

I expected Alyssa to argue, because she's the only one of us altruistic enough to be okay with that. But she didn't. Maybe her anger at me has spread to the rest of the world.

We agreed that we would pull over and open the box when we were far enough away, but now that we're moving, Henry flatly refuses to stop.

"We're almost there – why stop now? We can all hold out for another hour, right?"

"Yeah, we can wait," says Garrett, who suddenly became Henry's lapdog when no one was looking.

And since no one wants to show less self control than a ten-year-old, we all accept it.

"But if it's more than an hour, I'm kicking you in the head until you stop the car and let us get water," announces Jacqui. I'd be happy if she started kicking him in the head right now, but I keep that to myself.

I look through the car window. There's a haze that hangs in the air, thick and caustic. All of Southern California is blanketed in wildfire smoke. The dawn is angry crimson, and the sun – which has now risen enough to peer out from behind the mountains – is practically maroon, looking more like a blood moon than the sun.

We haven't put music on the radio this morning. Instead we switched back from satellite to the standard stations. Most stations are either offline or have triggered the emergency broadcast network, so it's the same thing almost everywhere. Mostly stuff we already know. Evac centers are at capacity – people are to go straight to overflow facilities, blah blah blah.

We keep listening to the broadcast, because I need to know about the fires. Three are burning far to the east – one completely blocking the road to Big Bear Lake. Two are burning in Castaic, more than fifty miles west of us, threatening access to Castaic Lake – which millions from Los Angeles are trying to reach.

One report talks about relief coming to beaches again sometime today, but there's no way to know how successful this second wave will be. I imagine World War II and the

Allied forces storming the beaches of Normandy, but with water instead of weapons. An operation like that would take months to organize. Whatever they're planning today, it's doomed to fall far short of what's needed.

"If there's fresh water at the beach, maybe we should go there instead," Henry says, having no idea what the rest of us have already been through.

"Just drive," Alyssa says, not wanting to explain.

We're only down in the aqueduct for half an hour before we emerge and follow a foothill road far enough from civilization to be beyond most roadblocks. Finally we come to a sign that says NOW ENTERING ANGELES NATIONAL FOREST, with a red placard that says FIRE RISK: HIGH. Big duh.

It looks like there actually had been a roadblock here – cones and plastic barriers – but they've all been pushed aside and the site is unmanned. Apparently, the personnel were needed elsewhere. We keep driving, and the road begins to wind.

"It's not far now," I tell everyone. "About ten miles up, look for a dirt road off to our left. Drive slow, because it's easy to miss."

"I have a headache," announces Garrett. As if we all don't have headaches.

"It's from the smoke," Alyssa tells him, although it's probably more from the dehydration. "I'm sure there's Advil at the bug-out."

"There is," I tell her, but she doesn't even acknowledge that I spoke. She's disgusted to be in the same car with me. I guess I would be, too. Of course, if it were the other way around – if she had a drone and looked in *my* window – I'd be flattered. Unless she was laughing. No, I guess I'd feel just as creeped out. I should probably just let her beat the crap out of me, and get it over with. But I suppose in our current situation, crap-beating is not a priority. And now I feel stupid for even worrying about it. As if my humiliation means anything in the big picture we're facing. And yet in my moronic head, it does. Stupid.

"Is that the road we're looking for?" says Jacqui about fifteen minutes later.

"Yes," I say, although to be honest, I'm not a hundred percent sure. But we'll know soon enough. "Turn here."

Henry veers off the paved road and onto the narrow dirt path. The truck barely fits between the trees, and the road is rugged. The truck's suspension absorbs the worst of the bumps, but it can only do so much. My brain rattles against the walls of my skull. Garrett moans, telling Henry not to go so fast, but he's not going fast at all.

"What are we looking for?" Henry asks.

"We'll go over a ridge, then back down into a valley," I tell him. "Eventually we'll come to a dry, rocky wash. Once we're there, turn right and follow the wash for about three clicks."

"Exactly what is a click?"

"A kilometer."

"And then we'll see it?"

"We won't see it," I tell him. "That's the whole point of a bug-out."

Ten minutes later we come to the wash, and I breathe a secret sigh of relief, because it means this was the right dirt road after all. Henry turns right, and we follow the rocky path, avoiding the boulders and ditches along the way. Finally we come to an upturned tree stump with a red ribbon caught in its dead, gnarled roots. Only it's not caught, it's tied there. It's our marker.

"Stop," I tell Henry. "We're here."

We get out of the car and I lead everyone up the embankment of the wash, and back into the forest. About a hundred yards in, I stop.

"We're here," I tell everyone.

"We're where?" asks Jacqui. "I don't see anything but a whole lot of trees."

"Is it underground?" asks Garrett.

"Nope." Then I just stand there, waiting, wondering who will be the first one to notice.

Alyssa's the first. I was betting she would be. She gasps and points. "There!" she says. "It's mirrored!" She runs a dozen yards ahead, and the rest of us follow. As we get closer, the illusion weakens, but only because the glass has gotten dirty.

Our bug-out is a small A-frame structure — the mirrored side walls slope so that they reflect the higher reaches of trees, instead of reflecting people who might be approaching. It's an exceptionally successful camouflage.

"I suddenly love your seriously disturbed family," Jacqui says.

Just like at home, there's a hidden key. It's in a knothole in a tree, although it takes me a few minutes to find the right tree, then a couple of minutes more to poke into the knothole, dislodging a spider and a bunch of other unpleasant critters that have taken up residence there. Finally, I reach in and pull out the key.

I stride triumphant to the door — which is also mirrored — and slide the key into the deadbolt lock.

"Welcome," I say, "to Castle McCracken!"

31) Jacqui

How many lifetimes have I gone through since the riot at the beach? I'm used to life changing in the flicker of an instant, but the Tap-Out has left every single moment a threat. How I live now is not the same as any of my yesterdays, and that void that always taunts me is now a moving target, making me lose all sense of direction.

But right now I don't care about any of that. All I care about is having a nice long drink. Doesn't even have to be cold. It just has to be liquid.

Our unlikely crew of accidental survivors now stands outside Kelton's family bug-out, while Kelton makes a big production of opening the door.

"Welcome to Castle McCracken!"

"Just let us in already," says Garrett.

Finally Kelton turns the key and pulls the door wide.

Castle McCracken my ass! The bug-out has bugged out. The place is a mess. There are cans on the ground, clothes tossed everywhere. Empty cereal boxes dumped on their sides. The place is small, but seems even smaller with all the junk spread around it. It's like a bear slipped in through the keyhole.

"This isn't right..." says Kelton. "We didn't leave it this way..."

"When was the last time you were here?" Henry asks, examining a spoon with peanut butter caked on it.

"Maybe a year ago?" Kelton says, like it's a question rather than a response.

It looks like I'm the only one with the courage to speak the obvious. "There was a break-in."

But Kelton shakes his head. "There's no sign of that. The lock was intact, and it's not ransacked."

"Looks ransacked to me," says Garrett.

"Yeah," agrees Kelton, "but not in the way a burglar would."

Exploring deeper, Kelton pushes open a door to a bedroom. Two beds. One is made, the other disheveled. There are comic books on the floor.

Kelton seems to reel out of his skin. "No!" he says. "No no no no no!"

He doubles back, pushing past the rest of us and to the kitchen, pulling open cabinet doors. The cabinets are virtually bare.

"No no no no NOOOO!"

He kneels, pulling open a trapdoor, and drops inside. We can only watch his panic, not wanting to make it our own. He bumbles around down there. I can hear the ponging of jugs – and he hurls up a couple of them up. When I look down, there are a whole bunch of plastic jugs down there. Empty. All empty.

"If it's not a break-in, then what the hell happened here?" I ask.

"My brother happened here!" he says, with so much anguish in his eyes, I have to look away. "This is where Brady must have been living! We knew he lost his job and bailed on his roommates. We thought he might be living with his girlfriend. It never occurred to us that he might come here. Where he knew there was food and water enough to last for months…"

And I realize that "was" is the operative word here. "Was" is the difference between salvation, and doom.

32) Alyssa

This is not the end of the world, I tell myself. *This is just a glitch.* And now I'm grateful that Henry was so obstinate about not opening the box of ÁguaViva. With all the forces that have been mobilized to bring relief, it will be a while until the supply chain can meet the demand – and the ÁguaViva will get us through that time. There will be people – lots of people – who won't be able to hold out that long, but we won't be among them. Thanks to Henry. He wanted so badly to be the hero. Now he is.

Kelton keeps digging through the storage space below, pulling out every plastic water jug, trying to get even the tiniest drops out, but all the jugs are open, and any moisture that had been left in them has long since dried up.

"I can't believe Brady did this!" he wails. "How could he do this? He knows better!"

"*Knew* better," corrects Jacqui, and I hit her hard enough

to generate a warning glare, which I return with equal ferocity. Has she already forgotten how terrible Brady's death was, or is she so callous that she just doesn't care?

Jacqui turns to the pantry and starts pulling out Styrofoam noodle cups. "Well, at least we have plenty of chicken-flavored Top Ramen," she says. "'Just add hot water.'" Kelton groans.

I turn to Henry, who has been unusually quiet through all of this. He offers me a slim, pained grin, and I try to offer him one back that's not quite so stretched.

"Some alkaline-infused goji berry mineral water sounds really good right about now," I tell him.

"It does, doesn't it?" he says, with a little chuckle.

"Kelton, give it up," says Jacqui. "The bug-out's a bust. Back to the truck."

Kelton is reluctant. He keeps digging through the same empty jugs, like he's going to find something different. Finally he gives up. He climbs out of the crawl space and kicks the jugs in frustration. They make a sad noise, like muted church bells. When we leave, he doesn't even close the door, because what would be the point?

We make our way down to the truck, which still waits for us by the upturned stump, and Jacqui hops in the back, pushing things out of the way until she gets to the box. She hoists it and brings it out, setting it down. The corners are a little dented, but otherwise it's intact. She attacks the tape with her nails, but it's thick strapping tape, and there are multiple layers.

"Does anyone have a Swiss army knife?" She turns to Kelton. "How about you, Survival Boy?"

"Yeah, there are plenty of knives back at the bug-out," he

says, but none of us, least of all Jacqui, wants to wait that long.

"I'll go get one," Henry volunteers, but he's overruled.

"Forget it," says Jacqui, and holds out a hand to him. "Keys, please."

Henry takes a step back from her as if there were a weapon in her empty hand, but Jacqui's wriggling fingers are insistent. I'm pretty sure I know why he doesn't want to hand them over. Once Jacqui has those keys, she's never giving them back to him. In the end, he relents, and hands the keys over to Jacqui. I wonder why he didn't just take over the task of opening the box himself – after all, it's his box – but the thought flits out of my mind before I even have time to really consider it.

Jacqui finds the sharpest key and starts slashing at the tape, then sawing it, then stabbing it.

"C'mon!" says Garrett. "Hurry up!"

Jacqui grunts in frustration. "What idiot tapes up a box like this?"

Finally she gets a good size hole in the tape and starts working it larger, until she can get her hand in and rip a whole flap off the top of the box. Then, with the box finally open, she just stands there. Instead of reaching in and pulling out water bottles, she just stares into the box.

"Aw, you gotta be kidding!" she says. "No freaking way!"

"What?" I say. "What is it?"

Instead of answering, she dumps the box over, and out spill hundreds of glossy brochures.

ÁguaViva! Hydrate with Elegance!

Pictures of slim, happy people jogging and a glistening mountain spring that makes my soul yearn to be in the picture.

The sight of the pamphlets hits me like radiation. That is to say, I feel the sudden blast of this terrible truth, yet I know the full ramification of it hasn't settled in yet. But it will. I think to the empty jugs in the bug-out. Then flash to the people behind the football field fence so desperate for water that they would sell their souls for a thimbleful. And then I flash to the rush Henry was in when he traded the box to get the truck keys back. How he wanted to get away as quickly as we could. Before that soldier opened the box. And I realize that this is not just a tragic mistake. Henry knew. He knew all along. Which is why I'm not entirely surprised when Garrett says:

"Henry's gone!"

33) Henry

In life, one should always have an exit strategy for any given situation. I've always known this – lived by it, even – but in this particular instance, I was caught woefully off guard. It never occurred to me that the bug-out would be a nonstarter. Because as much as I dislike Psycho-Ginger, I believed he had our backs. Serves me right for letting my guard down.

In a perfect world, no one would ever have opened that box. It would have been like Schrödinger's infamous cat. As long as the box stayed closed, there might actually have been water in there. At least as far as the others were concerned. And who's to say if their reality was any less real than mine?

But when the box was opened, that all became moot. If I had my wits about me, I would have slipped out and taken off with the truck the moment I realized there was no water in the bug-out. I should have abandoned any and all hope of being this ill-fated group's glorious savior, cut my losses, and bailed. But I hesitated. And that hesitation cost me everything.

So now I'm left to stumble through the woods, no vehicle, thirsty beyond belief. I remember the way we came. I know how far it is back to civilization, if you could even call it civilization anymore. My plan is simple. I will make my way back to Charity and her freeway commune. I will make myself an indispensable part of her little collective, and I will receive enough water to survive. It will be a long, difficult trip, and although I have doubts as to whether or not I can make it, I have to try. It's all a matter of risk tolerance, and in this volatile world, what other choice do I have?

But before I even get back to the road, I'm tackled to the ground. My first thought is that it's a bear – but then I realize it's much worse.

34) Kelton

People trying to escape don't act in the smartest of ways. For example: Henry Not-Roycroft. He took a direct path away from the truck – straight up the slope of the wash. But to get back to the road, he'd have to turn right once he reached the crest of the little ridge – so, just like in hunting a small-brained quadruped, I triangulated his course and ran the hypotenuse.

I scrape my knuckles on a rock pretty badly as I'm taking

him down, but the pain is a good kind of pain. It helps me to focus my anger where it belongs.

Now I've got him pinned with my knee on his xiphoid, making it hard for him to breathe, much less move. Quickly I clamp my right thumb and forefinger around his windpipe. I've seen this in demonstration videos, so I know the theoreticals, but in practice it's different than I imagined. The windpipe doesn't stay put. It shifts and slides around. It takes a moment until I'm sure I have it. I know because I can't hear him breathing. With all the air pushed out of him with my knee, it will only take about ten seconds to render him unconscious. Twenty seconds to give him brain damage. Thirty seconds to kill him. My fight function is now engaged. That, combined with my rage and my thirst, leaves me uncertain of which of the three outcomes I want.

"Kelton, enough!"

I snap out of it at the sound of Alyssa's voice and release Henry's throat, grateful that she was there to make the right decision for me, because I know I might not have. Henry gasps and coughs and gasps again. There's no fight or even flight left in him now. He's little more than a rag doll on the ground, just as he was when I dislocated his shoulder.

"Call off your goddamn pit bull!" he rasps.

"It's okay, Kelton," Alyssa says. "He's not going anywhere."

And so I let him go. Not because I want to, but because the orders Alyssa is giving me now are the first things she's said to me all day.

By now, Garrett and Jacqui have arrived. And it looks like I'm not the only one harboring homicidal intentions, because

Jacqui pulls out my gun and aims it point-blank at Henry's forehead.

"I will be solving so many problems if I pull this trigger," she growls.

"Stop it!" demands Alyssa. "Killing him won't solve anything!"

"All right, maybe not, but it'll feel really good."

"Put that away!" Alyssa yells, but Jacqui is not following anyone's commands, least of all Alyssa's.

And then Henry begins to grovel for his life. "Please," he whimpers. "I'm sorry. I'm so so sorry for everything..."

"The only thing you're sorry for is being caught," says Jacqui, which is probably true.

And then Garrett, feeling this betrayal more deeply than anyone, says, "Do it! Do it, Jacqui!"

Alyssa reels at that, horrified. "Garrett!"

"Do it! He deserves it! He lied to us! He tricked us! He pretended to be our friend!"

As I recall, Garrett had also wanted me to pull the trigger on the blond water-zombie at the beach.

Now a stain spreads across Henry's crotch. He's wet himself. Not much of a stain – he doesn't have much water in him. I have no sympathy. Maybe I will if Jacqui shoots him. Right now, not so much.

Jacqui looks at Garrett, almost as surprised by his outburst as Alyssa is. Then she ejects the magazine and fires the bullet that's already in the chamber into the sky. It echoes back and forth between the mountains around us.

"What is wrong with you?" Alyssa yells.

"If I didn't shoot it in the sky, it would be in his skull right now," Jacqui says.

"More likely the ground right behind his skull," I point out, being that it's such close range.

Jacqui storms off, and Alyssa burns Garrett a glare. "Go with her. Make sure she doesn't do anything stupid."

"Like I could stop her."

Alyssa holds her brother's gaze, and I know what she's thinking. *Are you broken, Garrett? Has all of this broken you worse than it's broken the rest of us? And if the gun was in your hands, would Henry be dead now?*

"Just go," she says.

Now it's just me, Alyssa, and Henry. He's recovered enough to make a run for it, but he doesn't even try because he knows I'll just take him down again, and he's deathly afraid of me. Funny, but no one has ever actually thought of me as a legitimate threat before. No one's ever called me a pit bull. Mostly, kids like Henry have either ignored me or seen me as a joke. But now I'm Kelton the Intimidator. If I survive this, I'll have a shirt made.

"I just want to know why," Alyssa says.

Henry can't look at her. Good. He doesn't deserve to look at her anymore.

"If I didn't have something to offer, you would have just left me there in Dove Canyon to die along with everyone else!"

"So you lied."

"I never said there was water in that box. You just assumed."

Alyssa looks like she might kick him. That look is sweet revenge. Almost as good as if she actually did kick him. But since she doesn't, I do a little bit of my own tormenting.

"If we change our minds, there's a shovel back in the bug-out," I say. "And the ground here on the ridge is soft enough to dig a grave…"

"I'll make it up to you!" Henry pleads. "All of you. I promise."

"Just shut up, Henry," Alyssa says. "Or I swear I'll get that shovel myself."

35) Alyssa

Henry may have killed us all.

I don't want that thought in my head. I want to focus on the solution, not the problem. But the thought keeps worming back in, undermining every attempt to rout it out. I think of all the things we might have done differently if we knew there was no water in that box – including leaving Henry in his fancy air-conditioned house. But who am I kidding? If I knew he had no water left, and he wanted to come with us, I would have fought to bring him with us.

But had we known, maybe we would have made a real back-up plan. Now we have nothing. Nothing but despair and that singular nagging thought: Henry may have killed us all.

We take him back to the bug-out with us – because if we just let him go, he'll probably die before he gets out of the woods, and I don't want that on my conscience. Jacqui insists on binding his hands so he can't do much of anything – and so he won't forget he is now under house arrest. I don't argue with her because maybe it's the right move. I trusted Henry and look where it got us. Even Kelton agrees that it's better having him under our watchful eyes than out there where we can't see what he's up to. From this moment on, the best policy is suspicion on all fronts.

In the bug-out we strategize our next move. Garrett is despondent, just slumped in a corner. "I'm conserving energy," he says. "Isn't that what we're supposed to do? Conserve energy?"

"We have enough gas to get back to the freeway," I tell everyone. "We'll find Charity, let her know what happened. She'll help us."

"If she hasn't been taken out by marauders," says Jacqui – a ray of light, as always.

"I have a better idea," says Kelton. Then he searches through a few drawers, until coming up with a map. He spreads it out on the small kitchen table.

"We're here," he says, pointing. "And Charity's there – about thirty miles away. But look at this." He brings his finger to a long, Y-shaped lake west of us. "The San Gabriel Reservoir."

Jacqui scoffs at it. "Haven't you heard? The reservoirs are all dry. That's what you get for looking at an old paper map."

"Yes," says Kelton. "The Cogswell and Morris Reservoirs are gone – but the lake behind the San Gabriel Dam is maintained for firefighting aircraft. I'm sure of it."

"How can you be sure about anything?" Jacqui snorts.

"Because it's why my father chose this spot for the bug-out. It will be way down from its usual level – but there'll still be some water there."

By checking the distances on the map, I can tell it's just ten miles west of us – much closer than going back to Charity.

"We'll have to go totally off-road for a while. We can cross this ridge here," Kelton says, dragging his finger along the paper, "and pick up East Fork Road here. That will wind to the lake."

"Sounds like a plan," says Henry from his spot in the corner. Jacqui kicks him – not hard enough to hurt him, but just enough to make it clear his input is not welcome anymore.

"Are we all game for this?" Kelton asks.

The answer is no, but no one admits that. Because if we want to live, it's the best choice we have.

There are a few backpacks and drawstring bags around the bug-out. I gather them up and hand them out. "Let's look around and grab things we might need – but don't weigh yourselves down."

I'm about to hand one to Henry, but he holds up his bound hands and shrugs. If I want him to participate, I'll need to cut him loose. So I don't give him a bag.

Then Jacqui does something I'd never expect her to. She gives Kelton back his gun.

"Here, take it," she says. "I don't want it in my belt anymore; it's giving me a rash." Then she glances over at Henry. "Besides, I don't trust myself with it, considering our current company."

Kelton takes the gun back, surprised by the offer. "So you trust me now?"

"Absolutely not," Jacqui says. "But at least if *you* do something stupid, it will be your problem, not mine."

Jacqui herself is a loaded gun with a hair trigger – and the fact that she, in this moment, is able to recognize that, makes her seem slightly less mental. Maybe even trustworthy.

I open the pantry, trying to see if there's anything other than the dry ramen cups. Nothing, but that doesn't mean we won't find something lying around.

"We should probably eat anything we find that's actually edible," I tell the others. "We'll need the energy." I pick up the spoon with dried peanut butter, hold it out to Garrett, and he gives me a look of profound disgust. "Beggars can't be choosers," I tell him.

"Obviously you've never met the beggars in Laguna Beach," Jacqui says. "I happen to know several of them." And then she starts to mimic them in various different voices. "'Hey, lady, this sandwich has a bite taken out of it!' 'Excuse me, but is this bread gluten-free?' 'Just a dollar, dude? Maybe you could send me a little more on Venmo.'"

It sets me off giggling, which gets everyone else laughing. And it occurs to me that even in these do-or-die moments, there's still space for us to laugh. I guess that means we still have some fight left in us.

36) Kelton

There is absolutely no reason for me to take comic books with me. They will take up space, and I'm definitely not going to be reading them. But there they are on the floor of the second bedroom. The room that was supposed to be for me and Brady if our family ever had to use the bug-out. As I lean over to pick them up, I can smell his sheets. Sour. There's no air-conditioning in the bug-out — just a fan, powered off the same miniature solar grid that powers the lights. The fan probably drains the battery halfway through the night.

It smells like his room used to when he lived at home, a faint vinegary reek that would cause Mom to break out the Febreze on a regular basis. After today I will never smell that again.

I'm taking his comic books. I don't need them, but I don't care. I'm taking them anyway.

Then, when I look up, Alyssa's standing at the door. I don't know how long she's been there watching me.

I pick up the comic books and put them on the bed. I won't let her see me pack them. This is between me and Brady.

"My brother was a real screw-up," I tell her. "I mean, he uses up everything in the bug-out, doesn't answer our calls, and then shows up at home just in time to get himself killed. If that's not the definition of screw-up, I don't know what is."

"I'm sorry, Kelton."

And then things start coming out of my mouth that I don't mean to say out loud, but I can't stop myself. "I don't have a brother anymore. I might not have parents. I don't even know what happens if I live through this. I mean, if my parents are gone too, what then? Do I go to Boise to live with my goddamn Aunt Eunice and her cats? How is that better than dying of thirst?"

"Tomorrow is going to have to take care of itself for a while," Alyssa says. Then she adds, "Yesterday, too."

I know what yesterday she's talking about. I force myself to hold her gaze, no matter how raw and stupidly naked I feel in front of her – and make no mistake about it, this is the true meaning of nakedness. If I had no clothes on, that would be nothing compared to the kind of bareness that's exposed to her right now.

"Saying I'm sorry for that thing I did in eighth grade feels stupid – because sorry isn't enough. Sorry is almost an insult."

"You're right, it's not enough," she says. "People go to jail for stuff like that."

"True. But I'm a minor," I point out. "I'd have just gotten juvie and counseling – but yeah, I get your point."

I look down at the comic book in my hand, which I've managed to spindle without even realizing it. I lay it flat and try to smooth it out. "I won't even say, 'It seemed like a good idea at the time,' because even then, I knew it was a really bad idea."

"But you did it anyway."

"Haven't *you* ever done something really stupid, and you knew it was stupid but did it anyway?"

She bristles at the suggestion. Maybe because she's never done anything so entirely stupid and misguided in her whole life. I realize she has not once asked me *why* I did it. Maybe because she knows. The truth is, loneliness and hormones and parents who keep you like a fish in a bowl can do weird things to a person. Life through a fishbowl lens is only one step away from life behind the lens of a drone's camera.

"It was the creepiest thing I've ever done, and I was so disgusted with myself, I never did it again." I hope she believes me, because it's true.

Then Alyssa asks me the last thing I expect her to ask.

"So what did you see?"

"Huh?" I say, not because I didn't hear her, but because I'm not ready to go there.

"You looked, you saw. I want to know what you stole from me that night."

I wonder what she's expecting me to say. I wonder what she *wants* me to say. It doesn't matter, because I just tell the truth.

"It was the week of that air-band contest at school – you remember that?"

She groans. "I try not to."

"Anyway, you and your friends had been practicing a routine, lip-synching some ridiculous pop song, but I guess you couldn't get the moves right because that night you were in your room by yourself. You turned on the song, and you were practicing in the mirror."

"Really?" she says flatly. "Is that what you wasted your drone on?"

"You were using Kingston's brush as a microphone, but dog hair kept whipping in your face, and it kept throwing you off. I remember thinking, *Here she is, looking in the mirror, watching herself doing something so silly and so dumb, but she doesn't feel dumb about it at all. But me? I can't even look in the mirror and do* anything *without feeling like an idiot*."

"That's where you're wrong, Kelton," she says. "I did feel like an idiot. But I did it anyway."

Then she asks me to stand up for a second, so I do. I'm facing her, not quite sure what this is about … until she suddenly hauls off and slaps me.

This is not your ordinary slap. This is like a Major League Baseball swing, with a wind-up and full follow-through. My head whips nearly around with the force of it. It leaves me in shock. I can't even speak, and I know there's going to be a puffy red handprint on my left cheek for a good long time.

Finally I find my words somewhere in the far corner of my rattled brain. "I guess I deserved that," I tell her.

"Yes, you did," she says.

"Are we even?"

"No, we're not."

I sigh. "I didn't think so."

"Part of your punishment is that we'll never be even."

And I get that. The worst part about doing something inexcusable is that you can never take it back. It's like breaking a glass. It can't unbreak. The best you can do is sweep it up, and hope you don't step on the slivers you left behind.

But then she leans in and places a gentle kiss on my stinging cheek, like a mother kissing a little kid's boo-boo. She leaves without a word of explanation – and I come to the grand realization that from now and until the end of the universe, if I live a hundred thousand lifetimes, I will never understand girls. And somehow that's okay, I think.

PART FIVE

HELL AND HIGH WATER

37) Jacqui

My mouth is dry and tastes like I've been chewing the soles of old Nikes. It tastes like I've been sucking mud. Moist, glistening mud. It's actually enticing. Never mind an ice-cold can of Dr Pepper dripping with beads of condensation – I'd definitely settle for mud right now. Funny how the needs of your own body redefine the parameters of what you'd settle for.

I climb behind the wheel again. Whether Alyssa likes it or not, I'm the one who has to drive, because Henry sure as hell isn't. And as neither Kelton nor Alyssa are anywhere close to having a license, they have no other choice. It's either that or walk.

"My father felt I needed to earn the privilege of driving," Kelton says as we get in. "But I think he was afraid of giving me too much freedom."

Alyssa's reason is more self-imposed.

"I put off getting my license because of soccer practice, homework, and the fact that I know my parents couldn't afford to get me a car right now, so what was the point?"

"For people who want to survive," I tell them both, "you made some pretty useless life choices."

"Oh," Alyssa snaps, "and your choices were good ones?"

"Just shut up!" yells Garrett. "Everyone just shut up!"

And so we do. Because grumbling at each other isn't helping anything. And besides, our voices are all beginning to sound raspy. Pushing air across my vocal cords is hurting more and more, and I know it can't just be me.

"When this is over," Henry says, as I start the car, "I hope we'll all be able to let bygones be bygones."

"When this is over," I tell him, "it will be my absolute pleasure to never see any of you ever again. But you especially."

I put the car in gear and turn on the useless fan. I'm not exactly sure of the time, but it's much hotter than it was when we arrived. Ten in the morning, maybe? Eleven? Kelton points out that even nonfunctioning air-conditioning makes us burn gas faster, and I tell him where he can shove his useful information. Gas is not the problem anymore – we have more than enough to get us where we're going. The problem is, we're facing a classic example of *You can't get there from here*. The map showed that the road we took into the forest turns away from where we need to go, so the only way to get to East Fork Road is to either backtrack twenty miles, or go through the woods, which, according to Kelton, is only a four-mile trek.

One of the maps Kelton brought shows elevation and the steepness of the terrain, so we know how to get there without falling off a cliff. Unfortunately, it doesn't show trees and boulders. We have to meander like a Mars rover to forge our way through the woods, weaving a slow and unpredictable path.

"I don't even know if we're going the right way anymore,"

I say – only realizing after it's out of my mouth that I've said it out loud.

"We are," says Kelton, although he doesn't sound too confident.

Then, halfway down the next slope, a bright yellow plane rips overhead. My first instinct is to jump out of the car to shout and wave like a deranged island castaway, but before I can give in to the impulse, the plane is gone.

"That's a firefighting craft," Kelton says excitedly. "See, didn't I tell you? It's going the same place we're going – which means we're headed in the right direction!"

It's the first bit of encouraging news we've had in a long while.

We continue to zigzag up and down the hills. Every bump hurts. Not just my head, but my bones. Whatever it is that lubricates joints I think must be in low supply now, because every moving part aches. My fever's gone, so I know it's not that. It's the thirst. Has to be.

"Watch out!" Alyssa yells.

I slam on the brakes and turn left to avoid hitting a tree that seemed to have leaped suicidally into our path. Yes, I know it must have been right in front of me, but I'm just not seeing things right. It's not that my vision is blurry, it's just that my brain isn't doing a good job of creating the full picture. As slow as I'm going, I'm going to have to slow down even more. Suddenly it seems like going back to Charity would have been the better idea. But it's too late now. At this rate, we might not reach the road until dark – and the thought of that fills me with such misery, I have to fight it with fury. How dare this forest be so hard to navigate? I think to the parts of it that are burning down, and although arson is not in my personal bag of issues, I have no sympathy. Right now trees and nature are the enemies.

38) Henry

My wrists hurt from the plastic tie cutting into my skin. What do they think I'm going to do if I have my hands free? Strangle someone? Well, maybe I might. Now.

I'm up against the right side door. I could try to lift the lock when no one's looking, open the door, and throw myself out, but what good would that do? No, my fate is tied in with everyone else in this truck. Until the moment it isn't. I must keep my wits about me, because there are always opportunities. Even when all options seem to be gone, fortunes could change at any time. I must be ready to seize the moment when they do.

39) Kelton

Headache, rapid heart beat, exhaustion, burning eyes, dizziness. I know the symptoms of acute dehydration. We could go maybe six or seven more hours without water now. Then we fall into a coma. Then we die. Simple as that. How much water will it take to save us? More than a thimbleful, less than a cup. It won't really hydrate us, but it will keep us from dying.

It will give us time. But I don't think there's as much as a cup of water between here and our destination. We have to get there. Period.

Right now, our lives depend on my ability to navigate and Jacqui's ability to drive. But what if I'm wrong, and the San Gabriel Reservoir is as dry as the rest of them? Do we just lie down on the cracked, dried mud of the lake bed and call it a day?

I find myself thinking about all of the second- and third-place ribbons and trophies in my room. Everything from robotics to marksmanship to chess boxing. My father said it was okay to have a few of them up, but didn't want me to display the rest. He felt all those nonwinning awards would be "a shrine to mediocrity," and such a thing was beneath me. But my mother overruled him, so the wall was enshrined. On good days I could look at it and see the accomplishments. On bad days it was a reminder of all the ways I am deficient. So I guess they were both right.

But when it comes to survival, all I know is that there are no second- and third-place trophies. There's just the gold, or the ground. And I don't think the others realize how close we are to the end of the line.

40) Garrett

Where are you, Mom and Dad? Are you as thirsty as we are? I think I'm gonna die. But if you're already dead, I'm not so scared. Except I *am* scared — but not so scared if you're there and you're waiting for me. And if there's water.

Or does thirst follow you there? What if that stupid longing for something cold and wet doesn't go away even after you die? I could swallow a river right now. I could drink Niagara Falls.

My eyes are open, and they hurt when I close them, and they hurt when I open them again. The corners where tears come out feel like someone stuck a pin in them, they're so dry. So I squint, trying not to open my eyes too wide. I see the windshield and I think, for a moment, that it's a TV screen and I'm just watching TV. All of this is someone else's pretend life. It's like I fell asleep in front of the screen with my eyes open. And that's a good feeling. And so I let the feeling linger until it feels a little bit true and I feel a little bit better.

There are people talking now, but I don't think there's anyone actually speaking, and that's how I know I've started dreaming – but I'm still awake, too. I don't know what that means, but then I think maybe, just maybe, this is what it's like when you start turning into a water-zombie.

41) Alyssa

Just don't think about it. Make yourself not think about it. I remember hearing somewhere that the human mind can only hold three things in conscious thought at any given time. And if I fill up all three spaces, I won't think about how thirsty I am.

Think about the reservoir. No, because that will just make me think of the water I don't have. Think about school and that last bit of homework I never did. And biology. Mitosis. Meiosis. Protein synthesis. It all requires water. Not helpful.

Subject one: soccer. I'm driving toward the goal. Passing back and forth. And wonder of wonders, Hali actually passes the ball to me instead of hogging it. Good. Good.

Second subject. Geography. I think of states. Countries. My father got me a geography coloring book when he found out that the asinine California school system decided they didn't need to teach geography anymore. A coloring book? Really? And yet it was great. I would think I was procrastinating, when in reality, I was memorizing the geography of the world. France is green and looks like a man with a goatee and his nose in the air. Egypt is a yellow trapezoid with one right angle, and looks like the cornerstone of a pyramid. Greenland is blue, just to be ironic. So soccer and geography. Good.

Subject three. What is subject three? Spanish. *Si, Español. Pedro tiene la bolsa de Maria. ¿Donde está el baño? ¡Quiero agua! ¡Por favor, agua agua agua!* This isn't working.

I turn to see that Henry is watching me. I wonder what he's thinking, and then I realize I don't care. Soccer. Geography. Spanish. That's all I can care about right now.

"I'm not the terrible person you think I am," Henry tells me. "If you met me in the real world, I know you would have liked me."

"But we never would have met, so why does it matter?" I point out. "You live in a mansion in a gated community and go to an expensive private school. What are the chances that we would ever have met?"

"It's not a mansion," he says. "It's just a house. And we

341

might have met if you came to visit your uncle." He looks off into space as if imagining that alternate reality. "If we had met, I would have asked you out to a fancy dinner, and I'd be sweet and considerate, and listen to everything you said. And when I wasn't listening, I'd be charming you with my sparkling wit."

"Sparkling..." echoes Garrett wistfully, and I know he's thinking of something cold with bubbles.

"You would have liked me," Henry says again.

"I *did* like you," I remind him.

Henry sighs. "Past tense. Maybe I can make it present tense again."

I don't answer him. Right now I have no interest in connection with anybody. The only thing I want to connect with is liquid across my lips. I could fall in love with a glass of water much more than a human being right now.

Jacqui suddenly stops the car.

"Are we there?" Garrett says weakly. "Please tell us we're there."

"Quiet!" Jacqui says. "Do you hear that?" She rolls down her window the rest of the way. The stench of smoke is stronger now than before. I wonder if the winds have shifted in our direction. Now, with the windows down, we can all hear what she heard. There's music. Someone's playing music!

42) Kelton

This could be a really good thing, but there's a voice inside of me – most likely my father's paranoid voice – telling me to be careful. That things that seem too good to be true always are, without exception, too good to be true.

"We should check it out," says Alyssa.

"I'll go," I tell everyone, before someone else volunteers.

"Always the Boy Scout," sneers Jacqui – and although I expect her to argue, she says, "Fine. The rest of us will stay here and enjoy the nonexistent air-conditioning."

It's an indication of how much the thirst is getting to her, if she's willing to let me take charge of a situation. But volunteering for this has nothing to do with my being a Boy Scout. It has to do with caution over curiosity – which I have right now much more than any of the others. I am just paranoid enough to hedge my hope, and that could be something that saves us.

It's torturous getting to the top of the ridge, even though it's not all that steep and it's just a few dozen yards ahead of us. My legs are weak and I'm dizzy, but I can fight that. For now. As soon as I get to the top, I hide behind a tree and peer out. The music's louder and now I recognize the tune. It's *Kashmir* by Led Zeppelin. That familiar relentless beat and exotic, yet somehow ominous riff fills the air. Robert Plant's voice wails above it all like some sort of religious chant.

There's a small camper down there – an old one. Rusty. Must have been there for a long time. This is a bug-out – I recognize that right away. Nothing as elaborate as ours, but a bug-out all the same. Two men sit out front in folding chairs. They have weapons – nasty ones – which isn't surprising. They're roasting rabbits over an open fire. How stupid to have an open flame when everything's so dry – but I sense that consequences are not a high priority for these men.

And then one of them lifts a water bottle to his lips.

The power of my craving is like an electrical surge. It's almost impossible to resist. I want to hurl myself down there and grab that water – even though I know I'll get shot trying. But somehow that doesn't seem to matter as much to my zombie-brain as grabbing that water. It takes every ounce of self control I have to stop myself and curtail my biological imperative.

There's something wrong here, that voice in my head says. I look for something incongruous in the scene to confirm my analysis, and I find it. Because there's a purse on the ground, items dumped. No sign of its owner. My neck hairs raise. This isn't just a bug-out, it's a lair, and we have to stay far, far away. See, I've been to plenty of prepper conventions. There are basically two kinds of preppers. First are the ones like me and my family. We arm ourselves and stock up, but only to protect ourselves from the chaos. Then there are the ones who *bring* the chaos. They wait for things to fall apart. They long for the lawlessness. Feed on it. Because there's nothing more exciting for them than the moment the world becomes their own personal video game.

Those are the kind who play loud music in the woods that can be heard for miles, just to see who it attracts. They are the wolves waiting to see what kind of prey comes calling. But just like their open flame, they have failed to consider the consequences. Because if it's another predator who shows up instead of prey, these two can be picked off with a couple of well-placed shots.

A twig snaps, and I spin to see Alyssa coming up behind me.

"They have water!" she whispers – she's seen it, too.

"Shhh!" I tell her, because the song is fading. We hold our silence, hold our breath until the next one starts. They didn't hear us. Dear God, I hope they didn't hear us. As the sounds of another Zep tune begin to blare, I move Alyssa farther away.

"We don't want anything to do with that water," I tell her.

"But —"

I can't take the time to explain to her now. I grasp her shoulders. I look in her bloodshot eyes. "You have to trust me," I tell her.

And she does. Reluctantly, but she does. And we return together to the truck.

Jacqui's kept the engine idling to keep the fan on, even though it's just blowing hot air.

"We have to get out of here," I tell her as we climb in. "Don't gun the engine. Just leave as quietly as you can."

"Why?"

"I'll tell you later," I say, "but we have to leave NOW."

For a moment, I think Jacqui might cave and accept my assessment of the situation, but Alyssa feels that she has to explain. That's not what we need in this moment. What we need is speed and stealth.

"There are a couple of guys down there. Kelton thinks they might be dangerous."

"Do they have water?" Jacqui asks.

Alyssa hesitates, and that tells the others all they need to know. Jacqui opens the door and gets out of the car. While I can resist my zombie urge, Jacqui's all about impulse, and I can see her turning. I get in front of her before she can make a mistake that will likely get her killed.

"We're maybe an hour away from the reservoir," I remind her. "Then we'll have all the water we need."

"Sounds like these guys are a bird in the hand," Jacqui says. "So let's make them share."

"Don't you get it?" I hiss. "They are not the sharing type, and they have guns that are bigger and badder than my Ruger!"

And suddenly a new voice enters the conversation. One that's been mostly quiet.

"Alyssa … I don't feel so good." Garrett stands just beside the truck. He wavers for a moment like he's on the deck of a ship weathering a storm. Then his eyes roll back, his knees give out, and he collapses.

Alyssa hurries to him. I help her pick him up and put him back in the car. Henry gets out of the way so we can lie Garrett down on the back seat.

"I think it's okay," I tell Alyssa, who has forgotten anything else now but her brother. "His blood pressure's probably low, and he stood up too fast, that's all. He just has to lie down for a while." I hope I'm right.

That's when I realize that something has changed. It takes a moment for me to realize what it is. The truck is no longer idling. The engine is off. Not only that, but the keys are gone. And so is Henry.

43) Henry

There is no turning back, and no margin for error now. The opportunity presented itself and I took it, simple as that. Now I must follow through. Game theory suggests that success favors the decisive. Taking any action is always better than taking no action at all. So while the others argued and dealt with Garrett, I did what I had to do. Alyssa will not forgive me, I know, but I find that bothers me less than I thought it would.

I follow the music, crest the ridge, and see the two men in their encampment. I hurl myself down toward them, falling to the ground and scraping my palms. I am on all fours and out of breath. They stand up and look at me, amused that I've tumbled into their presence.

"Looks like we got ourselves a lunch guest," one of them says, but I'm not interested in their lunch and they know it. Because my eyes are fixed on the bottle of water that one of them holds in his big, hairy hand.

When it comes to survival, there are harsh rules that go against the niceties of gracious living. Like in an airplane when the oxygen masks drop and everything goes haywire, they always tell you to put on your own mask first before helping others. But what if there's only one mask, and you're the one who gets it first? Well, I suppose you feel bad for the others, but whatever you do, you don't give that mask away. You breathe, and you breathe deep.

"What can we do for you?" the one holding the water asks.

"Today..." I say, too winded to finish the thought, so I try again. "Today is your lucky day."

Then I stand up, force fortitude to my legs, and begin negotiations.

44) Alyssa

I stay with Garrett, not willing to leave him for a second. Kelton races off to track Henry, while Jacqui desperately tries to hotwire the truck – but it's just not working.

"Old cars are easy," she says. "But newer cars have a damn digital verification chip, and I don't think I can get around it!"

I know this is a terrible thing to say, even think – but right now I wish Jacqui had shot Henry when she had the chance. Why would he take the keys? What was he thinking?

Then the two men from the rusty bug-out come out of the woods in front of us – and I know where Henry went ... and exactly what he was thinking when he went there.

"Hey there!" the taller of the two says. "Having some car trouble?"

In spite of the friendly greeting, there's nothing else friendly about them. Up close these men are intimidating, and intentionally so. They're muscular. They look like maybe they're thirty, although they're weathered in a way that makes it hard to tell for sure. The shorter one has tattoo sleeves. Not artful ones, but ugly ones. Scrawled words and symbols, and all in the same bluish black ink. The taller one has a shaved head and a scar that cuts diagonally across part of his scalp. We're always told not to judge a book by its cover, but there is nothing ambiguous about these two. Some people lack the imagination to do anything but embrace a stereotype and let it define them. These men lead violent lives, and they're happy to let the world know it.

"Easy to get lost when you're off-roading," the one with the shaved head says. "Is that what you are? Lost?"

I quickly look around. Kelton isn't back from his search for Henry. It's just me, Jacqui, and Garrett, who's still unconscious in the back seat.

"We don't want any trouble..." I say, although out of the corner of my eye, I can see Jacqui ready for all sorts of trouble.

"That's good, that's good," says the inked one. "We don't want trouble either. But I'm afraid you're gonna have to step away from our property."

"Excuse me?" says Jacqui.

Then the inked one holds up my uncle's key chain. "We just bought it," he says. "Your friend sold it to us for a nice guzzle of water."

The bald one laughs when he sees the look on Jacqui's and my faces. "Yeah, we poured it right into his hands and he sucked it all down. Some of it spilled on his shoe, so he took his shoe off and licked the rubber dry. Damnedest thing. Then he took off down the mountain, one shoe on, one shoe off. Funny kid."

And I think how unfair it is that of the five of us, Henry's the only one who's had water. Probably enough for him to get out of this forest alive.

"I'll ask you one more time," says the inked one. "Step away from our property." And he pulls out a no-nonsense handgun.

He's not going to use it, I tell myself. *It's to make a point.* Like everything else about these two, it's meant to intimidate. But I will not give in to the intimidation.

"We're going to the San Gabriel Reservoir," I tell him, not moving away from the door. "Let us get there, and then you can have the truck."

The inked one shakes his head. "Already a done deal. Nothing more to talk about."

"Now hold on," says the skinhead. "Let's not be hasty." And he drags his eyes across me, looking me up and down like I'm something up for auction.

That's when Jacqui makes her move. She launches herself at the inked one, trying to grab his gun, but he's quick. He uses moves on her like the ones Kelton used on Henry – but this guy is stronger, faster. His moves are second nature. Jacqui doesn't stand a chance. He uses her own momentum against her, twists her around like he's leading her in a swing dance, and forces her to the ground, pulling her arm at an unnatural angle, leaving her on her knees grimacing and grunting in pain.

"Play nice, now," he says, and he doesn't release her arm, which keeps her incapacitated.

Meanwhile, the skinhead hasn't taken his eyes off me. He moves closer. "Sucks for you that your boyfriend sold you out to save himself."

"He's not my boyfriend," I say reflexively – but I wish I had said nothing.

Because the skinhead says, "Even better," and he keeps moving closer.

I try to knee him in the groin, and he reacts by lurching

forward, pressing up against me, pushing me back against the side of the car, and leaving my knee no leverage.

"We could share our water with you, if you'd act a little more civilized..."

But by the way he's pressing up against me, I know his idea of civil is not the same as mine. I can smell his breath now. Cigarettes and Doritos. I don't think I'll eat Doritos again for the rest of my life. I try to struggle, but I'm so weak from dehydration now, it's useless. I've never felt this helpless, and it's an awful, awful feeling. Because I realize he can do anything he wants to me now, and I'm not going to be able to stop him.

"Don't you worry your pretty little head," he tells me quietly. "We'll go back to our camp, and it's all gonna be okay."

Then suddenly Garrett's there, jumping out of the car, and grabbing at him.

"Get away from my sister!"

He bites the arm that's holding me – and this burst of energy that Garrett has must give him superhuman strength, because it's like the bite of a shark, leaving a bloody, gaping wound.

The skinhead screams in pain and pushes Garrett to the ground. I try to use the moment to break free, but he's got me wedged so tightly, I still can't move.

"You little shit, what did you do?"

Then the inked one looks at the blood pouring from his buddy's arm, and he turns, pointing his gun right at Garrett.

"Nooo!" I yell—

And the world ends with a gunshot.

45) Jacqui

I see what's happening. I see all of it, and I can't stop it. I can't even get up, because the goddamn tattooed bastard twists my arm whenever I try to move. All I can do is curse at him and threaten what I'll do to him when I'm free.

I see the other one advance on Alyssa. I see her try to stop him. I don't hear what he whispers to her, but it can't be good. Then Garrett sits up in the car, finally conscious, with no idea what's going on – and seeing his sister cornered by the skinhead, he leaps right into the middle of a situation that's only going to get worse.

The skinhead is screaming from one hell of a bite, and the inked asshole, almost like it's a reflex, aims the gun at Garrett like he's about to shoot a rat that wandered into their camp. And in spite of the pain I tug my body around, screaming, because if I can throw this guy off balance, his shot will go wild.

A gunshot goes off, and suddenly his knees give out, and he goes down, and there's blood on his face – and there's blood on Garrett's face too, but Garrett isn't dead. And I realize that the blood on Garrett's face, dripping from his mouth, is from the bite he gave the skinhead. But the inked asshole's blood is his own. He's on the ground with a bullet hole in his forehead just above his left eye. He shudders once, then goes limp.

And Kelton stands ten yards away, arm extended, his gun at the end of it.

The other man freezes up, shocked. "Jesus H. Chr —"

But he never completes the invocation of his lord and

savior, because Kelton shifts his arm, fires again, and the bullet hits the skinhead in that space just beneath his nose. The exit wound splatters blood all over Alyssa's face. She's already screaming, so she just continues. I don't think she has any idea yet what's going on. All she probably sees in her mind is her brother dead on the ground, because that reality seemed so big a moment ago, it persists even after reality shifted elsewhere. If she lives through all of this, she's probably going to have nightmares about that moment that never happened for the rest of her life.

The skinhead crumbles. I get to my feet, and Alyssa finally finds her way back to the real world. She steps over the dead skinhead and goes straight to Garrett.

"Are you okay? Are you okay?" She wipes the blood from his mouth, reconfirming that it's not his.

He nods. And she hugs him in a way that sisters never hug brothers, except when they're almost shot in the head.

I go over to Kelton, who still holds the gun, eyes on the two men like they might still be alive, maybe because they kept their brains in their asses. Finally he lowers the gun. I think he might start shaking, or break down in some way, but he doesn't. Not at all. I hate the fact that he had to save us – but the situation could just as easily have been reversed, with me being the one to save the day. And as much as I hate to admit it, Kelton – who has actual training with weapons – is probably a much better shot than I am.

Kelton takes a deep breath, and then another. "Get the car keys, and get their guns," he says calmly. "Then we'll go to their camp and get their water."

"Good thinking," I say, noting how different this kid is now than the Kelton I met at the beach. I'm not sure which one I dislike less – the goofy loser who can't fire a weapon, or the kid who can kill two men in cold blood and not break a sweat.

Well, none of us are sweating anymore. And we're not second-guessing each other either. We're finally in that single-minded place where we do what we have to do, whatever it is.

Turns out only the inked one was armed. Kelton takes the gun and looks it over. "Desert Eagle with a muzzle brake," he says. "Much better than mine." He claims it, and offers me his gun. I hesitate, because I don't want it anymore.

"I'll take it," says Alyssa. She still has blood splattered on her face. I decide not to mention it.

"You sure?" Kelton asks.

She nods. "No one's ever going to put me in a position like that again."

"What about Henry?" I ask.

Kelton looks at his big, shiny new gun and shrugs. "I'll save a bullet for him," he says.

And for the life of me I can't tell if he really means it.

46) Alyssa

If I think too much right now, I'll lose my mind. There are two dead bodies in front of me. Can't think about it. My brother was almost murdered. Can't think about it. My parents might be floating facedown in the Pacific Ocean. Can't think about it.

What I *can* think about is the water that I know is just up the ridge and down by an old rusty camper.

"Alyssa…" Garrett says, just as he said before he lost consciousness before, "I don't feel so good."

"We're getting water," I tell him. "It'll be okay."

"But … but I can't get up. I can't move."

His voice is even weaker than before, and I think back to what Kelton said last night. How right before you die, your body will fight it. You'll have a burst of energy – the body's last attempt to save itself.

And it dawns on me that Garrett just had that burst of energy. Which means he could be only minutes away from closing his eyes forever.

"We have to hurry!" I say to the others, not sparing another thought for the dead men. I pick up Garrett in my arms, and although I barely have the strength to hold up my own weight, I bear his as well, as we make our way toward the campsite.

47) Kelton

It was different than I thought it would be. I expected it to feel monumental. Like ripping a hole in the universe. But it wasn't.

Pop! Pop!

Simple as that. Now two men are dead, and we're alive. I wasn't angry, like I was back in our house when I almost turned a shotgun on our marauding neighbors. I wasn't scared, like I was when the water-zombie kid on the beach was trying to suck the water right out of Alyssa's mouth. *Pop! Pop!* Done. Move on.

Like I said, these guys were feeding on the chaos, living by video game rules. And in a game, when you defeat an enemy, what do you do? You take their weapons. Which is exactly what I did. Is that why I don't feel anything? Because I'm living by those rules now, too?

We reach the top of the ridge and look down on the campsite, to see that the campfire, without anyone to watch it, has gotten out of control. The brush is burning. The two lawn chairs are burning.

And the fire has reached the cooler beside them.

It's burning, giving off a rancid chemical smell. The lid is open, and I can see splashes as the water bottles inside begin to burst. "Oh no!" Alyssa puts Garret down. "Don't move! I'll be right back!"

Alyssa, Jacqui, and I race down, trying to get to the water, but the fire is too hot.

"God damn it!" Jacqui tries to reach through the flames, but screams, curling her hands. She's burned herself. Still, she reaches in again. The second time must be so painful that she backs away, wailing, in pain. "No!" she screams. "It's not fair! It's not fair!"

"Look for something we can use to pull the cooler out of the flames!" I say.

But Alyssa's looking toward the camper. "This might not be all the water they have," she says. "I'll check inside."

She runs around the growing fire to the camper. The wind is blowing in that direction. It's only a matter of time until that's on fire, too.

"Okay, but hurry," I yell after her. And I begin searching

for a branch large enough to reach into the flames and pull out the burning cooler.

48) Alyssa

I throw open the door of the camper. It doesn't smell good in here. I didn't expect it to. It doesn't look all that different from Kelton's bug-out on the inside. Food containers and dirty clothes. And something I wasn't expecting at all.

"Benji, is that you?"

I follow the voice to the trailer's bedroom. There's a woman in there. Old. Sick. A floral print housedress. Fuzzy pink slippers. She regards me with suspicion, pulling the covers over her.

"Who are you? Where's Benji? Where's Kyle?"

"They … they sent me in," I tell her. "They sent me in for the water."

Her suspicion grows. "They got all the water already in the cooler! Who are you?" she asks again.

I look around the room, refusing to believe there's no water left in here. She sees what I'm doing, and she realizes that her suspicions are justified. She begins to look a little bit scared.

"They didn't send you! Get out of here! You're trespassing! Get out of here now!"

I know she doesn't have a weapon of her own, because if she did, she'd have already reached for it. I have one, though. But I won't threaten an old woman with a gun. That's not who I am.

My eyes scan everywhere, and I see things I don't want to see. Because on a counter by the bed, she has set up a miniature version of what must sit on her mantle at home, wherever that is. There are pictures there. Two boys. Different ages. One grabs my attention. A faded picture of the same two boys in Mickey Mouse hats, making faces at the camera. And I realize. Benji and Kyle. They were brothers. I don't want to know this. I don't want to know that they ever wore Mickey Mouse hats. I don't want to know that someone has pictures of them on her bedside table. One of those little boys was going to shoot Garrett. The other one was going to rape me. Wasn't he? *Wasn't he?*

"Is that smoke?" the old woman says. "What's going on out there!"

"You can't stay here," I say. "You can come with us." And the second I say it, I realize that if she does, she's going to see her two dead sons lying in front of the truck.

"I'm not going anywhere!" she says, not grasping the bigger picture. "Do I look like I'm up for a hike?" She purses her lips and shakes her head. "You better get out of here before they come back. Nothing they hate more than trespassers."

And then I see it! A plastic cup of water on a window ledge, just out of the woman's reach. She sees that I see it. She gauges me, it's a standoff … and she lunges for it.

I lunge too, but she gets it first. She clutches it to her chest, and I grab for it.

"It's mine!" she says. "This is my water, not yours!"

The water sloshes in the cup as I try to grab it from her, spilling over the edge. I can't grapple for it, because if I do it will all spill out.

"Benji! Kyle! Help!"

I grab her hand, trying to stop the water from splashing. She takes her other hand and tries to push me away. Then she moves the cup toward her lips. I know this is all the water she has. All the water that's left. If I take it, this woman will die. If I don't take it, my brother will die.

So I do something terrible.

I slap her. I slap her hard. It makes her lose her focus, and I'm able to slip the cup from her hand. More water spills over the side. There's not much left now – an ounce, maybe two – not enough to quench anyone's thirst, but maybe enough to keep my brother alive.

I back away from her. "The fire's almost at the door," I tell her. "You need to get out of here."

But even if she does, what good will it do? She's out in the middle of nowhere, alone. If the fire doesn't get her, she'll die of thirst out here. But still, I turn my back on her and leave. Because I have made my choice. If she has to die for my brother to live, then I will take her water and leave her to die. Henry was right. Sometimes it's the monsters who survive. And now I am the monster.

49) Jacqui

My hands! My hands! How stupid could I be! My hands. And still, I want to push my arms through the flames to that cooler that burns there in the middle of hell. My fingers and palms are already swelling with blisters, the pain resolving into a dull throbbing.

Kelton returns with a branch and pokes it toward the cooler. He hooks the end around the lip. *My hands! My hands!* He pulls on the stick, and the cooler moves half an inch. He pulls again. It slips another half inch closer. He tugs harder — and the whole side, half-molten, rips open, spilling water into the fire.

"No!"

The water steams, and as the steam clears, I can see the few remaining water bottles at the bottom of the ruptured cooler melt, spilling the contents out pointlessly. Uselessly. It does nothing to quell the fire, because the flames just close in and the remaining sides of the cooler collapse. It's gone. All gone. And when I look up, I can see how far the fire has spread. The winds are fanning it. One more fire to add to the ones that are already blazing in the mountains around us.

Alyssa bursts out of the trailer, leaping over the flames that are about to engulf it. She's holding something. What is that? Is that a cup? She holds it like it's something precious. And it is.

I could take it from her. I could catch up with her and take it. And drink it. Quench this thirst that burns even more than my hands.

But I won't.

Because I know that water's not for her.

I won't take it. Because even though I've seen everyone around me lose their humanity today, I realize that in this moment, I have finally found mine.

50) Alyssa

Garrett is exactly where I left him – on the ridge above the burning campsite, leaning against a tree. His head is lolling to one side. His eyes are slits. He might already be dead. I can't see him breathing. He might already be dead!

"Garrett! Garrett, I'm here."

I kneel beside him. I lift the cup to his lips. I pour a little in. What if he doesn't swallow? What if he can't swallow? Because he's already dead?

Water dribbles out of the side of his mouth. I was too slow! I should have pulled out the gun and shot that woman the second I saw the cup of water. That's what I should have done! It would have saved me ten seconds. Ten seconds that would have saved my brother's life. Swallow, Garrett! Dammit, swallow!

Then he coughs. He coughs! His eyes open the tiniest bit wider.

"It's water, Garrett!" I tell him. "Swallow it!"

"I'm trying," he rasps. "It's hard."

He closes his eyes. He forces a swallow. I pour a little more in his mouth. He swallows again. I pour all the rest in. It's easier for him to swallow the third time. He doesn't look any better. He's not any stronger. But I know that water is in there. Water absorbs into the body faster than anything. It will be gone from his stomach in minutes – even faster when he's this dehydrated. His body will suck it in like a sponge.

"Is that all you've got?" he asks, and I actually laugh.

"There'll be more," I tell him.

Only now do I look back down to the campsite. Jacqui

and Kelton are climbing away from it toward me. The fire has already spread to the trees at an alarming rate.

"Did the old woman get out of the camper?" I ask them, now that my tight sphere of concern can extend beyond my brother.

Kelton looks at Jacqui then back at me. "There was an old woman in the camper?"

I look down to the campsite again. The trailer and the brush all around it are fully engulfed in flames. The door is still open, the way I left it. I hear no screams. But what could I do about them, even if I did? The path to the camper is completely blocked by the fire.

"We've got to move," Kelton says.

So I bend down, pick up Garrett, and go back to the truck, trying to forget I ever saw this place. But that's not going to be easy.

51) Kelton

Jacqui can't drive. Her hands are swollen like balloons. She tries to touch the steering wheel and wails in anguish. Between Alyssa and me, I am the lesser of two evils behind the wheel. She doesn't have her learner's permit yet, but I do. In spite of my father's insistence that I need to earn the right to drive, he's taken me to empty parking lots. According to him, I've totaled about twenty imaginary cars while trying to navigate those lots. Good thing all I have to worry about now are trees.

I put the car in gear, with Alyssa beside me – she can work

the four-wheel-drive stick, while I put all of my attention into the normal driving part.

We lurch and grind gears. We scrape trees. We bounce violently over rocks. Jacqui curses each time she reflexively uses her hands to brace herself. I catch Garrett in the rearview mirror. He doesn't look as terrible as he did before. He just looks bad. Like the rest of us.

I'm tired now. My lungs burn from the smoke I inhaled at the campsite. Carbon monoxide. It bonds to your red blood cells like oxygen, but unlike oxygen, it doesn't let your blood cells go. They become useless. That's why people die from smoke inhalation. They don't have enough red blood cells left to carry oxygen to the brain. I'm still conscious, so I know however much I breathed in, it's not enough to kill me. But there's plenty of other things lining up to kill me right now. Including my own driving.

It's so hard to keep my eyes open. But I have to.

We come over another ridge and start down a slope. But this slope is steeper than any of the others. I should have been looking at the topography map! I should have known this.

"Careful, Kelton!" Alyssa says.

I hit the brakes, and we start to skid. We're at a steep downward grade now. Maybe thirty degrees. The wheels barely find traction. The brakes are useless. Nothing's going to slow our descent. I just have to somehow keep us from hitting trees and boulders.

"Kelton!" yells Jacqui. "You're losing it!"

As if I didn't already know. I turn the wheel right. We sideswipe a tree. A sharp turn left. We bounce over a boulder so big, I hear it scrape on our underbelly. And as bad as I thought the grade already was, it gets steeper. There's nothing I can do now. Gravity has taken over. I grip the wheel, brace myself.

A loud bang. A flash of white.

A pain in my gut and chest, like I got kicked in the stomach.

I gasp, can't get enough air. Maybe the carbon monoxide got me after all.

No, the wind is knocked out of me, that's all. And the airbags have deployed. And we're not moving anymore.

"Is everyone okay?" I hear Alyssa say.

"No," says Jacqui, which is her way of saying yes. Garrett just groans and tells me I suck at driving.

I kick open the door. Immediately I smell gasoline. "Careful," I tell everyone. "I think we ruptured the gas tank."

We're on a road now. Narrow, poorly maintained, but it's a road!

"This must be East Fork Road!"

At least that's something. I walk around the truck, but it's barely walking. My feet are dragging. Everything hurts. My head feels like it's going to crack in half like an egg. I want to lie down so badly. So badly. Just for a minute. But I don't. Because I know that feeling. I know what that feeling means.

The truck is done. It looks like it's been through a demolition derby. One wheel is flat, another one is turned completely sideways.

"The reservoir is about a mile that way," I say, pointing west. "We'll have to walk the rest of the way."

"I think I can make it," says Garrett, the only one who's had any water in two days, but Alyssa and Jacqui look at me like I just pronounced a death sentence.

Jacqui shakes her head. "I don't know if I have a mile left in me, Kelton."

"Don't think about it," Alyssa says. "We just walk, and keep on walking. Even after we feel like we can't, we just keep on walking."

So we stop talking, and we start walking. West. And I find myself taking the lead.

Because I have a sudden burst of energy.

52) Alyssa

Walking. Walking. One foot. Then the next. Then the next.

I am not alive. I am not dead. I am something in between. Shuffle. Shuffle. Step. Step. How far is a mile? How many steps? It doesn't matter. I can't count. My higher brain functions have mostly shut down. I think about nothing but the water up ahead. I allow it to pull my feet forward. Step. Step. Shuffle. Shuffle.

And the others are the same. Kelton is a few feet ahead of us, but I can see the way his feet move, that it's not a normal gait. It's the same dragging shuffle as the rest of us. For a few minutes it looked like he had his second wind, but he's slowing down.

I think we're water-zombies now.

Smoke pours through the trees, creating a haze in front of us. I start to cough.

"How much farther?" I ask. It barely comes out. It doesn't sound like my voice.

No one answers me. My guess is that there's maybe only a quarter mile to go ...

... but the smoke gets denser. Less than a minute later, I see flames up ahead.

Is this from the campsite fire, or is it another fire? I don't know why it matters, but somehow it does. Like the flames are driven by the angry spirits of Benji and Kyle and their invalid mother.

The fire has already leaped to the other side of the road. Now this narrow road looks like the black tongue of a great beast of fire about to swallow us. *Which is worse,* I wonder, *death by fire, or death by thirst?* How can you choose the lesser of two evils, when both evils are too great to measure?

"We can't get through," says Kelton. "We'll go north, back into the forest, to the right of us."

"That's away from the water," Jacqui says.

"And from the fire," Kelton responds. "We'll go around it, and reach the reservoir from the north."

But getting around the fire means adding at least another half mile to the journey.

"We're almost there!" says Jacqui. "I can see the water!"

I think that must be a hallucination, because when I look into the furnace of the road up ahead, all I see is smoke and flames.

"I think I can make it," says Jacqui.

"You can't," I tell her. I know it's not what she wants to hear, but you can't fight a wildfire with willpower. You can't intimidate flames.

Then behind us, I hear an explosion. A mushroom cloud

of black smoke billows into the sky.

"The truck..." says Kelton. There was gasoline pouring from it when we left it. If the fire has crept in behind us and ignited the gas, then we're cut off. There's nowhere for us to go now but up the slope to the right of us. North, around the flames.

"There's water just ahead," Jacqui insists. "I know there is. I saw it." She looks to the flames sweeping from tree to tree. "You can't outrun this. The only way to that water is forward." Then she looks at her swollen, red hands. "What's a little fire, anyway?"

She holds eye contact with me just for a moment ... and I know that she's going to make a run for it. She will either reach the water, or the flames will consume her. Either way, this may be the last we will see of each other. I want to say something, but I don't know what to say. *Good luck* sounds so trite and pointless in the face of this. I guess she feels the same way, because she just nods – an acceptance of all things not said – then turns and shuffles down the road. A few more steps and she lifts her feet instead of shuffling. Then she's running. She's actually running! And the last we see of her is her back as she disappears into the smoke.

"Alyssa, come on," says Garrett.

"We should have stopped her..."

"We couldn't," Kelton says. And I know he's right. All we have are bad choices left to us now. Jacqui made her bad choice. Now we have to make ours. I look to the north. The hillside is steep. I have no strength to climb it ... but I will. Somehow I will.

53) Jacqui

The heat teases my cheeks. It has the power to singe, to sear, to incinerate, but it holds back. Now it just teases. Tickles. It plays with me.

The slope changes. The road now heads downhill, and I keep my legs moving because I know that water is just at the base. The others were too short-sighted to see it; they were looking at the fire, but not through it. It blinded them. And now I'll be the one to get the first sip. Hell, they'll be lucky if I don't swallow the whole reservoir by the time they make it there. *If* they make it there. I may be the only one, because I was the only one willing to challenge the fire.

I will not look behind me: All that's there is dead forest and smoke. Now the heat pulses around me. Or it's just my heartbeat, but it feels like the relentless churning of a living furnace. A god of fire that must be fed.

I trip on a branch and take a nasty fall. The branch is on fire. It has fallen from a tree that's burning above. The tops of the trees around me are all burning, and through the smoke to my left and right, I see walls of flames surging forward, igniting bark on every trunk. The air is cooler down low, but only slightly. The smoke burns my lungs a little less. I pick myself up and run, but stay as crouched as I can so I'm halfway in the better air.

Now my entire body throbs. The heat is done playing, and although the flames still aren't on me, that doesn't matter. I can broil just as quickly as I can burn. So I move faster to beat the pain.

The wind whips in every direction, sparks helixing all around me, and that's when I hear it—

… Jacqui … Jacqui …

It's the gust at my back whispering my name, the burning breeze at my cheeks. The same wind I've always felt my entire life – the Call of the Void – but now it surges not just before me but all around me with self-satisfied omnipotence.

And for the first time, it actually scares me.

I've let the void taunt me and tempt me all my life. I will not let it take me. Finally, with all that is left in me, I will fight back against it!

The flames are now surging across the road, completely blocking my path. Every tree is ablaze – but just beyond the sheet of flames, I see something sparkling – twinkling – in the firelight.

The reservoir!

Salvation beyond a veil of hell.

They call that purgatory. I can accept purgatory if heaven is beyond it.

… Jacqui …

The pain is beyond imagining now, but still I run. I can't keep my eyes open – so I clamp them shut, and when I do, I find myself staring directly into the void. I am barreling through white flame and absolute darkness, the nexus between life and death. The void is beginning to take my body, and I know exactly what comes next. It wants my soul.

But it won't get that without a fight.

I don't slow down. I don't accept the pain. I crash through the burning void toward the waters of heaven.

54) Alyssa

The fire chases us uphill. Every time I look back, no matter how far we've climbed, the fire is no farther away. But it's no closer to us either. It's matching our pace – which means we can't slow down, not for an instant, because if we do, it will overtake us.

There's a wind now, but it's not coming from behind us. It's blowing against us from the top of the hill.

The fire's pulling down air, I think. *Sucking it in, to feed it.*

I immediately get a vision of the beach. How the incoming waves create an undertow, drawing back the water from the shore. We are caught in that undertow now with a massive wave behind us surging forward, and the image is so powerful, and my mind so weakened, I get muddled. The popping sound of boiling sap and the throaty breath of flames blends together into a deep roar that sounds just as ominous as a storm-torn sea, and I think for a moment that I am there at the shore, running from an all-consuming tsunami. It's only when I look at my brother climbing two paces ahead of me that I remember what we're doing and where we are. But I wish it were water chasing us. Even saltwater. If I were at the shore now, I would drink it until it killed me. Like any other water-zombie.

When we began up the hill, the three of us were side by side, but Garrett, the last one to have water, has pulled a few yards ahead, and now Kelton has lagged behind.

"When we're ... when we're at ... at the top," Kelton wheezes between labored breaths and coughs, "we'll ... we'll turn left ... cut across to the ... to the..." He can't find the word. "... to the..."

"Reservoir," I finish for him.

"C'mon!" Garrett yells. He's even farther ahead now, frustrated that we're not keeping up with him. "We're almost there."

But the top of the hill looks like miles and miles to me. I turn to see that Kelton has fallen even farther behind. He leans on a stump now, trying to catch his breath, embers from the fire falling around him like flaming confetti.

"Kelton!"

"Just a … just a…"

I make my way back to him, halving the distance between me and the fire.

"Just a … just a … sec."

It's so hot here, it feels as if my clothes will ignite. It feels like my dry skin will spontaneously combust.

"Little rest…" says Kelton. "Just a … just a…"

"No!" I yell. The mention of the word "rest" makes my knees want to fold. It sounds so, so good. The roar of the waves. Rest. Toes in the cool cool sand. "No!"

I grab Kelton and practically hurl him over the stump.

"I gotta … I gotta…" he mutters.

"You gotta MOVE!" I help him off the ground and start his momentum. He has not come this far, and seen the things he's seen happen to his family, just to falter in these last moments and die.

And somehow, putting Kelton at the center of my effort helps me overcome my own desire to drop where I stand.

We continue upward, and I realize that this is my burst of energy. The last one I'll have before there's nothing left to give. I hope Kelton appreciates that I used it on him.

I can't see Garrett anymore. He's far above us, but I hear him calling my name, and I focus in on that … until Kelton's legs give out on him again. He's not just leaning and heaving to catch his breath this time. He's on the ground, flat. He can't even push himself up.

"S … safe room," he says. "Get to … get to the safe room."

He's delirious, and there's nothing I can do about that. The thirst has started to shut down his brain. There's only one thing I can think to do. One thing that might get his lifeless legs moving again.

"I'm not letting you stay here!" I scream at him. "Which means if you don't get your ass up that hill, I die, too. Is that what you want? You want me to die because of YOU?"

His rheumy eyes meet mine. An ember falls beside him, setting the dry grass on fire. He pushes himself up on all fours. He scrambles forward. It worked! Putting me at the forefront of his thoughts drew out what little energy he had left, just as when I had focused on helping him – and I realize that this is the true core of human nature: When we've lost the strength to save ourselves, we somehow find the strength to save each other.

We finally, finally reach the crest of the hill. I find it hard to believe I'm still alive. I don't feel it. I feel like I died a hundred yards downhill, and now my spirit is trapped here, doomed to haunt this place, reliving the climb, and the thirst, and the flames for all eternity.

Garrett stands on a flat boulder, still out of breath, looking west. I join him. From this high vantage point, we can see the reservoir! It's maybe only a quarter mile below us! Kelton was right! He was right!

… But the fire has snuck in, insidious, determined. It now rages at full force between us and the reservoir. How could the water be so close, and us still be unable to reach it?

"North!" I say. "Around it!" The words barely come out. My tongue is a piece of leather in my mouth, my vocal cords brittle paper. We can still head north and get past the fire. Climbing the hill was the hard part – downhill will be easier, won't it? We can still loop around the fire and double back to the reservoir.

But then I look to Kelton. He's lying facedown in the dust.

"No!"

I make my way to him. I roll him over. I can't hear him breathing over the roar of the approaching flames. So I force his eyes open, as if seeing his eyes will mean that he sees mine.

"Kelton! Wake up!"

Finally, he begins mumbling, but it's not words, it's just guttural sounds, faint clicks and hisses. His eyes roll into his head, and I know that he's just a few minutes away from dying. And I know that I can't stop it. And I know that Garrett and I can't carry him, no matter how hard we try.

"Alyssa…?"

I turn to Garrett, who has taken a few steps down the other side of the hill. North. The direction we have to go if we want to live. But when I join him there, I see what he sees, and it makes everything as clear as the water we can't get to.

There isn't a slope on that side of the hill.

There's a cliff.

A sheer drop – at least fifty feet. There's no way down but the way we came. Which means we're cornered.

Garrett looks at me with such despair, it nearly overwhelms me. I see him begin to sway and waver. His shoulders go a little limp. Whatever energy he had left has been stolen from him by this revelation. I quickly grab him and pull him back from the ledge before he can swoon off the cliff, and I hold him tight.

"It's going to be okay," I tell him.

"No it's not," he says weakly. "You know it's not."

I do know. But I won't confess it. Not to him. Instead, I lead him back to the flat boulder. It looks like an altar. A place where our hope was sacrificed. Garrett turns away from me, brings his knees to his chest, pulling himself into a ball. He looks toward the reservoir and the water we almost reached. That's the image he wants to hold in his mind now. Not his life, not our family. The memory of water.

The sound of the approaching fire is deafening now. The sky above us darkens with smoke, like night falling early.

Suddenly I know what I have to do.

I've heard that the worst way to die is by fire. I will not go that way if I don't have to. And I will not let my brother be burned alive.

So I pull out the gun that has been shoved uncomfortably in my waist ever since Kelton gave it to me. I almost wanted to leave it in the truck. I almost chucked it when we started up the hill, because it was so cumbersome. But something told me not to. Never in my life have I been so horrified, and yet so happy to be holding a loaded gun. I hide it so Garrett doesn't see, and he lets me put my other arm around him. He leans in to me. He sobs, but no tears come out.

"I want to go home," Garrett says. "I want it to be last week."

"So do I," I tell him. Was it only just a week ago?

Downhill, a burning tree falls with an explosion of embers that sail skyward, over our heads. Seeds to spread the fire elsewhere. I bring the gun to Garrett's head, but not close enough to touch, because I don't want him to know.

"I love you, Garrett," I tell him, and he echoes it back. It's the thing brothers and sisters never say to each other until they find themselves in a moment where nothing else can possibly be said. Then I grip the trigger, feeling the gun's weight. But I hesitate … and hesitate some more … and then Garrett says, in the faintest of whispers:

"Do it, Alyssa."

He doesn't look at me. He doesn't want to see the gun or me. So I press the muzzle against that space between his ear and his eye, where the hair is short and soft.

"Do it. Please…"

I will be strong, if not for me, then for Garrett. I will save him from the flames. And then I will save Kelton. And then I will save myself.

SNAPSHOT: LOS ANGELES FIRE DEPARTMENT BOMBARDIER 415

The water bomber glides just meters above the lake. Like a pelican, it swoops down gently, slicing the tips of little wakes until its open bill is fully submerged, scooping nearly a thousand gallons – all within seconds. The pilot and his seabird have made this trip countless times in these last couple of days. He was given direct orders by his tactical supervisor to fill up at the San Gabriel Reservoir and make water drops on the fires between here and Lake Arrowhead, twenty miles east. The blazes that block the path to Big Bear Lake have already claimed countless lives. He can't do anything about that, but at least with the fires threatening the road to Arrowhead, he can make a difference.

The pilot pitches the nose of the seabird up from the reservoir basin and together they soar. He gapes at the fires surrounding the reservoir, surprised they've grown this far. Sometimes when a brushfire grows out of control, fire authorities set a backfire – a controlled burn – that hedges the amount of destruction a wildfire may cause. But this fire doesn't seem to be one of those, he notes, getting closer. This is the real thing. But he's only here for the water. They'll set another battalion to work here. Right now it's a lower priority. His drop point is much farther east.

Putting out these fires is beginning to feel like a never-ending game of whack-a-mole. Or at least that's how he tries to see it – it's easier that way.

Every time he makes a trip to refill from the reservoir, he has to fly past an overcrowded evacuation center. Each time he sees all of those people there, fenced in and helpless, he's had half a mind to just drop the entire payload of water on them. But that's an inefficient use of resources. He can save more lives by dousing fires. So he's been choosing to fly a little higher above that evac center. High enough that the people look like ants. It's an attempt to set a backfire to his own empathy – whatever it takes to prevent his conscience from burning him alive.

But now, as he leaves the reservoir, he sees something odd. It looks like there's someone running through the fire!

The plane had just done a steep climb from the reservoir basin – maybe it's just his imagination or a head rush from the climb. But just to be sure, the pilot banks left, doubling back to get a better look.

And sure enough, someone is sprinting through the flames.

A girl.

What is she doing out here? What possessed her to challenge a forest fire?

Then his eyes are drawn to the top of a bluff, where he sees others. They're trapped against the edge of a cliff, the fire burning toward them.

He weighs his options. He reaches deep. This is not his drop zone. His orders are very specific. Yet even though he's already begun his ascent, he realizes he can't just let this go. He's flown too low to jettison his humanity.

_____

55) Alyssa

My finger is firmly curled on the trigger, when the deafening wail of the flames gives way to a scream. No, not a scream. Something else.

I know that sound.

It grows into an earsplitting mechanical resonance that changes pitch as a shadow passes overhead.

Then suddenly the billowing smoke is shredded by something cold and wet.

It falls upon us in a single massive deluge that only lasts for a couple of seconds, but it's enough to drench us, to soak the ground, and to wound the fire.

I hurl the gun to the ground. Instantly it has become my enemy. I lick my hands, I lick my arms, I bunch my hair, pull it around and suck on it.

Water!

It tastes of ash, but I don't care. I swallow. My throat screams in pain, but I swallow again and again.

Garrett is on his knees licking the boulder, catching tiny rivulets that course down its side – and then I see that there are dips and indentations on the surface of the flat stone. Spots where the water has pooled!

I push my face into one of the shallow basins so hard,

I nearly break my nose. I draw the water in. Then I realize there's something I've forgotten. Someone. I tear myself away to look at Kelton. He hasn't moved. His sneakers are still smoking – the flames had been that close to him – but now the fire has retreated about a dozen feet. White steam now belches forth, blending with the black smoke as the fire licks its wounds.

I dip my hands into one of the indentations in the rock, scooping up water, but I barely get any; the pool is not deep enough. Still, I try to carry what I have to Kelton, but it dribbles through my fingers and is gone by the time I reach him. I can't bring it to him this way. I must find another way.

When the answer comes, I almost laugh at myself at how simple it is – and yet a week ago, I would never have considered such a thing. The box I lived in was simply too small to think that far out if it.

I go back to the boulder and once again push my face down into the largest pool, sucking in a mouthful of water. But as much as my body wants me to swallow, I don't. I hold it. And I hurry to Kelton.

I get down on my knees, leaning over him. I pull his mouth open with one hand, and press my lips against his. Then I force the water out, into his mouth, giving him a different kind of resuscitation. I pull my mouth away, push his jaw closed, and wait.

Nothing.

And nothing.

And then a gargle and a cough! Water shoots up out of his mouth like a fountain, but I put my hand over his mouth, and force it closed. Let him gag! Let him choke! But let him swallow!

He writhes weakly, gagging on the water, forcing it out of his lungs, and with nowhere else to go, it pools in his throat again – and I see his Adam's apple go up and go down. He's swallowed.

I run back to the boulder, draw in all the rest of the water that's pooled there, and go back to Kelton again. His eyes are slightly open – he's faintly aware. Once more I press my mouth to his and force the water out. This time he brings his hand up, gently holding my shoulder. I feel him actively sucking the water from me, and I let him, until I can feel him swallow, then I let him go and lean back to catch my breath.

He looks at me, still only halfway conscious. The moment is ripe for some sly remark, but we're both beyond that kind of thing now.

"Rain?" he asks.

"Plane," I tell him.

"Hmm. Even better." Then he rolls over on his side, coughing, but that's fine. He can cough as much as he wants now!

I look to the fire that still rages, but for the moment is at bay. Garrett now lies face up and sprawled out on the boulder, looking to the hazy blue sky. We could die happy now, our thirst finally quenched. But maybe we won't be dying today.

Kelton sits up. He's sucking on his sleeve, getting all the water he can from it, and I decide to do the same to my sleeve.

Meanwhile, I watch as the plane returns to the lake, skimming water from its surface, filling up for a second run.

PART SIX

A NEW NORMAL

SNAPSHOT: DISNEYLAND, 8:57 A.M., SATURDAY, JUNE 25TH

Main Street has been washed clean of wildfire ash, the Haunted Mansion has been cleared of vagrants, and the green phalluses spray-painted on the beloved character mural have been scrubbed off.

It's been almost two weeks since the Tap-Out officially ended, and it's taken that long to get things up and running again – not just here, but all over Southern California. But the Magic Kingdom is at the forefront of the effort to restore life as we knew it.

With so many "cast members" not returning, there are a lot of new hirees – including an eighteen-year-old ticket taker at the front gate whose mother forced him to take a summer job. The recent catastrophe cost the family a fortune in insurance deductibles. Everyone is expected to contribute.

"It will be fun," she said.

But it hasn't been. Instead, it's kind of been like finding out that the Tooth Fairy doesn't exist, or catching Santa smoking cigarettes in the Macy's parking lot. Perhaps it's because the entire park has looked practically post-apocalyptic. No character costumes, no electrical parade, no jazz band in New Orleans Square. And no guests. This has been the longest closure since the park was built. There was simply too much damage to repair, too much infrastructure to rebuild. Not just here, but everywhere. There was looting here, but not as much as one might think. People didn't care about clothing, or technology. There was only one thing they were looking for. Food concessions were torn apart searching for that one thing. The one remaining water feature in the park – a fountain in Tomorrowland – had become a Mecca for lost souls, who drank the chlorinated water until it was gone. The spin doctors in the corporate offices are planning to rebrand it the Fountain of Life.

The big news being pushed is that nobody died in the park. That's saying a lot. There's probably no other geographic area as large that can make that claim.

Tons of people are being heralded as heroes all over Southern California. Like the power plant manager who quelled a riot in Huntington Beach, and the mysterious good Samaritan in Tustin who saved a whole bunch of people at a nursing home, then disappeared. The ticket taker would like to say he himself was a hero, but he didn't do much of anything beyond survive. That was hard enough.

8:58 a.m.

He stands at his spot at the turnstiles, counting down the minutes until Disneyland opens up again, marking the first official day of normalcy. On the other side of the Emerald Gates, the lines wind out of sight, and he realizes why people are here. Why they need to be here.

More than two hundred thousand souls perished during humanity's hiatus. The highest fatality count from any non-war event in the history of the nation. Yet even that number somehow feels remarkably low, and the fact that it isn't higher is a miracle – or at least, that's what people have been reaching for. The silver lining. Why else would so many need to be in the one place where magic still exists? Where hope is eternal? Where dreams never die?

The clock strikes nine.

The music fades in, right on cue – enchanting the crowd – and then the sparkling Emerald Gates open, welcoming humanity back to the Happiest Place on Earth.

———————————————————————————

56) Alyssa

Soapy sponge, wet washcloth, dry towel, repeat.

A pounding at the bathroom door.

"Alyssa, come on already!" says Garrett. "I gotta take a dump!"

Soapy sponge, wet washcloth, dry towel, repeat.

"Use the downstairs bathroom!"

"I can't! Dad's in there!"

The sponge, the washcloth, the towel. One arm, one leg at a time. I will get clean. It will just take a little effort.

Garrett pounds again. "What are you even doing in there?"

"I'm taking a shower."

"I don't hear the shower running."

"Then you're deaf."

He's not deaf. The shower is not on. But there's a sponge for soaping, a washcloth for rinsing, and a towel for drying. I stand in the shower and reach over to the sink, which is half filled with warm water, like a basin in the days before homes had running water. With the water heater finally replaced, we don't have to boil water to warm it anymore. And with our neighborhood's water turned on for two days a week, it means we can shower. I know that. But I just can't do it. I can't bring myself to spray my body and watch it flow down the drain. Maybe another day. But not today. Today it's a sponge, a washcloth, and a towel. I'm happy with that. More than happy, I'm satisfied.

"We'll be leaving soon," I call out to Garrett. "Are you ready to go?"

"I'm ready to use the bathroom!"

The crisis officially ended two weeks ago – just a day after Kelton, Garrett, and I were air-lifted out of the forest and dropped off at Lake Arrowhead, where the entire community had become one massive evacuation center. But only for the people who managed to get there, which wasn't easy. We were treated for smoke inhalation. My lungs hurt for a week. They're better now.

I dry my hair, put on a robe, and let Garrett into the bathroom, where he starts taking care of business even before I completely vacate. Typical. And yet nothing feels typical anymore. There's a new "normal," because our lives are punctuated by weird air pockets of the surreal.

Like when we went back to Costco. The shelves were restocked as if nothing ever happened, with a stupid sign out front that said YES, WE HAVE WATER!

But even though the store is the same, people are not. Since the return of life as we knew it, I've found there are four kinds of people now, all easy to spot – especially in the aisles of Costco.

There are the oblivious ones, who go about their lives like the Tap-Out was a dream that waking life has completely washed away. Maybe they got out before it got bad, or maybe they just exist in a constant state of denial. I find them hard to relate to. It's like talking to aliens pretending to be human.

Then there are the ones like us, who lived through it and are still facing the PTSD of it all. They linger in the aisles, marveling at the sheer magnitude of products and the organization it took to get it all here, no longer taking anything for granted, and guarding their carts as if their lives depended on it.

Then there are the fulfilled ones. The people who found something in themselves they didn't know was there. Heroes in the rough. Now they talk to strangers, look for opportunities to help. They've discovered they can truly be of use, and don't want that to stop just because the crisis is over. I admire them. The Tap-Out left them with a calling they didn't have before.

And finally there are the shadows. These are ones who move through the aisles silently, avoiding eye contact, afraid at every step that someone will recognize them and accuse them of whatever horrible, unspeakable thing they did to survive. The ones who can't look at others because they can't face themselves.

It's the same at school. We all went back a couple of days ago. Even though school would have ended by now, they have to finish the year. "Healthy closure," they said. Because a water-zombie apocalypse is not truly over until kids go back to school.

Three teachers had perished – two beloved, the third not so much, but everyone cried for him, even so. Thirty-eight students were lost – including the school's star running back and the girl voted Most Likely to Succeed. But those weren't the only empty chairs. There were dozens upon dozens who simply hadn't come back, and might never come back. My friend Sofía, for one. Who knows if I'll ever see her again.

And the shadows were there, too. Kids who are wraiths of their former selves. Hali Hartling, for instance – who kicked hard, lived large, and was always at the top of the social pyramid. Now she moves quietly through the hallways, and I suspect has completely lost her edge on the soccer field. I suppose I could have become a shadow, because I did plenty of things I am not proud of, but I made the choice to wear it not as a brand of shame, but as a badge of honor. If I'm scarred, then they're war wounds, and I will not cower from them.

When it comes down to it, there's nothing "normal" about our new environment, and I wonder if life will ever be the same. Will we ever be able to put the past behind us? Will the shadows find redemption? Will all the fulfilled heroes go back to their less altruistic selves? And will I ever stop having nightmares about my parents?

It doesn't help that the truth was almost as awful as a night terror.

Mom got knocked out during the riot at the beach. She collapsed, out cold against the hot sand. The crowd was savage. She was trampled, three of her ribs were broken. Her left lung was punctured, and she suffered a grade three concussion. She was lucky that there were still paramedics around to bring her to a hospital, or else she would have died.

Dad was arrested because he was fighting to get to Mom, and it got bundled with all the rest of the violent behavior of the mob.

Turns out they both ended up in the perfect places. The

hospital was a high-priority location, so it got the first water deliveries, and county jail, being a government facility, never had its water shut off like all the municipal water districts had. Funny that jail was one of the safest places to be. It was hard on Dad, though – not knowing what happened to us, or to Mom, not to mention whatever craziness went on in there. He won't talk about it. I don't blame him.

They both got home before we did, and suffered their own hell waiting to find out what had become of us. But we finally got in touch with them, and they met us where the buses bringing people back from Arrowhead dropped everyone off.

It's a moment I replay over and over again in my mind, although the memory registers more viscerally than visually. The *feeling* of the memory. Maybe because my eyes were too blurred by tears to see much of anything. The feeling of home in the smell of my mother's shirt as I cried into her shoulder. The sense of safety brought by the touch of my father's hand when he rubbed my back to comfort me, just as he did when I was little. The blanket of comfort that was carried by their voices – voices I thought I might never hear again. We all just stood there in a parking lot – I don't even remember where – holding each other until nearly everyone else had left. I wasn't even embarrassed. I could have stood there and held them till the end of time.

Uncle Basil's back with us, too. Alive and well, just as we told ourselves he would be. We're determined to start calling him Uncle Herb more, although he has his own ideas about that.

"Call me Uncle Sage," he told us, "because I feel a whole lot wiser than before."

I'm sorry to say that Daphne didn't make it. He still tears up when he talks about it. I really think they loved each other. But our uncle, who had been wallowing in his misfortune for so long after losing his farm up north, isn't wallowing anymore. He's found a second wind in life, selling, of all things, ÁguaViva. He's even doing a commercial for them. *ÁguaViva saved my life.* Talk about turning lemons into lemonade.

I join my mom in the living room to watch the news. It's a press conference. It seems every five minutes there's another press conference.

"The governor of Arizona just resigned," Mom tells me. No surprise there. Everyone who had a part in shutting off the flow of the Colorado River into California is facing criminal prosecution. Officials are being indicted on everything from criminal negligence to conspiracy to commit murder.

"And," Mom says, "they finally found the good Samaritan who saved all those people in that nursing home."

"There were lots of good Samaritans," I point out, thinking of the Water Angel, and the pilot who dropped water on our fire, and that rabbi and the priest who both led thousands of people on a pilgrimage to the promised land of Big Bear Lake just before fires closed in behind them, blocking the way for others.

"Yes, well, there can never be too many good-deed-doers," Mom says.

I glance at her to see that she's taken the bandage off her forehead. Seven stitches. They don't look as bad as I thought they would.

At the sound of running water, I glance into the kitchen.

Garrett has come downstairs and is filling Kingston's water bowl. He does this every day now – something he never did when Kingston was actually here. Now he sets it outside every morning with food. Some days he goes off alone, riding his bike in the hills, looking for our dog.

"He'll come back," Garrett says. "When he thinks it's safe, he'll come back."

I want to believe that. I want to believe that maybe someone else found him and has given him a new home. Dad offered to get us a new dog. "A rescue," he said. "Maybe a dog whose owner died in the Tap-Out, and needs a family like ours."

But Garrett won't have it. As if taking in a new dog is some sort of admission that Kingston's gone for good.

After Garrett fills up the bowl, he turns off the water. But then turns it on again, watching the faucet, watching the water flow down the drain. Then he turns it off. Then turns it on. Then turns it off, then on, over and over. I should be mad that he's wasting water – after all, we still have all the same restrictions as before. No watering lawns. No frivolous use. But I'm not mad at Garrett, because I know this is not about him intentionally wasting water. It's that he's mesmerized by it. Not by the water itself, but by the sheer power to be able to make it flow, and make it stop with the simple flick of the wrist.

He catches me watching him and looks away, a bit red-faced, caught in his private, guilty moment.

"Ready to go?" I ask him.

"I've thought about it," Garrett says, "and I decided I'm not gonna go."

"You sure?" I ask him. "You might regret it later."

"Yeah, I might," he admits, "but I'm sure."

He leaves so he doesn't have to talk about it anymore. I'm not going to pressure him. If he doesn't want to come, he doesn't have to. So it will just be me and Kelton.

And a few minutes later, Kelton arrives, barging in unannounced, which has become a fairly normal occurrence. He's actually been crashing on the couch here some nights. He's got his reasons, and they're all good ones. I don't mind him around.

"Turn on the TV!" Kelton insists.

"Already on," I point out.

"You've gotta see this!" He grabs the remote and switches around until he lands on a different news station ... and on the screen is a face I thought I'd never see again.

We're looking at none other than Henry Not-Roycroft, being interviewed by a reporter. Henry, larger than life on my TV. I always thought "jaw dropping" was figurative – but my jaw actually does drop.

"Oh, look," says my mom, "this is what I was talking about – that's the good Samaritan."

The caption reads *Henry Groyne*.

"Groyne? His last name is *Groyne?*"

Henry speaks proudly. "I just did what anyone would do."

"Not everyone would run into a burning building with nothing but a towel over his head to rescue people," says the reporter.

"That was in Tustin!" I yell at the TV. "He was nowhere *near* Tustin!"

"Shush!" Mom says. "I want to hear this."

On screen Henry shrugs, like he hasn't just taken credit for something he couldn't possibly have done. "In this life, you see what must be accomplished, weigh your options, and then embrace the opportunity."

"But why did you wait so long to come forward?"

"It's not about me. It's about the people I saved."

"You've got to be kidding me!" I shout.

"It gets worse," says Kelton, who must have already seen this on another station.

Now the report cuts back to the studio, where the anchor smiles for the camera and says, "Henry is an eighth grader at Access Alternative Middle School, proving that you're never too young to be a hero!"

"What? He's a WHAT? He's in *eighth grade*?"

"He does look a bit old for his age, though," Mom says, cheerfully oblivious.

There isn't even a word for how utterly speechless I feel. "He said he was driving since he was thirteen…"

"Yeah," says Kelton, "which was, like, three months ago."

My mom looks at us as if we just arrived from Mars. "What are you two talking about?"

And since neither of us wants to spiral down the rabbit hole of this particular madness, we excuse ourselves and go outside.

Kelton and I grumble and moan about it, trying to filter our whole experience with Henry through this new lens, and decide it's not worth it. So we end up laughing about it, and choose to move on.

And pretty soon, Kelton will be moving on too, one way or

another. There's a big FOR SALE sign on Kelton's lawn – a lawn that you can actually see now, since the security gate was rammed down during the not-so-neighborly neighbor attack.

"How are things?" I ask him. I know it's a loaded question.

"Good," Kelton says. "I'm breathing. That's a thing. And it's good." There's a silence that lingers between us, but it means something now. What, I'm not sure.

Kelton's parents are splitting up. He says it was inevitable. He almost seems relieved. His mom already moved out and took an apartment a few miles away.

"My mom wants me to live with her," Kelton tells me.

"Do you want to?"

"Well, it's either that or go with my dad to live with his sister in Idaho."

"The one with all the cats?"

"Yeah." He looks off toward his house. I can't imagine what it must be like staying there now. How could you cook in that kitchen with the memory of what happened there? How could you sit at that table? It makes sense that they're selling – although I don't know how much luck they'll have. Too many homes have FOR SALE signs now.

"My dad got rid of all the guns," Kelton tells me. "He didn't sell them – he destroyed them. Every last one. Part of his way of mourning Brady, I guess. I don't think he'll touch one for the rest of his life."

I think to my own brief ballistic history, right after those men attacked us in the woods – how I took Kelton's pistol, and how I was fully prepared to use it. How I almost did use it to end our lives. I don't even know what happened to the gun after that. I hope it was destroyed, too.

"Anyway, I'll stay with my dad until he heads to Idaho," Kelton tells me. "He kind of needs me more than my mom does right now. It might not look it, but my mom's the strong one."

I nod. "I get that."

We sit down on my lawn, looking across the street at the Kiblers, who are "supervising" their kids as they play maim-the-sibling or some similar game in the street. Kelton and I will be leaving in about twenty minutes, when my dad gets back, because he's driving us – but knowing him, he'll be late, what with all the new business. Before the Tap-Out, he was struggling, but now the insurance biz has seen a fresh surge. Suddenly everyone wants disaster insurance. Go figure.

"We're not making money off of people's misfortunes," my father is constantly reminding himself, and us. "We're protecting people from *future* misfortunes."

As we wait on my lawn – which is still brown, and will never be spray-painted green – Kelton turns to me and asks me a question.

"So, like, what are we?" he asks.

I shrug. "Survivors," I tell him.

"No, I mean what are we to each other?"

"Oh, that."

This feels like it should be an awkward conversation, and yet it's not awkward at all – which makes me realize exactly what we are to each other.

"We're old friends who've known each other for, like, a hundred years," I tell him. "It's just that ninety-five of them happened in one week."

Kelton smiles. "I like that."

But then his smile fades. His eyes seem to be looking far off, past the Kiblers' feral children. Past our neighborhood entirely. His eyes become moist.

"I killed people, Alyssa…"

I've been waiting for him to say something about that. Waiting for two weeks. I'm glad he finally said it, so I can tell him what I've wanted to all this time. "You did what you had to do, and that's all. We *all* did what we had to do, and that's the end of it. Besides, the forest burned, Kelton. There's nothing left, so no one's ever going to know."

"But *I* know."

"So do I … and you know what? I forgive you." Then I add, "I forgive you for that more than I forgive you for the thing with the drone."

That makes him smile again. "Your priorities are way out of whack, Miss Morrow."

I lean over sideways and bump his shoulder. He bumps me back. Then he looks at me for a moment, pondering. Considering.

"Three years from now," he says, "when you break up with your first college boyfriend, you'll call me and I'll stay up all night talking you through it."

"Possibly," I admit. And then I say, "*Seven* years from now, when your first computer start-up company goes belly up, we'll go out that night. I'll make you laugh, and keep you from getting too drunk, and convince you to get to work on your second tech start-up."

"Possibly," he admits. "And *twelve* years from now, you'll

call to tell me that you want me to be the godfather to your first kid."

"Possibly," I concede. "And *twenty* years from now, we'll all go on vacation together, and our spouses, or whatever, will get jealous that we're spending too much time talking to each other, and they'll run off together."

"Possibly," he concludes. "And *thirty* years from now, when you're running for reelection, and I've made my third fortune, I'll take you dancing, and it'll be all over the tabloids." And then he adds, "Of course, they'll be holographic by then."

I have to laugh. "Of course they will."

He smiles at me. "And *then* maybe we can ask again, what we are to each other?"

I hold out my hand to shake. "It's a date."

But instead of shaking it, he takes my hand and kisses it, like someone who is actually charming. And I think, *Yeah, he might get to charming one of these days.*

"Wow," he says. "I finally have a date with Alyssa Morrow. I can die happy."

We both laugh, and it feels comfortable. It feels real. And it makes me feel a little sad that we might not get to dance together for thirty years.

Dad pulls up, amazingly, on time.

"You both ready to go?" he asks.

"Never been more ready," I tell him.

You see, just yesterday when I got home from school, my mom looked at me strangely – which she's been doing a lot of lately – but this time there was a clear reason. "I just got the oddest call," Mom said. "There's this girl at a burn unit way

398

out at Foothill Hospital ... and the weird thing is ... she gave your name as her emergency contact. I think they might have the wrong Alyssa Morrow."

I know for a fact that there are five Alyssa Morrows in California. I know for a fact that they found the right one. And it doesn't surprise me that Jacqui kicked the fire's ass.

Kelton opens the car door for me, but trips on the curb as he does – which is perfect. In fact, I'd have it no other way. We get in and set out on our familiar, unfamiliar street and head off into a world where fresh roots are already growing deep in the fertile ruins of what used to be.

Wasn't it Jacqui who told us the human body is sixty percent water? Well, now I know what the rest is. The rest is dust, the rest is ash, it's sorrow and it's grief... But above all that, *in spite of* all that, binding us together ... is hope. And joy. And a wellspring of all the things that still might be.

ACKNOWLEDGMENTS

Dry has been an amazing project to collaborate on, and there are so many people to whom we are grateful!

A heartfelt thanks to our editor, David Gale; editorial assistant, Amanda Ramirez; and our publisher, Justin Chanda, for trusting us to write a novel together, and for their guidance every step of the way! Everyone at Simon & Schuster has been incredibly supportive. A special shout-out to Carolyn Reidy, Jon Anderson, Anne Zafian, Michelle Leo, Anthony Parisi, Sarah Woodruff, Lauren Hoffman, Lisa Moraleda, Chrissy Noh, Keri Horan, Katrina Groover, Deane Norton, Stephanie Voros, and Chloë Foglia.

And, of course, Jay Shaw, for such a fantastic eye-catching cover!

Thanks to our book agent, Andrea Brown; foreign rights agent, Taryn Fagerness; our entertainment industry agents, Steve Fisher, Debbie Deuble-Hill, and Ryan Saul at APA; our manager, Trevor Engelson, for all their hard work setting up *Dry* as a film; and our contract attorneys, Shep Rosenman, Jennifer Justman, and Caitlin DiMotta, for wading through the endless fields of legal kindling.

Thanks to the film team – Marty Bowen, Isaac Klausner, and Pete Harris at Temple Hill, as well as Wyck Godfrey and Jon Gonda at Paramount.

We'd also like to thank our friend and colleague Elias Gertler, for believing in this story from its inception; Barb Sobel, for superhuman organizational skills; and Matt Lurie, our social media sensei.

Thanks to you, our cup truly runneth over!

ENJOYED *DRY*?

We'd love to hear your thoughts.
🐦 #Dry
@WalkerBooksUK
@WalkerBooksYA

📷 @WalkerBooksYA

Arc of a Scythe 1

SCYTHE

"A true successor to The Hunger Games" Maggie Stiefvater

SCYTHE

NEAL SHUSTERMAN

What if death was the only thing left to control?

In a perfect world, the only way to die is to be gleaned
by a professional scythe. When Citra and Rowan are
chosen to be apprentice scythes, they know they have no
option but to learn the art of killing. But the terrifying
responsibility of choosing their victims is just the start...

Arc of a Scythe 2

THUNDER HEAD

It's been a year since Rowan went off-grid.
Hunted by the Scythedom, he has become an
urban legend, sniffing out corrupt scythes.

Citra, meanwhile, is forging her path as Scythe Anastasia. But
conflict amongst the scythes is growing, and when her life is
threatened, it's clear that there is a truly terrifying plot afoot.

The Thunderhead observes everything, and it does not
like what it sees. Will it intervene? Or will it simply
watch as this perfect world begins to unravel?

**A shattering tale of murder,
maths and the mind**

Seventeen-year-old Pete Blankman is a maths
prodigy. He also suffers from severe panic
attacks. He takes refuge in the love and support
of his family, but his life is crippled by fear.

Then, the unthinkable happens. Pete discovers that
his mother has been stabbed and his twin sister, Bel,
is missing. Dragged into a world of espionage and
violence where state and family secrets intertwine,
can Pete's exceptional skills and instincts save him?

**"A dizzying rollercoaster of a novel"
Will Hill**

We were all surprised when the vuvv landed the first time. We were just glad they weren't invading. We couldn't believe our luck when they offered us their tech and invited us to be part of their Interspecies Co-Prosperity Alliance.

Several years on, jobs are scarce due to the rise of alien tech and there's no money for food, clean water, or the vuvv's miraculous medicine. Adam and his girlfriend, Chloe, must get creative to survive. Since the vuvv crave "classic" Earth culture, recording 1950s-style dates for them to view seems like a brilliant idea.

But it's hard for Adam and Chloe to murmur sweet nothings when they hate each other more with every episode. Soon enough, Adam must decide how far he's willing to go – and what he's willing to sacrifice.

NEAL SHUSTERMAN is the *New York Times* bestselling author of more than thirty award-winning books for children, teens and adults, including *Scythe*, *Thunderhead*, the Unwind dystology, the Skinjacker trilogy, *Downsiders* and *Challenger Deep*, which won the National Book Award in America. He also writes screenplays for motion pictures and television. Neal has four children and lives in California. Follow him online at www.storyman.com or on Twitter: @NealShusterman

JARROD SHUSTERMAN is the author of the short story "UnDevoured" in the bestselling *Unbound*. He writes for film and television, and his talents extend to directing films and commercials. He was the story producer on the television movie *Zedd— Moment of Clarity*, and he and Neal are adapting *Dry* for the screen. Jarrod lives in Los Angeles but enjoys traveling internationally, and is currently studying Spanish. He can be found on Instagram: @JarrodShusterman